1981

Jessie C. Matteson, R.N

I, JAMES LEWIS

BOOKS BY
GILBERT W. GABRIEL

I, JAMES LEWIS

JIMINY AND HER LOST SONNETS

BROWNSTONE FRONT

THE SEVEN BRANCHED CANDLESTICK

FAMOUS PIANISTS AND COMPOSERS

I, JAMES LEWIS

BY GILBERT W. GABRIEL

DOUBLEDAY, DORAN & COMPANY, INC.

GARDEN CITY   1935   NEW YORK

PRINTED AT THE *Country Life Press*, GARDEN CITY, N. Y., U. S. A.

CONTENTS

OVERTURE TO MR. ASTOR'S OPERA

I

Overture to Mr. Astor's Opera

I, JAMES LEWIS, dead and standing forth in Heaven's court before the blinding fairness of the throne of God, relate these things out of bewildered memory of my life so lately left behind.

I that was James Lewis, orphan and childless, fleck of the dust of commonest humanity, rebel son of a dull age and a raw, unsettled land, bachelor of arts who sailed a world away to count the skins from little beavers' backs, lover of life and of all men living, with the blood of three hundred Indians upon me . . . I who sang Mozart with Mozart's own librettist and with the same voice wheedled for Mr. Astor's pelts in the stinking cedar lodge of the flat-headed chieftain, Comcomly . . . I whose fingers trembled to touch the pretty Perrault's cheek and yet were like avenging iron when they thrust flame to the powder store, and whose eyes that hunted beauty beyond a warehouse bin are now torn out and flung by my own act into a cold, strange sea . . . I, stripped soul of him that was James Lewis, come into the presence of God, with His terrible bright gaze upon the page whereon I now must write and tell these things from out my life. . . .

And a man's life, though it seem no fuller than the laughter of an infant angel, is all of a man's life, and all that he may remember.

2

There was one Captain Thorn, master of the *Tonquin*, erstwhile lieutenant, U. S. navy, and hero of the fleet

3

against Tripoli, with red, wind-stitched cheeks and a sense of duty that lashed like a devil's tail. I was his chief clerk aboard, and something like his spy.

He chose me because, of all the clerks, he hated me most. He hated me because I was, like him, an American and a New Yorker and yet spoke—so he oathed I did—like a Tory, like a Hamiltonian senator, a damned unbearable pedant. When Mr. Astor described me to him as a schoolmaster something in his little gray eyes immediately told of how, in his own few school days, some tutor had birched him for being so bad at his grammar, and of how, with his proud young bottom smarting behind him all the way down from Trinity to Whitehall Slip, he had run away to sea.

In the ship's cabin, months after our first meeting, he told me that story in full. We were hugging around the Horn at last, with a sleety gale spent astern, and the islands of Diego Ramirez sinking into the long, almost endless day. The air had the hungry cool of near-by Southern ice fields, and midnight of New Year's Eve would be no darker than a restless, unbelievable dusk in the furrows of both seas.

The captain had found the cabin lantern lit. No one could possibly have burlesqued his passionate and overbearing show of discipline as he ordered me to haul it down.

"That's that young Perrault fool of yours," he said. "Fine boy y' got me, Lewis. I've told 'm time 'n' again, but . . . our best sperm, 'n' he goes on lightin' it 'n' lightin' it against my absolute command. What the devil's he think he be?"

I fumbled the little glass plate open and blew the light out. There, order was reëstablished, economy had triumphed. I should have to lecture Perrault on the duties of a proper cabin boy. They all called Perrault my boy.

"Just needs a bit of talking to, sir. He's really all right. Unsettled by the weather but . . . we'll make a man of him yet, sir."

Two things made me smile to myself as I hung the still hot lamp back above the mess table. How solemnly he had swallowed my last remark, for one thing. As solemnly as though he were sitting here at the table head, host to the partners for three stiff meals a day, their undying enemy for every twenty-four hours, conscious of their eyes on his strong, munching jaws when these damned landlubbers could not eat, as he could, a regular fare of sea-soured fowl or salt-porker and molasses. As solemnly as all that he had taken to himself my prophecy about making a man of Perrault.

But secondly I had smiled because, when I reached the lamp loop back over its hook, the glass had given me back a black, indented little portrait of me. I had seen my own nose, comically long and sharp, piercing the smoked bugle of the little chimney, and the way my thin chin sloped off doubly weakly, of both its own accord and in the dimple of the glass. I smiled . . . what else was there to do about it?

Yesterday, as ever so often, Ovide de Montigny had happened to meet me in the steerage and called me the old stork.

"Perrault probably had orders from the partners, sir," I assured Captain Thorn. "What with the holiday and all that . . . I suppose they thought we might have lights to-night."

This fight with his passengers, Mr. Astor's famous partners from the North-woods forts, had begun on our very first night out about the cabin lantern. One had only to touch a taper to the wick and he roared about the goddamned waste of it, the disrespect, the downright insubordination against all naval custom and his command. He began, sure enough, to roar again now.

"But it's only the New Year, sir, and our rounding the cape they're celebrating. They'll all be abed by one or two."

"Yaw, will they? 'N' wantin' eiderdown 'n' lavendered linen, too, no doubt. Abed by one 'r two, the British pot-licks."

I thought he would curse himself dry and be done with his tiresomeness for that day. He was moving towards his stateroom, but stopped in the doorway, turned around upon me, and was off again.

"One 'r two what? O'clock? God 'n' all the admirals, man, don't y' know y'r ship's bells yet? You're as bad as the worst of 'em, for all y'r fancy learnin'."

And so forth . . . and Mr. Astor should know just how bad . . . and what a sweet pack of seasick fools we had aboard. Fur merchants 't thought themselves the captain's superiors and gibbered against him with their bastard Highland monkey-talk. Lazy, craven French voyageurs, filthier 'n any Indians they'd lived and swigged amongst, boastin' how they could take their canoes through boilin' rapids and then green-faced and ill all over the deck at the first poke of a sea breeze. Saucy little clerks out o' Montreal billiard halls and taprooms, struttin' with ex-schoolmasters from Tory colleges, all runnin' to write their memoirs at first sight of flyin' fish.

"'N' all bound for God knows what on the wild shores of a hardly charted Indian river, to do 'r die . . . 'n' do what but filch 'n' squander Mr. Astor's good money?"

Something dogged and respectful had come into his voice, as it always did when he spoke of Mr. Astor, the *Tonquin's* owner, the expedition's financier back home in New York. Captain Thorn was your true navy officer.

Heels thumped over our heads. The Canadian canoe men were dancing. Their fringed leggings and slovenly, gay blankets whipped in the dusky breeze of a festival night which refused to grow dark. Paddle songs came down the hatchway, melancholy preludes to the sudden shrill burst of a Scotch bagpipe.

The partners, Messrs. M'Kay and M'Dougall and the Stuarts twain, were there with their Trinidad punch in contempt of all the captain's indignation, sharing tobacco and cheer with the voyageurs and the fawning Montreal youngsters. Bits of Gaelic and heathenish French blew down into the cabin, and the tipsy scuffle of moccasined feet.

Mr. Thorn listened grimly. Then he crooked a thick, completely calloused finger into my nankeen, and pulling me into the stateroom, closed the door on their noise.

"Old Noah had the better o' me," he said at length. "Noah understood what the apes 'n' tigers were sayin' of him."

His quarters were kept awfully tidy. All weather, he insisted on the rubbing down of his berth and lockers. An old Nantucket sofa jammed the recess, a monstrosity of horsehair and walnut, with furniture polish always shining damp between its eagle claws.

He poured us each a precise half glass from his private Teneriffe stock. He wiped the bottom of the bottle before he'd set it down on any varnished part.

"I ought to thrash the whole lot of 'em whoresons, Lewis. I ought to, by God. Introduce 'em to the gunner's daughter, or dump 'em on the next barren island they hanker to see. 'N' you, too, Lewis, with yer mild, holy-stoned sort of talk, yer six syllables t' every word, you more 'n any of 'em. You 'n' that pretty little cabin boy you're f'rever coddlin'."

He was a squarish man with arms and shoulders too big for the rest of him. He bulked so brutally . . . and the incongruity of his watery, infantile eyes in a face so up-turned by the wind, so red and seamed and hostile, must

have appealed to me then for the first time. I watched him
a good while. In the pearly, unreal light of this freezing
midsummer dawn down at the bottom of the world he
watched back at me.

"Allow me, sir, to wish you well of the year eighteen
eleven. A swift voyage North, sir, and Oregon within the
month."

"None too swift for me," he answered haughtily, "or
for the good of John Jacob Astor."

3

In the Putnam County village whence I came Mr.
Astor's name had once meant nothing. Even to me, who
had spent two college years in New York and sometimes,
between my Latin and philosophy, had seen the name in
the gazettes and on the boards of warehouses along the
muddy waterfront, it had meant less than little.

For lack of harder things to do, I had gone back to my
home township and taught school.

They had given me my keep, and time to read and to
play idly an old spinet which had somehow drifted into the
schoolhouse and stayed. I had no kin there. My parents
were dead long ago. But there were quiet valleys and deep
green views towards Connecticut over the maple tops and
soft marshes, and many children from the simple farms
around. I must have fancied myself a Jean-Jacques of the
New World. I was all of twenty-two years old then.

The farmers in this pleasant country had had their land
from the new state government: small woodlands, neg-
lected pastures and bramble patches, sold at low price to
honest Whigs and veterans of the war. They had made
fertile and bright fields of them. Decent townships were
already springing and pricking the valley view with a
glint of little roofs, and of far-away windows like pinned

stars by night. Young orchards reddened on the hills
where the fled patrician, Roger Morris, had once chased
the fox and let his park of fifty-thousand acres go rot to
the greater glory of King George.

But across the plowing and the freshly springing corn
the farmers bellowed to each other the strange news of
1809.

One Mr. Astor, furrier, banker, tea and timber merchant, city millionaire, had just bought the heirs' rights
of dead Morris in England, and of doddering Mary Morris,
too, and was going to go to law and the Legislature for
his due. Land, tillage, and all trespassing houses, every
stone fence the farmers had put up meanwhile, he could
and would claim for his own. This first year we all laughed.

I recalled the fat storehouse on Liberty Street, and the
name of J. J. Astor printed so fatly across it. One evening,
too, when I sat playing the old spinet for sweet, uncounted
hours, I had happened to notice the names of Broadwood
and Astor, London, on its key plate. It reminded me of
all those notices I had seen in the newspapers in my
college days: a Mr. Astor had always been sending another ship here, with no concern at all for the Embargo
of 1807, or announcing a ship from there with tea and
cassia aboard her, or had had a consignment of muskrat,
wolverine, and marten from the English curers . . .
millionaires must deal in so many things and places,
evidently.

Talk, too, in front of the farm ovens about a butcher
named Astor who had trundled around Westchester thirty
years ago: older folk remembered a genial, pink-jowled
German from the Fly Market, buying what cattle he could
from the British and pushing his own wheelbarrow from
yard to yard. Some one of the same family, perhaps, if
not the identical man.

And more recently still, another Astor, as pink of face

but not so genial, all strong bones and sturdy neck and deep-sunken eyes below his dusty hair, with a pack strapped to his shoulder blades, trudging his way to the forests above Albany, to the sorry Indian coureurs around Lake George. This might be the man . . . this our million-aire proprietor. They recalled him stopping in at the General Putnam for a mug of Holland beer, munching and sweating gravely into the chunk of bread he had hauled out of his bundle. This must be the man.

4

Because I knew the city, a terrifyingly large place of nearly ninety-thousand souls by now, and was not to be cowed by its thirty-two churches, its markets, theaters, and ever-restless ships, they made me their delegate to seek out and interview this unknown Astor. They mis-trusted my age, but I was full of college honors, and of that readiness to argue which only teaching school can give.

They loaned me an old mare, fit for a Quixote, and I rode her for three and a half days into the town.

On the door of the heavy-pillared, plain brick house at 223 Broadway a brass plate carried his name. I talked my way into his vestibule. He was finally at home to me. He sat back from his tankard of beer and his draughts board, but he went on smoking his pipe with its painted porcelain bowl between his knees, eyeing me and my dusty shanks over the gray sausage rolls of smoke which hung in the plump silver candelabra.

He had the wine-colored cheeks of a man approaching fifty. In the planing candlelight his face seemed cut out of stuff of a sheer, peremptory strength. His concentration flattened every word I tried to say.

When he spoke at all he spoke bluntly, deeply, with an

explosive German accent. It was perfectly true, the late
Roger Morris and his eighty-year-old widow had had but a
lifetime lease on their huge Putnam County holdings.
Their heirs had sold him a permanent ownership for
twenty-thousand sterling.

I began to describe the hardship he would cause. The
injustice to old soldiers, to soldiers' children whose fathers
had left them only their fouled muskets as benefits of a
long war. I thought myself attaining eloquence. He was
not amused by my appearance. He drank with his nose
deep in his silver beer mug. He heard me out.

He had already made up his mind to let the farmers have
the property back from him for three hundred thousand
dollars and the usual interest. He would not press them.
He did not need his attorney's assurances that the courts
would prove his claim correct. His title was only a matter
of time.

Ten, twenty years might be spent that way . . . all the
more expensively for the present squatters. In the end
he'd have either the money or the land. The farmers, since
they'd sent me for a message, might as well be advised to
start saving their pence now.

He announced all this without a single lapse into humor,
passion, or self-doubt. His small, powerful face nosed in
and out of his smoke, but his eyes never quite emerged
from the pits below their bushy brows. There was no
arguing with such a chin; when I began to plead a morality
above the law he sat comfortably still, with lips like
bronze which opened only to clamp occasionally closer
around his pipe stem.

"You talk well, young man," he said in the end. "Like
a genuine Heidelberger—and too well for your errand."

I stood facing him beyond the game board, looking at
the invulnerable force of him in his stout satin-bound
chair. The candlelight shone back from the arms, and

from his stock and pin, but most broadly from the sober, heavy satin of his waistcoat. When he nodded me good-night, I caught, too, the damp gleam of that thick red neck at the back of his strong hair.

"When your good farmers show their gratitude by throwing you out, come back and see me again. I will give you work to take the talk out of you."

And then, over his bent head, almost like its shadow on the wall behind him, I saw a hanging beaver skin, a beautiful, luminously smooth, unblemished specimen. It looked an incongruous ornament to such a room. His household god, I thought, his banner in honor of his millions in the fur trade. . . . I had a hot desire to tear it down and slash it across his hard, crammed face. He caught me looking at it.

"A good pelt," he said fondly . . . except that he said it thus: "A goot pelt. Most berfect I haf efer seen. In Canton id voult pring fife huntret tollers."

5

Pelts. Here was another world for me to live in. A world of skins torn from the steaming bodies of things of the wild: beaver, fox, sea otter, bear. So that the dandies of London should have smart luster to their hats, and Philadelphia ladies own fashionably savage rugs to tuck about them in their tasseled sleighs, and old mandarins of a far-off China might edge their ceremonial robes with splices of rarest fur. A world of bins stacked with the corded bundles of beaver, of dusty sunlight of the warehouse finding soft answers in the glint of peltry, of tawny backs and trap-bitten, dangling paws and edges of torn bellies where, in spite of daily beatings, the moths gorged themselves to sleep.

For, true to Mr. Astor's prophecy, I had come back to

my schoolhouse to find a notice already flapping from its door latch: the children would be needed at the looms and in the fields against the probability of such hard times, and school must wait until the settlement of the impending lawsuit.

They had managed to come to that conclusion while I was conveniently away on their own errand.

Indoors, a solitary boy of eight or nine was sitting with tear-soiled cheeks among the deserted benches. I gave him his last reading lesson and a jack-in-the-pulpit I had found beside the ford, kissed his little Dutch brow, and sent him home.

Then I made a small bag of what I had there of woolen stockings, a pair of buckles the villagers had given me last Christmas, my Voltaire and college Virgil, a few prized pieces of music. They all went easily against my shoulders. This time I would have to walk into New York.

Along the noon-dappled road wild honeysuckle grew profusely, so that my heels were always in the fretted shadows of its blossoms and marauding bees. There was a ringing of frogs and spring insects across the pasture, and I caught myself trying to establish keys, and even to wring melodies out of the high, gay uproar. Heart of hearts, I was not so sorry to be done with teaching the alphabet and atlas to slow-witted little gapers.

Though when, one sunny-roofed house I passed, I saw two small faces staring after me with noses flattened to the windowpane, and round eyes which must have followed my back all the way to the next turn of the road, I felt a little guilty and would have halted to bid good-bye. But the father farmer, polishing his boots with tobacco-stained spittle on the doorstep, pretended in his embarrassment not to see me . . . and I went on. A thrush sang his crystal benediction from a woods ahead.

Five days later I stood again before Mr. Astor. This

time in his counting room. On the wall above his desk hung another rare and glossy beaver skin. With the unhesitant, deific humorlessness of one who has made his bargain and will still have the best of it, he engaged me as a clerk-apprentice of the new American Fur Company, and had me taken over to the bins to thwack pelts.

"Dot," he said in that thick, crushing speech of his, "vass how I, doo, began to be a millionaire."

6

My thin, silly wrists were stiff from the weeks they had been wielding rattans in the warehouse. Throat and nostrils labored against caked dust. The smell of tanning was strong in my clothes.

But this once I had forgotten all these things and was blessedly happy. I was at Mr. Dunlap's benefit in the Park Theater, watching the new American play, *The Indian Princess, or La Belle Sauvage*. Transparencies across the arches of the building had lured me into its hot, damp hall as soon as the day's work was done. They had announced a concert, too, of classical music by some of the city's most celebrated foreign singers.

So gala an occasion had packed the pit early with men and noisy boys. We sat on the close board benches, staring under the clustering Liverpool brass lamps at the promenade of gentry in front of their fashionable boxes, our mouths watering to the distant clinking from the bar at the back of the third tier, where the town molls and pickpockets and holidaying coachmen sprawled and guzzled.

The play itself meant precious little to me, true: I was no longer a child, and these solemn speeches rolling out of the mouths of Pocahontas and her tribesmen to make a Redskin Iliad seemed to me only childish. Of Indians, real Indians, I had neither love nor hate nor any first-hand knowledge at that time. . . . Nor probably ever shall have, please the Almighty, I remember musing as I stood up with the others when they stretched and ogled between acts.

And as for the songs they'd inserted to make a popular affair of it, they were for the most part patriotic rubbish. It was the evening's finish which enraptured me. This was what I had been waiting for . . . perhaps all my years. It was a first singing of some arias from Mozart's *Nozze di Figaro*.

A first singing, at any rate, to me. No doubt the elegant Signor Comoglio who arranged winter concerts of Italian music in Miss Gervais's ballroom in the Commercial Coffee House had included excerpts from Mozart ere this. Out of honor to the equally elegant Mr. Dunlap, whose theater the coffee house adjoined, Signor Comoglio, M. Perrossier, Mlle Perrault, and others of their concert company would oblige with appropriate selections from Haydn, Paesiello, Pleyel, Cimarosa, and (by special request of one of the wealthiest patrons in New York) Mozart.

So that I heard at length this lovely piece from *Nozze di Figaro*. . . .

The delight of it stayed with me as I walked up Park Row and the Bowery after the performance. It was raining, a warm, early summer rain which had almost extinguished the street lamps and left the ground a dark, abominable trough underfoot. But I can recall how, until I reached my room in Chatham Street, I noticed little except the shine of wet leaves on the trimmed poplar trees, and how these seemed to me the magical reminders of a moonlit Spanish garden of Count Almaviva where I, too, sang along.

Sang Mozart's dear music as I marched my lanky, somehow lightened bones home through the Bowery muck. Sang directly into the rain-sopped face of a suspicious old watchman. Went on singing, smiling with what I sang, remembering it was the music of Cherubino, the mischievous boy in the Almaviva's household . . . and remembering, too, the slim, silky hoyden who had sung him on the stage just now.

Her name meant nothing to me. A playbill had announced it as Juliana Perrault, and she must be a favorite of the town, to judge by the specially illuminated scenery Mr. Dunlap had furnished her, and by her almost brand-new clothes. Perrault . . . French? Juliana would be Italian, though. But what did her name matter—or her nationality, either—when she sang as she did, and looked so much as if she had sprung, a gayer young goddess, up from Mozart's foamy music?

Her impish figure strutted along with me across the night, and all that was Mozart was in my memory of the way she had appeared in her boy's clothes, the way she had sung with white, uplifted throat, seemed almost to be singing with me now.

Though once I must have stopped and been for a little while silenced, hearing only the drip of the rain and the rough suck of my boot heels out of the sidewalk. This was when I also remembered looking up during an intermission to the lighted boxes, and how I had seen there in one of the central and most cushioned ones the ruddy, tight, satin-stocked face of Mr. Astor.

7

The American Fur Company, incorporated for a million dollars, charter of the Legislature of the State of New York, 1809.

Negotiations with the great Northwest Company of Canada . . . negotiations which turned into blunt defiances within a year. Buying out of the mighty Mackinaw, its merger with the American. June 23d, 1810, formation of the new Pacific Fur Company between Alexander M'Kay, nabob of the Northern wilderness, explorer to the furthest mountain pass and Western river, chief of those chieftains whose names had painted the fur trade with proud Scotch plaids, and plain John Jacob Astor of New York.

Astor's dream is safe on paper. A whole world shall know of it soon enough.

A President of the United States gives his thanks and unofficial sanction. In snowy Fort William the banqueting Britishers drink their mulled wine mixed with a strange worry. In the rough little outpost trading towns of Michilimackinac and St. Louis the voyageurs and the trinketed squaws stop carousing to listen, hiccup, and scarce believe. Russians watching for sea-otter herds from their cannon-studded rocks of Alaskan Seetka will have the news whined them across the dragon-daubed poops of relief ships out of Kamchatka, and old Baranoff's serfs and Kodiaks will have surly beatings for their next meals instead of raw rum and blubber. Into the brown hubbub of the Thames the tidings sail, and there will be jealous conferences in the colonial offices of London and St. Petersburg and sullen Madrid . . . and there will be a fury of outwitted ministers and affronted kings which means world fame for John Jacob Astor.

On the Western coast of the continent, high northward where the Columbia joins the sea, the new fur company is to station. We hear of it in the warehouse, Matthews, Farnham, others of the young clerks, and I.

The Columbia River. As an ex-schoolmaster I have to explain them where it is, though I am not so sure myself. When we were children, before Gray's voyage, we had all called it the Oregon. Only one famous expedition had so far traveled down it to the sea. What they had seen, encountered, escaped . . . over our lading lists and scales we gossip all day about the wonder and boldness of it.

We begin to bet each other sixpences as to which of us will go. In the warm noons we run along the waterfront, where there is a constant hammering from all the ship-yards and the sky's edge is cross-stitched with many new masts. We set up prize bottles for the day's latest news. We are always running in and out the gazette offices to see what's on the hand press.

Mr. Astor will equip a great overland expedition. Mr. Astor will send another and even bigger expedition simul-taneously by sea around the Horn and up the Pacific. Mr. Astor will recruit from the celebrated fur personnel of Montreal, snatching leading gentlemen from the Nor'-westers' group and giving them opportunities for new wealth and power in the wilderness of Oregon, where Mr. Astor's millions are going to build a handsome trading center among the Indians and have a hundred tributary trapping posts along the unknown streams and up the island clefts which face the Arctic.

Mr. Astor has had Mr. Jefferson's congratulations. Mr. Astor is reported to be buying or building a most admir-ably suitable ship. Mr. Astor has lately had lunch at the Tontine with His Britannic Majesty's chargé d'affaires, Mr. Jackson, has eaten nothing except one huge dish of cole slaw, drunk only one quart tankard of Hudson brew, and listened to not a single word of the irate Minister's expostulations on behalf of all fur-wearing England. Mr. Astor has bought an excellent piece of East River property where, it is to be presumed, he will assign a warehouse to the particular collection of first-rate goods for exchange with the savages on the imminent expedition. . . .

And so Mr. Astor, the little German butcher's son, hunts the beaver.

And so the remnants of hundreds of suddenly slain men drift in the riled straits to-night, and sink, rise, drift, and sink again in horrible dismemberment amid the floating

spars and the soaked tatters of a thousand beaver skins.
Along the shores the funeral fires of the howling Clayoquots cast bloody glow upon the bloodier water.

Months to come, when he hears of it, Mr. Astor's firm
cheek may mottle a bit . . . but he will not miss the theater
in the evening.

OVIDE

II
Ovide

MY REVERENCES to the great M. Voltaire. It was my occasional reading in that volume which I had of him that
kept alive my poor, gawky knowledge of French. It was
my French which finally assigned me to the *Tonquin*.

I had had my year's trial in the warehouse. Good-bye
and good-riddance to the beating-stick. I was a full-
fledged clerk attached to Mr. Astor's office, his secretary
in certain matters that needed a particularly cautious
correspondence: in the enlistment, for instance, of the
coming expedition's French-Canadian personnel. I was
always sending small equipment drafts to Mr. Astor's
Montreal agent, who was always relaying confidential
receipts thereof from men who made their crosses beside
such strange, outlandish names as Antoine Belleau and
Jacques Lafantasie.

I sometimes thought vaguely of enlisting myself. I was
young enough. I had no ties. I knew furs, now, and how to
judge and handle them. I could be no more lonely in
strange countries than here in New York. A hundred
pounds' reward . . . a heroic short-cut, perhaps, to . . .
whatever it was that all the men around me were working
to.

Farnham, from the warehouse, had already enlisted.
He could even be a partner and get married to that
wealthy Boston girl of his when he came back. He already
patronized Matthews and me. He was sure Mr. Astor
would be able to spare us. We really ought to . . . the New
World needed new life, and anything to keep the British

23

off our Western coast. One needn't be especially brave and strong . . . look at himself, he didn't pretend to be a Hercules.

But it was at me that both of them were looking, and grinning as they looked. I knew it. I once tried, too, to speak to Mr. Astor about it, to ask him whether he thought I ought to sign to go.

He was busy with the Putnam County matter that day. His neck was fiery red. I could not get a sentence out. My knees creaked foolishly as I went off with his afternoon beer mug and a letter to the Legislature.

I left the office an hour early. It seemed to me a great risk to take. If I had not been so disturbed I should never have dared to.

Summer had come again and baked the brick faces of the buildings in the Bowery a dusty brown. New wine shops did noisy business along green Canal Street, and the Park and all the uptown Gardens were filled with tired, hot strollers.

I liked the Battery best of all. Here there were grassy promenades, the cool sight of sail tops and extensive waters flashing to the sun, and of the Moro and glinting tiers of guns on the Governor's and more distant Gibbet Islands. Here some freed Negroes used sometimes to gather on the breathless wharf ends and sing blissfully while they sweated. Here, on not too stifling afternoons, the rich of the city would drive down and sit stiffly in their open carriages under heavy beaver hats and parasols, and the damp horses tugged at their checks to lower their muzzles to the grass.

Here I saw today the little Cherubino of the play, sitting high in carriage cushions next a fat, sunken old banker.

I had been to the concerts in the City Hotel as often during the winter as I could afford, hoping to hear her

sing again. I had haunted the Little Lyceum on Warren
Street, and even the MM. Pepin and Breschard's circus
where she might have been one of those who sang numbers between the flaming trick of the Infernal Horse, the
hornpipe on the tight-rope, and the pantomime of the
"Battle and Death of General Malbrook." When Vauxhall opened its summer season with a promise of concerts,
burlettas, and duets I rushed there almost nightly at
first, had my fill and more of fireworks and ballads . . .
but no Mlle Perrault.

Yet here she sat, bright eyes beneath her bonnet, and
a young throat as white as the June day around her. I
must have stared at her so awkwardly, she noticed me and
laughed. She called her patron's attention to me. He, too,
laughed, his old face pleating in upon itself under his
glossy brim, and he put his snuff leisurely away to pat her
hand.

I remembered having seen the old buck once or twice
in our counting room. He could pass through to Mr. Astor's office without introduction. He wore his frills starched
back to show large diamonds. He laughed very loud.

I had turned away. Neither he nor his little diva re-
marked me any more. I was trembling . . . miserable,
furious, but at myself, because I did not know why I
was trembling. One of their plump horses close to me began to piss, and I felt the splatter of it on the backs of
my calves before I could jump aside.

The next morning I signed to join the expedition to the
Oregon wilds.

2

My landlady, an anxious churchwoman, turned on a
tap of exclamations when I told her. She had troubles of
her own, the Lord had elected to try her sorely, and now
I should be turning back her best room in times like these.

She did hope I was not telling her lies and vacating my lodgings only because the baby had cried so much last night. I had always been so gentle with the baby and seemed to know so much about them, I must know how they suffer of their colic and have to howl it out.

I assured her I had not even heard the baby, that I loved the baby, that I was at all times satisfied with my lodgings, their commodiousness and respectability, and their tidy view across the suburb, and that I should not dream of leaving her house to go anywhere else than the Columbia River. No, the Columbia River was too far away, unfortunately, to permit me to come home of nights. The Columbia River was . . .

I stuttered after her into the kitchen, where the crib stood toasting in the stove glow, and gave the baby my thumb. Tiny fingers clutched, slipped, grew sticky, and held me fast. The Columbia River was far away.

I must not think she had not appreciated having one of Mr. Astor's employees among her tenants. I had always been a dependable young man, even if not a churchman, and had never tried to bring wenches into a decent house, like the so-called gentleman on the floor above, who had brazenly complained about the drains, used to try to do. I had been so thoughtful of the baby, and she and her husband, tired and abed of a hard day's worry when I came home, had often said to each other how good it was of me to go upstairs on tiptoe, and what a good husband and father I'd make some good girl some day.

There was a pleasant smell of strong soap and cooking foods. The baby had pulled up my thumb to suck. When I leaned over I had the fragrance, too, of freshly washed flannel and a foolishly young flesh. I volunteered—I had done it several times before this—to stay at home a while and watch the crib. My landlady loved the Wednesday vespers.

"You should go to church yourself, young man. A studious, diligent young man like you, with no bad habits. You could easily come to know God."

I thanked her gravely. I wondered what God would look like when one got to know Him. But I was too shy of her to wonder aloud.

She had on her bonnet in no time. She was blowing off a dozen anxious directions as to which pot to stir, which to let rumble, and what to do about the baby. . . . She did hope I was not going to fall in with wild companions on this mad voyage. I wasn't, if she might say so, the sort of young man to go playing pirate or Indian-fighter, like her cousin who'd been scalped, or to gamble my life away among ruffians and adventurers.

"I haven't the least idea," I said. I was quite apologetic. "I only know some of their names. Names like Lafantasie, Ovide de Montigny . . ."

"Frenchmen," she said. "Papists, I'm sure. Or even revolutionists, perhaps."

There, I was already a lost soul. I should never know God.

Plainly sorrowing for me, she went off to her vespers. Evening glimmered behind the kitchen garden. Now and again came a slow clop of hoofs down the street, the grating of wheels against little stones loose in the road. The heat from the stove made me drowsy. I napped to the soft tapping of a kettle cover, with my thumb nested in a pink, tiny paw. Had I reached into my jacket pocket for the old Latin poet I should have waked the baby. And it was grown too dark to read.

I half dreamed some parading imagery of names, strange, flashing names of those whom I was yet to know, to meet and be on brave, gay terms with in some time yet to be. Names like Lafantasie, Roussel, De Montigny, Lapensee . . . and God.

3

We were to be ten to twelve clerks, most of us due from Montreal and from past experience in the trapping trade with the Nor'westers. No more than three of us from New York. Though not yet twenty-five years old, I should probably be our oldest.

I was bound to the service of the company, land and sea, for the next five years. I should have five hundred dollars at that time's end, plus an annual equipment of clothing of forty dollars' worth, and then all reasonable expectation of promotion, even a partnership, when my clerkship expired.

These were fair terms. Mr. Hunt, just before he started North to enlist the overland troop which should meet us at the mouth of the Columbia in a few months' time, assured me how fair they were. I had been sent down to see him off on the Albany Post. He carried saddlebags, a paddle, and a hymn book for the trip thereonward. We talked quietly while waiting the post horn. I had a letter of final instructions for him from Mr. Astor. Mr. Wilson Price Hunt swore by his Mr. Astor. So did we all.

Thanks to Mr. Astor, the fur trade would wear a new look now. There would be such millions in it as the Nor'-westers had never dreamed of. There would be trading stations flying the American flag all up and down the Missouri and Columbia. The Indians would pour in past the stockades of new masters, new and more generous dealers than they had ever met before, rejoicing in an amity of fair play and honest goods, value for value of trinkets and cutlery and stanch woolen blankets in exchange for their treasury of rare skins. We should be Christ's witnesses to the heathen, we Americans. Wealth and power and the North Pacific shore as our rewards, and God's loving image displayed to all the Indians.

Mr. Hunt believed these things . . . and I know nothing of where he is now . . . he and that collected band of woodsmen with whom he was to cross the savage leagues of a whole continent. But his belief transfigured his gentle, already gaunt, harassed face and gave it the thousand gleams which sunlight gives the snow. He will never know how much I envied him his smile.

I gave him Mr. Astor's letter-of-credit. To the blowing of the horn and the storming of the coach around the corner I remembered that he knew some French from his sojourning in St. Louis, so I shouted him an excited, absurdly careless, "*Au 'voir.*"

Au 'voir to him. And *au 'voir* to all his cold, errant, famishing cavalcade to join us.

4

The *Tonquin* lay off Brooklyn Basin, where she had lately been on the stocks. Mr. Astor had chosen her to suit the special occasion: she was a chubby three-master of three hundred tons burden; and even such an inlander as I had sudden pleasure from my first sight of her when, with Farnham and Matthews, I rowed across in the white Sunday calm of August fourth.

Small pleasure craft were drifting in the Bay. Many lay close to the sunny side of the *Tonquin*, for the whole city seemed to know of her, of her ambition and far destination. Many more floated lazily behind, loath to leave the vicinity of the Battery, its music corps, its bright Sunday clothes in mosaic against the trim brick and fresh swards of the shore.

The Canadians were coming. They had landed at the northern end of the city last night, shelving their huge canoe and camping in a river street-end under the round eyes of the cottagers with a great fire and foreign jabber

and song. To-day they would reëmbark and make their
official, celebrative entry. They would paddle the whole
course around the city to treat us to a sight of our future
companions.

News had already galloped down the Hudson road,
these past two days, of their jolly advent. They had
come all the way from Prairie de la Madelaine in their
big Indian skiff of birchbark, portaging and paddling
down Lake Champlain and the river, past wondering
Dutch farms and the lazy little Hudson villages. Sometimes they had owned the towns for whole nights of whoop-
ing and dancing the Dutch steps and their own, and of
finding what girls would go how far for a second-best
ceinture fléchée behind the hedges of the bowling greens.
In advance we knew them for gay dogs.

Their extravagant French names went prancing through
my head. I should risk my life beside a man named Ovide
de Montigny. I remembered from my college reading how
a quaint, infamously great poet called François Villon
had had a friend by the name of Regnier de Montigny,
reckless blackguard of an honorable family, son of that
Jehan de Montigny who had followed the Dauphin's
fortunes, and how this Regnier had been known to all
as Regnier à Coquillard, as a cheat, a player of marelle,
a tavern murderer. Ovide . . . Ovide de Montigny, of that
same tribe, perhaps. What would he be like? What could
a gangly, long-nosed schoolmaster from Putnam County
find to say . . .

Our rowboat grazed in a herd of its fellows, cracking
bows and giving off thump and laughter, all oars splatter-
ing in an indolence of long waiting. It grew noon-hot.

I had rowed a little while, but I was bad at it. Matthews
succeeded me, but he was no better. We roared at the
idea of youths as soft-handed as ourselves signing up
for a voyage around the Horn, up to an utter wilderness

. . . roared a little too loudly, of course. Farnham, the New Englander born, sat solemn in the stern and could not be heckled into laughing along. There are as many ways to confess fear as to hide it.

The sunlight, I remember, lay under the water and drank of the green dark through long, straight tongues of gold. When I leaned over, watching, I saw how Matthews's oars broke these into brilliants which sucked away in tiny whirlpools. I must have been wondering of the water of other bays, of the surfs and involved, murderous rocks and unimaginable shore lines we should meet, and of the copper bodies of the savages flashing through the spume. Some hag had cursed me on my christening day with the gift of imagination.

There were cheers and quick packing of crowds along the Battery. All the yawls and rowboats that could make headway were already working in towards that point. Down their line it approached, the big canoe of the Canadians.

Nine men impelled her, their paddles advancing in carnival rhythm on her either side. Nine stout, unwearied men, dark as Indians and as luridly dressed, with feathers and many colored ribands in their hats. They were singing as they came, their song in time with their strokes. But I could guess this only from their open mouths and their paddles. The song itself was drowned under the crowd's welcoming shouts as she passed down the midst of us.

A few months later and I should understand more fully these playful, boastful children of the woods and rapids. But they would never stir me again as they did with this merry, mock-heroic arrival of theirs. The dancing heat over the bay fastened on their barbaric shirts and set their colors afire. The sunlight took charge of their supple swaying, made each flash of their blades a chivalrous feat.

Farnham and I seized oars together. We managed to bring our boat into the fore of the canoe's followers. I recognized the blackened, gnarled face of Alexander M'Kay, the deputation's famous commander. And, when they were past the festive Battery and rounding towards Long Island, I saw how all the new roof-tops, quays, and open windows on the East River, too, and even the bare ribs of unfinished ships in the building-yards, were alive with little figures, watching, waving hands and scarfs and beavers, with a noise that came so faintly over the water, it seemed but an old, lost echo of the excitement quickening my heart.

On the Battery itself I distinguished the tiny carriages, the tiny people in light clothes standing up in them to watch over the toy horses' heads. I thought of a shrunken old banker tapping his snuffbox complacently and cackling along with his little diva, and I rowed two big blisters into my soft palms.

5

Fair outside of Brooklyn village were the quarters Mr. Astor had taken for the dozen voyageurs and the eight Canadian clerks. They would be less cramped there, less mischievous, too.

There was evidently some anxiety about their behavior during the two or three weeks before we hoped to sail. Mr. Jackson, His Britannic Majesty's chargé d'affaires in New York, was already suspected of much inquisitiveness about so many English subjects bound for a rich peltry country which Great Britain had always considered potentially her own. Fishermen had risked the fog at Sandy Hook to put in and report the prowling of one of His Majesty's armed brigs.

It was I whom Mr. Astor delegated to Long Island to tell the Canadians they must take immediate oaths of citizenship of the United States. It was a ticklish message. It needed other French than mine. I did my foolish, perspiring best with the language of Candide. The voyageurs spoke a language of the woods. We were all laughable—and laughing. I sorely missed an interpreter, and was friends at once with him who volunteered.

Ovide de Montigny. He kept one hand upon his hip, half buried in the gaudy worsteds of his belt, while his other hand uncovered his bright, rebellious mane with a flourish of fine ceremony. I fidgeted with my own hat. No one had ever taught me to take it off like that to another man.

So we met. So, at first meeting, I adored him . . . abysmally. He stood in the farmhouse window, lounging a little, facing the sunlight and the white flash of the bay's water, his long hair afire, such an accomplished smile upon his features as though he were a hero of the stage in the footlamps' circle. He was the handsomest youth I had ever seen.

Most of the rest of the clerks from Canada were of Scotch blood—or bloodlessness, rather—plain, white-eyelashed young relatives and sons of friends of the partners, overgrown cadets of the Highland families which had waxed so quickly rich and influential in the Montreal fur mart. Ovide de Montigny looked none of that breed. He knew what he looked. The whole height and grace of him were in his smile.

The voyageurs shrugged their thick shoulders below their capots. They did not mind what flag they sailed under. They wanted their pouches kept full of tobacco screws. They liked girls of all nationalities who liked men with shoulder muscles like theirs. They did not care.

The young clerks would have given me trouble: they talked with solemn burrs in their mouths, they managed to argue like prigs and parliamentarians. They must ask

The M'Dougall's advice about it. They had been warned back in Montreal to remember that Partner Duncan M'Dougall was the high word of the clan. I gave them some high words of my own. I had almost to take on my old rôle of schoolmaster with them. With all, that is, except De Montigny.

He outdid the voyageurs at French carelessness. He played the young seigneur . . . but of the wilderness. In the forests around Whitehall, at the foot of Champlain, the canoe party had taken him aboard. He must have spent years in Paris to put so fine an edge upon his speaking.

We all sat down. The hot, low room of this Dutch house where the clerks were billeted was full of a gleam of varnished pine and boxwood bowls and pewter. Through the open doors came the smell of the garden and the bay shore, of smoke swinging indolently from the fire in the next field where the voyageurs had insisted on camping outdoors.

De Montigny leaned back in his chair, the argument over. From heaven knows where he had brought out a beautiful pair of old pistols which he intended to carry along on the voyage, and he was looking them over with a dandy's concern which seemed all the more gallant of such a huge, browned fellow.

I was thinking how best to remind him without offense of Captain Thorn's advice that none of us should stow private firearms or steels without permission. Only yesterday they had had me into Mr. Astor's office to check the requisitions for the gun rack and the powder run.

"M. de Montigny, I trust you will not take it amiss . . ."

It was as though little turtles' heads, stretched to the sunlight, sprang suddenly back beneath his brown, domed eyelids. He seemed almost offended before I had said half a sentence.

". . . not take it amiss if I . . ." I had to finish it in some

way, even if not at all the way I'd planned . . . "if I inquire,
are you descended of the famous De Montigny family who
. . . there was Jehan de Montigny who followed the Dauphin's fortunes . . ."

He laughed. "Oh!"

I had pleased him mightily. The tiny turtles' heads returned lazily towards the sun. "I suppose so," he conceded.
"My father was full of such lore, an' most proud. . . . When
he caught me with my first squaw he made the woods
around our *manoir* ring with his sermon on *noblesse oblige*.
Then he packed me off to France to a school for the
aristocracy's sons. I did not stay there long. Schools . . .
ah, pardon me, they tell me you once taught. . . ."

"Not at all. I assure you."

"But, dear sir, I should have known it without their
telling me. You wear your horn glasses with such a guaran-
tee of learning. An' you do not smile easily, sir. One should
be careful not to cast rash memoirs into so serious a face
as yours."

He said it charmingly. His words had the ring of a rôle
in a gracious play. They left me more and more humbled.

"You must stay the night with us here," he next suggested. "You shall have Franchere's bed. Franchere is a
dull boy who intends to keep a journal. He and his notebook leave us for a tour of the city with some New York
friends. He never thinks to ask any of us to come along. I
am sure his bed will prove more inviting than himself."

That was a well turned bit of wording, that last sentence.
If I did not think so, I could see that De Montigny himself
did. My own thoughts were on another De Montigny, on
Regnier, son of Jehan, Regnier à Coquillard, the reckless
blackguard, cheat at the games of women and marelle, and
tavern murderer in company with one Villon, poet. . . . I
sat straight in my chair, rubbing a gloss nervously into my
nose, but I did not mention Regnier.

"Perhaps you would like to come over to New York, instead." He had hinted he might enjoy that. I hoped he would. I wished I could overcome my bashfulness before him. "We—we can catch the ferryman within an hour."

"My dear Mr.——" De Montigny's glance came slowly up from the barrel of the no doubt empty pistol which he was aiming humorously into the next room, where a half dozen of the young Scotsmen now sat hunched and jabbering Gaelic among themselves.

"Lewis," I said. "James Lewis. It's a common enough name in our United States."

"Popular, perhaps," he forgave me cordially, "but not common. Well, Mr. Lewis, this is most kind of you. I have seen many cities abroad, you know, an' I fancy that some of them are even larger an' slightly lovelier than your New York. But, *qu'importe*, I'd go almost anywhere to double my distance from that pack of parvenus in the next room. So if you can direct me to a reasonable chamber——"

I cried out in protest that he must share my own. My landlady would not mind. On the contrary . . .

He thanked me with an almost royal nod. "—and can promise me that there is such a thing as a theater where a gentleman who has attended the Comédie Française may be made to forget his years since among the pines and beaver traps and fat squaws, and his years ahead in this madder place for which we sail. . . ."

A theater? My heart bounded to this fellow. To the theater we'd go. And I loved him dearly, without care or cavil.

But both the playhouses were still closed for the summer. I was sorry. I feared New York must seem a small, provincial town to him. With faint heart I suggested what few other pleasures I could think of.

Of course, I could personally recommend a visit to the

new American Museum, only recently opened a few doors
from my room on Chatham Street, where there were wax
horses, life-sized, and mammoths, scripture groups, and
some rare vials of preserved reptiles. Perhaps he would
prefer a panorama. Or at the Circus, I added anxiously
when I saw him yawn, he might see Manfredi and Menial
among the favorite acrobats. He was handsomely un-
impressed by any or all of these.

"To tell you the truth, my dear Lewis James, or James
Lewis, or whatever your plain, sober, schoolmasterly name
may be," he said, "I have already formed a tender attach-
ment to an establishment right here in Brooklyn, an inn
garden not far from here, close by the ferries: an excellent
place . . . if a little shabby. You probably know nothing
of it, for you live only across the river, and that is always
the way. Besides, I can see that you're not a naturally gay
liver. But they have really good liqueurs there at Mr.
Green's, and in his Military Gardens last evening I heard
some delightful music."

"Music?"

"Ah, so you have your luxuries? Music. Good."

"It is my love."

I must have said it in so fervent a way, it much amused
him.

"All the better. The evening will be easy to divide.
You'll enjoy the music, I the young creature who makes
it. We'd best agree on that before you see her. Else you
might fall in love with her yourself, and I should have
to——"

He waved the pistol at me, and misjudged my surprise.
Laughing: "Dear James, did you think it was loaded . . .
yet?"

But I suddenly had no notice to waste on his teasing.
"She—the young . . . singer?"

"Certainly, a singer. At least she sings. A pretty little

thing like that, what else would she do for music? Play a
viole d'amour? Not in public." He had another turn at
laughter. His large eyes skimmed the room, merrily
patronizing all the empty benches before they rested on
me and demanded applause for his latest pun. "Sings at
Green's on odd nights. She's the toast of all the officers
there. Or was, until I . . . you should see her."

"In costume? Cherubino's?"

"What?"

"Boy's clothes? So that's where——"

"Ah, then you have seen her."

"It may be that I know the lady," I told him . . . so
solemnly that he checked his grin. "Not precisely know
her, of course, but have seen and heard——"

"Oh, so she's a lady? Either you're sadly smitten,
James, or we're talking about different charmers. Mine, in
the intimacies of our first fondness, our first dip of the
bottle, made no great ado about admitting herself . . . oh,
well, the dear little beauty, she's been down on her luck
and her bed-sheets often enough of late. Your town has
not devised much other welcome for stray opera singers."

I stammered something. "Is it Mozart she sings?"

"Possibly. Something Italian. I'm no impresario. It
was her looks that caught me."

"Is she dark, slim," I said, "and . . . her throat . . ."
But here was a question I could not complete, I did not
know why. I waited a long pause, then gave him another in
its place. "And this is only your third night hereabouts?"

He lay back and howled. "While you, I suppose, have
been coveting her acquaintance all your life! Poor old
James, don't despair, wait and see what your five years in
the wilderness will make of you. You'll come back a lion for
the ladies."

I was between punching his head and hanging my own.
I did not mean it to sound as bitterly as it did: "No num-

ber of years will make me an expert whoremonger," I replied.

His hand came swiftly up as he pulled the trigger. The
pistol flamed and roared at me. My beaver tore off my
head, spun crazily upon its brim along the floor behind me,
a bullet hole burnt through the crown.

As I started for him, he was already laughing again.
"Good God, James, do you think I had the least idea it
was loaded!" But then, jumping out of his chair and
standing brilliantly to face me as the low room filled with
our scared companions:

"Green's Military Gardens . . . I shall be there until
midnight, any midnight, sir, and damn drunk, too, in case
you care to call me out."

"Mr. Lewis!"

Accident, jest, or downright try at murder, it had sickened my nerves. At the sound of my name from the doorway I wheeled like a scared cat. In the thinning smoke,
breaking its slow drift to the outer air with his stocky,
bristling body and red face, stood Captain Thorn.

"Your French is too good, Mr. Lewis. It exceeds your
common sense. Return to New York at once."

I tried to explain. I burst into tears.

6

The fortnight ere we sailed had already lengthened to a
month. The *Tonquin* was loading with strange goods and
necessaries: separate parts, for instance, of the small, coast-
wise schooner we should build when we reached the Columbia, and innumerable trading truck and knacks and iron-
ware which were to go into the main post we planned on
the Oregon shore.

We clerks spent all these sultry days chasing her pro-
visions up the quay and out into the lighters.

Until dark, once, I counted the stowing of blue beads and tobacco twists, knives and red blankets, hundreds of cheap but bright red blankets, to please the Indians' tastes. When the last of these still lay above the hatch in the sunset they, and all the deck around them, had the affronting glow of warm blood, the puddled liquor of a wanton and preposterously wholesale murder.

The next morning I went down with the armorer, Stephen Weeks, to check the piling of our powder kegs in the run beneath the cabin. We had a full supply of casks— too many to stow chine and chine—enough to take care of the *Tonquin's* own energencies after she should divide with the partners' fort and sail on North. More than enough.

"Ten cannon'll have to have big appetites to eat up all this black gruel," old Weeks complained.

For, though we were pierced for twenty, we carried only ten good guns. Wooden ones, wholly sham, were being made by the Russian carpenter, Koaster, for the forward portholes. We'd never need cannon, iron or wood either, or any such large amount of powder.

A few days ago I had helped distribute muskets to the cabin and forecastle racks. I had hated handling them. They had been much heavier than they looked. I had stood lifting the long barrel of one of them slowly, absently up and down, remembering a scarlet astragal sprayed across the snow from the bullet-mashed head of a baby rabbit which one of my boys had shot in the school yard. And how wretched I had been, unable to teach all the rest of that day.

Old Weeks piled his kegs the length of the powder run. The black place took on immediately the blacker smell of its contents. I helped him with the roping. I counted in the dark. Too many . . . he kept on complaining of too much gruel to take care of, and that we'd never blow off a quarter of it.

"No telling," I answered him, content to answer anything at all if only we might hurry and climb back soon out of the close, loathsome darkness of this tumor in the deep breast of the ship.

Scarlet and black and the tarry, sulphurous smell of sudden death, and down in the hold the sheen of heaven on common little blue beads in their tuppenny bags.

7

Mr. Astor had sent for me. I had not often the great man's confidences, but when he must once or twice have wanted a letter of particular risk and college polish composed for him he would summon me above his usual secretaries. This time to his home, between the day's work and the dinner hour.

I came in from the wharf in the worn, streaked clothes of my labor there. They were the same clothes I had had on me all my days in the warehouse when beating pelts, and the same Mr. Astor had seen whitened by the country roads when I first came to him a year ago on the farmers' behalf. I cannot explain why I took such satisfaction in my shabbiness. It was half a contemptuous subservience, half defiance, perhaps . . . and, at any rate, a great waste of attitude. For he scarce looked at me at all.

They showed me into the same rich, artless room I had been in before. Mr. Astor sat again in his big, satin-covered chair, with the same plump bush of silver smoke growing through the fat branches of the silver candelabra from the big pipe clamped into his lips, and the soft light reaping the same insolent luster from his stock and waistcoat.

Had nothing happened, nothing changed, to declare it

another year? Mr. Astor, I knew, was so and so much richer in China tea and English sterling and real estate along the city's fringe; yet here he sat with his early evening beer pot and his pipe, his game of draughts already waiting for an after-dinner tourney, and he spoke again with that thick, ironic accent of the indomitable German.

And I in the same soiled clothes, with breeches streaked a little the more brownly in His Millionaireship's service . . . and here was our anniversary.

But down on the river the *Tonquin* creaked and strained upon the ropes which held her towards the shore, her timbers chatting on good terms with the tide which would soon take her and her fifty strange shipfellows and her stranger cargo out into the bay and away . . . and I should be one with them and with her and with all the unforetold adventures of our circuit. To this, thanks be, the year had brought me.

My eyes must have sought Mr. Astor's across the room, while past and future played invisibly upon the checkerboard between us, but his eyes were merely little tunnels into the harsh cliff of his brow and gave me no greeting at all.

"Mr. Lewis," he said, "I want you to prepare two letters for me. One to those four of my partners in the fur company who sail for Oregon. The other to Captain Thorn. I do not care to have the contents of these letters bandied about. I have no ambition to make school books or masterpieces of them, either, mind you. But they must be worded so that they will command for me during the entire time of the *Tonquin's* absence. I expect you to compose them tactfully, impressively, unmistakably."

The large words did not come easily to him. They exploded around his pipe stem like hard fruit splitting in the frost. He pointed me to a fat desk on his left. Paper, ink, and quill were waiting. I sat down, waited. I knew how deliberate he would be with his way of giving me my memoranda. He held a gulp of beer a long while in his mouth before he finally swallowed it and began.

"First, the letter to the Messrs. M'Dougall, M'Kay, David Stuart, and Robert Stuart. This letter will enjoin them to maintain harmonious relationships, not only among themselves, but with all others subordinate to their direction, and with all they encounter in travel and trade. They themselves should make unanimity their ideal. I expressly recommend that all differences of opinion among them concerning the aims and interests of the voyage should be decided by majority vote."

The pause, while he took breath, was upheld by the meager bubble of saliva boiling in his pipe, and the twin buzz of some summer insect against the chinks of light in the heavy window shutters.

"The Indians. I have dealt with Indians many years. The Canadian gentlemen are not so superior to me there that they cannot accept my advice. I advise them strongly to take care, once you have reached the Oregon . . . the Columbia. . . Fort . . . to see to it that you all impress most favorably the savages among whom you must live and trade. Tell them I hope you will find the Indians kindly disposed, but that you must all be ever watchful and cautious of them. Because I know the Indians from my youth. . . ."

Sounds of gentle city life came in to us: the brisk clopping of smart horses' hoofs down Broadway, the random voices of promenaders across the park, the soft click of leaves of young poplars along the walks, the call of a flower girl like a tail to the kiting resonance of St. George's chimes.

Indians, Mr. Astor was speaking of. Indians on some far Pacific inlet which probably neither he nor I could give exactly on the map. Only a few months forward and I . . .

but even the knowledge that all these solemn, circumlocutory things he was dictating must apply to me, too, and to the saving of perhaps my very life, could not make them seem less stodgy and bizarre. Indians . . .

"Next, my letter to Captain Jonathan Thorn, First Lieutenant United States Navy, on furlough to command the *Tonquin*. The usual naval compliments, of course. Acquaint him with my hopes for the health of himself and his crew, and for good-humor aboard ship. I leave it to his special management to prevent misunderstanding. Write, too, how particularly careful he must be on the coast, and how he dare not rely too much on the friendship of the natives. Recall him General Washington's instructions to St. Clair, saying that all the accidents which have yet happened arose from too much confidence in the Indians. Have you that quotation right, Lewis?"

"Sir? Oh, yes, Mr. Astor, entirely." So I had, but only by the grace of that faculty to listen with half-open ear which men attain when they are hot and weary and must put up politely with voices and topics as outlandish as these.

On the desk, atop a neat, fat pile of the day's mail, lay an opened circular of the coming season in the Park Theater. Even while I wrote I could read over the edge of my own page onto this other which heralded the arrival of the great English actor, Mr. Cooke, and his intended repertory of celebrated tragedies before subscription audiences of the most fashionable people of New York. The theater itself was being newly decorated *à la mode*, in tasteful combinations of fawn, white and gold, with exquisite recesses of French gray and purple. A new era for the drama in America and for the fortunate box holders, limited to leaders in the city's social . . . Mr. Cooke's fame, it scarce need be advertised, throughout all Europe . . .

"Read me your notes on that Thorn letter."

I started to read them. "Very well. Yes." He shut me down on the fourth or fifth word. "Very well. I want to be explicit with the captain. In the event of savages approaching the ship, even if they display the most peaceful appearance and willingness to trade, no more than a few at a time should be allowed on board."

"Yes, sir." I should make it most explicit. He said, exp-p-plishit. His spittle sprayed his pipe bowl. "No more than a few at a time."

"Let him always remember the boarding netting I am furnishing and rig it against the Indians on the least . . ."

I had never heard of a boarding netting. I made some listless marks for one in my notes. A long ink blot passed like an eye bandage over my mind's picture of the theater, the mighty Mr. Cooke as Hamlet, the audience genteelly exalted in cushioned boxes of French gray and purple and gold. Mr. Astor in a most central box, with his strong, wine-colored face above his satin stock, insensitive but full of a knowledge of owning . . . knowing, as none who craned their necks from the pit to have a glimpse of him could know, why it is that the world and all brave things in it, arts, adventures, the lives of little singers and lank, romantic schoolmasters, must all belong to men with thick red necks.

"Bring me those letters to sign to-morrow night. They will be delivered aboard the *Tonquin* the day you sail. I have wanted you, as a responsible employee of the expedition, to know their contents. Under ordinary circumstances, to keep quiet about them. That proves my trust in you, Lewis."

I should have been grateful. But there was a little spray again from his last words. It came all the way over to my paper. I wiped it away with the side of my hand, and the ink smeared. I rose and, while I folded my notes, made shift to bow. But he was through with kind words before

he began them. He sat back, patting the beaded belly
of his beer mug . . . and something in the way he did it
reminded me of another day, of another old banker patting
the little Perrault's hand while they laughed at my rustic
staring.

"You may go now, Lewis. The partners are dining with
me at seven."

"Yes, sir."

When I was at the door he exploded again. "You are
not a man for the wilds. You look half starved before you
start."

So he too laughed at me—or would have, had he had the
gift of laughter. He would not have thought it a gift.

"I can use you right here at home," he said. "But you
want to go?"

And when I answered him, "Yes, sir," and began to
protest how early I had been among the applicants, he cut
me short again with his, "Very well," and flipped me out
of his life forever with a stubby red thumb.

"Very vell, und pring me pack a berfect peaver pelt.
More berfect als dot one, even."

On the wall behind his powerful head it shone, his love,
his household god, his one torn prayer to beauty . . . to
beauty profitably crucified.

8

Between Ovide and me no quarrel could last. I even lied
for him on days when he was absent from the wharf. I kept
a schedule of the clerks for Captain Thorn, and never put
the mark I should have against De Montigny's name.

"That is noble of you, James," he said when I told him
of it. "Now I presume you will go on and ask me where I
have been these forty-eight hours."

He was binding his great mane of hair, Indian style,

to keep it from flying over his face. In the evening he would undo it again and bury his big, quick hands in it up to their wrists to shake the locks loose, to make himself the lion again, the perfect Parisian revolutionist.

We were on the dock's open end, where the morning sunlight made a white unity of wood and water and a spar-webbed sky. De Montigny looked at me lazily, smiling as he spoke, knowing he teased me, and that I should never, for ten times all of Astor's millions, ask where he had been.

"The sooner we are loaded the sooner we sail," I said.

"And if you sail too soon to suit my pleasure, I suppose you will sail without me."

"I suppose nothing of the sort. You've signed. . . . There is something in the world besides your pleasure, Ovide."

He finished with his hair. He flung it back and stretched himself magnificently. "Not for me," he replied. "Not this week."

But while he leered it his eyes kept roaming the dock, as though I were too inconsiderable an audience for so good a show; his trick of collecting new hearers without their knowing it never failed him. Gabriel Franchere came up to ask me of a stack of hardbread, galley-bound, which had somehow disappeared from the lighter. A painstaking, worried chap, filled to the roof of his mouth with correct little facts and virtuous French protestations. Franchere treated his problem as though it threatened a whole army with starvation.

Ovide looked from one to the other of us, then up into the blue, and yawned.

"*Voyez*, the poor, spent moon," he said. "There is nothing so dead as the moon by day."

Last night, with my elbows digging at my window sill, I had watched the moon for a long while. It came back to me now how hot the night had been, how stale the land breeze over the roofs and in parched gardens, and how, once she was clear of a gate of black chimneys, I had watched the moon burning among burning clouds, with thousands of her sparks blown up and down the sky around her. First she had been red, and the tree tops had run with the wind to keep abreast of her. Then she had turned to gold, and all the misers in their city attics must have watched her flight covetously, mumbling to themselves as they bit their drooly lips and dreamed of following in her rich wake like greedy sparrows behind a plow. Then, at last she had grown blazing silver. . . .

Franchere disapproved of his fellow Canadian. He blinked after one short glance into the sky. "M. de Montigny," he said, "permit me: I am here to ask M. Lewis——"

"Listen to that, Lewis. I give him the moon and he still asks for hardbread."

He enjoyed his quip immensely. It seemed actually to annoy him that Franchere, at whose expense he made it, did not enjoy it too. He was wasting himself on a dull audience. He specialized on me.

"Dear learned James, the way you stand there with your long nose tucked into your shoulder blade . . . so wisely, like nothing so much as an old stork. Is it only worms and baby-clothes that storks care for? They never peck at the moon? I was sure you were watching her last midnight."

"Her?" Damn him. "Who?"

"Why, the moon, of course. Who else? The lovers' moon."

Aye, I had watched. Until long past midnight I had watched. I had seen her turn to hot silver, unshadowed, naked, lying back desirous on the soft night, a moon for shameless, happy lovers. But, damn him, I would not tell him so.

"I was with someone you know, Lewis . . . guess who
. . . and we laughed . . ."

He must have known he was taunting me. He was doing
it purposely, but not primarily with malice, only insistent
that I enjoy it as much as he himself did. He raised his
voice above the rattle of carts along the river street. There
was something tipsy, crazy, cruelly successful about his
shouting.

"We laughed as we looked at the moon, Lewis. First
we looked at her through our glasses lifted between her
and our eyes. That gave her the color of a young girl's
lips."

He told it with a little belch and stopped to taste the
morning-after sourness of his mouth.

The color of a young girl's open lips, until they put their
glasses down, spilling them carelessly perhaps around the
couchside, and saw the moon as silver as she really was,
the color of nothing except a young girl's trembling throat,
the round white mirror of her rising breasts . . . and there
must have been little moons drowning in each other's eyes,
as little moons go singing down among the reeds of summer
wood ponds. . . .

And aye, damn them, they had laughed. And here it was
my silly part to try to keep him from ever knowing how,
as I had sat there at my window looking over the white
town's roofs, it had almost been as though I heard them
laughing, a delirious and boastful ecstasy, and almost
seen them somewhere far across the city, lying high and
white in locked delight upon the white youth of the sky
. . . and how I had closed my shutters with such a crash
as to bring a watchman running up the street . . . and
then, when his footsteps were distant, how I had opened
them again to that full-flooding, shining torment of the
moon.

"It's in those boy's clothes of hers I love the little bitch best, Lewis. You've seen her like that . . . when she rigs herself up in those boy's breeches, and stands there, laughing, head up, Lewis, and laughs . . . you've seen her like that. That's when I want to put her in my pocket and carry her along to the Col——"

"Aye, as in any old operette!" I remember how sarcastic I sought to be.

"M. de Montigny," said Franchere, "we are not interested in your foul amours."

Ovide planted his feet apart with rather absurd care and steadied himself against a pier-end pole. I realized how wild a time he'd made of it the last few evenings, and that he was still a little drunk.

"No, we are not?" he mocked, and meant his look for me. "Do not misunderstand me. I did not pick up any strange habits in France. It is women I love. But a woman in boy's clothing . . . dear James! Good old James!"

I turned away, sick of his liquor-rank breath and his wild, paradoxical handsomeness. Franchere had begun to scold him shrilly. Two or three steps, and I heard the scuffle and yell behind me.

I flung around again. Ovide was grabbing at Franchere's collar when I shoved myself between them. His other arm was up and, as I collided with him and he lost his footing, he clutched with it for the pier pole. His hand met a green slime; furious face, shoulders, somersaulting legs raced it down into the water.

He was climbing out again before we knew what had happened. Dripping, joking, treating it all as a rare lark, all resentment immediately forgotten, he sat in the sun for a few moments like a great wet dog, while he undid and spread his sopping braids.

From a next dock some waterfront loungers cheered him for his expert swimming, and he was completely pleased.

"Here's something charming for your journal," he sang at Franchere.

"Oh, no, I promise you . . . on my word of honor . . ."

"All right, little preacher, run me up a glass of hot rum from that shop over there." He searched the sky whimsically for his moon, dead or alive.

After which he set gayly to work, with his damp clothes moulded to his muscles, and outdid any three of us all day. Next morning he was missing again.

9

I delivered Mr. Astor's letters at his door. He was already gone out to the famous partners' banquet in the Assembly Rooms.

As chief clerk I had had the honor of an invitation to appear there at nine-thirty, meet the gentlemen, share the speeches, the good-night brandy and cigars. I was not a full-fledged officer, however, and could not have been expected to sit down to dinner with the most distinguished guests the city offered. Well and good.

Two hours for my own supper somewhere, meanwhile, and for something even better: for leisure, a careless, aimless saunter, a chance to think without need to account for my thoughts or to check myself present.

But, in streets where I walked, the sly windows opposite the sunset seemed all to have red beasts slumbering behind them, and a red glare lapped the bricks slowly to the roof lines.

I was uneasy and morose, and knew myself for a coward. The incident with Ovide this morning had unnerved me more than I would admit: I kept telling myself it had all been only funny. I found myself walking down to the Brooklyn ferry . . . Not so far from its other landing, on a little hill above the dusty Long Island road, I knew there was Green's Military Gardens. I kept daring myself to take the ferry. I faced about angrily, walked uptown again, with a new trepidation riding me as a little Dutch imp had once ridden me pick-a-back in the schoolhouse days, shrieking down my collar, little fingers hooked into my windpipe.

I hastened, with nothing to haste me. I found an old stick and ran it along the Broadway fences as I walked, stubbornly, mechanically counting the noisy flow of pickets.

Counting, counting things, kegs, blankets, trinkets, always counting costs.

The stick split short. I hurled the remainder of it into the brown dark. The sunset was now gone from all but St. Paul's steeple, which smouldered like an old torch inverted in some enormous afrit's unseen hand. Perhaps he, too, would soon hurl his pastime impatiently away.

I had reached Mr. Astor's house again. From close beyond it the oil flares of a shilling peepshow touched his pillars and his brass door plate with a new, dancing light. I hurried by.

The show was the year-old exhibition of paintings by the Signor Gorme, four hundred square feet of canvas, depicting the Bay of Naples and the Battle of Trafalgar. Not an ordinary panorama, the board read, but a series of masterpieces by an artist renowned over Europe, Russia, and all Eastern Empires. Incidents hitherto undisclosed of the most glorious victory in naval history amid the world's loveliest scenery. There was still more lettering, top and bottom, but the flares had smoked it above and little boys had kicked and scrawled and committed nuisance on it below: the whole entryway wore the sad, shabby look of a lost cause.

In the ticket booth an old Italian blew into a flute. When I came up and laid my coin in front of him, he did not bother to rake it up; only nodded while he went on playing, his tune squeaking a little with the surprise of having actually attracted still another customer.

But there was only one beside me, indoors: a fat, hot farmer who stood in the middle of the hall, fanning its stuffiness and his own odor of the barnyard with a broad-brimmed hat, his slow Dutch eyes pasturing in the flats of paint around him.

They were bad daubs, I knew, and the colors of water and heaven seemed to have been laid upon their hugeness with huge brooms. But such blues . . . sang like flutes. And along an all too verdant Posilipo, and in the base of a sugar-dipped Vesuvius, white temples of antiquity crumbled under the unstinting sun and confided their centuries to drowsy poppy fields and a serene sea. I had no reason to be reciting Virgil at them, but reason or no . . .

The farmer was staring me over, I kept my lips still. He was from Putnam County, the father of one of my favorite pupils in the past, and we had recognized each other.

"Mr. Lewis!" He started to hold out his hand, realized the hat in it, fumbled, went on fanning himself. The embarrassment of the meeting wrung fresh sweat from under his cheek bones. "How are you . . . Mr. Lewis?"

I gave him back his greeting. I took pleasure in a little irony about it. I remembered my last day in his township, when he had let me go trudging past his farmhouse without any word or pause while he blacked his boots.

I guessed at once why he was in the city, in this neighborhood, quite next door to Mr. Astor's. Harder times than ever on the farms, the knowledge of Mr. Astor's legal ownership lying like sharp, discouraging stones in every furrow, and the children already mean and spiritless from too early labor.

"Well, Mr. Lewis . . ."

"Well, Mynheer. And welcome to New York."

"Well, Mr. Lewis, 'n' you live here?"

"On and off, Mynheer. At the moment, yes."

"Truly, do you? Well, well, Mr. Lewis. We all . . . often
. . . You're doing well, Mr. Lewis?"

"Oh, excellently. So well that I am soon going to
Oregon."

"Where?"

"To the mouth of the Columbia River." But this must
have meant even less to him. "The Pacific Coast."

Beads started from large cheek pores again. I thought
it his difficulty of locating the Pacific, but I did him an injustice. For he rumbled slowly: "But we've heard . . . that
is the expedition of John Jac——"

"Right."

"But, no . . . well, after all he has done to us. To you,
too, Mr. Lewis. Well, yes, to you, too. It was his fault that
we had to . . . well, wasn't it? And here you are . . ."

He was as inarticulate as all of his breed. He was suspicious of me. He backed a little away, examining me over
his barn-brown jowls as if I had suddenly revealed myself
Beelzebub.

"He would not even see me to-day, your Mr. Astor. I
was sent by all of them, just like you were once, all the
way to New York in our busiest farming time, and, well
. . . he would not see me for a minute."

"That is like him," I said. "He treats all squires like
that. He keeps kings' ambassadors waiting for days."

"I only wanted him to know how hard it will be for us
. . . but, well, I couldn't get to speak to him. I couldn't even
see him."

"I know. He is a great man. Didn't you know? He is a
millionaire."

"Well, yes . . . so it will be easy enough for him to wait
until we give in to his terms. Now we'll all have to go to

law, instead. Yes, you'll see, we will all go to law. He directed me to his lawyers. He would not even see me." The poor dunce thought of his ripe, busy fields, which he had had to leave on a busiest day to come jogging down here for a brusque snubbing, and which were really Mr. Astor's fields. "Well," he said. . . .

"Men like Mr. Astor are the law's best friends and customers," I said. "The law is on his side. If not yet, it will be. You'll find that out."

He did not know what to make of that remark. Neither, indeed, did I. Why or how it had burst from me I had no idea. I glanced at the fat farmer, sorry for him, ashamed of him, annoyed, amused, ill relishing this turning of the table of our meetings. Those sweat drops in the creases under his eyes might almost have been tears.

I looked away, to the opposite wall. There hung the battle pictures: Trafalgar, ships aflame and sinking, ships with their sails in shreds, their masts toppling to the broadside cannonades, flags pierced but cheerful in the upper hell of bombs and mangled rope and musket men. Ships locked together in embrace as cold as the sea's waves, as hot as the fire above the waves, bedded in fury and terror and a lust of gore. Abominable, sickening, crude paintings, with a thousand things wrong with their workmanship, red paint slung in every spare crevice of them, and men like maniacs rampaging in the red.

Whatever befell us, it would not be like this. That was my first thought. But my flesh jumped, and I felt as though the veins down my legs had changed into long worms and must crawl outside my skin. I cursed myself silently and turned back to my farmer.

"You, Mr. Lewis . . . on Astor's expedition. Why? Well . . . why?"

"Oh, to get to be a partner quickly. To become a millionaire." I waved to the poppies and turquoise water of the

Posilipo. "To have flutes and viols playing for me while I banquet in my old marble temple in an ever warm and gentle land."

I was the stupider of the two of us to joke like that. He thought me mocking him—or crazy. All his chagrin of the day, the jogging and shooing and worrisome rebuffs he had endured, cooked in his moist face.

"Tory!"

It was the worst thing he could find to call anyone, poor lump. Then he hawked and spat an umber phlegm at me, and, partially revenged on Mr. Astor and the Law, creaked out into the street.

I cleaned my coat with my handkerchief—it had served me right.

Then I stood staring at the vermilion horrors of Trafalgar. I was a long while before I realized that I was searching for something special: for a boarding netting. I must see what a boarding netting looked like. . . . "Let him always remember the boarding netting and rig it . . ."

The farmer had left the door open, and a breathy, grieving music floated in.

IO

I managed to arrive at the partners' dinner in the City Hotel when it was nearly over. Segar smoke was in the bad air, clutching at the pompous curtains and columned doorways of the Assembly Rooms, settling in the white, tablelong troughs between rows of many indistinct but no doubt renowned heads. The savor of heavy dishes, come and gone, stayed on. Decorousness had swollen into solemnity; solemnity was by now an unhappy drowsiness. The collective drowsiness of a hundred overfed, flatulent notables who went on smoking and sipping and digging their heels into their own insteps to keep awake and look undoubtedly sober. Mr. Astor was celebrated for his dislike of drunken-

ness. He would be even more offended by any exhibition
of it than by anyone's premature departure.

Those were the partners beside him at the head, of
course. Two on his right, two on his left. And there were
speeches making . . . anyone's departure would indeed
be premature.

Mr. M'Kay I knew from the far glimpse I'd had of him
in the big canoe, the day of the voyageurs' arrival. The
younger man next him must be David Stuart. David's
uncle, Robert Stuart, would be one of the other, fatter pair.
Then the fourth was Duncan M'Dougall, The M'Dougall,
chief of his clan's Canadian branch. They had arrayed
themselves in Highland costumes, these last two.

The M'Dougall was standing, finishing some sort of
declamation, as I tiptoed in. He could be a mighty fellow—
or a fool. It was hard to understand him from here; the
drone of his Scotch rubbed at everybody's ears like loose
wool.

He was giving the guests a piously unabridged history of
the glories and profits of the Northwesters, that great
British company whence he and his fellow Canadian partners had been induced. This very banquet of buffalo
tongues, venison, beavers' tails, brought down at great
trouble from the shores of Superior, was only a small copy
of the famous revels in Montreal or at Fort William, when
the Northwesters gathered in their pomp of a new peerage
of the rich, fur-bearing wilds.

Yet, here were he, M'Kay, the Messrs. Stuart, all, all
willingly severing themselves from all these past advan-
tages, sacrificing even their fealty to the Crown, nay, their
very covenant with Heaven above, to go out under new
company colors, to become Americans, Astorians. . . .

Heads turned his way. Half of what he was saying still
stuck to his fat tongue, or in the puffed folds of his plaid
diagonal. But the other half was proving itself of that

wallowing gracelessness and unconscious insult which will make the most wearied assembly sit up and listen in grim, damning humor.

It needed a gawk like me, perhaps, to wonder why there are so many round-faced, full-bellied, fat fools on earth . . . and what it is that steams from their chafing flesh to make them gabble like this. I thought of the farmer who had just now spat at me. That was only instead of the blown speech he had not had wits enough to compose. I preferred even him to this one who, with the looks of a merchant at a masquerade, could go on complacently toasting himself with the wrong, wrongest possible, speech.

There sat Captain Thorn. He was not at the head of the table with the partners, but in the middle of a row below. Maybe mere oversight had seated him here, maybe some incipient spite of which I had as yet heard no gossip. At any rate, he appeared openly aggrieved. He did not lounge or yawn, as those around him were at length allowing themselves to do, or give the prating M'Dougall the benefit of one commiserative grin. He sat erect, his face claret-dark, his jaw muscles running like mice beneath a tight coverlet.

He, too, was a heavy man, but his bulk was bleak and his fuming cold. When he saw me he beckoned me to him.

"Mr. Astor's orders," he said, "we sail on the mornin' o' the sixth. Have our Noah's Arkful o' clerks aboard afore dawn, 'n' see there's a likely cabin boy among you, too."

"Very well, sir."

"That's clear? 'Bout the boy, I mean?"

A trim young man, seated next the captain, gave me a long glance. I thought I recognized Mr. Washington Irving, the lawyer and humorist whose *Father Knickerbocker's History* had taken the town by its nose last year. He had on a plum silk waistcoat and an elegant pearl pin. It was plain to see that he and the sea captain had never

exchanged a word the evening long, had not the least
interest in each other, never could have. He kept his kind
eyes on me.

"'Bout the boy, Lewis, y'understand . . . I want one."

"Very well, sir. If you want one, sir."

The M'Dougall was winding up his monstrous speech
with a memoir of smart trading in the Athabaska country,
in the Rocky Mountain House, all across New Caledonia,
in mighty Britain's name. When he finally subsided a little
applause spattered the groan of many chairs. Even this
little was too much for Captain Thorn. He fairly bellowed
his final direction to outdo it.

A likely boy, useful and respectful and no damned little
whoreson landlubber like the parcel his passengers had
brought along from Canada. That gave me the clue at
once: he had probably been quarreling with the partners
already about our many clerks, and over the necessity for
a cabin boy of his own.

"To be sure, sir. . . ."

"A real hickory young lad, Lewis. No four-eyed, seven-
syllabled schoolmaster like you, either, mind you."

I caught Mr. Irving looking me over and over as he
tamped out his segar with his heavy gold fob seal. He was
so kindly and elegantly entertained. When he overheard
that I had been a schoolmaster he seemed to enjoy an
especially humorous resolution.

"Oh, no, sir, a—a—not like me," I stammered at the
captain. "Good-night, sir." My long legs got me swift
away.

"Good-night, Ichabod."

I was down to the table's foot before I realized that it
was not Captain Thorn who had answered me like that.
But then, who had it been? Ichabod? What did that mean?
I looked back over many shoulders, through the smoke
bank. . . . I saw young Mr. Irving still following me with

his kind, mirthful eyes, as though it were he who had said it. Ichabod?

I waited a moment in the rear of the room, listening to the elder Mr. Stuart, whose turn it was now, proposing a toast to all those minor members of the expedition who, of course, were not asked to be present to-night in such distinguished company, but who came all from excellent Scotch strains, or were celebrated voyageurs from the Northwesters' most treacherous waterways, all loyal Americans and brave Astorians overnight in emulation of their employers, whose stanch Highland traditions . . .

Our Noah's Arkful, the captain had called them. And who'd supply the dove of peace?

I shambled out. I kept wondering what I could possibly do about the captain's snappish clamor for a cabin boy. And what the devil . . . Ichabod? Ichabod?

II

Two days until September sixth. By the evening of the fourth the *Tonquin* was fully loaded, her load vouched and listed, her personnel and embarkation papers ready for the naval supervisor of the port, Commodore Rogers. He had promised her safe convoy off the coast. This would be the government's amen to Mr. Astor's scheme.

The talk in the coffee house that night was all of frigates, British seizures, and American protests. Ebenezer Fox, our first mate out of Boston, was an affable man, moon-faced and modest. He talked mostly about his nine-year-old son. It was odd to hear his cheery vow that there'd surely be war if we were interfered with.

"War?" I said. "With boarding nettings and such?"

"Aye, well, war's not the worst. I've got a worse dread of the Columbia we're bound for. I'd an uncle got drowned right on the bar of that river, what d'ye think o' that?

An' here I am, matin' it up to the very same . . . aye, well."

A full-bosomed serving wench behind him laughed and ran her fingers over his bald spot. "Aye, well yourself, Yankee," she said; "you talk 's they all talks when they're leavin'. Have another round of Jamaica 'n' forget the family f'r year 'r so. It's a tar's life."

Mr. Fox leaned back and slapped her playfully and did order another round. He said it was good rum, though not so good as Medford, of course, and he had promised Mrs. Fox not to touch any of the poor stuff we'd find on Owhyhee, and he'd advise us the same. Aye, well.

There were Farnham and Matthews and I, done with our last trip between wharf and warehouse, and glad of that. There were Mr. Mumford, the second mate; and Thorn, the captain's brother, who had lately joined the crew. We had brought old Stephen Weeks, the armorer, along with us, and he in turn had brought the ship's carpenter, Johann Koaster. We were already something of a clique around the jolly moon face of Mate Fox.

"No good sailing weather," said Weeks. He had a blackened gray beard, as though gunpowder had been blowing in and out of it for years, and his ears were clogged and almost useless.

"We'll drift for a week in a calm like this," said Mate Mumford. There was something spiteful about the way he said it. He had already had a disagreement with the captain, and a reprimand . . . he could not discuss it here in the same taproom with the captain's brother.

Johann Koaster, the Russian carpenter, stared from one to another of us, trying to understand the restlessness which underlay all our curt remarks.

The windows were open on John Street, and a heat as heavy as furriers' glue came in. There was no breeze. A square of the hot, uncolored city night, like a puppet-show stage. A pair of beaver hats went by, pushing much small-talk before them. Then a drunken coachman, cut off at the waist by the window-sill, blowing his nose on his sleeve. Then, like a prize Judy, a town woman on her way to the waterfront stopped in the middle of the little stage and grinned in at us . . . "Sailor boys, duckies, sailor boys."

But the night was still young, and three of her front teeth were missing, and we waved her on. Farnham, more fidgety than ever, was showing great interest in Mate Fox's matrimonial advice. There was a deaf man's vacancy in old Weeks's gaze. Mate Mumford sat biting his lips, watching the captain's brother.

The feeling came over me of how far apart each of us was being driven from the others by the mere knowledge of how long, how closely, we should soon be cooped to-gether. As though no amount of rum we swilled could . . . I was growing thick-minded, foggy, drunk . . . could swill away the mesh of hostility which each soul weaves and raises and ties tighter and tighter around itself in times of most unwilling, uninvited loneliness. As though each of us had run up his own boarding netting . . . Christ, his boarding netting against all . . . these gory fears and tipsy disgusts which swarmed in the pressing faces of all others.

Koaster had not made a sound. He sat next to Farnham, and I could feel how he annoyed him with his simple silence. He had both his huge hands around his tankard. When he lifted it I saw that three of his fingers were gone. He was a gigantic man, and he looked from one to another of us in a meek, dumb agony of loneliness. I remembered having seen a live ram floating in the river tide the other day, its black muzzle bubbling and sinking to its eyes. Koaster's eyes were like that ram's—and when he looked at us out of them he seemed to see no more of us than he understood of why we laughed and joked in such brittle

ways. What he saw instead . . . what memories of a boyhood in some Black Sea town where America's name was
less than a myth among the serfs, and Oregon's unpro-
nounceable and entirely unknown . . . I cannot tell. Or
could not, then.

But his tool-chopped hands brought his tankard down,
he dried his mouth with the end of his hawser of blond
hair, lurched up as dumbly as ever, and out and after the
old whore.

Whoops from a table hard by the door. A half-dozen of
the French voyageurs sat there in a noisy, lurid circle of
their own. The three Lapensees I knew, Nadeau and
Jeremie. They had come over on the ferry for a last, ex-
tended spree. They were all brave in deerskin and striped
worsted again, in spite of the heat; their hats tossed with
new feathers and ribands, the spoils of Brooklyn conquests.
They never strolled anywhere without kitchenmaids'
waists in the crooks of their arms and a parade of awed
urchins behind them.

I got up and went across to drink with them. I was unsteady in my walk. A table between them and me seemed
to lean out purposely to trip me. It was at me they laughed
now. I assumed much dignity. I did not enjoy my question:

"Where is Ovide de Montigny?" I asked them.

Nadeau shrugged and looked at Jeremie. Jeremie smiled
and looked at the brothers Lapensee. It was an all too old
question, perhaps. An all too public joke.

"*Eh bien, où est Ovide de——*"

"*Qui sait?*"

"*Moi.*"

"*Et moi.*"

"*Moi aussi.*"

They began to sing it. They put it impromptu to some
ballad music they all knew, made a ribald canon of it.
They knew where Ovide was as well as I did, and they'd

prove it. They were younger children than any I'd ever
had under my birch switch. I drank with them. Twice.
While the roundelay lurched into verse two.

"*Eh bien, où est la 'tite chantresse? Qui sait?*"

"*Moi . . . et moi . . . et moi aussi . . . je sais où est la 'tite
chantresse . . . Ovide et la 'tite chantresse.*"

"Every evening," said Basile Lapensee expansively.

"You have seen her? With him?"

They shook their heads, no, as they sang. No, they had
none of them seen her. Nor him with her. Him they saw
sometimes at the billets, I supposed, and he talked, told
. . . while he did his bright hair and smiled down on the
circle of them around him, he told them everything, I supposed.

> "*Youpe, youpe, sur la rivièr*',
> *Ovide est mon chevalier*——"

They all laughed loudly. They loved their new rhyme.
It went with their oldest paddle song. I had another drink
with them.

I did not care a snap. Once I had heard her sing, once
she had giggled at me from her rich keeper's carriage, and
that was the sum of it. Nothing. And I was nothing as a
chevalier . . . had never been one . . . and, once out of sight
of New York, nothing from nothing would amount to . . .

> "*Ovide, mon grand chevalier,*
> *Vous ne m'entendez guère*—
> *Youpe, youpe, sur la rivièr*'."

"What long white faces these young Yankees wear," ob-
served Jeremie. He used the heathenish patois of his woods,
and must have thought the few French remainders in it
would escape me. When I swung towards him they all
roared their glee into their song. I wanted to be very
angry. We had another drink.

We drank to the day after to-morrow. The voyageurs sang, "*O jours si pleins d'appas* ..." They had an endless repertory. They filled the hot tavern with ballad after ballad of life in their canoes, of rapids seething under the pines, of miracle flights and savior paddle strokes among the black teeth of whirlpools, and of warrior Ottawas and amorous Pierce-Nez squaws. Their boasting grew too turbulent for tunes. Give them a wild white river, and we should see what feats of skill and bravery the voyageurs employ.

I was fully drunk now. I remember promising them a wild white river in a tone of promising children the play-things they've been howling for. "*Youpe, youpe, sur la rivièr'* ..."

I got myself back to the other table. The two mates were leaving, arm in arm. Farnham had already gone.

"Gone to spend to-morrow with his young lady," explained Matthews. "A very proper young lady, of course, that's Farnham. He'll very properly marry her when he comes home again, he says. He would, aye, he would. You've no such lady around, have you, Lewis?"

I shook my head ... it did not shake well.

"No, I thought you hadn't. Well, neither have I, none of that sort. But whenever I want my beef pie——"

> "... *mon chevalier,*
> *Vous ne m'entendez guère,*
> *Vous ne m'entendez pas.*"

"There's a damn smart young widow's been kind to me on and off, and I'll go let her cook for me to-morrow—I shan't have a beef pie like hers again for five years, I suppose. She'll cry. They all cry. The best way to stop their tears is in bed, I've found. Haven't you?"

I tried to shake my head again, but plain drunkenness made it sag sideways.

"Haven't you anyone like that, Lewis?"

I yanked up. Be damned if I'd let him pity me. But he was only amused—and I was used to that.

"You're a queer old stork, Lewis."

My eyes caught the tip of my nose and watched the comical peck it made as my head went down again. Like a stork's beak, as thin and prying and foolishly vermilion as a stork's. Is that what he had meant?

All of us look like various birds or animals . . . what a marvellously trite discovery!

Yes, but we do. And when one is drunk one sees as never before. One sees the greed and jealousy and all the foolish cowardice which file a nose sharp, and the slobber shining on weak lips of sudden caricatures. . . . One more rum burning down to my stomach and I'd be philosopher enough to smile back into the faces of them all and know them for pink pigs, dogs in a street-corner heat, vain ravens in circus caps and ruffs.

Matthews was gone, too. They must have left me alone there. The serving wench brought me something more which I kept upsetting without trying to. When she wiped the table she rubbed herself against me like a lazy cat. Cat, whiskers and all.

I have a memory, faint as breath in a cold room, of finding a note in my pocket from Partner Duncan M'Dougall: a note which had been sent me in the early evening, and which I had crammed away because I had not liked the first few bumptious and peremptory lines of it . . . something about taking orders from him and not from Captain Thorn, and under no circumstances to let myself be bullied into signing a cabin boy.

The paper was sopping with rum. The writing ran, black inklings threw wet veins out across the little amber pools and became a map of wild, unnumbered rivers. The liquid soaked away, the map became a moist, blurred face.

I laid my own face down upon it and it filled my eye,
became the huge, puffed, grotesque face of The M'Dougall.
Ever so sly a face, the face of a fatted fox, perched on his
thick neck.

And I saw other necks, separate, unattached, inhuman,
yet immediately recognizable. Thick, red necks, rooted
with coarse hair on bulging ridges and around the crater
edges of old boils, sweating in the folds of sullen flesh.
Necks which were more than channels between body and
brain or mere troughs for food and breathing. Necks growing like great, squat, scabbed oaks out of the swamp, vast
with the freely sucked strength of the ever hostile ooze
. . . the everlastingly thick necks of the domineerers.

Then, like a white swan's lifted into sunlight, like all of
a June day around her, the neck of a young girl, slim,
audacious, shining, with an aria of Mozart's trembling in
the throat, a song within a song.

I was in the street. Someone was helping me. I shook myself free. I knew where I lived. I was a maudlin, scrawny
booby, but I'd not be helped or pitied. I did finally reach
my room. My pockets had been picked.

I lay down in the hot, twirling darkness and shook with
a loathing of all the faces which still brought their hot
snouts close against my cheeks, and with a fear more indefinable and unhappy of the voyage so soon ahead, the
unfathomable years . . . if years there were to be . . . ere
life should hawk me up through the great neck of the unknown and spit me out, forever out, far and forever.

12

Deep in the night I burst awake again, unsteady,
parched, and with a penitential headache. I lit a candle and
gulped water. I began to lurch around the room, picking
up this and that familiar thing which must go into the small

bundle of belongings I should be allowed to bring aboard. I did it very gravely, as if gravity were a brilliant excuse for the useless things I chose, for the way they went slipping from my hands, for the black pain between my eyes when I bent down to scoop them up again.

I found my old Voltaire. A single volume, an odd portion of the *Dictionaire Philosophique* which I had had at college. It was my darling volume, and none should part me from it. I rocked as I opened and began to read from it. I sat down on my mussed bed, under the candlelight. The random print gathered into words, into long sentences.

"If you could disturb the destiny of a fly, there would be no reason that could stop you from making the destiny of all the other flies, of all the other animals, of all men, of all nature; you would find yourself in the end more powerful than God."

I was too befuddled to gain much from that, then. I'd sharpen my wits against it some other day when my wits were rid of rum and deserving of such exercise.

I could only sit hunched and swaying over the page, the stinging paragraph, resentful, ill from stomach up to tongue-tip, brooding bestially on beasts and men and God. God of the heaving seas, and of forests swarming with things of fur. God above the Noah's Arkful of our voyageurs, young clerks, partners with kilts for tassels to their paunches, Yankee seamen with wind-sewn jaws. God even above Astor . . . and when I thought of that I laughed aloud and rolled against my bed table, so that the candle toppled, the light ceased, and my laugh died in a new darkness.

I did not try to strike my flint again. I sat in the mean, damp heat of the fading night, my fingers scratching the page a little while, then still and sodden as the rest of me. Through my shutters on Chatham Street a firefly had erred into the room. I watched the prick of its unexpected

flight around me, half-dozing, my senses as intermittent
and haphazard as its tiny glow.

The page in my lap was suddenly dappled with a green-
gold light. The insect rested, crawled an inch onward,
rested, and each time its tiny haunches glowed and were a
lantern among strewn, half-buried words.

". . . the destiny of a fly . . ." And then I could almost
hear the dry rustle of its feet as it clicked its way down
the paper. Another crevice of soft, cold light, and the
delicate body of the little thing above the more delicate
shadow thrown by its own shining.

". . . the destiny of all the other animals, of all men . . .
you would find yourself . . ."

My thumb should grow rigid as it approached the page.
A hard, thick, domineering thumb of destiny, taking its
casual pleasure in the little crunch of dainty, futile
mechanism under its flat nail, and in the sudden moisture
of the smear. To disturb destiny, to be destiny itself, more
powerful than God.

The book slipped and closed between my knees, fell to
the floor as I myself fell back upon the bed.

The room grew full of a steaming dawn. Soon the sun
thrust its white blades between my shutters, and my last
day in the city had begun. When I leaned over, recovered
the volume and opened to the page once more, I could see
that it was still neat print and unsoiled paper, innocent
of any cruelty.

My eyes hurt with childish gratitude that I had lost my
chance to be the fate of a fly.

13

By noon I was on the ferry, bound for Long Island,
where I had advised the clerks to convene. I had long
since rolled and strapped my bundle and said what few

good-byes I must. I was responsible for the attendance of us all. I might as well be at the billets as anywhere else.

The ferrymen knew me from many trips now. There was so little wind, they had to row quite all the way across the river. They eyed me curiously over their oars. They knew all about the *Tonquin*.

The New York shore line simmered beyond a lengthening stretch of hot brown water. Craning, I made my valedictory to the trim little wharves, the dusty poplar trees and a steeple pasted behind them, and to the hard little houses which edged the Battery with sunny brick. Made it and unmade it. I recognized the conspicuously stout new warehouse with John Jacob Astor's name across it.

"You'll be wanting us at midnight to take the last of you out?"

"Maybe. Yes, midnight or thereabouts."

From Corlears Hook the shipbuilders' stays, a long, bare row, sent out to us a throbbing of hammers and mauls. It was a care-free sound from here. Under the piles of some waterfront building, so tiny at this distance, tiny men were dumping cartloads of earth, creating land out of pinches of stone and dirt . . . and that seemed the most miniature and fanciful of tasks from here.

An hour ago, on the steps of the rooming house, my landlady had let me hold her baby all the while she had tried to give me a long-winded Godspeed . . . if I'd only been a good churchgoer, a nice youth like me, and now sailing off to sea with no kin to wave me good-bye and no minister to warn me of the thousand sins and dangers of the sea, the sea, the sea. The baby, sweet-smelling as new grass, crowing, plucking at my mouth with those ridiculously little fingers, had refused to be given back. I had had to stand there listening to a sea dirge for a nice young man, an employee of Mr. Astor, my arms unaccountably forlorn when she took the child away . . . a highly educated young man like me, who seemed so fond of babies and could have stayed at home and . . .

Farnham was waiting at the Brooklyn end of the ferry, sitting neatly on the knapsack he would bring along. Mates Fox and Mumford had already gone aboard with the captain, he reported. The partners were due any quarter hour in the Astor firm's cutter. Even Matthews, full of the best beef pie and rosy reminiscences, had put in his appearance.

"And De Montigny?"

Franchere, loaded with clothes and blank-books, tried to shrug his shoulders. Farnham had a quick look at me, as if, having seen me so tipsy last night, he must class me forever with Ovide among the damned. When I yawned, the whole of Boston in him triumphed.

"De Montigny has not been seen for three whole days."

"No?"

"No. Your fine French hero——"

"Never mind, Farnham, go take these boatmen and get aboard. Don't worry for De Montigny."

Franchere walked me over to the farmhouse where they would all be, the rest of the lads under my care. Don't worry for De Montigny . . . but I did, myself. Franchere was anxious to tattle me something.

When I quickened my pace, a brown powder spurted from underfoot, and apples on low, overhanging branches turned suddenly lusterless, gray-streaked. Dust of the road, the fine, light, somehow friendly dust which is the decent end of all things clinging sensibly to land. A thrush sang across the fields, bringing back to me some other time when I had walked in the flecked sunlight into new adventure. There had been nobody to worry about except myself, then.

Near the farm garden the voyageurs lay stretched and dozing, as gayly colored as any of the flower clumps, indolent as any of the leaves. In the doorway Pillot was cutting himself a pocketful of quills. A group of the other, younger clerks lounged indoors, lax with so much waiting. I told them off. Ross, M'Gillis, M'Lennan, Wallace, and the rest.

"Where's De Montigny?"

There was no straightforward answer. Pillot blew the feather-parings from his fingers. Two of the others passed remarks in Gaelic, giggled. Franchere cleared his throat at a high pitch behind me.

"Very well, then, only tell me this: Does he know we go aboard to-night?"

This was just what Franchere was so anxious to report: "I told him so two nights ago when I met him in the village."

"Then you did see him?"

"Yes, but—he was climbing into the carriage at that moment. He was plainly in his cups. There was a woman with him. No—" flushing and hasty, as though he would anticipate the question—"I did not get a look at her. Ovide was most insolent to me when I stopped him. He seemed to think——"

"I don't care what he seemed to think. Where was he bound?"

"He did not do me the honor of saying. He will probably desert us even before we start, and I am happy not to have his confidences."

I glared at the beautiful young prig and at them all. I thumped my bundle down on a bench.

"Take this along for me when you go out to the ship. And go out as soon as you please. I'll find De Montigny and bring him on board. Then I hope he'll spank the whole tender pack of you gossip mongers."

It was now midafternoon. I walked back towards Brooklyn village. A cart gave me a lift a little of the way. The

driver talked of cattle and crops and the cheapness of real
estate on this side of the river. Farewell to these grubby
topics, I was thinking while I listened, with my eyes on
the dust-lined wrinkles in the rumps of his old horse,
hearing everything he said interrupted by a crazy, contemptuous, lovable voice, which kept shouting, "Green's
Military Gardens . . . any midnight, sir, and damn drunk,
too. . . ."

14

Close to that polite resort of the Long Islanders the cart
set me down. In the inn yard, under the galleries, a few
tables were already spread for an early evening meal.
Yellow chairs and tabourets crowded the lawn to a rustic
fountain and an orchard heavy with fruit. Neat English
awnings laid their purple shade upon the nooks where
naval officers and stout young subalterns from the fort
sat sipping against the humid hour.

I looked for De Montigny in vain. I made an ally of
the waiter. Yes, he knew whom I meant. The handsome
young monsieur was well known to them all here.

Yes, yes, the monsieur who was the chevalier of . . . ah,
correct, and many thanks for my shilling. But neither this
monsieur nor Mlle Perrault was here as yet this evening.
Would they be? He dared say they might. Mademoiselle
was undoubtedly scheduled to take part in Signor Comoglio's concert, customary to the summer weather. Here, I
must have a handbill of it . . . and thank you, and would
I not meanwhile have a seat and some refreshment? Close
to the fountain would be most . . .

I sat down. I did not want to be drunk again to-night.
Head and stomach both rebelled against the possibility
of that. I had very little money, too: only a few dubious
old paper dollars which the pickpocket had spared me,
not so much out of mercy as from fastidiousness. I ordered

something light to eat, something still lighter to pour down with it, to keep me patient.

The sky grew slowly golden, and at length red, so red that the apples which hung in its fringe seemed motifs made from the same fabric. The fountain pool took up the hue.

Carriages hummed by beyond the highway hedge; sometimes one halted and sent another party of beaver hats and parasols into the yard. From within the inn drifted the click of billiard balls. Out here, the cheerful crunch of gravel paths, of tableware clinking in the open, of voices swirling under the trees. In the overhead branches a gardener was beginning to light little globed candles.

I could enjoy it immensely. To-morrow I should not have it to enjoy. The waiter excelled in conveying the management's apologies that there would be no concert, after all. Signor Comoglio declined to begin without Mlle Perrault, who had failed to appear.

Then Ovide would probably fail to appear, too. I leaned on my elbow and sighed. It was nearly a sigh of relief, now. Oh, very well, and I could furnish my own music, too.

And I hummed. At least I thought I hummed. I must have been singing loudly . . . loudly enough to catch the attention of someone at a table just across the fountain. He bounded up for a look at me. I would not be cowed. I went on with my aria.

He was a little old gentleman. In the blue of the evening he looked very dark. A foreigner, Italian perhaps, or Spanish. A Jew, I conjectured. The devil with him. I was through with such as him. I was saying good-bye and good riddance to all these old fops who wore greasy waist-coats and many gold chains and reaked of pomade from such a distance.

But then, suddenly, he was standing in front of me, his bottle in the tuck of his right arm, his cane thrust up in the other, his hands clutching excitedly at hat and old white overcoat and whatever of food he could bring along.

"Mozart, sir! I am infinitely your debtor for the compliment."

He had large, liquid eyes. He put down his plate on my table, dragged up a chair. He handled his poor English with extravagant care. He was as shabby as he was ornate.

"I dine with you, sir. I dine with any man who honors me by singing Mozart. You do not know me, sir. Lorenzo da Ponte, sir. Occasionally tutor of Italian to your young New York numbskulls. At the moment keeper of a failing grocery shop in Elizabeth, New Jersey. *'Basta!'*"

He was already seated, comfortable, eating while he talked. He did not wait to be assured that I had never heard his name before and did not know him. *'Basta* it was. He waved his truffle in midair.

"But Da Ponte, sir, was librettist to Wolfgang Amadeus Mozart. Librettist and inspiration to Mozart in his most celebrated and delightful operas." He crammed his old mouth, put down his fork, shook out his tattered wrist laces. "And I, sir, am that Da Ponte."

15

It was close upon nine when the waiter told me in an undertone that the monsieur I expected had come in. The message caught the old gentleman and me in the middle of an air which, with heads together and all our attention on his imaginary baton, we were whistling in secret duet. I stopped, but he went on, unheeding. A few irresolute seconds, I joined him in our sarabande once more.

"M. de Montigny . . . you know, sir, the gentleman you . . . he is in the taproom, drinking. He seems to be waiting for someone. Perhaps for you, sir?"

No, not for me. For someone . . . else.

I waved the waiter away, and this time did not interrupt my whistling. We finished the suite, and after it the glasses. Then sat back smiling on one another, still curious, still surprised, bashful for our antic enthusiasm—and still more so for our bashfulness. Then, leaving speech behind, we wiped our lips and began again, softly, gravely, jealous of the neighboring loiterers who overheard us.

"This lovely thing from *Don Giovanni:* do you know it?"

Of course I knew it, but not as my Signor da Ponte did. When it grew too beautiful for piping through screwed lips, he flung his mouth wide and sang. He had a few big yellow teeth left, and his voice seemed to catch and shred upon them. But he was singing music at whose birth he had been present, words he had himself composed in the magical years when he and Mozart . . . or so he said, and I believed him.

Some day, in some quiet corner of the sky where the twilight bides its hour, my soul and his may meet again, and mine shall be in danger of knowing certainly at last whether he was simply a fluent old mountebank sponging a meal, or whether he was truly all he boasted of being: genius, gentleman, professor, artist, poet, famous lover. I did not know then—and, rather than know now, I think I shall rush upon him, hug and smother his confession against my shoulder while I whistle him a welcome of celestial Mozart.

He had told me a hundred stories of the poor, dear Wolfgang Amadeus. Stories out of hearsay and his own experience, of Mozart the young prodigy of an imperial court, the adored stripling of Paris, the merry, inexhaustible collaborator, the tender, careless friend, pitiful, enviable, sickly, poverty-ridden, prodigal, so brave. Stories of Mozart in the opera house, his whole life in pawn to the beefy Schikaneder, his heart spread out before each twittering prima donna, his pen scampering among his music notes like a young god amid the dust of stars.

I saw, through his telling, a gentle old city of Salzburg napping between vine-green hills, with the roof tiles and the rain-browned marble of its residences below a great bishop's fortress, and monks come down steep streets, and burghers sunning themselves in the crisply cobbled square before an ancient cathedral. I saw the little house where Mozart was born, and here where he lived when an unknown lad, and how from this high monastery sward he looked out in the evening over the valley palaces and the singing stream to the upflung fantasy of the Tyrol . . . and I wondered what impromptu which could never have been caught on paper had rushed to his pursed lips in answer to that sight.

Vienna in its gayest days, the Paris of yesterday's monarchy, imperishable Rome: these, too, were backgrounds extraordinary to the old gentleman's recital, stations of the Grand Tour I traveled in his company that night. Night in the small, common garden of a Brooklyn inn . . . yet, thanks to an old man's loosened tongue, night in a hundred splendid places where I had always dreamed to be. The happiest night of my life.

The tables around us were emptying. The glass globes above us smoked, shuddered, and, one by one, went black. The innyard gallery grew deserted, and the dimness of the hedges brought the dimness of the sky down to earth's lowest rim in a single piece.

I paid for what we had eaten and drunk. Most of the little money I had left went to the waiter for our privilege of sitting on undisturbed. I need only keep a single dollar for the ferryman.

"Once, in Naples . . ."

I remembered that huge, crude painting of Naples,

ruined temples under the silvery olive trees beside a
jeweled bay. And the Italian poppy field, blood red before
the gleaming portico. And this transferred my memory
immediately to the opposite wall, to the red, grotesque,
uproarious obscenity of that naval massacre. . . .

"Once, in Naples, when I was as young as you, but
already famous, and had the most romantic head of jet-
black curls to lay on many a white breast . . . for even
that expert rascal, my courtly but somewhat stingy friend,
Casanova de Seingalt, had had to compliment me on my
effect upon the ladies, while Cagliostro . . ."

But his flamboyant, meanly mended clothes were gone
from view, and his face was only a blur of lesser darkness
in the dark. Now and again some link or facet of his
jewelry would reply to an unseen beam. His eyes were
there, too, as though they were the eyes of the fountain
plashing somewhere behind him. When he sang, an old
tooth shone. Nothing else of him remained for me to see.

Again the waiter: "The person for whom your drunken
monsieur has been waiting . . . she has arrived. They are
preparing to go."

"Go where?"

"He . . . he is not easy to understand just now, sir.
He talks about a ship. But very low, sir . . . monsieur is
talking so quickly, very low. About a ship."

"Oh. Then that's all right."

Ovide, as young as I or younger, would lay his romantic
mane on a white breast for a last time, but he'd be aboard
by sailing time. What else in it was any business of mine?
And be damned to them.

The last of the other guests had gone. We could sing
aloud under the slumbering, lightly breathing trees. Now
and then the soft report of apples dropping from undis-
tinguishable boughs, the idling of a warm night wind in
a wheat field hidden by the misty road, the confidential

chuckle of water in the vanished basin behind us. Otherwise we sang into a nothingness of sight and sound, where our fond voices were all space, our pauses the tick of all time, and life knew no other evidence than this of amicable and unearthly song.

"The Requiem Mass—do you know it?"

The light shadow asked it of me from far away.

"Mozart's last work. You should know it. Something like this." He began it, but it was too much for his old, unstrung voice. "No, Lorenzo da Ponte will not desecrate it. You should hear it in church, over the vaults where the great dead lie. My Mozart's Requiem. Death came to him in the shape of a sorrowing gray stranger who ordered him to write. . . ."

There was long silence between us. My old friend went on:

"Death has so many shapes, he comes to each of us in different guise. I have lived to see such great ones die . . . as great as I, some of them. I, librettist to Mozart, poet to royalty, philosophic pamphleteer and an unrivaled scholar in the Latin languages, have lived to keep a grocery shop in a little New Jersey village, to prod cabbages and polish tomatoes for my too few customers. Death will come to me finally, I am sure of it, dressed as a round, rough-handed housewife, who will decline to buy my laurel wreath because it was not plucked just yesterday and will make poor seasoning for Tuesday's soup."

He enjoyed his pleasantry more than I did. I touched his hand on the table, but then quickly withdrew mine. I had not realized how old his fingers would feel, or how cold, or the bite of the several rings he wore.

His white hair glimmered . . . or was it the mist?

"Death should have come to Mozart like a young girl, laughing, light-footed, teasing, promising, with the tiny images of an upraised wineglass in her eyes. That was the

Death he would gladly have gone with, instead of with a rigid, gray-masked stranger who could only thrust him money and say, 'Hurry, hurry my work!', as though to a hangman, to a street sweeper. . . ."

I was sure of that rigid stranger's face behind the mask —and of the thickset, strong body pushing under his cloak to the shameless strip of his fiery chin and neck. Death must have been such a man to Mozart. I said nothing.

"Death is as chance as Life. To this one Death comes like a writhing bundle of bleached bones, to that one like a star behind a raging fire. For most men Death is a dark. Some see it in the shadow of the wings of a great bird, and some in the golden face of a torn Christ. Some . . . who knows? . . . there must be some so fortunate and gentle, they hear it in a song."

He began to sing again. Trembling at first, then calmed and unrestrained, I joined him. The dark and the deeply welling shadows in the dark and the one white star above them were all gay, rapturous melody.

16

I had still an hour before daybreak when I reached the ferry landing.

The old gentleman and I had parted with absurd reluctance, and with many stout promises to meet again. He called me his son, and had no idea of my name, my business, or my destination. It was part of the lark for me to tell him nothing of the *Tonquin* waiting in the river, or of Oregon at the journey's other end. I saw him up to his room at the inn. To-morrow morning he must be at the market for an auction of up-state fruit; in the forenoon he would call at Columbia College in regard to their founding a professorship of Italian in his favor. Was this really true? Was any of it—and what matter if it wasn't?

He kissed me farewell, I walked into the shut, lightless village with a new gratitude spinning my spirits.

It had been only an interlude. I might have met him any other night than this. I might not have met him at all. I should never see him again. I should think of him seldom, and then lightly.

I had to wake the ferrymen. They tugged sleepily into the bay, offshore of the rotted stumps and the low, stale marsh in the yellowing coves of the fog. Here and there a lantern shook its reflection down into the water around a blurry wharf end. Across the river New York was void and wiped forever out.

We worked against the night tide. There was no wind. The oars dipped into black, lusterless quiet, creaking and complaining rhythmically. For a little while the shreds of music lingering in my head kept pace with their noise of wood against wet wood. Then this accompaniment gnawed its way to the top and was all I heard.

A little dawn breeze puckered the water. The sky was rubbing its eyes. Hurry a bit, now. I had said I'd be aboard by midnight, four hours ago.

The lifting vapor showed us the *Tonquin* just ahead. We were making straight for her bow. In the brown half light she spread her structure like a brooding bird and looked fantastically large.

Like a bird, but no bird I had ever seen or heard of, dreamed of. A creature to fly through black, destructive clouds, with talons trailing in upheaval and damnation. Her wings were boned with slanting cannon, and the round, apocalyptic faces of the lighted ports stared out from under her smoky feathers. The quarter-deck gave her a low, flattened head, the bowsprit a beak savagely awry.

Red day sheeted the water between us and her. A sail was climbing the foremast, a red crest of anger. We were almost under her figurehead, a little indecipherable shield

which glowed bloodily in the dawn. This was all of her
small, hard, brazen body; but the huge wings jutted and
flared from it and beat upon the dawn with sudden, angry
shadows.

Death . . . "Some see it in the shadow of the wings of a
great bird . . ."

"We're here, young fellow."

Yes, we were here, young fellow. We had swerved alongside, the water creasing and bubbling as we closed against
that high wooden wall. I passed the ferrymen my dollar.
They helped me over the thwarts, got my hand upon the
ladder for me, pushed me up. Above me the ruddy face of
Mate Fox looked over the rail, growing larger and jollier
as I climbed.

"Fine time, you young limb." He hauled me up into
the clamor of the busy deck. "Singin', too, by God, singin'
away!"

17

There were less than sixty aboard, crew and all. But
the *Tonquin* was a small boat.

The din of orders, warnings, and abuse was already
stupefying. The sailors had almost to pummel their way
to work among us. Bewildered, bad-tempered, we trod
on each other's heels, herded awkwardly away from the
coils and loose riggings, glowered and barked at each other
for the pack of uprooted, unseasoned strangers we were.
And the crew goddamned us all.

The pilot had brought some last letters aboard. The
partners, nursing their mussed dignity in a corner whence
they could glare up at the captain, had received one of
them. The captain, glaring down on the partners in the
broil of his commands, received the other. I knew well
what they were. I sniggered with curiosity concerning
what they'd think of my fine Astorian hand. I was jostled

out of any chance to see how much either party had time to read. I went looking for De Montigny.

The morning breeze died before it was half born. The sails wilted. The weighed anchor slimed the ship's side like a newly caught monster, and the slime stank and dried in the brown sunlight of the bay.

Here lounged De Montigny in the cabin hatch, handsome, contemptuous, amused by the hubbub around him, smoking a long Havana so calmly that it held its ash for several inches. As I came towards him he pretended not to have seen me. Some sailors lumbered between us. When they passed he was gone, vanished. Only a little spray of gray particles clung in the fresh paint of the hatchway.

The voyageurs tumbled, bumped, and overran each other like bottled dragon flies. They kept wandering aimlessly into the yellow-painted place abaft the forecastle where they and the other common passengers would bunk; then out again, ill of the stench of tar and the low, evil-colored walls, baffled by their own forced idleness on idle waters, some of them already nauseous from the greasy heave of our drifting . . . yet as gaudy as ever, as cheerful, noisy, and inveterately noticeable.

We anchored in the evening calm off Staten Island. Then our first meal aboard. I sat at the head of the clerks, and purposely kept the place next mine for De Montigny. We should be friends in spite of him. He could not dodge my beck this time. He was cordial, charming; we linked arms when we were through and started for the deck together. It was an elated moment. Some tiny people were waving to us from the soft shore. I loosed my arm from Ovide's and waved back.

He was suddenly gone again.

A sailor came by bawling my name. The captain wanted me. I was to stand by and wait his convenience within the hour. I knew what his convenience would amount to. I had forgotten to ship him his precious cabin boy. Not altogether forgotten, either . . . after I had sensed what an immediate wrangle the remembering would entail.

As chief clerk I was custodian of the company books, all the inventories and specifications which must land with us in Oregon, the course charts which were to guide us there. These were stored in a little cubicle off the cabin. I had had Koaster rig me a bunk there. There was just room enough for that.

I slipped down there, away from the confusion and the shrill after-dinner sickness of the green Canadian clerks, for a few minutes of composure before I should have to stand up to Captain Thorn.

As I passed through the cabin he was already battling crudely with the partners. He had ordered the light out there at eight o'clock sharp, as on all men-of-war. The Scotch gentlemen would take none of his discipline. They'd have him know here and now . . . the whole quintet of them were on their feet, scarlet, fuming, voraciously offended. The fat M'Dougall was shouting his belly away. The captain's fist was under David Stuart's nose. So much for Mr. Astor's plea—and my fine penmanship. On the very first night.

I slipped into my closet, drew the door quietly shut behind me, grateful to have escaped their enraged eyes.

It was dark, dark beyond all certain knowledge of where to step next, darkest of all around the porthole which held back the watery dusk and which looked like a dead moon. A dead, spent moon. . . . I remembered Ovide braiding his abundant hair and laughing, prating of the moon's life and his loves. . . .

A little noise startled me: a crackle of paper, then a slide of books from their jarred stack. Rats? I thought of foolish tales I had heard of rats on seabound boats. Repugnance shook me. I kicked out into the dark.

Something leaped, squealed, stood at bay.

"Who's that?"

My only answer was the silhouette which blotted all lucence from the porthole. The face of a human, which, turning towards me, lost all features. I heard a quick, dry, rapid breathing.

"Who are you? What in hell's name——" I had found my flint at last. I could scarcely strike it.

But the first spark gave me her white throat lifting her white, amazed face, and the glint of satin of her torn Cherubino costume, and then her young chin thrown back when she laughed in recognition of me and my frightened looks.

18

I did not attempt to make a light again. We stood staring, unseeing, sensing each other's surprise and automatic hostility in the closet darkness.

Numberless questions, challenges, accusations retched me. I managed at last to stammer the most stupid of them, but she would not reply.

In the cabin beyond my door the captain and the partners kept up their fight. The captain's voice trumpeted of ships' irons for one and all. Or be damned to them and get ashore and back to their British consul, if they didn't like it. Lights out or the irons, sirs. It had come to this, the first twelve hours afloat.

And opposite me in the dark a young strumpet of a stowaway giggled and hiccupped drunkenly and disdained my questions.

"How was I to know it was your private room, you fool? I had been somewhere down . . . deep down there, hiding all day among the barrels . . . I could not stay there any longer. Out there those angry men . . . they did not notice me. I darted in here."

As in any old operette.

"I am hungry, lonely. I want my . . ."

Her Latin voice had the hot, swift stealth of flames. When it touched me my fury exploded.

Her Ovide. She wanted her fine, gallant Ovide. Her chevalier who, to cap a last debauch, had brought her aboard into the confusion of such a boat as this and crammed her down into the hold, the powder run, God knows where. Why, why? What was he thinking of? And she, was she gone absolutely mad? Did they take all this for act one of any stale old operette?

"Do you know where we are bound? For how long? The sea, the wilderness, sailors, savages—has he told you of these things . . . and what will happen if we do not somehow get you ashore to-night?"

Once more she only laughed. Her laugh mounted a slim, proud channel which I could not discern, but which the bones of my fingers cracked loudly lest they should clutch.

"Laugh, you little idiot, laugh again . . . as you always do at me. No, of course not, you have no answers to waste on a gawk like me. Save them until I fetch your handsome pimp and——"

She struck out at my voice. Her slap stung the corner of my mouth.

Outside, the insulted partners were replying in chorus to the captain. I could hear The M'Dougall squealing threats of firearms and a Yankee head blown off if anyone tried to put him into irons. Thanks, now, for their silly rumpus. They could not hear the sudden weeping of the girl.

"I wanted to come. I, myself . . . I begged him, took him in my arms and kissed him, kissed him, crying as I cry now, until he had to promise."

"Undoubtedly," I said.

"I had thrown away everything else . . . it was not his fault. Maybe he did not really want me to come at all, but I made him say yes. As women can . . . I made him bring me. Maybe we were a little drunk, crazy . . . it is a grief I cannot describe, such a parting forever. It would have been forever after we had . . . so wildly . . . I cannot describe it to you, no, not to a fool like you."

My cheek still smarted from her blow. This tumultuous, many-toned hysteria, theatrical, alien, an unreal treat. No, I was not the fool for her to describe it to.

"See, see—" though she knew I could not see—"I am a boy. A young boy, clothes, stride, everything. On the stage I often play the boy. I can so easily . . . where and how I live mean nothing, if only——"

"Hush!"

The cabin had grown quiet, the grand wrangle over at last. The crack under my door went black; the captain had evidently won his point and was reaping his darkness.

"Give me your hand, promise, promise . . . I love him so. It would be like death without him. You . . . could not know. But be our friend, help us, promise. . . ."

"Keep still!"

I pressed back, out of her pitiful reach. Her sobbing stopped. She told me months later of the toy dagger she was reaching for at that black, desperate moment. There were heavy footsteps across the cabin.

The door caught me between the shoulders as Captain Thorn flung it open.

"Lewis! Where the hell've you been? I gave you orders to ship me a cabin boy. Where is he?"

"Here, sir!"

Two voices. We had cried it together.

19

Sandy Hook, two mornings after, and a fair southwest breeze filling the sails for a first time. Good-bye to the

pinch of yellow land on the horizon, good-bye to the navy
frigate which had given us convoy past the British patrol.
For me, good-bye to my chart closet where the cabin boy,
Perrault, would sleep each night behind a locked door.

And the open sea, a clean, green pastime of the wind,
with Franchere watching it ever studiously for the first
flying fish to commemorate in his diary, and the whole
band of our valiant voyageurs puking fervently into its
waves.

III

The Islands

NO, BY GOD 'n' all the admirals, we'd not put in at the
Cape Verds, no matter how worried the gentlemen might
be about their water rations. F'r Jonathan Thorn was a
tar 'n' a hard-head, maybe, but no Tory's fool. The Cape
Verds coast 'd be barnacled with English ships-o'-war,
'n' no healthy vicinity for an American bottom with so
many born Britishers aboard . . . 'n' captain's compliments
to Mr. Dunkie M'Dougall, The M'Dougall o' Clan
M'Dougall, no less, 'n' he'd kindly observe the etiquette
o' the quarter-deck 'n' mind his own damned business . . .
'n' c'd go suck the bilges if he was as thirsty as all that.

I took care to edit Captain Thorn's reply to the partners' petition. The weather from the African shore had
sent the mercury up to 94 degrees of Fahrenheit, and had
robbed us of breeze and motion, and was no weather for
spite and insult.

I laid great stress on the captain's sincere regrets. I
assured the gentlemen how sorry he was that the water
had had to be reduced to a pint and a half per man, and
that yesterday's cornmeal pudding had wanted molasses,
and that the last fowl from the gangway coop was gone,
boiled up and irrevocably eaten.

Even so, when The M'Dougall heard me come to paragraph the last, Captain's regrets, but it'd be impossible to
put in at the Cape Verd Isles, he pounded his open Bible,
he pulled out Mr. Astor's proxy, he broke into Gaelic and a
fat, sweaty pout . . . and he called me the captain's man.

I had my denial all ready. But the deck was blazing

91

where The M'Dougall and the Messrs. Stuart squatted
in noon powwow, and the voyageurs' circle under the
mizzenmast was listening and grinning; and a shark we
had taken yesterday, October tenth, from the several
around us in the white calm off the African shore, was
being slit and opened in the galley, so that an ugly smell
came across the heat and mingled with the smell of soften-
ing tar from all our boards.

I turned away with only a hasty bow. It must have
been an awkward one. The voyageurs were chuckling
aloud. Ovide lounged with them, and he smirked along.
The single grave face was Mr. M'Kay's. The celebrated
leather-bonnet smoked a long Cree pipe with a red stone
bowl. He was the idol of the voyageurs. He paid no attention to me.

So be it, I was the captain's man.

2

I was also—an equally accidental honor—Perrault's
keeper. It was I who had had to shear her, find a pair of
boy's old overalls for her, instruct her in the cranky duties
of the cabin . . . though these were few enough, superfluous
and proof of the captain's autocratic ways in wanting a
boy aboard at all.

It must be I, too, of course, who'd encourage her to
play monkey in the rigging in her time on deck, to keep
her as distant as was sensible from the eyes and instincts
of half a hundred rough-edged men . . . and from the pos-
sessive gallantry of one handsome, bright-haired lover in
particular. I, of course, who'd trust her to bolt the chart-
closet door behind her every night, and then must lie
drumming the canvas of my hammock when I'd wake
towards dawn to the creak of Ovide returning to his
hammock next mine.

I had moved here into the junior clerks' quarters abaft
the forecastle. As their senior I had a good enough excuse
to do so. They'd need a chief clerk's minding. They'd
resent me, naturally, as spoilt children do a proctor. The
Canadian clique would try Gaelic and lofty allusions to
the better manners of school teachers in Montreal on me
for a sleepy while.

Ovide would lie, a lazy sculpture, with his braids in his
fists, and, smiling, watch our feet go up and down against
the yellow paint of the walls and the dusk of the ports
with each swing of the ship through the early night. He'd
pretend not to hear me, perhaps. He would close his eyes
luxuriously and be asleep.

But four or five hours later, when I awoke with a sullen
start, I'd not need to glance towards Ovide's hammock.
It would surely be empty again. The dull, sour air from
sea-damp clothes, from lungs of youths sleeping away,
snoring back into the stuffy dark, into the smell of tar . . .
and Ovide's hammock rustling blankly to the rocking of
the ship.

I tried several times to say something to him when he
returned. I could not, for shame, for fear that he would
twit me for prying, for playing the shocked spinster, the
outwitted duenna so fatuously, and for seeming almost
jealous . . . why, of course, almost jealous of him and his
little . . . cheap, silly little slut, with her slim white throat
thrown back on the pillow, my pillow . . . the two of them
giggling, whispering, clasping, kissing, his shining hair
over her little shorn head in the black secrecy of the closet
I'd given up to her, on the berth I'd vacated to keep her
self-assured and safe . . . safe from . . . us all.

I must have old Weeks make me a new lock and key to
my chart room. I must shake my head from on high over
the danger of losing some of the valuable maps, and not
trust her to bolt the door herself any more, but lock her

in from the outside every evening, so that . . . and, above
all, I must not, could not speak of it to Ovide when he
came back just before the dawn, lest he should see what
I'd done to my brittle fingernails by drumming and
scratching at the taut canvas of my hammock, and then,
of course, should think me jealous . . . me, jealous . . .
me, of a whoremonger and a little masquerading whore.

Now was my turn to pretend to be asleep. I'd hear him
stretching handsomely beside me, and the happy weariness
of his long yawn, and the satiety behind his slow, deep
breathing while his sculptured legs went up and down
across the tarry, stuffy advent of the day

3

The winds stayed light, the November weather in-
creasingly hot. We crossed the Equator. We saw occasional
sails, a large, twenty-gun brig, a Portuguese Pernambuco-
bound, and little sails pinned far off upon the calm. We
crossed Capricorn on the fourth before a fine breeze.

We had a canary bird, spent and with a broken bill,
aboard with us for three idle days. Koaster, the carpenter,
carried it around in his tool-pocket, which he had padded
with hectic woolen ravels from the voyageurs' *ceintures*,
and whittled an exquisite little cage for it out of hen-coop
slats, now that the chickens were all vanished into the
stomachs of the cabin mess. But the canary flew away to
die, and the gigantic Russian blubbered for hours and
knew too little English to be able to tell us how he felt.

But moon-faced Mate Fox, whose watch it was that
night, saw to it that Koaster had a double grog with his
souchong tea at supper time . . . and explained to me how,
as many a time as he'd sailed out of Boston on a voyage
as long as this, he himself had grown terr'ble lonely for
his young lad, for his home with its garden that must be

all autumn leaves by now, and how often he'd made pets
of China mice, roaches, anything at all, just so's to have
some little living thing beholden to him. . . . Mate Fox
stammered when he told me this, and I could see the blush
on his round, kindly cheeks through the evening of the
open deck . . . but Lord, Mr. Lewis, one got so foolish
on a long, hard voyage like this that anybody, anything
alive . . .

I nodded. I patronized his sentiments—and him, too,
the pink, gentle, sober, friendly fellow.

I listened without listening to some interminable yarn
he began to spin thereafter about that uncle of his, or an
elder brother or someone, who'd been drowned on the
bar at the mouth of that same Columbia, that mysterious
River of the West, as they'd called it in those days, not
so long ago . . . aye, the same Columbia we were bound for,
Mr. Lewis, and his uncle or his brother or whoever it had
been had left a large family, for the Foxes were all family
men, and his body had never . . . but no doubt I'd not yet
seen a man lost at sea, had I?

White lace foamed on the colored velvet of the sea, and
when I leaned upon the rail and looked down our side I
saw the drowning green-gold glint of the sequins of phos-
phorescence. All the water wore an operatic dress. From
high in the rigging above us someone was singing into the
warm breeze; the breeze blew back to us foamy snatches
of her song.

"Voi che sapete che cosa e' amor . . ."

The captain came by, and his metal buttons gave Mr.
Fox his evening stare.

"Y're idlin', mate. Y're hobnobbin' with the passengers,
'n' it won't do, mate, 's I've told ye twenty time afore,
it won't do."

"Aye, sir. It's only Mr. Lewis, sir."

"Oh, I see, it's only Mr. Lewis, sir." He was a heavy
mocker. "Well, you, Mr. Lewis, if y've no more learned
things to do just now, y'll report to my stateroom with a
couple o' sturdy quills and make ready f'r the Owhyhee
post to Mr. Astor."

"Very well, sir."

I had already filled a quarter of a notebook with the
complaints he intended to send home about the gross
familiarity of the Messrs. Stuart with the easy-going
voyageurs, about the stubborn condition of the lubber
nests 'n' their sea-sick occupants, about Partner M'Dougall's upturned snout 'n' criticism of the mess fare, 'n'
the constant petitions to put in at every pleasure port 'n'
barren island just around the bend of the horizon, 'n'
the young clerks neglectin' their inventories, 'n' the
sniggerish idleness 'n' insubordination 'f one 'n' all . . .
aye, absolutely one 'n' all.

'N' a school teacher f'r captain's clerk who was, he
must say, as foolish a pedant as never lived. He had
called me this in the midst of my note-taking, and I had
actually, gravely, put it down. I did him the silent favor
of correcting him on paper. I made it "as ever lived."

All the artisans from Canada were so many carriole
drivers, draymen, barbers, barkeeps, culprits. He knew
their worthlessness, 'n' Mr. Astor must know it, too.
'N' what they asked o' the *Tonquin* was a thieves'-
market on the forecastle, a tavern in the main-top, 'n'
aye . . . a Covent Garden opera on the poop.

This last for my humble benefit. Once or twice he had
heard Perrault singing in the shrouds, had looked up and
snorted with some small satisfaction that so slight and
lubberly a lad should be already at home and reckless in
the ropes. But her singing . . . as he heard her singing
now . . .

"God's sake, Lewis, if that boy o' yourn must sing, teach him to sing like a man."

He never joked. It would be months before I should see him smile for a first time. I managed one swift glance at him in the dusk, and his stocky, testy righteousness stood firm against the possibility that he suspected what a funny thing he'd said.

"Aye, sir, I'll try. I'll teach him a lower key."

Teacher, teacher . . . Ichabod, as the plum-waistcoated Mr. Irving had called after me. I must follow the captain to his awfully neat stateroom, take down his interminably growly, dogged, infantile complaints in a notebook with a polished wood cover, clip the errors and the accents from all he said, make nicely grammatical sentences out of his spites and oaths and honest loyalty to his shipowner, his taskmaster, his millionaire-on-high.

I said the bumbling Mr. Fox a slow good-night, but he had grown nervous under the captain's eye and scarce knew whether he ought to answer me. I watched for a moment the white lace foaming on the night-black of the sea. I heard Perrault still singing aloft, the puffs of the song which the warm breeze made sound so casual and imperfect, and I saw Ovide de Montigny lounging back, looking up into the ropes and laughing at the Southern night's disclosure of her tiny shadow fluttering in a web of stars.

Teacher, tattle-tale, duenna. Aye, sir, I'll try. . . . I followed my captain down.

4

The wind changed to the northeast that night, and a storm hurled itself upon us over a sea which seemed all on fire. We had five days of violent churning in the thunder and the rain, of waves which swept our bow deep down and deluged the cabin through the heat-pried seams of the deck.

Once, on the fourteenth of the month, I remember how they had to unfasten the hatch to lower us a helmsman who had had his ribs smashed by the wild spinning of the wheel. And how, beastly with nausea, thirst, tedium, the rage and unacknowledged fright of close imprisonment in a swinging cage, we all howled up at the sudden square of rainy air, at the wind which howled back in the hatchway and pushed another animal down among us. And how the sky shifted and rattled behind this glimpse, a small red pane with the black lightning of bare masts and spars upon it.

We beat to windward, now. The gale continued till the twenty-first. The sea churned up many marine plants, and grew opaque with the mud of the Rio de la Plata, and water birds flapped slantwise out of nowhere. Our water-still clogged. We were reduced to three gills per day to wash our salt beef down. We saw our first penguin —ah, Franchere, rush to put that down!—and were but a hundred and fifty leagues from the Falkland Isles.

Before the dry-mouthed partners could prepare their petition the captain himself gave orders to make ready the anchors.

"Land, land," Mate Mumford's dim bawling through the long December dusk. In the morning we should see the iron-gray, barren rocks, should send the first mate and some of our gentlemen ashore . . . and up bobbed Perrault from her service on the latest cabin conference to say that among them I should go, and she and Ovide should go . . . think of it, good Lewis, she and Ovide together on the land, in the tent . . . oh, yes, with me, of course, but . . .

And the wind tore at her foolishly large boy's blouse, and at the short, sea-screwed curls which were growing so

fast again across her forehead, when she threw back her
throat and laughed, laughed, until Ovide laughed, too,
and I . . . I, too.

All we had of our first landing were some wild geese
and a pair of shot-riddled seals. No fresh water, reported
our mighty Nimrod, The M'Dougall, who came back
from his reconnoiter gorged with duck meat and penguin
eggs. We needed three days to cool the captain's temper,
to put to sea and tack about, this time to gain good anchorage and a clean, bubbly spring in, said the map,
Port Egmont.

5

Men had lived here and were long since gone. Of the
settlements which both the English and the French had
tried to make here in the dip of the harbor rocks only this
one hut remained, the weather-whitened, sea-scooped
leavings of an old fishing cabin.

I was content to be alone. Three months of the raucous,
moody intimacies of shipboard, of menial errands and
silly embassies between the swinging cabin and the heaving
quarter-deck . . . and of never one minute of privacy to
open a beloved book.

The air was full of stalwart noises: of the basso surf and
the miles-wide click of grains of sand in the rout of the
shattered waves; of our cooper's hammer on the filling
water barrels down there in the spring cleft where the
salt-white grass gave way to a clump of sedge and cress,
a dark vein on the brilliant deadness of the rest of the
island shore; and of penguins, penguins in clamorous,
busybody protest all around me.

Often, also, the sporadic noise of musket fire from over
the dunes and tussocks, from the south side of the island,
where the Messrs. Davie Stuart and Dunkie M'Dougall
were putting a closing glory on their three days' carnage

among the seals and birds and shy Virginia foxes, and from down the beach where Ovide took pistol postures and pot shots at the baby seals sunning on the coral.

A toy *Tonquin* lay awaiting us, far out. We must be back aboard her in a few more hours. The last water kegs would go out to her in the whaleboat. Ours, three quarters up the pebbles and tipsy in the sunlight, was the small-boat. From here I could see the chill mess of shot-torn, dead birds which the hunters had brought in last night and mounded between the thwarts, and the parade of scolding penguins in the radius of their stench.

A few more hours, then. I had already struck our tent. I could sit idle or read . . . though my book stayed shut, forgotten . . . and pleasure myself with the novelty of solid rock and homely grass under my heels and haunches, of my fingers in the sand, of solitude and grateful thought-lessness in the bleak, white glitter of the sun.

But there was one thing I must do. I had promised myself to do it before we'd row away. I had borrowed a jackknife from the ship's store yesterday to do it with. Between the old whalebone hut and the sea two graves were wasting: there was a driftwood cross toppled over the head of one of them, and I could make out the letters FRAN—for Frank, perhaps, for François?—wind-rubbed, erased by many years' spray and flying sand. Over both graves the salt had formed stiff ripples, and in the raw groove between them penguins hatched and squabbled over an old pair of sealskin moccasins.

I cut a second cross out of barrel-wood, tied stave on stave with a string of water weed, and set the first straight again with the letters newly scratched into its arms. FRAN—and that was all I could do, the best I could do, for either of them.

Who had they been, of what ship, what land, what time? . . . Had they died here ashore and had a cortège of funeral-coated penguins . . . of hunger or murder or in the glittering, thundering surf? . . . Four letters of an uncertain name was the fullness of the history they had left behind. All else belonged to the wind.

"What are you doing there?"

It was Perrault, come upon me from around the hut.

I held up my book. I did not want her to know what a maudlin thing I had really been engaged on . . . and then, too, I did not want her to see the dead. Instinctively, I could not have explained why, but such young, gamin-gay eyes as hers were not to be darkened . . . and then of course I was immediately cranky with myself and her for this necessity to shield her.

"Reading," I said.

"Oh. What are you reading?"

"The Æneid."

"The——?"

"Virgil's Æneid."

She was unenlightened. "Oh," she said again. "You are very wise, Lewis."

But she smiled and looked far down the beach as she said it, as though she knew he'd soon come marching hither who would show us how little wisdom counts in women's eyes.

I stood up and started with her down the beach to meet him. She trotted to keep pace with my long legs. She would not slow us up for all the world. At the far tip of the long white scythe of sand Ovide was firing out at the seal rock. He had not seen us yet.

"Aeneas was another famous wanderer, like you and me," I said. "He adventured everywhere, over the water——"

"He was tall?"

"Oh, undoubtedly."

"And brave?"

"Very."

"And——"

"And handsome, too, of course."

"Of course. With bright hair braided——"

"Well, now, let's see." I brought up Virgil.

"And a famous pistol shot?"

"H'm, something like that. In those old days——"

"Oh . . . good, dear Lewis, what a funny old *professore* you are!"

Mother penguins flapped stumpy wings and gossiped indignantly about us as we passed their nests in the rugged grass; and where the waves flattened to leaf-thin spume upon the beach the larger king penguins waded behind us, waddling, upbraiding, prodding us with their strong bills, a company of constables in court dress arrayed against these two strange, pink-faced trespassers on their field of stranded fish-bones and the small, scuttling things of the salt and rocks and sand.

"This Æn—pronounce him for me, Lewis."

I pronounced him.

"He . . . had his ladies?"

"Certainly. All brave men have."

"Yes, certainly." A rich color, freer than a flush, glowed under her sea tan. It could have been no natural modesty which made her hesitate: "But . . . he loved them . . . faithfully? He——"

"Was an adventurer, a wanderer, I told you."

"Oh." She jogged along with her little fists lost in the tarry pockets of her overalls. Her eyes stayed fast on the far curve of the beach. She stumbled over a gray tussock, paid no heed to a penguin's lecture and sharp nip. "Then, I suppose . . . he was always wandering away? Yes?"

"Always. That was his fate."

"His fate? It had to be?" She added something in a slipshod, impetuous language of her own. Neapolitan, I guessed. There was an operatic gibberish she always used when English proved too cool. Then: "You mean, he could not help it when he grew . . . tired of them, and was . . . and went away?"

I had no clue to the kindliest answer, so I made none. Our scrunching heels took up the pause, and her too large boy's clothes flapped noisily. They made her look more slight than ever. From the other side of the island the wind brought us several black bursts of musket fire. The doughty hunters must be bagging their last prey.

I looked away to the *Tonquin*. The whaleboat had reached her a quarter hour ago, and the kegs were probably all hoisted. We'd best be rowing out to her soon.

"See!" Sure enough, from the ship's side a ball of white cotton shot suddenly and spread into the wind. We did not hear the sound of it until a second later, and then only distantly, and I wondered whether the partners could have heard it at all against the breeze and the strong surf on their side.

"The signal," I said. "Let's go find the gentlemen. They may reward us with a musket ball, but there'd be the devil to pay if they kept the captain. . . ."

"Ah, wait." She did not turn about, but stopped short, and I saw how she gauged her lover's leisurely approach. He must notice us by now.

". . . Now I remember, Lewis. But yes, of course, now I remember your Æneas. And Dido, that was her name. She was a large, fat prima donna, and the maestro's mistress, and she died on a flame-colored couch, surrounded by cunning steam pots, in a beautiful new white satin gown of the directoire style which showed her breasts as full as Roman wine skins."

"What in the name of——"

"The opera, silly, the opera I sang in. All about Queen Dido and your brave but bored Æneas. I was only the queen's confidante, but I had a lovely song to sing, and a beautiful new gown, too . . . well, almost new, but not satin, of course, or so . . . so directoire."

"Whose opera?"

"What do you mean, whose? A famous opera. The tenor——"

"Who composed it?"

She shrugged her young shoulders. "I shall sing you things from it some time. We had a great success with it in Venice . . . no, in Vienna, it must have been in Vienna, because I remember the little margrave with such an embonpoint who gave me a gold bracelet which I . . ." She held up her narrow wrist, so close to me that I could not help but see the exquisite monogram of blue lines under its tan, and how they seemed to throb. . . . "While in Venice the maestro himself was my adorer and would certainly have let no one but me sing the prima donna's part. But, oh, no, it was never a question of my voice, you know."

Why did she laugh so excitedly? Ovide was within fifty feet of us now. I echoed her. "Yes, I know," I told the penguins and the baby seals and the climbing white sails of the distant *Tonquin*. "I know."

"It was only that I was so young, and in Vienna they prefer their primedonne to be grandmammas with full wine skins for br——"

"What?"

Halted, she had made me halt with her. Her dark boy's head was thrown well back, and my eyes strove to avoid the enigmatic merriment of hers and the youth of her throat and shoulder when she tore her collar open.

"See for yourself, good Lewis. I could never be such a fat Dido, could I, Lewis?" She pulled the loose blouse top wide apart with a pretty shrillness. "See, I——"

Ovide was upon us, between us, with his next swift

stride. He grabbed her hands and bent them back upon
her throat, closing the shabby blouse they had been opening, quilting her saucy flesh with his bright, unbraided
hair. Angry, he laughed at her. Sulky, he held her so
pressed to him that he could not see the triumph which
flooded her upraised face.

Her vulgar little trick had worked. He held her wholly
off the ground.

"*Bien*," he said, "but you must not corrupt our old
stork. He is no match for a charming slut like you, my
love. . . ."

And, laughing, they loved. And laughed more than ever
when he set her down and they saw how the bird which
was dangling at his belt had left a sticky bloodstain on
her shirt, a mark which soaked and stayed tenacious to
her heart.

So they stood a moment and forgot me and all else.
Now I could turn away. Awkwardly away, unnoticed.

The ragged sound of a second gun from the far-off
Tonquin. Her sails were up and filled, and she was moving
out before the wind. Moving, leaving us.

I could not realize with the first instant what it meant.
My shout came out of sheer dismay. It made a futile dis-
sonance with her shout, and his, and with the shouts which
blew down to us from the bleak hill above the beach
where the partners were returning, puffing, grossly laden
with carcasses and vainglory, from their regal sport.

We ran. We all met at the small-boat. The lovers and I
had run without regard among screaming, fleeing penguins,
straight over the two wind-bare, salt-white mounds and
the two poor crosses.

6

We rowed for three and a half hours. Blistering, heart-
breaking hours, with the treeless island soon out of sight

behind us, and the *Tonquin* calmly widening the waves between us in the fore.

"I'll nie forgive the villain," gasped the scarlet M'Dougall.

"Y'll nie haf a chance t'," sobbed sweaty Davie Stuart.

They might have saved their breath for the oars. They spent it on ridiculous shouts, threats, commands to the far-off ship to stop and put about for us, prayers for some miracle to strike that wretch dead before he could wreak his diabolical malice and leave us stranded on those dead rocks astern. They made fat, useless rowers. They doubled their bellies noisily and almost upset us in the gray swells beyond the surf.

Ovide and I swung away without words. If we could not reach the *Tonquin*, we could at least keep within sight of her a little while. They would see us aboard, see how desperately we were trying . . . and, damn them, how contritely. . . .

Perrault crouched between the thwarts, parceled with muskets and a canvas roll and as many of the hunters' birds as they'd insisted we must bring back to prove their zeal and diplomatic generosity. The small-boat was only twenty feet of keel, but they'd insisted.

We'd never have gotten them into the boat if we had not agreed to the seal, too. They'd been all for standing and shivering boot-deep in the surf and bawling gory nonsense at the *Tonquin's* dwindling poop for hours and hours. That rascal Thorn had planned it to keep us eating salt beef instead of fresh duck, that was it, that was all . . . and couldn't abide the idea that they'd captured the first fine sealskin . . . and they'd nie come along with us a-chasin' o' him without we'd agree and take the seal.

So there it sat in the stern, an absurdly propped carcass, with its flappers at rest above the red, draffish billow of its bullet-holed underside, its small, snouty head and mustaches cocked away: it had just the look of a plump old gentleman at a banquet's end, his best white waistcoat dribbled with port wine.

And there it stayed until we were out of the spume, away from the ledges and grunting through deep water. Then, rowing closest to the load, Ovide swung his oar in a circle clear of Perrault, caught the old corpse a crunching smack and toppled it into the sea. The lightened stern leaped and spun away to the next wave. The precious partners bellowed. Perrault laughed . . . and adored.

Behind us, in a gray-green marble trough, the old seal tipped slowly, slept with its flappers at peace and its mustaches up and bright, while under it, each oar stroke away from it, an oily red wadding spread upon the sea and signaled the gulls screaming from the sky.

It was better rowing now, almost decent headway. The wind was with us, even if it was with the *Tonquin*, too.

Ovide rowed illustriously. He was buff to the waist, and his wet back's muscles threw sleek, playful loops up to the level of my eyes as I rowed behind him. This was heroic of him. Everything he did with his body he did so well, so rejoicing. Over the white leapfrog of the bunched strength of his shoulders I watched little Perrault watching him, too.

There were times when even the partners kept still, when the sense of a tiny boat sick-keeled and slithering in such an irreconcilable sea, on such an extravagant chase, silenced The M'Dougall's Biblical lamentations and all the elder Stuart's Athabascan wrath. Towards evening the *Tonquin* sailed out of sight, and there was neither ship nor land riding on the slow gallop of the black, sun-saddled waves. Night would come, and cold and terror.

It was Perrault who first saw the *Tonquin* when she turned and came back into the wind to pick us up. Then the partners saw her and broke loose again into both sacred and profane rage. They were safe, they were rescued, but their vanished seal . . . and their raw palms and splinter-laden seats and simmering cheeks . . .

We boarded a sour, glum ship, greeted of none, none reaching across the rail to help us up, to explain, even to scold us. Things were evidently grown too hostile for any further bawling. A sailor hustled me down at once into the captain's stateroom.

He sat there, a burly shadow, mounted on the shine of the long twilight and the shine of stiff horsehair of his couch. He took his time surveying me.

"Back aboard, aye, Lewis?"

"Yes, sir."

"All o' ye?"

"Yes, sir."

"Y've pen 'n' inkwell?"

"Why, no, sir, I'm only just . . . I'm to get some, sir?"

"Get some, man, get some. 'N' the notes f'r my letter to Mr. Astor. I've somethin' interestin' to add t' it. Leave the door t' the cabin open, I want the gentlemen to hear it 'n' know. Know how I waited all the mornin' f'r 'em to finish up their fancy tarantaras ashore. 'N' how, by God, I certainly expected to leave 'em there f'r good riddance 'n' f'rever."

"Did you, sir?"

"I did indeed."

He did indeed. And the cream of his jest was this, though he brought not the dimmest smile to it: that one of the persons he had certainly expected to leave there, thousands of miles from bearable life on a dreary, bird-spattered rock, would have to stand respectfully before him now taking notes on the malicious righteousness of his intentions.

I could have thrown the inkwell in his face, as Luther had done to the Devil. But this one was not yet a full-

grown devil. He suffered . . . from humorlessness, from
dogged loyalty and righteous indignation he suffered, and
was only neat and dutiful and irascibly small.

"Standin' off Falkland Isles, afternoon o' December
eleventh, 'n' I'm obliged to report to Mr. Astor 't one
o' the passengers, Mr. Robert Stuart, objectin' to the
departure o' the *Tonquin* without awaitin' f'r his uncle,
Mr. Stuart, had the mutinous impudence to pull a pistol
from his frock coat 'n' place it at the captain's head,
sayin' he'd blow his, the captain's, head . . . aye, my head,
the son of a buggerly bo'sun, he'd blow my head off if I
failed to turn around 'n' stand toward the small-boat 'n'
pick the party up again."

"Oh, sir, so it——"

"So it was. High seas mutiny, 'n' that's what it was.
I want Mr. Astor to know it all, to be warned o' the worst
of 'em. . . . Make nice little sentences of it, Lewis, lavender
'n' polite regrets 'n' all that, but, by God, that rebellious
upstart made me turn round 'n' keep an Astor voyage
awaitin' on a lot o' bloody ducks 'n' lazy . . . Here, what's
the matter with y'r hand, Lewis?"

"Sir?"

"Y'r hand, man. Y' can't write properly with a lump
o' skinned meat like that."

"I'm sorry, sir. I'm not used to such rowing races. I
pulled all afternoon."

"So you did. Aye. . . . Let me see it."

I put down notes and prettifying instruments and held
out both my hands. They were swollen out of their usual
boniness, hot and aching, running with the stuff of many
red raws. I thought he could not see the painfulness of
them through this shiny dusk. He said nothing. But at
length he twitched himself higher on his couch, and a
curious chuckle rattled around his little stateroom's walls,
a sound so pitilessly enthusiastic, pleased, that I could

not immediately believe it had come out of his strict, wind-planed face.

He had not been the least bit sorry for me. He had forgotten for once to tell me to be careful not to spill an ink blot on his polished wood when he'd seen the red soreness of my split knuckle pads. He had actually liked the sight of my smashed blisters. Maybe the Devil was in him after all.

Overtired, I lay awake interminably that night. My hands were on fire under their grease and rags, and my head swung and bobbed in comic, loose fashion, in rhythmless answer to the mustaches and small, snouty head of a blood-dribbled seal at which the captain chuckled, hoarsely, humorlessly chuckled. And out of the heaving marble of the waves floated such trivial theorems as this: the presence of Ovide in his hammock next mine throughout all the night, asleep like an indifferent baby and never once waking to go on tiptoe down the cabin darkness to the chart closet and the adoring little slut who waited there.

7

We had a man down with scurvy in the steerage. Captain and partners quarreled about his cure. Our salt fare and stinginess of water got the blame.

It would be quite two months before we'd drop anchor again in Owhyhee. The Patagonian coast was so much nearer. Why couldn't we make . . . it was landsmen's fear of sickness and no frivolous whim for pleasure jaunts or hunting parties, they told me to assure him . . . but we couldn't, he growled, 'n' we wouldn't, 'n' t' hell with 'em.

The man with the scurvy grew well again. On the fifteenth we saw the high mountains of Terra del Fuego.

It was lucky we had not had to put in anywhere along this awful shore, I confided to Jeremie and Laframboise in the voyageurs' circle, since Patagonia is all iron deserts and volcanoes and inhabited only by tremendous giants who drink fire from the craters. I was horrified that they believed me. I wanted to shout apologies down the round holes which their open mouths made in their blowing beards. They never forgave me for confessing it a fable.

Ovide yawned and sulked. High above him in the ropes a quaint doll clung dangerously and watched the brown toss of the coast, the keen wind upon her clothes; but he did not look up at her until he caught me doing so.

"You are very bold . . . at fables, old stork," he said. "I can tell some, too, but all true ones. That's the differ-ence between . . . romancers. Mine would all be true, of . . . well, of war and the woods, and Paris and its beautiful, hospitable women, and women everywhere, all colors and stations, strumpets, comtesses, squaws. But yes, squaws, too. They have their own charms, yes, *mes frères?*"

He appealed to the voyageurs. He took their assents and grins for granted. They idolized him, and he knew it. He was not trying to convince me, only to tease me. He had long ago learned how distasteful this sort of talk must be to me. He'd punish me for my fairy tale.

"One time in the Hudson's Bay country an old chief's squaw, with blubber and pemmican crumbs all over her mouth . . . she was surprisingly good at it, if you know what I mean, dear Lewis . . . though I'm afraid you don't, do you?"

I turned and walked slowly away. He should not see how he had distressed me, or that I heard the general sniggering I left behind.

A sailor, Verbel, bumped against me, swore, went on working. The crew took its attitude towards us landsmen from the captain.

The ship's bell told the time. I collected my nerves and came back to the circle.

I, James Lewis

Mr. M'Kay was talking now. He so rarely talked. Someone had evidently asked him about the overland expedition, Wilson Price Hunt's procession to meet us at the Columbia, and the route it was probably taking. He used the deck seams for longitude lines. He crouched with leathery, gnarled face over a miniature land. His pipe stem pointed the Missouri, the Platte, the Rocky Mountains house, the Arctic Unjighah, and there were a thousand miles of forest no white man had yet explored, and here was a traverse of the Black Hills, and here the Mandans dwelt, and here the Shiennes fled the Sioux . . . and wherever he showed us an Indian tribe it seemed to me as though his lowered pipe bit lingered an instant and sent a thin wisp of smoke up from the boards.

On this river they'd paddle, Mr. Hunt and his party, and up this one, too, and come on horseback across here, foot when the horses grew into lamed skeletons or on . . . d into some thieving village . . . and here, disappeare . . . dered, taking to canoes again in the white, starving, bewil . . . desperate snake twists of great rapids . . .

I remembered Mr. Hunt's gentle ways, and the cheery casualness of the "*Au 'voir*" we had given each other when I had seen him into the Albany post coach that spring afternoon. And how happy he had been that we should be Christ's witnesses to the heathen, we wealth-bringing, civilized Americans.

A musical note threaded the sunny breeze along the deck. The ship's bell again. An hour was gone by since Mr. M'Kay had begun to talk. Fables . . . his had been the best of them, by far.

They would stagger under flights of arrows as black as swarms of gnats. They would eat horse and cur and moc-casin, and maybe each other, and be lost so many times, betrayed and crazed, completely lost, before they'd finally find us in our riverside fort.

Fables. The finest of them, this, and our pleasantest hour on the sea. So probably none of us wholly believed it. Not then.

8

Thickened weather, a fuming storm, drove us towards the Horn. All the long days before Christmas our bow was in and out of water. Green, glassy masses rolled down upon us out of cloud and rain. Whence we landsmen were penned, the roar of huge waves assaulting, retreating, smothering all our screeching wood, flinging our boxes everywhere around the slick-wet boards below hammocks and berths, seemed a racket invented for our special torture. No doubt there have been worse passages around the Horn, but never worse passengers.

Captain and crew being now too busy to bother with us, we managed a few ugly moods among ourselves. Those murderously yellow bulkheads of our clerks' quarters, the seesaw and the drip, the airless, soggy pressure of this sight of the same few yellow faces in the churlish light of the Antarctic midnight . . . and the ever dark smell of tar.

Ovide had grown languid beyond bearing. He avoided Perrault. At me he snapped and, when I'd give him a half-minute's chance, jeered for the benefit of all our fellows. Was he yet jealous of me? He had no reason to be. I wanted to tell him so . . . when I saw the hurt and dumb confusion in her eyes I wanted to tell him what a dolt he was, and what a scoundrel, too . . . but that would have brought on another sulky scene, more taunts and theatricals, and another of those brave plays of his by means of which he always dazzled himself out of boredom.

To-morrow the world would wear a blue sky again, and our shuttling masts would stitch bright fleeces to the

azure, and the sun be golden again upon young hearts.
. . . Lord, was I these lovers' keeper?

Instead, to-morrow was destined to be a day of dead
gray calm, the sails hanging idle, as loose as a spaniel's
jowls, and only the current carrying us within dim sight
of the cape, five or six leagues distant. A sullen day for
everyone, of worry and incapable drifting in a flow three
miles an hour strong, of bawling and barking from the
foggy quarter-deck and watches against the slow suction
which gripped us towards the cloud-slung rocks.

We were not to see the cape entire. Even when a land
breeze gained us fair offing and a free view, the vast
shore swelled with cloud shapes, a purplish gray fantasy
mutable and gusty high in the gray air. I remember how
I stared at it from behind a rain-grained port, and how
long I watched the wind carving this pendent moisture
into new and huger faces, and how one face lingered for a
full, baleful minute above the sun-torn remnants of the
fog.

It was the face of someone I must recognize, must hail,
challenge . . . yet someone I had never seen. I laughed
aloud when I finally knew. That broad, translucent, philosophic brow across the sky, a cumulus upon a core of
cape rock, and the hot, narrowed brightness of the rifts
which were his eyes, and especially the thin lips of contorted stone scoffing, epigrammatizing down upon a waste
of noisy gales and sloven mists . . . I had learned his strange
features by heart only a few nights ago while trying to
read him in the pearly evening light on deck.

There was that odd volume of him which I had along,
and there was all the babble and chaff and sailors' business
of the deck around me, so that I had not really been able
to read, but only to stare at M. Voltaire's face, at the
engraving on the soggy frontispiece which made him so

dim and prodigious . . . as this vast enlargement made him now upon the sky.

It was he, for quite a minute it was his gigantic self in nebulous grotesque upon the sky, with sunken old cheeks already in slight dissolve as they recited me that paragraph of his, that unforgettable paragraph which a drunken monologue of my New York days had made peculiarly mine: something about a fly, the destiny of a fly. If I . . . how had he written it? . . . if I could disturb the destiny of . . .

He was a shapeless, unacknowledgeable dump of cloud and rock knob when I looked again. To the very bottom of the world I had come sailing to meet this monstrous effigy. Old doubter, flouter, truth impaler, melting weakly in the wind.

Our breeze changed to the southwest and we beat into storm. Under the lee of the islands of Diego Ramirez we saw a large schooner helpless, her sails like a moth's torn wings in the cold, late sunset, but never could hail her. For a week we fought the contrary weather, and the captain ruled and ran us with no amen excepting an occasional belch from The M'Dougall's tortured stomach.

Then, at length, the wind hauled round to the south, and we swept westward, all allowed on deck in the genial Christmas morning to bear witness to our passage into the new ocean. Perrault, too: a silent and confounded little Perrault who stood next to me at the rail, as instinctively far away as she could from the moody temper of that mastiff in the manger, Ovide de Montigny, and who, hiding under the stoop of my shoulder, never minded that I saw her sob, saw how her silly tears went down in infinitesimal sparkle when she leaned far out and giggled to disguise them, and how they were our first libation spilled to the Pacific.

9

I did not wait to slip on my shoes that February daybreak when I heard the lookout call his sight of land. I
made for the bow and stood behind Mate Fox's lumpy
back.

A great pink flower hung on the horizon, its lower petals
floating open on the sea. Midair, when the first sunlight
found it, its stamen burned with white dazzle; and this,
Mr. Fox informed me against the wind, was the summit
of Mona-Roah, mountain of Ohehy, signal to all comers
to the Sandwich Isles.

We watched the wonder of it ripen, the petals grow
flushed and heavy with the day and drop slowly down.
Then the hills were uncovered, and their tints of dawn
and lessening distance wove into upland greens, the
quenching green of mountain sides turbulent with swift
verdure, jungles of palm and cane and tropic vine.

"Wait a bit," said Mate Fox, "you'll smell the peppers
'n' all."

I could have sworn I smelled them already. Out of
the chalky blue trough to starboard a bird rose in a
burnished helical and flew ahead coastward to chatter
the news of our approach.

"Ohehy." I kept trying to pronounce it in the seamen's way which Mate Fox used. "You've been here before?"

"Aye, time, 'n' time."

"And the captain—has he, too?"

"Well—" cautiously, with all of a sailor's glum respect—"I couldn't say for sure."

"Last night," I explained, "Captain Thorn told me
he may have to distribute small-arms amongst us when
we go ashore. He said all savages are . . . savages."

"Maybe." And then, with his pink, shy cheek turned

half away from me and chubbier than ever in this morning light: "But . . ."

And straightway launched into another of his long, sentimental stammerings concerning all the world he'd seen, the many far, lonely ports he'd put into where some folks might've thought the people savages . . . pagans they certainly were, sometimes, and heathens in their home habits, and there might be some bad ones among them on the waterfronts, loose ones, as there always are wherever idle sailors are . . . but he'd always found the world and all people of every color in it somehow satisfactorily good and kind and . . . and decent.

I said, "Of course."

Many others had joined us on the deck. He brought his voice down to a mild, bashful drone. The purple flower of the dawn was dying in a blaze of gold, a peak with an exotic name blew scarfs of birds and tingling scents to greet us, and the good mate went on droning me meek, rueful platitudes on the universal goodness of the decent life. There was that uncle of his, for instance, who'd been drowned on the bars at the mouth of the Columbia, he'd been a fine family man, like all the Foxes . . .

I leaned a little back from him, so that only a quarter of what he said should reach me. I was amused, vexed, then inevitably ashamed of my superciliousness. I saw my young monkey, Perrault, scrambling into the fore-rigging with her overalls ballooning and a white, tight face.

"Now, there's that young son of mine, Mr. Lewis, no bigger than Perrault, there . . . my son's no pretty one, though, for he's mine, got a fat little face like mine when I was that young, eats hearty and fast like I used to, hasn't got the least idea how much I love him, but . . . Lord, what else does anyone live for, Mr. Lewis? To love and to die. Decent love, I mean, of course."

"Of course." How many more times should I have to say, "Of course"?

"The last time I came in from round the world he'd just found a bit of broken mirror, and there he sat at the window flashing it at me as I came up the walk, just sitting there young and naughty, grinning, flashing it straight into my eyes until I trod all over my own feet and into the rosebush . . . he hadn't meant harm, of course, the young imp, just . . . and when his mother made me spread-eagle him I just snapped my belt in the air and made a lot of noise, not really touching him with it, you know."

I assured him I knew. And I did know. Apple-cheeked faces of little Dutch school children against the school-yard snow.

This side of the funny man must always touch me. I listened with a knowing tolerance to his protest that what had hurt him most was when he had had to take the boy's bit of glass away from him, but that he'd give it back to him, he'd secretly promised it, some day soon . . . perhaps when he was back in Boston from this very voyage.

Ahead of us the land formed silently, and the intervening sea was overlaid with the fresh hush of a harbor still too far away for any stir or noises. Lord, would the good man never leave off his worthy sayings?

"That's all that death amounts to, Mr. Lewis. Somethin' to serve love like that . . . decent love, of course. There's only love and death in all. . . ."

Of course. Of course. Of course. But I had not the least idea what death could look like, nor ever had known love . . . of course. Out of the mouths of fools and dullards . . .

To windward, where the shrouds were taut in the rigging directly above us, we heard the sudden bow-string twang of the rope to which Perrault had been clinging, and then at once the streaming terror of her cry as she shot out and down into the sea.

10

So quickly, so surprisingly, it happened. The stunned deck raced past the frothing spot where she had sunk, and when she rose again we'd left her far behind.

I tried to cry out and cried nothing. I stood crushed against the rail, watching the dwindling bobbing of her inflated canvas clothes which, like a ludicrous breeches buoy, kept the lower half of her afloat in the soapy green swirl of our wake.

Stupefaction had exploded into uproar. Cries came from all parts of the deck. Cries for a man overboard, for the ship to heave to, for a rush to the boats, for us to hurl things, anything, everything, at hand into the lather's groove astern. Cries of the wood and canvas as our wheel ground around and our sails rebelled. All the cries and impulses of pandemonium . . . my own cry dead in my mouth, and my own immediate impulse dead before it could be born, drowned already in the plumbless seething of the water into which I stared when I had swung one foot across the rail.

"The lad's head down, he'll smother," someone yelled past me.

The lad. Perrault. Perrault out there in the green-blue churning, smothering, drowning. Chairs, barrels, benches, hen coops streaked down, splashed and swirled behind us in a torpid spread. I pulled, as if out of quicksand, to pull my other foot across, to leap without this necessity of looking, to avoid the sight of this boiling nothingness of the face of death in the water below me . . . but I looked and looked.

Someone came rushing up the hatch behind me, slammed

me back again flat upon the deck as he vaulted, and, with supple swiftness and his shining hair undone, sprang down into the wave.

Now I, too, could cry out. Cry to the wretched, traitorous coward who was ever resident in me, and whose shocked nerves fired and shamed and agonized me while I lay in a faint of fright and released my sickness all around me on the deck.

II

The lowered quarter-boat, from which men had thrust me away as a nuisance, rescued the two of them out of the wash of spinning débris.

Ovide had reached her long before the boat could, righted her, held her pinned high to the hen coop's spewing slats. He had laughed—Farnham and Matthews told me so long months later—when he hoisted her unconscious, wave-lax little body upon their oars and grabbing hands, laughed to their cheers as he seized the listing gunwale and heaved himself in beside her.

And to our cheers, the gruff applause of the whole ship when they returned the boat alongside. Muscle-moulded, dripping, he climbed back aboard, holding her dripping to his moulded chest, one arm in careless spread across the risky secret of her sex, the other thrusting his way through all the arms which would have shared his burden.

"Rum, idiot, rum!"

He shouted it at me as he smashed by me to the hatch without even noticing the open blanket I was holding. Under his soaked locks his eyes burned with personal triumph, with impatience at any possible hitch in the perfection of his play. I stumbled in the blanket, stumbled down behind him . . . in the puddles they left on the steep hatchway and across the cabin floor.

He laid her, white wet face upwards, on the closet

berth. He paid no attention to me when I came running back from the cabin store with the bottle spattering upon my hands: he only grabbed it, put it to the blue twist of her lips, poured, lifted it, and swigged from it himself . . . straddling and leaking sea water in huge rivulets across the maps there, laughing at me when I closed the door and said that none must see how we revived her.

She stirred, coughed; water ran pitifully from her mouth and nose. The plaster of soaked clothes gave a queer sob as he wrenched it up from her breasts. He was tearing the blouse collar back from her throat . . . white, whiter than ever I had imagined.

"Here, you, James Lewis, or Lewis James, or whatever . . ."

He wanted me to help him. Me. Me, with my eyes suddenly bloodshot and averted, my fingers hooking back into my own wrists to suppress their helpless shaking, all my native awkwardness become a flushing misery as I turned away towards the door.

"*Nom de* . . . man, half-man that you . . . have you never undressed a woman in your life?"

His play was over. He was wet and tired and beginning to be drunk. All his exultance in our cheers above had given way to savage exasperation and contempt.

A low moan of reviving senses swelled the slim throat on the bunk below us, pressing him to flagrant rage.

"Afraid . . . of a woman's nakedness, or what? Of drowning in a woman's navel . . . Get out, out!"

He flung the door open and me out. He kicked me out, and I sprawled on the cabin floor, abject and stunned, my spine shrieking from the impact of his kick, my head cracked hard against one of the partner's berth boards and sunk in ignominious stupor next The M'Dougall's china night-pot.

From far away I heard him slam the door.

12

Over the Karaka-koua bay where we had anchored
the moonlight lay in seamless luster, the molten stuff of
shining and unstinting magic. Such silver I had never seen
before, palpitant as a sleeping lightning, solid upon the
sea, liquid to the land, all the escarpments, clefts, and
coral surfs surrendering their daytime substance to its
heatless alchemy, and all the stars raked out of the palm
trees' lofty fermentation, away into white engulfment by
the moon.

I watched from the bow. Franchere had found me
churlish company and left me alone. Alone I was pleased
to be . . . if anything could please me after this long
day.

Fair ahead of our bowsprit a silver cliff flung its four-
hundred feet of sheerness up to the exquisite fret of a solitary cocoa tree. From the amphitheatrical, profuse land
around us the spicy scents of curious foliage and swift-
ripened fruit poured down upon us in a heady blend the
bouquet of the white liquor of the moon.

The huts were dark, drenched in the splotching palm
shadows on the low lava arms of the bay; but sometimes
I heard singing . . . above the grating swish and squeak
of the sailors' brooms and squilgees tidying the deck behind me I heard the warm, healing voices in strange song
from the shore.

All afternoon, while we slapped past the coast, they
had been around us: brown, audacious bodies, flower-
slung and glistening with the watery reflection of the
sun; high gabble of their eagerness to barter with us as
their paddles brought their dragonfly pirogues up close
to us in buoyant chase; the brazen clamor of them on
the deck where, for the first time, we set up shop and
traded . . . needles, beads, iron rings, anything in chor-

tling trade for the fruits and clucking poultry they had brought along.

That was my afternoon's chore, my singular knack, I found: to count the exchanges, balance them quickly, correctly, in the ledger in their midst.

For an inch-blade chisel a whole hillock of cabbages and yams. For a rusty, broken-toothed saw, long since discarded by Koaster, a heaping thanks of watermelons, breadfruit, taro, and bananas. For no more than a cock of the head and an uncertain grin a skein of white, dream-smelling flowers, of flowers still cool of the mountain slopes in their morning green, still glowing of the copper bodies on which they'd been awaiting us.

Some of the sailors had been saving their grog rations for this sly time. Smashed gourds and trodden garlands lay kicked into the scuppers, and around the forecastle afterwards, and a drunken girl's tapa girdle had jumbled itself, crisp and thin as a snake's last year's skin, down the deck and flat against the taffrail.

They came around us still when we were inside the harbor, diving with fuddled glee for the ha'pennies and tinny buttons some of the voyageurs were throwing out, following our anchor down to the coral bottom in fourteen fathoms of water, climbing our chains in flaunting clusters until the cathead above them grunted with the strain.

The M'Dougall had been shocked . . . piously, to be sure, and with great dignity, but with his plump tongue licking the excitement from the air. The elder Stuart had declared we should have got out the boarding netting.

Now there was peace again, loneliness and quiet.

Silver the fronds of the leaning palms above the silver beach, and the singing fragrance of white flowers opening upon the banded hills in answer to the moon. All my senses mingled into this one sense of silver shameless and yearning everywhere, naked upon the night, until it was almost my nostrils that sucked in the song, my ears that breathed the peppery, sweet redolence of the land, while my eyes turned upwards in the arc of the white flight of a dream.

But even as I looked, a cloud which was greenish as putrescence fawned on the perfect ripeness of the moon, swarming and violating it, bloating it into the lopsidedness of execrable, lewd burlesque. And behind me the brooms and squilgees scraped at the malodorous remains of the deck's holiday, and sailors ground their chilblains into the squashed flowers.

I grew aware of the throbbing ignominy of my soreness where Ovide had kicked me . . . kicked me out, as though . . . and had slammed the door.

I felt the sweet cleansing of the sky. But I did not look up any more. In front of me, a startling, splitting sound, the abused cathead cracked. I jumped back.

Someone came running up the deck. Mate Mumford— it was his watch. What's happened? What now? He rammed his face into mine to see who I was.

"The cathead, sir. They were all over it this afternoon. I was just——"

"All right, don't get frightened—" damn him—"it's nothing serious. Cap'n wants you, Lewis. Cursin' after you all night."

"Me?"

He was amused at me. Maybe whimsically sorry for me after my morning's exhibition.

"Aye, you. You're to luff down to the powder run and check kegs for old Weeks in the morning. We'll be distributin' small-arms——"

The powder run. Black and quiet as the core of hell. "I'll go right now, sir."

"Now? Why, you . . . how can you see?"

"Oh, never mind that, sir." A crazy nostalgia beset me,

a haste for the dense, bitter airlessness and black discomfort of that secret place where I should be unseen, unsensed. I could not wait to reach there.

"But——"

"Oh, there'll be plenty of light from the cabin, sir. Moonlight, if nothing else . . . look at it."

I would not look at it any more, myself. I'd give them a lifetime of full moons for one night in that sulphurous, stifling burrow, the one sure refuge which my swart mood wanted. An Astor would have snapped at such a trade.

"You're a queer one, Lewis. Well . . . but don't try any tricks with flint 'n' steel too near the powder."

That was an excellent joke. I enjoyed it as much as he did. More. Mr. Mumford had seldom inspected the run, had no idea that, long before we left New York, Weeks had shown me the old flint he would actually keep hanging at discreet height above the kegs against God alone knew what emergency.

I went straightway below.

13

I lay there. In the cramming narrowness, beside the stowage of the powder casks in their bung-up and bilge-free order, I lay with my nostrils flattened on the filthy boards and my lips stretched back to avoid the taste of black, gritty powder flakes in the tar seams of the floor.

For an hour or two the window over the ladder had worn the grimy pallor of something less than light which came from the cabin lamp. Then that, too, extinguished. I lay in the evil-smelling, still, compressing stomach of a whale, in the acrid core of hell where there is darkness more burning than fire, nothingness beyond all torment, and gradually I relaxed my lips and let them feast upon the sour black dust of the floor.

My reverences to you, M. Voltaire, arch-crucifier of the truths of destiny, most debonair apostrophizer of the Unknown God of flies and men and universes long pre-destined, where a man's little life is all of a man's life and all . . .

How many centuries before the world was born had it been ordained that I, the sore lank body of James Lewis, should lie here wearily, ill of the seas and the deceptive night, and of the hundred bewilderments and hurts of this *opéra bouffe* Æneid for the creatures of Noah's Ark, illest of all of my own self . . . that I should lie here under the round, firm kegs of instant disaster in the pitchy center of my own distress, and see myself as never before, as the new and necessitous Me must see me?

I . . . now I must count the times, the hundred times . . . once, for example, when a young slut had laughed at me over the glossy carriage horse's back and I could not shamble fast enough away. Again, when a dull-witted Dutch farmer had spit his stained phlegm at me in dumb resentment. And when a gallant youth whom I might have killed, might have adored, flung me out with contemptuous laughter, kicked me out. . . .

To episodes like these, then, must all of the Me that was life within me have been born? To what else?

This gawky, blank respect of mine for the pot-bellied partners who sermonized me, for the infantile-eyed captain who cursed me and misused me as his buffer, his informer, spy . . . and for him, the butcher's son with the thick neck and the many millions of dollars and fine furs, who was master and deity over us all . . . and over my servile, futile sentiments, the timidities of a weakling in absurd dismay. . . .

Teacher, teacher, teacher, swearing his sore hide and his hurt soul away to the stifling dark. Swearing his sudden self-transformation into that new Me, necessitous, assertive man, millionaire-to-be, whoremaster, bully of his own fate and the fates of all the other men in crowds around him. I must be that Me.

I swore it. I beat upon the firm, round bellies of the casks, regardless of their contents, and swore it as I lay there and fought the niggardly alternative of self-extermination in the dark. I swore it, I should learn to beat like this upon whole villages, countries, worlds, until the grains of accident tight-packed within them must obey my fist and sift, leap, roar for me and signalize to God that each man's destiny is as great as the Me which his own need hurls forth.

I swore it. I . . . the fly.

14

There was shore leave for most of us the next evening. We were bound for the native feast. Aye, we c'd go 'n' be damned t' us. We went. The partners in special state, of course. Laird M'Dougall in such plaids as shamed the sunset all around him.

Ovide and pale little Perrault went together in a large pirogue with two curved pieces of timber lashed across its bow and a proud spritsail of woven grass. Matthews went with them, and there was room for one more.

But I hung purposely back; climbed down into a smaller craft, instead, where my only white companion would be our woebegone boatswain, Anderson. The captain had been berating him again all afternoon—Lord knows what about, this time—and Anderson would keep quiet enough to suit me out of sheer moroseness.

Or so I had expected. But once we were clear of the ship and sweeping inshore to the broad, wet whisper of the paddles, he began to whine and confide me his grievances.

He had a lout's face, small and weak and awfully complected under his seaman's beard; I had to watch it for

the next ten minutes over the magnificent backs of our
native paddlers . . . watch the pink scabs and pistules
showing in the roots of his hair while he went on complaining of his under-dog days, his rotten luck, Thorn's stinginess and meanness and stinking temper.

It was as good a time as any to stop feeling sorry for
such people. There'd be no surer way to stop feeling
sorry for one's own self. Though he wasn't a half bad-
looking chap, or wouldn't have been if . . . but I shut him
up.

"Well, then, Jack Anderson, if that's how things
stand with you, why don't you desert?"

One of the antennæ of long twigs which the canoe's end
dragged behind for equilibrium whipped out of water
with the suddenness of his alarm.

"Sit still, you bloody fool!"

If he saw my grin he would not know what it was about
. . . how easy it was to call people things . . . lest they called
you them first.

"Who says desertin'?" he protested. "Sick 'n' tired
's I be, 'n' spoilin' fur a fair deal, why, s'help me, I've never
once——"

"You lie! You've been thinking of doing it ever since
we sighted a green shore. You've heard tell of these
Sandwichers. They never have to work as you do. The
food drips down from the trees. It's summer forever.
The women are handsome and hot for white men, even
for men like you. Look there . . . on the shore, waiting for
us with flowers and children's smiles, already half naked
. . . and a poor devil like you that's been a half year at
sea . . ."

"Don't talk like that, Mr. Lewis!" He could not get
over his fear that our paddlers must somehow understand
what I was saying. Besides, he must assure me of more
sterling motives.

"It's not that, Lewis. It's the captain. You've heard
him, how he's treated me. I wouldn't ever 've thought on
it if he—he 'n' all those fatheaded redcoats he's always
. . . Jesus, why does he have to take it all out on
me?"

"On you?" I must have smiled broadly as I looked
away towards the growing palms and the colored crowds
awaiting us. "On you alone? Because you are the puny
fool fated to be crushed between them. Because you
haven't the sort of face that means a fight."

He scratched ruefully at the mild sores in his beard.
"I know it," he said, "but it's not my fault. . . . Are you
thinking on it, too, Lewis?"

"On what?"

His lips went through a comical business of pronouncing
it soundlessly: "Desertin'."

"No, of course not. Not I." I felt suddenly immensely
tolerant of him, of his squeaky little face and pink scabs.
"Don't worry, though, I'll not tattle."

He breathed again. "Funny finding what a good one
you are," he said, "like this . . . at the last. . . . I wish I'd
known you better aboard. Maybe then it wouldn' 've
been so stinkin' hard. Maybe, if we stick together to-night
ashore, you can help me . . . keep a kind o' weather eye
out for me, you know . . . maybe . . ."

What was he asking me to do? Aid his desertion or guard
him against it?

The paddles were lashing us clear of a low spit where
turquoise water turned a milky green and spilled across
the gleaming burls of coral. I leaned back in the bottom
of the canoe, enjoying the final few yards of calm before
the surf began, and the picture of crowds and big holiday
cooking-fires between the surf and the voluptuous woods.
A triangular fish with a drowned rainbow on his scales
darted back from the shadow of our furled lateen.

"Maybe." I replied to John Anderson. It was no sort of reply, but it was enough for him. I was already one man's master.

15

We were the white men, the haoles, and they were our servants and worshipers. We were the strangers, the malihinis, and they our hosts, our friends forever around the cooking-fires' twirl of orange sparks, our lovers under the full moon.

We gorged ourselves and grew drunk. We watched them dancing under the great kamani trees beside the sea. The moon had escaped the stars and lay bare and panting upon every palm leaf, expectant of the greedy reach of the firelight's blaze up every tree trunk. The arms of the dancers had the slow, glowing sway of melting copper.

Jack Anderson and I sat a little apart, our backs cushioned against the slatternly, springy refuse of a giant fern. His eyes kept turning leerily for a look from mine, like a tipsy dog's will when he gathers the sight of one familiar human face above him through the fumes. But when he watched the dancers his whole little face became red, crawling fire.

The partners, groggy and drowsy, propelling their heavy guts before them as dignifiedly as they could, had retired with one of the priests and the village headman into a grass hut. It was hogs they wanted, thank ye . . . forty 'r fifty live hogs as fat and succulent and ready for roasting as these they'd had served up to-night . . . and laws or no laws, King Tamehameha or no Tamehameha, they were here to buy hogs at fair barter, damn ye, and hogs they'd . . . they were in small danger of being understood before they would give in to their stupor. The voices of the melé so gravely sung outside, the strange notes of the nose flute, the damp rustle of the dancers' warm feet

in the warm, damp jungle shrubbery, would only send
them fast asleep.

There were nineteen women and one man who danced.
They sang as they danced, and the hundreds of others
who sprawled around us, munching, drinking, watching
us with soft, friendly, fire-starred eyes, joined in the song
at vagrant intervals.

There was a young girl among the dancers with white
flowers trembling in her hair.

Across the savory smoke I caught a glimpse of Perrault
and Ovide sitting close together, amused, carelessly happy,
his arm in frank possession of her waist. Their shore manners . . . a bridal night such as they'd never yet enjoyed,
with the quicksilver shadows of the koa tree to hide
them from the jealous moon. No, there'd be no hiding
here, nor any need of it . . . nor use for jealousy. . . .

I swigged of the gourd of ava they had given me. I
could not learn the color of the stuff in this light. It was
warm and sweet-smelling and, after the glut of food we'd
had, it had a creamy, earthy taste. What was it made
from? I did not care . . . the effect of it was what I wanted:
the self-satisfied, nepenthal stupor that is the prize of
middle age and is untroubled by resentments or bereft-
ments or its own burning loins . . . or by anything except
the wherewithal of fifty fresh hogs.

Anderson, at my side, made queer noises with his terrier lips. I looked where he was looking—at the young girl
among the dancers.

Her tapa cloth had fallen free and swayed in dark folds
around her thighs. Loosened petals flaked her wet, metallic
skin. They rained upon her face, in the fire-tipped black
of her long hair when it raced its strands across her throat,
down her short, frenzied petticoat to the ground. They
were red in this light, silver in that . . . and she and the
flowers she wore were so much of the moon and the flame,

these petals seemed but large drops of the very warmth
and life of her wild, swaying being.

"I'd a nice little chat with that wench afore," said
Jack Anderson. He wiped his beard with the back of his
hand.

"I hope she understood you."

"Aye, well enough. They all know what y' mean."

I looked around the clump of clerks. Their eyes were
glued on the dancers . . . on this same one, probably.
Matthews had had the night of his life, nor finished it yet.
Farnham, Franchere, Ross, a prim, insignificant-looking
lot, trying to appear at home, to hide from each other
the beads of uneasy light which shifted and snapped behind their eyes. They'd hide them from their diaries, anyhow.

Over there, a wholly different species of mankind, some
of the French voyageurs rolled unrestrained among the
guava and the ferns, dragging the gleefully shrieking
women down with them in mock wrestling matches.
Nadeau had given his deerskin shirt to a fat young mother
to wrap her baby in. He had the woman up against his
hairy chest, his grasp already wrist-deep under her pau,
whilst all three of them, even the babe in arms, must howl
for joy and vigor.

The song had changed from a mele to a hula. The
measured wail grew swift, flailing, crazing. The dancers
gave their limbs to freedom. Torches of wax nuts sputtered in the excited hands of those around them and colored their seething and grave lasciviousness all anew.

The women's breasts were like those I'd seen on a
statue of the wolf which suckled Romulus and Remus . . .
God damn me and my pedantry! These breasts were of
hot, hungry flesh and torch-red skin. And under them,
like wells of fire, like eyes of the moon, the women's navels
were the trembling pivots of all their wild contortions.

Look at them . . . there, James Lewis, look . . . and break
at once all thralldom to cold ink and colder statuary. You
that had been afraid of drowning even in a woman's navel
. . . any woman's. You that are so different now, laughing,
jerking little Jack Anderson's gourd of ava away from
him when your own is empty. . . .

He let me have it with one of his regretful squeaks.
"Oh, aye, friend . . . take it, take it. But you'll help me
's you've promised. Y' promised it, friend, remember!"

"Aye, friend, I promised it." I said it so solemnly, he
had no idea why I finished with a chuckle. "Help you
how?"

"The girl . . . that girl there. Well, all the young bastards'll be after her, from what their looks say. But I've
already said things to 'er . . . sort of . . . what one says to
a jolly wench anywheres in port. An' maybe, when I get
'er 'n' know 's I'm a man again, not just a captain's
bilge roach, I'll feel all different about . . . you know . . .
what you guessed about."

There was something good about him, then, in his way.
Good . . . and pitiful and silly. He did not want to desert.
A girl in his arms, a pair of child's eyes looking up at him
in merry wonder, admiration, while he went on boasting
and bolstering his self-esteem, emptying his clogged, tired
little heart . . . maybe. . . .

The fires had been allowed to sink. They were smooth
mounds of embers that held together in their glow. Little
flames raced under their surfaces and left unquiet veins
of darkness . . . as in the hot red breasts of the native
women.

The dancing was nearly done. Only the strongest of the
young ones stayed on under the resuming, flooding moon.
I noticed that Perrault and Ovide had already slipped
away . . . where . . . Yes, Jack Anderson, poor little
wretch, I knew what you had meant.

I drank his gourd empty. The rich, earthy stuff tasted better than ever. Yes, Jack Anderson, with your terrier's face all moist and sore with a new desire, newly audacious to balance all your life hereafter on the wriggling of a woman's collar-bones . . . and expecting pimp's charity of me. . . .

"'Ere she comes, friend!"

Panting, she had left the dance. She stood a moment leaning for breath against a palm, and wore the same disheveled luster that lay over its abandoned leaves. She did not think to rearrange her tapa cloth as she walked our way. The loose folds of it over her full, strong thighs were snowy with petals.

Jack Anderson jumped up, plucking at me to do likewise. Come along . . . here's where I could help him. Matthews was already skirting the embers and making towards her. The rest were edging sheepishly over. She smiled at one and all, and the moon gave her lips a patina of hot good-nature and desirability. She was hot copper, half bare.

I cut in across Matthews, Anderson behind me. She smiled at me. Her eyes were large under her heavy, wet hair. Her arm was warm and yielding when I grabbed it. With my other arm I pushed the lot of them away. Jack Anderson trotted, yelping his thanks, by my side.

Under high, humid palm fronds, torn into the white sky, we climbed a short hill behind the fires and the sea. We staggered, laughing, breathing coarsely in our drunkenness, halted knee-deep in the low vines of a burning white flower which swept the crest. Down the other slope the thin plumes of wild sugar cane glittered and hummed. Beyond them a narrow, moon-blue band of the jungle's night shadow . . . and then the jungle itself, a black, unlimited, inseparable mass of upflung wilderness.

"All right, friend. . . ."

His voice squeaked. He was so grateful. And excited and untroubled and triumphant.

I looked at the girl. Her large, unconcerned eyes had the dark drench of foliage in them. She did not understand or care. Her ripe breasts parted when she breathed, and a flower of moonlight trembled between them. She smiled at him, at me, dumbly, good-naturedly. As I let go her arm her skin seemed to spring to hold my fingers.

"Y' promised . . . y' can go now like y' promised. . . ."

At least I did not taunt him. I gave him no chance to prolong the anxiety that retched him at last. As soon as he thrust his suddenly worried and puckered little face at me, I slapped out at it. I hit it with the side of my hand, and felt the small bones give and smart as they clove his beard and smashed the sticky chin beneath.

He fell and rolled a few feet down the inland dip. He got up, dragged out his pistol, but had no stomach to fire it. He stood staring up at us on our palm-wreathed crown of the hill.

He had the weariest, most hopeless expression on his little face that I had ever seen. Everything had gone out of it excepting pimply weakness. A wordless rebuke started coming from under his tongue; a sob, perhaps a hiccup, tweaked it short. He turned and fled, stumbling, floundering down the slope, in among the cane, where he gave us one last sight of his stricken face over his shoulder. . . .

The shadow of the jungle rippled over him, drowned him in black silence. I never saw him again.

The girl's low croon, the language that is half speech, half song, of a high-breasted dove, brought back my brooding to the hilltop. She laughed when I laughed. She stood with her hands in her hair, her cheek to the moon's, her whole torso restive and twitching softly. I felt the life of her strong thighs under the tapa when I seized her.

As I tore away this zone of bark all the white petals it had hoarded in its folds leaped free and raced us to the flower-mad earth.

16

This, too, I remember: how the dawn closed the flowers among which we lay and raised the heads of others that would scent the new day through the tangled grass. And how, waking and stretching her arms, she tried to teach me to pronounce her name, but drew me down and drowsed again while laughing at my slowness, and with the silver shoe buckle I'd given her for a keepsake clasped tightly in her large brown hand.

This, also: how the sunlight hurt my eyes as I came down to the shore, leaving her behind me deep asleep, her body sagging in final and oblivious contentment over the low vines. How the sea had a sound for men's ears, and carried a hard, scornful brightness across the beach, the overturned boats, the foreground of heaped, dead ashes and heaped, drunken sleepers all around. How the leaning palm trunks were already slashed with morning, and the tree ferns were freighted with brown decay, and the ground was a swamp of brown, inert nakedness and smashed gourds.

This, especially: how, while we waited lazily to be paddled back to the ship, we watched an old pair with stripes of quicklime in their hair manufacturing a new supply of the ava they'd given us to drink the night before. How they chewed the roots patiently between their old brown teeth and spat out the rich, earth-colored spittle into a bowl to decay under the strong sun. And how one of them was a white and sightless creature whom they called a leper.

And how that did not matter, either . . . any more than that she had not even tried to learn my name. . . .

17

Five gentle days we cruised among the islands, coasting from Tohehigh by order of its celebrated Governor Young, the king's white admiral and counselor, to the royal bay of Ohetity.

All we had had from Young were four black sucklings for the partners' mess, and a long, lazy tale of his seaman's luck and his native wife, in exchange for some tea and coffee and Madeira wine. None other than Tamehameha himself, the mighty Eri Tamehameha, lord and master of all the Sandwich Isles, could give us the fifty hogs, the good water, and the flock of brown men we wanted for our sojourn in the North.

We made for Wahoo in a golden weather, past Mowhee and Tahooraha, where the green hills had neither beginning nor ending in the sea, but seemed each to ride upon the sky for no brisker reason than to hang a garland there of cocoanut and breadfruit trees. Green, too, the bar across the Ohetity bay: the tender, ever-tossing green of palms above the coral and the spray. There we anchored on the twenty-first, with Captain Thorn damned if he'd take her inside the reef.

The canoes came out to us, were soon many around us. The long, leaf-like paddles flashed across the sunlight as they came; so, too, did the palm-oiled bodies of the men propelling them . . . so lightly and brightly they flecked the sunny water.

White men, too: a pair of Americans, a young Bordeaux Frenchman who told us he was the king's sons' tutor, and who struck up an immediate camaraderie with Ovide over the rail.

Then came the king's prime minister, Kraimoku, long-nosed, exceedingly statesmanlike, with a blue hussar's coat moulting under his maro, and a flower-wreathed beaver on his head, bearing His Majesty's invitation to the captain and equally important personages to disembark.

Those equally important personages, the partners, were not to be outshone. On The M'Dougall's advice they had all arrayed themselves in their Scotch kilts and plaids. I fear that Captain Thorn, clinging gruffly to his old, storm-worn sea jacket, must have cut a plain figure among them in the cannon-strung palace square where even the sentries sweated under great coats of blue and yellow braid; and that he must have got a certain plain satisfaction out of doing just that.

A fleet of pirogues was at their service. They disappeared behind the reef, a small, bobbing flotilla, the tail of which, I was quite sure, was a pair of pink, sunny rumps of someone trying to juggle himself on the slender canoe seat when the wind and surf grew disrespectful of the kilts of Clan M'Dougall.

Mate Fox was in charge of the little trading we'd do now. I had private work of the captain's to perform. I lingered on the inactive deck, unwilling to begin it. Captain's orders seemed always to suck me down the hatch.

Through the bay's gate I caught a glimpse of the little town, a hundred or so houses of yellow matting among the hillside trees, and the occasionally larger white buildings . . . the public store, perhaps, or the palace itself, a temple, a little wharf, a few old schooners idling in the blazing sun. . . . The two miles' distance between all this and us laid its little parody of cannonry and prime ministers and palace guards to rest in a green lullaby of miraculously fertile and untroubled land above.

A native had smuggled some home-made brandy to the voyageurs. Ovide went sauntering back and forth between them and the rail, impatient, snipping the awful

French of their jests with sulky monosyllables, as though he could not wait to be ashore and away from us all.

Perrault crouched near him, watching him with the intentness of a forlorn understanding. She looked humbled. Something was wrong again . . . anything . . . nothing to me, I told myself. I went below.

The captain's stateroom had the stale smell of little things in their right places. I knew precisely and immediately where to find the notes he had hidden for me. I must finish his letter to Mr. Astor. We should leave it here at Wahoo for the next ship New York bound. That might be months . . . but Mr. Astor would ultimately receive it, read it, and know.

His handwriting was Jonathan Thorn's whole life on paper. A slow, excruciatingly exact handwriting, a chart of rigorous self-discipline of one unused to forming letters, except when his temper bore his thick fingers down upon the lines in a fury of black illegibility. He could have written his final draft himself, but he wanted it worded and engrossed as impressively as a congressional declaration . . . and they'd given him a schoolmaster for his chief clerk.

. . . Contrary to orders, out of all rule, endangering of the ship's insurance, they had endeavored to make him break up the cargo and distribute articles of clothing unnecessarily among the Canadians from certain sealed bales. . . .

Oh, very well, he was the author, not I.

He had served them the best possible fresh and smoked meats in the cabin. Puddings, too. With what thanks? They had declared it . . . "damned hard they could not live as they pleased upon their own property, being on board their own ship, freighted with their own merchandise . . . and these the fine fellows who had boasted they could eat dogs!"

Leave that in, too, his very words. Pity only that I could not reproduce the vindictive splatter of black bile his honest writing used here. His latest notes were hastily added:

"Red coats . . . frantic gambols, foolish promises, wasteful gifts of wine, etc., to natives who cannot furnish us a single hog. . . . Taking clerks and men on shore to spot where Captain Cook was killed, and each fetching off piece of rock or tree touched by the shot . . . collecting ridiculously contemptible lot of curiosities and histories from natives and loafers, etc. . . . impossible to enumerate their thousand instances of ignorance, silliness, filth, etc., daily practised. . . ."

God save us from stout men with justice on their side! To hell with him and his righteous itch . . . his little stateroom stank of neatness.

I finished him up: long, curling, learned sentences and elaborate calligraphy, through which his wind-stitched, wrathy face still flared with honest Yankee indignation. Let him be right. Let him bore his great shipowner to death. Let me be present in imagination when the great Eri Astor, seated in equally humorless, satin-stocked state below his prize beaver skin, snorted at the length and methodical complexity of my transcription.

Here, through all of these golden days among the islands so softly green that they seemed but the print of dreams on lovers' sleep . . . notes, complaints, the sputter of a plain, just man against red coats and gambols. . . . God have mercy on his rigid little soul and all who'd dare offend its suicidal rightness!

Cheers called me to the deck again, and then the deafening crash of the four guns we fired for salute. The shore party was returning. A large state craft accompanied them, a double pirogue with two dozen paddlers. The water was winy with an afternoon splendor as they came across it, and their mighty paddles moved with a vigor and precision which were the envy of our voyageurs.

As it neared, we could see that a great chest full of firearms had been lashed over the center of the two canoes which formed this pirogue. And that a large brown man in a suit of garish old regimentals, with a sword at his side, took his ease on a once gilded chair among the muskets.

Bravo, the great Eri Tamehameha, Supreme One of the Sandwich Isles . . . he had removed his boots and carried them on his gold-buttoned paunch, while he trailed his plump brown feet in the water that ran high and foamy under him. When he came aboard, his toe prints shone as big as dollars on the deck. And after him came his three royal consorts with breasts like coconut pods, and hips as broad as bays, and the smiles of little children.

Partners and captain were back aboard, too, to give him a ceremonial reception. He tugged at his uniform collar, and his sweaty neck bulged up out of its restraint. He treated the plaid of the Clan M'Dougall to the honors of an only slightly inferior potentate. He followed the partners slowly around the ship, stopping a while with greedy interest in front of the old water-still attached to our caboose. Useless contraption, but he had never seen one before. He said something in a rich, imperious voice. He had called us his friends, his bringers of fresh wonders and improvements.

I had a chance to look long at him as he stood there. His big, hot body, drenching his old uniform below his arms and just above his belly, had fattened untidily with age. He must always have been stocky, bullish . . . his face showed it, and his neck. . . .

But it was not until I heard the captain behind me that my sense of complete familiarity with him was clear. I heard the captain growling at Mate Fox about the unsuccessful bargaining on shore, and that the old black savage, crown or no crown, was craftier 'n' grubbier after Spanish gold than any white man, Jew or German, he'd ever . . .

I began to laugh. How could his old operetta costume, his royal sword, and his blowsy harem disguise him when his neck grew out of his shoulders like that and was so thick with strong white hairs? How could his pigmentation blot out the bluntness of his brow and the sunken pits of his little humorless, indomitable eyes below it?

18

"All peoples," said Kraimoku, the lean, long-nosed prime minister, "are made happy in the power and riches of one man among them. All peoples attain their strength of life through the strength of their tyrant. Without the tyrant the people could not live. Before the coming of Eri Tamehameha to the throne there was not a single schooner in the islands, and Owhyhee knew not Wahoo nor Wahoo Tahooraha. Now, under the glorious rule of Eri Tamehameha, whose fleet is of forty schooners, and whose sails bring him yearly tribute from all the bays and littlest villages as far as distant Atooay, all the islands are as one nation, and all are Tamehameha's."

We sat in the sun-bathed palace yard, Kraimoku, the French tutor, and I.

I had been sent ashore with the articles of enlistment I had prepared for the twenty-four islanders we were hiring for the expedition and the crew. The prime minister must visé these, must have His Majesty's seal upon this and all our other, more important contracts concerning the purchase of live hogs and such. We waited while His Majesty held court of justice behind the sentried gate.

"And are the islands happier because they are all

one nation now?" I asked the suave Kraimoku through the tutor's courteous tongue.

"Ah, they must be," replied the prime minister. "Eri Tamehameha insists upon it. They must love him because he is mightiest among them. They must rejoice in him because he has conquered their lesser kings and been called cousin by the Eri George of England himself. They must delight in his grandeur because he is master of all their lands and keeper of all their waters, owner of each taro root they pull from his soil, each little fish they scoop from his waves. They must relish his riches because he uses them to buy more schooners to collect more riches. That is his rule."

I bowed. A very generous rule. A rule all gentlemen of wealth and power and fat warehouses and imperial ambitions might well remember.

"So loving a father to all his people is the Eri Tamehameha," continued his statesman, "that he once led his army across a great crater and surprised and slew his enemies by hundreds. Another time he fought a famous battle among the sacred needles of the Iao valley, so steep, so wild that no man in history had ever dared set foot there. Still another time he slew beside the sea, so that the blood of the kings he conquered ran on the wet sand as freely as the ink would run on the papers you are now clutching so nervously in your hand if you held them under yonder spring. . . . When one has gained the name of Little Buonaparte," he added, smiling at the white palace doors, "and has for one's prime minister a man of such admirable diplomatic qualities as to be called a Billy Pitt, one's people would be foolish if they were not very, very happy."

"*C'est tout, n'est-ce pas?*" added the dapper Frenchman of his own accord.

He had caught a glimpse of Ovide coming up from the

wharf, swaggering, immensely gay, a company of naked brown children trailing admiringly behind his yellow braids. They would be off somewhere together, these two Gauls.

"*Oui, c'est tout.*"

Where was Perrault? As usual, that was no concern of mine. "*Merci, monsieur. . . .*"

But His Excellency had one more piece of wisdom up his long, heinous sleeve.

"Among all peoples—" ah, the leathery old cosmopolite of the South Seas, he was back where he had started— "among all peoples there are three classes only. First, there is the Eri, he who commands and hoards and is happy in grand style. Second, there are the many, the countless ones . . . they might as well pronounce themselves happy, too. But, third, there are always a few who can neither lead nor serve nor will ever be happy. They can only philosophize. They have lean bodies and long noses . . . like you, my young friend, and like . . . prime ministers of happy . . ."

He did not finish it. I caught the curious twinkle of his eye as the sentries grunted up their muskets to a present arms and His Majesty came waddling out into the yard.

"From the Eri John Jacob Astor, richest of Americans, whose own scribe I am, I bring special greetings to the Eri Tamehameha, as of cousin to cousin, ruler to ruler, splendor to splendor. . . ."

And when they translated it to him, he gave me a slow, complacent, utterly serious nod of his bullish head, and he and his three wives sweated with pride.

19

A black-turbaned Hindu from Bombay, sitting in the face of the sun, weaving a rope of grass fibers for a hawser,

answered me in stealthy English as I neared the morai,
the native graveyard, up the lane of huge banana trees
beyond the town. That was their temple, he said, that
stilted, rickety thing of platforms and cane ladders and
old mattings drooping in the glare. But it was taboo.

An old priest was coming slowly past. He was bent
and senile, and his face was like a withered coconut, his
body above its kirtle a crumple of the black designs that
had been sown there when his skin was young and brave.

"Ask him," I said, "if I may look upon his gods."

The Hindu smiled into his long, dusty beard. "His
gods are poor idols with rotted vegetables at their feet
and the decaying flesh of slain goats and hogs around
them. Could true gods live in such a stench?"

"Nevertheless . . ."

The priest stopped before us, leaning on his staff, peering at us out of near-sighted, dark old eyes, making sure
that we were malihini . . . and that that was why we did
not prostrate ourselves in the spurting ground beside his
gnarled old feet.

The Hindu asked for me. The ancient shook his withered head. Even to those who worshiped and believed,
the sight of the face of Etoway was taboo. White men
had once seen his face, and they had swiftly died, and
Etoway had drunk their blood and eaten their flesh.

I took my cue from the Hindu's smile. "Ask him," I
said angrily, "what sort of god is this who has to take his
strength from the flesh and blood of men."

"Ask him," the priest returned, "what sort of men are
the white men that they have to take their virtue, so
I have heard, from the blood and flesh of their God."

I turned away and would have gone. The dusty Hindu
went on contemptuously translating for him . . . for us
both.

"God is many names in as many lands. God is Etoway

and many minor gods, bearing rain across the sun and fruit
to the tree boughs. God's mouth is red with the fire of
volcanoes, his brow is white with milk from the breasts
of young mothers, and in his hand he carries the black
of thunder, the silver of the sea, the dawn-color of the
juicy watermelon, the hues and shapes and images of
things that all men most fear, most bind their lives upon,
most seek in hunger and in love."

He waited a moment for my reply. I had none.

"Is your god then so different from ours? Look around
you. . . . God, above all else, is of the mystery of death.
In your land, ours, all lands, God must be the goal of
that sunless journey from the grave."

"Some of us have to go to the Devil instead," I answered grimly.

"The Devil? The Evil One? But he too is a god . . .
whom men must sometimes worship. . . . O, pale, foolish,
quivering young man, is not your god great enough to be
evil as well as good?"

I stared back into his old, half-blind eyes. How deeply
could he see within me?

The Evil One . . . he too is a god. I did not dare ask him,
was there an idol of the Evil One up there behind the matting and the sacrificial putrefactions, or what it looked
like. But I knew the very face of it . . . the forceful, unkind,
beefy face . . . of the god I worshiped now. I knew that
he, too, was the same in every land.

The old fellow went back among his graves. He might
have come out of one of them. The Hindu returned to
his weaving in the dust. I wandered down under the
green, heavy-laden banana trees, past the irregular, sweet-
smelling grass huts of the sprawling town, with the sun
sucking moisture from the back of my neck and . . . good
. . . scorching it red, toughening it. . . .

There was little Perrault wandering around, too, looking

for someone so lonelily, humbly. Damn him for breaking her spirit like that . . . and her, too, for letting him, the little fool. When she saw me she tried to ask me where he was . . . if I knew.

She followed me down to the wharf, to the empty quarter-boat tied there with a few natives dozing around it in the shade of the mangos on the shore. All its rowers had come up into the town for a drink. We climbed in and waited. The noon rebounded from the water like white fire.

"Sing while we're waiting," I said to Perrault.

She pressed her hand to her throat. "I . . ."

"Never mind, sing! When I want you to!"

"What do you want me to sing?" she asked listlessly. She had raised her hand over her eyes, ostensibly to shade them from the sun. She could not fool me.

"Oh, anything."

"Mozart?"

"Yes—anything."

But when she raised her slim throat to begin, I burst out laughing, shrieking, devilish with merriment.

20

It was the last day of February when we sailed. We had taken aboard our fifty head of hogs (for which His Majesty insisted on receiving nothing less solid than minted gold in his system of gracious exchange), some goats, two sheep, two boatloads of sugar cane to feed the hogs, as many more of yams and taro, fresh water snugly casked . . . and incidentally the two dozen Sandwich Islanders, too.

The deck was even more difficult and cluttered than when we had left New York. The live animals had had to be penned in the gangways, with boardings over them for the crew's work, and their refuse and noises were a constant affront to the captain's bridling sense of order.

Jonathan Thorn was in his prime, that morning. His compliments to the Eri, the sordid old son-of-a-black-bitch, but he'd encumbered us with the wormiest, foulest specimens of animal and vegetable in his whole damned kingdom. Particularly those natives for the crew. Look at 'em, now. . . .

They were tall men and strong, and would make great sailors in a short time; but at the moment, true, they clung together in a mute and almost tragic stupefaction, understanding nothing that the mates or coxswain bawled at them, seeing nothing but the green land beyond the bay, knowing only that it would so soon slip down behind the rim of a watery, blowing world and be lost to them for an eternity of three years. Three years . . . some of them, most of them, might come back fabulously wealthy with a hundred dollars' worth of merchandise at the end of that time, but now . . .

The pirogues thinned out around us. The captain had to threaten one of them that tried to smuggle some last liquor to the voyageurs. Its paddlers were like little children. As they darted their canoe away they sang and pelted him with flowers.

We waited for a last load of sugar cane, brought up in our own longboat which had been grounded by the ebb. A sailor was still missing when it did arrive and lashed alongside . . . Aymes, I think his name was. He followed in a canoe, but not until the captain had missed him and reached a climax of his rage. The captain ordered him into the longboat, climbed down into it, too.

I remember nothing of the sailor. I remember only the broad, thewy shoulders of Captain Thorn as we saw them from the rail above, and as he reached into the sunny pile of cane for a stick which whistled and sprang and glistened like glass as he began to whip the fellow. And the sharp dry cracks of the wood splitting on a man's head and upflung, unprotecting fingers. Fingers and cane grew bloody.

I remember how I kept seeing under the captain's arm, as it rose and fell in precise and terrible method, a distant palm, a little green emerald with the sunlight behind it, and how it sank each time a little further into the sea. The sailor cried with pain.

"*Tiens!*" shouted Ovide from beside me at the rail. That was brave of him . . . oh, yes . . . and fine and foolish.

The captain stopped and looked up. His face was scarlet. The stitches of it glittered with passionate moisture. There were little red flecks on his hands and chin. He was breathing deep and was happy. I had never seen him smile so before.

And, horrified, taut, trembling, I made myself say something under my breath. "Bravo!" I said . . . as the sailor went overboard, splashing, crying, imploring of the nearest pirogue. The Devil's disciple could say no less.

Slowly the green shores paled and died. The creak of the rising canvas was our only song. Ginger and hibiscus and all sense of the voluptuously growing land thinned from the air, and left only the keen smell of the sterile sea above, the smell of the ship and tar-stained hold below.

For two days, while we doubled the extremity of the island, we saw a silver peak upon the sky. Then, this, too, was gone, and with it the last water bird.

The new brown men worked in the riggings and looked back, seeing nothing, saying nothing, but remembering the shadows of tall palms shimmering on silver beaches, moonlight in a scented flood across the cereus clusters and the humming cane, hulas of bright arms and excited thighs beside the cooking-fires where the girls threw off their tapas and had no names, except the name of earth itself . . . happy, unstinting, ever-springing earth for men to wander, to riot on knee-deep among the vines, to lie in when sleep came in a golden dawning . . . earth hurled miraculously heavenward out of the sea, out of the hot red lips of Étoway the omnipotent, the god so strong that he could be both good and evil.

"Bravo!" I had made myself say, almost as though to the Evil One . . . for he also is a god.

We sailed northing into storms.

RIVER MOUTH

IV

River Mouth

THROUGH storms, with the bronze sky quivering like a gong, and sleety winds clawing our rigging, while the spray on our taffrail piled and thickened into ice.

None disputed the sailors' sole rights to the cold deck now. We juniors stayed gladly below when the partners would let us, or in our sour place abaft the forecastle, hearing through a constant quarreling of wooden walls and sudden winter the shrill bewilderment of half-dead pigs and the bawling of orders against the gale.

The cannon grew white beards. The portholes wore new windows of opaque, roughly toughened brine which left us dark and sightless, only the swing of our stomachs in the swinging pipesmoke telling us which way the ship rolled at the moment, and how badly.

Once, when I had been sent for to bring some inventory and settle another argument between M'Kay and M'Dougall in the cabin, I saw one of the islanders crossing to the mainmast like a cat on snow. They had given him an old oilcloth, and he would wear nothing else. His brown legs and bare feet came comically out below the blown swirl of it, and he howled with white teeth at the quick downhill throw of the sea. Behind him the deck's shiny crackle was fretted with the print of bloody toes.

From the quarterdeck the captain was calling for a double reef in our foresail. We had already struck our topgallant masts and topsails. The canvas would be like jagged iron.

2

Two weeks' imprisonment turned all tempers rotten.
Under the clamped hatch the air became a soupy
poison.

On their plans for the Oregon fort M'Dougall and his
crony, the elder Stuart, vented much scratching, pompous
ruling, and blot-letting and architectural argument. Out,
twenty times out, came Mr. Astor's old letter of appoint-
ment of The M'Dougall as the expedition's chief on land.
Twenty times Mr. M'Kay, hunching sardonic and taci-
turn of his full knowledge of the Indian wilds, could only
let a mouthful of smoke at this cursed letter through the
gap in his tightly clamped, tobacco-browned teeth, and
watch the smoke mushroom against the paper and fatly
glove his partner's fat hand. The M'Dougall was most
furious of all at him for saying nothing.

Another time it was a matter of blankets. They sent
for me to find out how many bales of them were in the
hold. Mr. Astor had had them stowed aboard for West
Coast trading, and each scarlet-striped blanket would
reap so and so many beaver skins among the Columbia
Indians and up Vancouver Strait.

But it was beastly cold sleeping aboard, now. Some of
the pet clerks had complained, and the partners themselves
were only too ready to receive petitions to rifle the bales
for blankets. They were passengers, they wanted their
due comforts; each of them probably wanted a new grudge
against Mr. Thorn, too.

They knew they'd have to apply to the captain. I
could tell from the way they talked of it how much they
enjoyed the prospect of his refusal, the growls he'd surely
give them instead, the ease with which they could there-
upon tease him into hasty, outraging courses.

Blankets, by Jesus . . . break the seals on Mr. Astor's

cargo to keep those buggerly lairds from catching a bit of gooseflesh!

It was plain baiting. He was worried—and we all knew it—over the side-arms he had distributed among us for our Island sorties, and which he must wait for decent weather to regather. He was worried about the long storm, the constant batter of bow and sides, the new fright and squalor of our freezing livestock, the crew all numbed and bruised and with mean sleet crisping in their beards and nostrils.

Worried but proud. Something heroic belonged to him at last. Heroic and incontestable, for he was master now. When he came below for his few hours' sleep his face wore the mottled blue and red of a steadily fanned and intense fire; the cold of his wet, rime-chipped clothes would make the partners draw their plaids closer about their shoulders as he stomped by. They had left the unregenerate sea for him to deal with. Let them not bother him with their goddamned little chills and blankets business. They'd know he was master now.

His hard, light little eyes, tiny icicles already melting on their lashes, looked over the table and the untidy papers and the gentlemen hugging their pipes and clutching their shawls like old women against the momentary draught down the open hatchway as he passed through, tired but glowing, to his stateroom. He would say nothing. He would not need to.

From the noisy way he walked, from his look alone, they knew the virtue of his hate for them, the triumph and the new, wind-fed strength of his scorn.

God rest his poor, torn soul to-day. And save all living men from the thousand little villainies of long days indoors.

It was one of the young clerks—M'Gillis or Wallace or one like them from Montreal, I cannot remember—who

first began methodically to goad him. The partners, yawn-
ing over their toddies, sick of their amateur drawings and
of wrangling among themselves for the next few days,
soon took it up. Whenever Captain Thorn went by they
managed to switch their talk immediately to Gaelic.

They would speak it in stage whispers, mock-mysteri-
ously, with large nods and nudges and weighty, suspicious
silences as he passed. Rare sport, a manly revenge. And
grease upon fire.

He had me into his stateroom. Behind the shut door
all his new self-satisfaction became a stripped, tired spite.
He lay back on his horsehair couch and mumbled himself
into a fast belief that they were actually planning mutiny
against him.

They'd only to start, by God, and he'd have every
Tory bastard of 'em chained 'n' spread 'n' cat-o'-nine-
tailed. Warm, they wanted to be? He'd warm 'em. He'd
teach 'em to go struttin' around with Mr. Astor's side-
arms, chucklin' their gibberish of how to steal Mr. Astor's
own ship. Aye, the bloody British liked doin' things o'
this sort . . . look at the celebrated mutiny of the *Bounty*,
for instance.

He was sure of it. He knew. Weather like this, and
they'd the livers to want to toil open the hold and pretend to bother about blankets . . . when it was really
powder and knives they were after, of course, and he
goddamned well knew it.

I began to assure him he was wrong. That was a waste
of time. In his bottomless lack of humor a red wish grew
and raged, a wish to believe, and he went suddenly to
sleep believing.

The man could sleep believing in a mutiny against his
life. Melted weather ran down the little brook beds of
his face, and when he breathed he sputtered wetness like
a baby whale.

3

Perrault fell sick and kept to her chart-closet berth. I had excuses enough to visit her there by day, but would not use them. Most often I sent Ovide in to her, instead. I had every right to order my assistants on such errands.

Ovide was surly about going, and I thought at first that he merely resented my giving him commands. I was still green at practising authority, and my voice squeaked.

I looked for him, one blowing evening, in the sailors' quarters beyond ours. He and two or three of the restless voyageurs had formed a new habit of trespassing there when they had no open deck to sprawl on. Laframboise owned a pair of dice, and Roussel and De Montigny had still some ribands and beads or a few Canadian coppers they could lose.

All hands were on deck except one. A seaman—a big, dense scapegallows named Adam Fisher, I think—had sprained his wrist and was trying to snatch some off-duty sleep behind their noisy game.

"Ovide," I said. I had to say it twice before he looked up. The dice had gathered some tar stain in their travel across the planks, and he was busy polishing them off against his knee.

"Ovide!"

This time he did look up, amused.

"Ah, *M. le Professeur?*"

"Since when have you had Captain Thorn's permission to make a gambling room out——"

"Since storks took to lecturing on morals."

I could let him call me anything he pleased. That sport would soon end.

"The captain has asked for the California coast chart, Ovide. You put it away this morning and know where it is."

"So do you, Lewis, better——"

"Perhaps, but please get it."

That "please" was my mistake. He stayed squatting over the dice, his fingers resting lightly on the floor against the unruly swinging of the ship. A man of his frame might have sprung at me with ease from this position. There was none of our officers around. The voyageurs were his friends, not mine.

"Send Franchere or Matthews or some little someone like that," he said. "Or get it yourself."

"Franchere and Matthews are attached to the partners. They have plenty to——"

His great, unbraided mane had come up, and his face grew full of mischief. "Or send Adam Fisher. He'll enjoy what he finds there."

At the sound of his name the bulky sailor started lumbering out of his berth, grinning back without knowing what to grin about, nursing his wrapped wrist. His huge blanched feet were bare, and his clothes had the reek of continual dampness next to his thick, hairy chest. He slid amiably, sleepily down into the dice game, reaching across Ovide for his boots.

"Why don't you frog-eating gamecocks let me sleep? Send me where? Where'll I go? Tell me that!"

Ovide de Montigny leaned back from him, his eyes catching and then avoiding mine across the seaman's stupid lurch, and telling me, in spite of all the hostility there was still in them, how immediately he had grown ashamed of himself again, annoyed that he had let such a companion into his game of teasing.

The ship threw Adam Fisher hard against him. Both crouching, they both went completely down.

For a moment they stayed down, grappling. Ovide was the first up, quick at once to smash his heel into the sailor's bare instep.

A bull's roar and Adam Fisher had him around the knees and down again, Ovide's head cracking sharply on a bunk edge as he tumbled. There was no room for real fighting here. And we were all upon them instantly, parting and haranguing them, laughing as overloudly as men always do when they have to convince themselves of the good-nature of a sudden, entirely causeless fight.

The two fighters laughed, too. They stood staring over our heads, panting hugely, taking stock of each other's hurt, of how the sailor had to hold to the bunk with the bandages dangling from his wrist, and with his sore foot off the ground, and of the red worm already crawling in Ovide's yellow hair and down his forehead . . . while the forecastle seesawed to the storm, and the two of them, this one out of exultant frenzy, that one out of goggling, blubbering slow-wittedness, joined our laughter.

"Now," I said nervously to Ovide, "there's no substitute left to send for that map."

He made a wry, mad face—and went. But, for fear of her very life, I went along.

4

It was only a small gash in his head, but it bled generously, and he would not stanch its flow. It must always be part of his code to pay no attention to his wounds.

We had to go through the cabin to reach the chart room, and he reveled, I could see, in the drama and amazement of his appearance as we passed the partners' table. The M'Dougall sat looking after us with a mouth like a cannon's.

"An' now what?" demanded Mr. Stuart.

I let Ovide go on ahead. "Nothing at all. A silly fight with a sailor. About nothing."

"Nothing!" The M'Dougall was purple above his

shawl. "Common sailors striking a—a passenger! Nothing!"

"One sailor," I corrected him. "And De Montigny's a match——"

They were all shouting at once. I did not finish. I followed Ovide hastily into the closet and closed the door.

Perrault cried out, too, at the sight of him: cried out in gratefulness for his surprising visit, and then, when he stood wildly over her berth in his boisterous dishevelment, she caught her breath and gazed up at him with foolish care. Her hands came out of the heap of old rat-ruined overcoats which I had found yesterday to cover her with, and stretched up towards his forehead.

That everlasting laugh of his was the only explanation she got from him then. I had to tell her for him. I mumbled a fancy lot about his fighting for her sake, to wipe her name from the greasy lips of a seaman who did not even know she was a woman. I made her see the comedy of that.

Her face, thinning and meanly pale for many past days, grew flushed. She smiled like a spoiled child, was immensely pleased, giggled. . . .

In Parma, she remembered, two fine bucks had once drawn swords over her fallen garter in the greenroom and might have come to scratches and punctures if she had not picked it up herself and shown them both the medallion of a third man, a favorite tenor, sewn into its ruffles.

She reached for Ovide's hand.

He was as pleased as she. My little half lie had made a hero of him again in someone's eyes, even if that someone was only a weather-browned ragamuffin who couldn't get enough of her lean arms around his neck, and who clung and sniveled at wrong moments and told tales out of slutdom. The pretty little piece couldn't help it if she was sick—maybe he was to blame for it, himself.

He began complacently to ask her health, and to give her playful wagers she'd be as good as new again as soon as the storm receded, and never to mind, she was his—always his—I could not hear what he called her, so closely he said it in the hollow of her throat when he leaned down.

His best audience, that was what she really was, I remember thinking. His best beloved audience . . . call her what he liked, with all the graces of his condescension, but he'd never have honest insight enough to call her that.

I found the California map. This time I needed neither a shove from him nor any sly meaning from her eyes to leave them alone. I shut myself methodically out into the mounting loudness of the cabin crowd.

The captain had come below. They stood around him, shouting, affronted, puffed, their cheeks a multiple mirror of his own blown red cheeks. They knew nothing of what they were bellowing about. And he had only the sailor's side of it. They were all down to calling each other every ugly name in blackguardmanship's dictionary.

"Here, you, Lewis!"

I started to hand Mr. Thorn his chart. He paid no attention to that. "Here, damn you, you were up there. Tell 'em——"

They did not want to be told. And I had no great ambition to crack my voice against their howling. But I tried.

The noise brought Ovide himself out. He was in a heaven of his own, the cause and center of a battle royal, the handsome blade that would cut our feudists forever and further apart. He struck a gallant attitude, conscious of his tallness above them all.

"Oh, it was a private matter between me and the seaman," he said, smiling. "By all——"

"Then let 'em fight it out atween 'em," shouted the captain.

They all shouted back. All but Mr. M'Kay. The old explorer waited for quiet to make the one quiet remark of all the uproar. And because he said it so quietly, it took on a grimness, a black finality of threat and ultimatum which I doubt he intended:

"If you say fight, fight it is!" said Mr. M'Kay.

Captain Thorn was past bristling. The stitches froze white around his mouth. He had heard what he had been waiting to hear from any one of the partners for months. This meant open mutiny to him . . . and the justification for all his autocratic malice and uprighteous spleen, past and future and forever more.

His eyes came straight to mine. His were gray ice and glittering with private victory. Had he not told me? Had he not dictated as much to me in his letter to Mr. Astor? My own eyes attempted to protest that he was taking Mr. M'Kay's remark too literally and strongly, that mutiny was furthest . . . but my eyes went down. They saw the thick red jaw atop his open pea-jacket as they went down.

Ovide had had his little play and was already tired of it. He turned back toward the chart room, fingered its door latch for a few luxurious seconds, then yawned, shrugged, sauntered away in the opposite direction, up the hatch.

All in one minute's spin he had been applauded, been adored, been bored. The life of all their living runs to little plays like these, the brave Ovides.

But it probably never even occurred to him that he had been the cause—and could, with a little less pose, less temper, and supercilious smile, have been the end, instead—of a feud which would henceforth admit no truces, no simplest decencies, and would go on widening, stiffening, blasting the very last of us. . . . How could he know what he had done?

Or know even now, for he still lives . . . and the living never know, nor the dead instruct the living.

5

Leaden skies pressed the storm down upon the waves and watched me perfecting my new duties of Devil's disciple.

In my own secret council chamber, my black refuge of the powder run, I had had it out with myself for sure, had decided . . . and did not need to tell any other man among us my decision. Nor tell myself it, either, many times over.

I was the captain's man, and knew it as well as he took it for granted . . . as well as all of them, partners, voyageurs, young clerks, now took it for granted, too. The captain's man and messenger, his suspected spy in the forecastle, his shadow up and down the hatchway whenever he had any business to do with the cabin. Perrault, his cabin boy, and I. Until Perrault was well again, back on sea legs and able to run some lesser errands, I alone.

Captain Thorn'd have no further personal dealings with the partners, nor they with him. His way past them to and from his stateroom was invariably prickly with Gaelic or, worse still, with silence in the shadows. They sent him curt messages through me, and insisted on written answers which must be kept and filed for Mr. Astor's possible inquiry. Their factions sat apart at the cabin mess, Captain Thorn motioning his officers close about him and munching his pork rolls with thick, dry jaws through the testy quiet.

Once, Mate Fox tried a bit of spongy peacemaking. He was ordered to go sit from then on among his friends the landlubbers. Official notes flew to enlarge that incident. Even here, with only a few feet of chipped crockery separating them, Mr. Thorn must send little Perrault down the pine board with a proper salute to Mr. M'Dougall. No other intercourse. An' no sniggering, damn you 'n' your little yeller girl's face . . . get down there quick 'n' deliver 'em this without tryin' to be so funny about it."

The days grew a little warmer again, and black rains burdened the wind.

March 16th, Captain Thorn, Lieut. U. S. N., Commanding Mr. John Jacob Astor's *Tonquin*, Columbia River bound, informs Mr. Duncan M'Dougall, senior partner on board, that we stand at latitude 35° 11' north, longitude 138° 16' west, wind shifting to S.S.W. and landing probable within the week, all passengers herewith duly notified for disembarkation at earliest convenience.

March 19th, Captain Jonathan Thorn, Commanding, etc., reports the necessity to lay to for a second successive night, and the inability to take observations in such headway weather. Captain Thorn insists on excusing himself from any further questions, and refers all passengers hereafter to his clerk, Mr. Lewis, for such information as can be properly given out.

March 22nd, Captain Jonathan Thorn, etc., compliments Mr. Duncan M'Dougall on having such remarkable eyes in his head and perceiving at three miles' distance the Oregon shoreline which Second Mate Mumford's glass had already picked up at twelve miles in the early morning while the passengers still slept. Mr. Alex. M'Kay's concern over the launching of the whaleboat to sound the channel ahead is uncalled for and against all proper discipline, and persistence in it will only force Captain Thorn to prove how prepared he is for any last-minute evidences of mutiny on the part of those who cannot mind their own business. . . .

I managed at least to leave out the goddamned from in front of that final word.

The rainy wind shrieked fresh from the northwest, and the sea fought high and wild along a wild, tall coast. To our journey's end the storm kept after us, snapping, wolfing, unappeasable until we flung it our first sacrifices.

Landsmen were not allowed on deck while the whaleboat was preparing.

Through the cabin ports we saw the swinging land, a great, shaggy head of forest grayness, pre-historic and incalculable, snow-scaled, knobby with harsh wilderness and capricious rock. We saw its long tongue of shallows lapping greedily in the combers just ahead; and, as we tacked away, saw the mist-dripping tail of many cold mountains far behind.

Land, land, the river, Oregon . . . Mr. Astor's land, and the high woods swarming with peltry and black rain. My head was out of a cannon port as we circled toward deep water again, and the weather assailed my eyes, filled them for one anguished moment with the foolish daub of a different seashore, all sunlight and crumbling temples among the poppies by a turquoise bay, lovely as a young girl's song.

Overhead I could hear the hammer and stubborn creak of the loosening whaleboat, shouts tattered and unintelligible in the wind, the curious cries of the Sandwich Islanders when gray birds came about them in the rigging.

6

Chief Mate Fox had the whaleboat in charge, and with him went Nadeau, two of the Lapensees, Ignace and Basile, and the sailmaker, John Martin. Not one genuinely able seaman would the quarterdeck spare them.

I had a few hasty words with Mate Fox before he went. He was in the galley, cramming his jersey pockets with biscuits and dried beef. His face was a green moon, blank and mild but filmed with the moisture of excitement which fat men's faces suffer. Captain's orders and he had to go . . . but look at that chalky sea, that bar ahead, and not one honest-to-codfish sailor along with him.

Captain's orders, in spite of all the partners' remon-
strances and Mate Fox's own earnest, stuttering protest.
It was Fate and that was all. Mate knew it. Mate's uncle
or cousin, someone of his Boston kin, had been drowned
on just such a stormy bar along this very coast ten years
ago . . . he'd told me that story time and time again.
But he couldn't blubber it now to Captain Thorn. He
knew Captain Thorn thought him a stuffed good-for-
nothing. And that Captain Thorn would only order him
to hurry up when the partners' petition for delay till
better weather was presented.

Mild, simple-minded, trying hard to keep up some fair-
day jollity, he went on cramming his pockets with food,
mumbling and mopping . . . while Nadeau came by with
the pair of old sheets which The M'Dougall had noisily
insisted they take along for emergency sails, and the two
Lapensees stood whittling down their oar handles, laughing, jabbering heathenish *au 'voirs* and guttural bets with
the other voyageurs.

Here was white water with a vengeance, the boastful
French canoemen's turn to prove themselves at last. In
went their canoe paddles, too, and their blankets, a pistol,
and a cooking-pot, in case of God knew what. Then the
heavier oars, the sounding plumb, and then themselves,
an uncertain, gangly few, clinging hard to thwarts and
oarlocks as the whaleboat sank down our side.

She passed my port. Her wood screeched on the *Tonquin's* wet wood, gave me the exaggerating closeness of
her little keel, then the dark profiles of shoulders and
faces . . . that round, rueful moon-face of Fox . . . as she
splashed and untied upon the sea.

We watched her throw away towards shore, towards
the four-mile stretch of foam across the river's mouth.
She climbed from the trough astern, righted herself,
sagged down again. The waves lifted her for little instants

into our sight, each time further and smaller, her five
people unrecognizable at their oars and rudder, then altogether indistinguishable in the gray seething of the
maddened shoreline and the rain . . . and each time less
personal, less ours or part of us, until all cheerfulness about
her died away, all indignation . . . and all question, too.

When evening came it kept the morose sound of soft,
continuous waves, of winds as tired as we were, and of all
of us proving ourselves famous prophets; now we had all
known from the first that the whaleboat could not succeed,
would never return. The M'Dougall had known it more
positively than anyone else, of course.

The captain did not come below at all. Night long, he
stayed staring into the squalls, at the silver particles of
the peculiarly frozen Oregon mist which danced upon the
dark, and at the gash of white, softly thunderous water
across the blackness a-bow . . . stared and searched until
a serene dawn gloated over the tinting peninsula head
and clearly showed him the shore again, the sea, and the
apparently unchanneled river mouth, and no trace of
boat or man whatever.

I sent Perrault up to him, a little past eight bells, with
a cup of hot rum. He sent her sharply back with it. She
said his voice had been icier than the air. He had told her
merely to tell me to collect the two voyageurs' and the
old sailmaker's things for auction, and to seal Mate Fox's
effects for stowage in the hold.

7

The hope we had of a calmer morning was soon forgot.
All that next day we fought a riled and sand-choked sea,
hauling off again and again into far, glum water, returning
ever with the current close the coast.

Ovide had come in to me in the officers' quarters with

some crazy scheme of his. He would go overboard alone
the next time we were nearest to the shore. What did I
think of that, eh?

A couple of tied slats from the gangway sties were all
he needed to keep him afloat, and a paddle to steer him
leeward of the bar. He could do what no brittle boat could.
Reconnoiter, no doubt meet up with Indians . . . Indians
were Indians, and did any man among us know them
better than he did? . . . he could parley and learn, perhaps,
the native passageway, signal us from shore, eh? . . . save
us all.

I looked up at him dully. He had slept well, damn him.
He was the only neat and lusty one among us to-day.
He had taken time to rebraid his hair. That fact alone,
had I never had two words with him before, would have
told me how much he really meant of what he now proposed. So handsomely, though, he proposed it.

"Ask Captain Thorn yourself," I said. "It sounds ex-
traordinarily bold to me."

He gave me a quick, gratified glance. "The captain's
no special friend of mine, as he is of yours, Lewis. I'm sure,
you've only to ask him on my behalf- ——"

"Since when do you need any man's permission to
throw yourself overboard and drown?"

I was going through the first mate's bunk box. My hands
were deep in the sour, damp old clothes which Mr. Fox
had left behind him. Ovide eyed me again, leaning back
against the mess table.

"Answer that from your own memory," he said.
"Whose permission did I ask when I jumped in after Julie
Perrault? Yours, perhaps . . . oh, yes, yours?"

"Hush!" The cabin was by no means empty, anyone
might have heard what he called her.

He began to laugh. "Hush!" he mimicked me, inevitably mistaking what I meant. "Never mind, my poor Lewis,

nobody expects you to come with me. I go alone . . . I always go alone on such . . ." His hands were brilliantly expressive.

"Are you serious? Or mad, or what?"

I had wanted to say, "Or only play-acting?" But that would have stung instead of flattered him, as every other exclamation flattered him. And what was the use of quarreling in this already raging gloom?

Besides, how could I be sure? He would fool me, impress me, keep me worrying for him, admiring him secretly, begrudgingly, until the day of our last handclasp. The way he shrugged his splendid shoulders now. . . .

I got up and pointed out the shorescape to him through a rain-stippled porthole. We could see from here a funnel of the sky, all mountain-rimmed and bubbly with gray cloud, as hostile as the confused, sand-gorging ocean which boiled in the river's black-toothed mouth.

"A raft of pigsty boards and one self-appointed hero in that great dragon's jaw——"

"Ah, Lewis, there you are, a great dragon's jaw! You beat me there. I could never have said it as classically as that. I must always leave it to you to be our romancer—in words."

I let him have his smile. I went back to the dead mate's bunk.

Another moment, and he would have been telling me, without the least misgiving, how he was our romancer in deeds, instead . . . that that was the difference between us, wasn't I aware? That I had one of those imaginations born of books and fancy tunes and bad wall-paintings, while he had only muscles hardened in the forest, eyes trained to nothing except whirlpools and gunfire and the frank glances of Parisiennes, ears only for the crude songs of vivandieres and yowling squaws. He would have put it like that to give himself a coat of modesty as well.

Another moment after that, and I could probably have goaded him with one or two words of incredulity and mock into hurling himself actually overboard, a hot-headed and preposterous nuisance, impossible to turn and rescue in our present plight. I knew that much about him by now. He would do anything to amaze any audience, one or a thousand strong. He would do more than anything to prove his pose.

Another moment . . . But I let him have his smile.

I had found a piece of paper in one of the pockets of the old jacket I was packing, and had recognized my own handwriting. It was Captain Thorn's most recent reprimand to Mr. Fox for indolence and laxity of conduct among the partners, a threat to erase his name from the log, which had been dictated to me only three or four days ago.

I did not show it to Ovide. He had lounged away, promptly all content that he had silenced me, awed and put me back in my place in the theater pit before the romancer in deeds. Quite as promptly, I knew, he would forget that he had ever proposed to rescue us so singularly from my dragon's maw.

He was right enough about me. Cape Horn like an old philosopher's beetling forehead, Ohehy a giant flower floating from the sky, Oregon a beast of fable with its tongue thrust into the sea and its tail of snow spikes . . . similes, similes out of schoolbooks and silly operas. Similes as tuppenny and tawdry as the bad daubs of Naples Bay and . . . and . . . I could not remember at the moment what that other painting had been in the Broadway peepshow. Never mind, as cheap as all that, anyhow, as untrue and unavailing.

Romance in word and thought, dragging trite imageries around the world with me like a calf still carrying its long since shriveled navel cord. Meeting arctic cold and tropic

blaze with the same old arias and allusions, accosting
every sudden living situation with the same old deferences
and self-disciplinings, fearing yet always hungering dryly
for all the actualities that were everywhere along our way,
for all the swanking and bullying and muscular gallantry
of my self-sufficient Ovide.

This was no season for rages and stale regrets. I had
had all that out with myself long ago in the ship's black
bowels. Noisome and bitter as that night had been, it
had given me my new life, the life of the lean, necessitous
Me who had punched a mean, pimply little man away
and lain gladly with his savage wench all night, emptying
my loins of envy and despair.

I had no further reason to be jealous of Ovide. Perrault
was a young idiot, smeared with vulgarity and self-conceit.
She deserved the treatment he gave her. Time was when
I had thought her throat a song of Mozart's.

Now it was my own turn to smile. For where was Mozart now? And the old man, Mozart's librettist, telling
tales all the summer night long to the tune of a deserted
fountain and ripe apples falling in the dark, while we sang
and made the night a respite from all reality, from all
time, a night when time had faded from my fears as gently
as his old face faded into summer dusk, and there was
only his old voice from some strange, sweet nothingness
where time was nothing, too. . . . Where was my old
charlatan now?

The cranky weather screamed against us. The tide and
the untamed wind fought over us as greedily as before,
mauled and spun and periled us all afternoon against the
river's entrance. This was my now, here was my whole
life in time, my completest, most pressing and real time,
I told myself. This was my turn to smile . . . at Ovide and
them all.

I went on with my work. Deep at the bottom of Mate

Fox's box I found, wrapped in a piece of old linen shirting, a cracked little looking glass. I sat a short while with it cupped in my hand, gazing hard into it, unable to see myself and blaming this fact on the unlighted cabin, but seeing well enough a young, chubby boy's face instead, pink cheeked, simple eyed, and full of mischief.

I tore up the captain's note. The devil's disciple could do him no shrewder favor. And, when I had sealed the box and seen it stowed, I grit my teeth and gave the little mirror to Perrault for her closet wall. She never asked whence it came.

The sea alone cried out all night to ask me why I had not at least hurled it after its dead owner. Or so I imagined —and that was my final indulgence in imagery.

8

Five men were already lost. We'd lose three more before we crossed into the river.

We lay a little north of Cape Disappointment, anchored against the current in thirteen brown, sand-curdled fathoms. Between us and Point Adams the water drummed ceaselessly on many reefs. For two days we had nipped and scurried, pushed our nose in, backed, fled, circled, pushed, and fled again. Misty noon or stone-gray midnight, the bar was a wall of yellowish violence we knew no way to pass.

First, early of the twenty-fourth, we launched the pinnace, Mate Mumford growling things into his long-grown, blowing beard as he monkeyed aboard her. Mate Mumford was back by noon, his beard now dripping like seaweed fresh from the breakers. The captain could go try his own luck against that sort o' sea.

In the three o'clock calm the Messrs. Davie Stuart and

M'Kay volunteered. They offered Ovide an oar with them, but Ovide had a distaste for partnerships in glory They, too, came back soon enough, drenched and spent, puffing a fine yarn about savages on the cape rocks and motioning them to pull around. But not a word of a possible passage.

Towards evening, though, with the breeze from the west, we raised anchor and made our long-delayed dash for it.

A last employment for the pinnace: to slap ahead of us, sounding our way, signaling us through the charges of spume and the half-drowned bars all burning with the sundown. No mate could be spared her, now. With the *Tonquin* close behind, her rowers need fear nothing worse than a wetting.

Two Sandwich Islanders were in her, and our three oldest mechanics—Job Aitken, the Scotch rigger and caulker, John Coles, our other sailmaker, and my gruff, deaf friend, the armorer, Stephen Weeks—three ancients out of a nursery rhyme.

I was one of those detailed to push them off. Their white hair whipped foolishly across rheumy eyes as they stumbled down between the thwarts. The Islanders' brown faces glittered like copper idols'. They were unused to our clumsy American oars. My hook was pure flame from the sunset as I held them from stoving against the ship's side.

A little pity for a cockleshell—I already had one foot over our gunwale, and they were straight below me, scarce a jump at all. But before I could get my other foot over I heard a girl scream out behind me.

Then it was too late again. The boat was splashing free, the captain roaring me back to the deck, and Perrault turning fast away, refusing to meet my gaze, with her face the one white spot in the evening's windy color.

9

We followed under easy sail. Six fathoms, four fathoms
. . . danger there, then a safe six again. Then four once
more, and the breakers dancing up our bow to the hard
tune of our bottom scraping over rock.

Six, they signaled . . . as the breeze strengthened with
the shadows and shoved us clear, almost abreast of them,
a pistol shot to larboard of them across the darkening
spite of the ebb tide.

Then four fathoms again, scant three, they signaled us
wildly as the breeze must carry us past. We were the wind's
game, they the tide's, and both of us worse than rudderless,
helpless in these breakers.

We struck twice, more violently than before. Deck and
masts shuddered, our bow flung up snorting each time with
a sudden mane of water. A great stone, high as our poop,
rose against us in the dusk, barely dodged our onrush,
fought us off from its steamy girdle of waves.

We shouted to the people in the pinnace to come back
aboard. We were leaving her behind. The gray air was
slashed with combers' spray, and the spray cut our cries.
Even if the pinnace heard us, she could not pull against
that tide any more than we could linger for her in this
gray sport of shallows, lurching rock, and surf as high as
geysers. We struck again, all our beams shocked and
protestant.

We pressed to the quivering rail, as out of reach as
possible of the masts when they might snap and topple,
and shouted, shouted . . . valedictory to the damned.

Six times our bottom slammed. Below decks the cabin
lamp jumped its hook and clattered down on The M'Dougall's open Bible. Something heavy had broken loose in
the hold. Ropes parted in the rigging with a piercing
report.

Six times we slid forward in the breakers, with two men clinging to our wheel and uprooting our smashed figure-head from the river mouth's deafening tangle. Distance had been transmuted into an immeasurable roar. Time was a throe of protests, a blind shouting into spray against all this concert of inevitabilities and convulsions, against all the unblended and unrhythmic noises of a little wooden world upheaving, chuting, careening on . . . a shouting for shouting's sake, a shouting against time itself.

In the pinnace far behind us they were waving arms. We could see nothing else of them than these tiny half arms waving above the water, as though she had capsized. We could hear no cry when she did actually capsize. Some of us saw the little white belly she gave to the dark as she spilled her crew . . . or thought we saw, and could shout no more.

We had refound the channel. We threw two anchors down into it, waiting the night wind and the flood tide. It grew wholly dark. Sight was taken from us. The cape lost all shape and whereabouts, the waves still ran at us from out of nowhere, and only the harsh straining of our wheel told us how much our anchors tugged and our bow was being swung back seaward in the black, wet air. We had let our best bower go.

Over there, beyond the horror of the bar, in the dense suggestion of long, low land which must be the night's sightless shadow of Point Adams, the pinnace floated overturned . . . or had they righted her? And which of them . . . the dark alone could tell which of them, of any of their foolish, Mother Goose crew . . . but the dark had larger things to tell.

For the dark brought a new night tide, a broad, grandiose, invisible benevolence of the singing flood, a new wind choral with power, a tide and a wind which spoke with the tongues of a great sea to distant mountains.

The dark had no voice small enough to tell of three old men spilled from a cockleshell, or of two Sandwich Islanders kicking naked in the cold.

We set free again. We rode the flood to shelter around Disappointment's coil, to good anchorage behind a long sand spit in Baker's Bay. We were officially on the river.

Midnight, we slept among the several empty bunks and hammocks, too weary to remark them, too sorry and numbed to talk . . . except when someone would shout out in his sleep, sob, shiver, and shout, shout. No, not I. I slept.

Officially on the river, midnight, March 25th, 1811, in Mr. Astor's name, his will be done, his commerce increased, his empire consummated and eternally secured, the while the wind marches sentry-wise between his seas and his forest uplands, and his good, obedient, tired servants sleep.

10

Old Weeks we found ashore, when our landing party searched the woods northwest of the cape. Old Weeks the armorer, naked and livid, his few old teeth churning with the early morning cold. He alone, of the white men in both boatloads, could be left alive.

He thought one of the Islanders still lived, though; but he had lost him in the starless forest last night, in the maze of black cedars through the further blackness, and had heard him whimpering piteously behind him as the frost writhed in his own puffed legs and his bitter, salt-soaked bruises.

The other Islander was surely dead. He had frozen to death in the half-filled pinnace. All night the little boat had joggled on the bar, after the three of them, stripped of their soaked clothes and fighting for her overturned gunwale in the foam, had managed to right her, jerk some water out of her, scramble up and in, bailing, drifting, bumping, bailing . . . until feet and faces, their naked bellies wet and fiery cold, the very water in their choked lungs, all froze.

When one Islander died, the other had thrown himself on the body, lying naked on his companion's lifeless nakedness in the puddled torture of the bottom of the boat, speechless and exhausted as the dead, his freezing arms around the frozen corpse, his shrunken lips striving desperately to breathe life back again into the crisping mouth and nostrils.

Washed ashore, Weeks had stumbled on ahead, screaming with the pain—and the relief—of making his legs move again in the forest quandary. He thought he had heard the living Islander sometimes, but only sometimes. He had heard him dragging his friend's body towards the trees.

It was many hours before we found him. He had pulled himself under some rocks, lay there with legs gashed and horribly swollen, his glazing eyes turned straight up towards the branches of a tree where, climbing somehow, he had managed to hang his dead companion's body away from the wild beasts and the little desecrations of the ground.

That evening the captain ordered Franchere and me to accompany the rest of the Sandwich Islanders on their funeral party. They were allowed small amounts of biscuit, lard, and tobacco.

They dug a pit scant inland from the surf, where the cedars started and the shadows of the forest ran gladly to the river edge. While they worked I saw another and stranger shadow on the sand; and, looking up, I saw the birch tree all cold gold in the sunset, with the frost still stubborn in some of its forks, and then the brown, glistening contortion of body and face which hung there.

The sun was strong upon him. It made a burnished ghost of him.

I had never known him well. These Islanders stayed strangers to us aboard ship. I could certainly not recognize him now. A brown man, one of two dozen, assorted sizes. I remembered a hot, lazy day in King Tamehameha's courtyard, when I had waited with long-nosed, cynical Kraimoku and the bored French tutor for His Fat-Necked Majesty to arrive and sanction his twenty-four subjects' departure, and to take his accustomed percentage of their enlistment sales . . . and the great palms and banana trees drowsing over the road to the old morai, where this poor devil might have been buried in his own kindly ground.

What did that matter? Any ground, anywhere. Death is not at all particular. Why should the dead be? I looked down. Franchere, sitting apart squat-legged as a Hindu, was busy taking notes. The Islanders had finished the grave.

They laid the dead man beside it on the sand. They placed their food beneath his arms. Under his chin and his genitals they stuffed little rolls of tobacco. He was provendered for whatever other world . . . whatever other world. Silently, with religiously closed eyes, they transferred him to the pit.

As they lifted him a little sand beetle scuttled across his chest. As if that mattered, either. . . . I think I was the only one to notice it. Franchere continued taking notes. They put stones and sand upon the corpse. The last cold sunlight colored the heap they made.

Then they knelt on either side of the grave in a double row, all turning their faces like lonely children's to the east. One of them must play priest. He went to the water's edge, scupped water into his hat, came back and sprinkled all his countrymen. He was reciting something now, and they all gave wild, low moaning answers, the universal, melancholy dialogue of litany over the dead. I thought I could make out the name of Etoway, their god . . . but the god's name never matters.

When they were through, they went quickly back to the shore, looking neither this way nor that, nor ever behind them. Franchere rolled his journal, tied it, stuck his crayon neatly into the knot of the string, and got up, dusted himself off, to follow them. I followed slowly, too.

I saw some little buds of flowers starting under the old black leaves around me. The rich woods' soil ran moist to the strand. This man's body would bloom quickly anew, have color and grace again, and pleasant scent in the shadows of great cedars. Far from the palms and warm, rioting ground of his youth . . . but far, too, equally far from the sterile, sea-bleached mounds with toppled headstones which are sailors' luxuries, or from the sea's own green and monstrous depths. I could not pity him. His Etoway was both good and evil, and in such a strong god's scheme it would not matter where his body lay, or when the beetles found it.

The ship stood small across the cove, drying her sails. The boat had returned to her since bringing us ashore, and was now grating up the beach again to row us back. She carried a new load. The Islanders waited, huddled and pathetic, while she spilled it.

It was the first lot of pigs from our gangway. Koaster, the Russian carpenter, was with them, with nails and tools to build them a temporary sty. He shouted joyfully, the pigs squealed, the sailors roared with laughter. In another moment the forest would be full of delighted grunts from snouts guzzling deep among the ferns, the trample of fouling hoofs, the cheery, promising sound of an ax on wood.

COMCOMLY OF THE ONE EYE

V

Comcomly of the One Eye

APRIL's first week was all of rain, a soft, slouching rain which curtained the mountains from us and gave the river around our keel a gray, monotonous jigging. But the deck grew clean, the spars glistened freshly; and when we saw the near shore we saw how the last of winter had been washed from its gruff rock and dripping tree boughs, and that the sun would have plentiful moisture of young stems and ferns and berry blooms to drink up through this dramatic soil.

Over there, beyond the rain, the village of Chinook Indian houses sent up smudges of squashed smoke against their shell heaps and the towering, wet hill behind. On the south side of the river, on Point Adams's long spit, the houses of the Clatsops stood close to sea, bare cedar boxes, so bare, so low to the horizon, they seemed to float there unattached to any worldly element.

Mate Mumford was sure he had caught some Chinooks through his glass, but his glass was rain washed and he could furnish few details. He saw the houses were all square and windowless, all enormous in comparison with the moving figures, and that strange things were cut into their fronts and on the tall poles along the strand.

The Indians waited, too. Across the rain, the bay, the gray, jigging river, they must have waited as we did, wondering were we humans, and whether it was we who had hid the spring sun from them . . . we, who, after all these months, should see spring again ourselves, smell spring again upon the hills and in the suddenly starry

thickets under transformed cottonwoods and cedars . . .
and for all the sun's sweet goods and healing charities be
thankful.

2

Then it cleared, and out from the Chinook village a
canoe rode towards us in the green, bright noon. In
circles, far at first, then each time closer, her many men
paddled her around us. She must have been sixty feet
long, a great, carved, multi-colored creature meant for
war or fierce seafaring or some most special ceremony,
and there were fully fifty or sixty men in her.

Her long, lanceolate paddles sang to the sun whenever
they came up. Her adzed flanks were red. The intricate
and majestic sculpture of her projecting prow, the scarlet
and orange and white of so many painted bodies which
leaned to her paddling, threw down reflections as gaudy
and uneasy as torches' into the river.

They brought her ever closer. We could hear the shrill,
nasal chatter aboard her. She was examining us at her
leisure.

We could see what her little men looked like, and how
they looked up at us from the rhythm of their ochred and
striped shoulders. We could not see their whole faces.
All except one of them wore bonnets of woven bark. That
one was doubtless the chief, standing high in the perpen-
dicular stern, who wore the scalp of a slain enemy . . .
and that was all he wore.

But over this grisly headdress, and over his body
smeared with colored fish oil, he was sprinkled with bits
of white down. This, then, was their sign of peace. We
should have peace if we wanted it. We should have
brothers among the Chinooks.

This was what it must have meant, for Mr. M'Kay was
ripping hastily into an old pillow he had found and filling

the air around us with feathers in reply. We should be brothers, white men and red, and our love be baptized gravely in goose feathers.

Their chief was a thick, crook-legged little old man. He had only one eye. Slowly, as we cheered him, he gave us their final sign of trust: opened his bare, greasy, lime-chalked breast to whatever spears or arrows we carried. His other, closed eye seemed the climax of a solemn wink.

But, even as he raised his arms, one of his tribesmen yelped with fright. A few days ago we had already moved our cannon up into the ports, prepared for anything. The shadows of the cannon, when the sun was just overhead, ran straight upon the water like the shadows of the wings of a gigantic bird. The canoe had come so close to us, its bow flamed in and out among these shadows.

Fear of what . . . even Mr. M'Kay could not explain it to us afterwards . . . whether they thought themselves about to be crushed by these black, overhanging bones of thunder, or whether it was rash sacrilege they were committing against some immemorial myth, or some more recent scandal of ships which spit fire from under their wings . . . but suddenly they all yelped along, lashed their fantastic craft away again, and fled for their huts across the bay.

I did not laugh with Ovide and the rest, or bawl cranky curses after them like the captain. It was my guess, they would be back again before long, still shy of our guns, of course, and down to littler, less impressive shovel-nosed canoes, but as anxious as ever to be our friends and brothers, bearing beaver skins and sea otters', shaking their wares high for us to notice, shrieking and counting excitedly on their fingers, begging to trade, to wrangle and profit and cheat . . . to trade as only friends and brothers do.

Our squall of feathers had subsided. I kept seeing one

placidly shut eye, one open, shrewd, intensely black and
Asiatic, in the fat little face of hideous stripes and fish-
oiled sleekness underneath a slain foe's scalp.

3

Dignity, that last refuge of lazy minds, made all the
partners' plans mysterious. They knew how, having
brought them to the land, Captain Thorn was only too
frankly anxious to be rid of them and up the Vancouver
coast on his own little exploring fling. It seemed to give
them a special satisfaction to stay aboard, to call the *Tonquin* their temporary quarters, to use her deck as a trading
table, to take their own sweet time and, now that we were
theoretically ashore, to nip at him with unwarranted
orders.

They bade him sail us across the river. He did so. They
asked for anchor down. Down it went. Now they'd have it
up again, and up it came for two or three miles of listless
floating on the flood, of staring into the foggy woods for a
point which would suit all their fine ideals of a home site.

Ross and Pillet had been sent rowing south. They came
back with no news except of the oddly white earth of
Point Adams, and how handsome this would be to white-
wash our inner walls when we had built the fort, and of
how poor and ugly and in awe of them the Clatsop villagers
had been, all filthy with rancid oil over their misshapen
faces.

Mr. M'Kay, Ovide, Matthews, Farnham, rowed north
at the same time, up through the jerky weather, rain in
the core of the mist, gray sunlight gnawing at the rain.

There was Perrault with them, too. The little fool had
let her hair grow long again, as though all danger of discovery . . . I must cut it for her to-morrow. Nursemaid to a
sickly, pouting prima donna. For an instant before the

fog reduced them to a splash of unseen oars, I saw how thin she had grown, and how her enlarged eyes, strangely fixed on Ovide across the boatload, now carried a look which would make it impossible to hide much longer the fact that she was a woman.

Ovide was smiling out at his oar blade. He knew she was watching him. Then they all belonged to the mist.

They had left stupid work for those of us who stayed behind. Sure enough, trading had already begun. All yesterday the shovel-nosed canoes, heaped with wet beaver skins, had been poling out to us. Little red faces, bulge-eyed from the horrible misshapings of their heads, squashed between rain mantles and conical hats of reed, had screamed incessantly up at us, gibbered with satisfaction over the penny nails, jackknives, and worthless empty bottles we had tossed them in exchange.

Their pelts lay stinking in the forecastle, waiting the drying of a decently sunny day. Meanwhile, number them, appraise them, note the rips, the arrow holes and trap marks, the sizes, ages, lusters. It must all go down into the book. Pelts are merchandise; merchandise is wealth; wealth must be counted.

I had Wallace and Franchere helping me. They had not served warehouse terms, as I had, and had to be taught how to stretch a skin and use their finger nails against the fur in search of thicket sores and lice eggs. This bending and scratching bored them. I gave them no rest from it. They had not served, as I had, a whole year in the snuffy dust and menial back-breaking of the road-way to wealth. Well, let them start now.

Once, when I looked up, I saw the captain in the door-way. He gave me a quick, sarcastic glance, but there was approbation in it—the only time I ever recognized it there —and then he motioned me outside.

Those two famous companions in diplomacy, the Messrs.

M'Dougall and Davie Stuart, were taking the last of our
small-boats for a mission of their own. They were returning
the other day's state visit of the one-eyed Chinook chieftain and his huge canoeful of savages. They were marvels
to behold. They wore their scarlet regimental coats, their
clan kilts, shrieking tarlatans tight across their bellies.
They must have seen us goggling at them from the rail.
They rowed off with difficulty—but also with infinite
composure.

"Do you remember those Christmas sausages in the
meat shops, sir," I said, "so fat and kingly in their colored
paper frills? . . ."

I had known this would burst his temper. He began
to chase my little sentence with a pack of hoarse, humorless rages. Yes, Christ Almighty, what a pair they looked
like, and how he hoped the Indians 'd let the air out of
'em, and would slice 'em and broil 'em before M'Dougall
would have a chance to pull out that British flag that the
captain knew he was carrying hidden under his kilt, the
goddamned traitor. Like Christmas sausages, by God, I'd
said it, like . . . as pompous as . . . as . . .

I watched his own broad face puff and redden in its
run after words. His old green pea-jacket was no match
for their masquerade finery, but he wore it with the same
stout pride. And the same faces . . . it would have given
him a fatal stroke to know how much the same as theirs.

I went back into the forecastle. The smell of damp pelts
was even stronger than that of tar. Wallace was idling.
He stood holding a jagged patch of fur. Even he could
know it was a beauty. The daylight stroked it with golden
fingers.

A perfect pelt. A good pelt. I took it and gave it a place
of honor on the pile. Mr. Astor would be pleased to know
we had had to pay only three nails and a sixpenny chisel
for it here.

I kept hearing that thick, crushing speech of his while we worked. "That was how I, too, began to be a million-aire."

A thousand thousand things happen in a lifetime. Time is never long enough to recall them all, the little things said without meaning and yet meaning all our future years, the careless things done and undone in the craze of complete disregard, the million million things which swarm upon our eyes, are seen, released, forgotten utterly until . . . until now.

I remembered so perfectly how he had said that. His gross, powerful accent was in my ears again. And over my eyes, as though it were dust that must fly by sheer habit out of any furs I handled, a speckling picture of New York in the neat summer, the old beaux sweltering under their heavy beaver hats, the young girls riding beside them in carriages Battery-bound. And a young, dark hoyden laughing down at me across the horses' lowered heads and the sweetly clipped grass.

To-morrow I must cut her hair. I must speak to her. Something actually, bodily wrong with her, whether or not Ovide . . . I must ask her.

To hell with her! Was I her keeper?

I snapped at Wallace. "You, there, get back to work." The mist oozed thick through the bulkhead, and the reek of our booty grew as acrid and choking as hot smoke.

4

Our proud ambassadors were gone three squally days. They were returned to us on the tenth in two large Chinook canoes, Mr. Stuart sitting cross-legged and placid in the high stern of one, The M'Dougall nothing less than a god of gracious plumpness in the other. Their relation of ex-periences lasted all that afternoon.

Scorning a heavy sea and full of their sense of duty to find us a proper site for the fort, they had set out across the bay against all the Indians' advice. A wave had upset them before they were fifty yards from the village strand.

They had been followed and rescued and pulled cordially ashore again by the slacks of their kilts. Since neither of them knew how to swim, they owed their lives to Chief Comcomly of the One Eye.

The way they acknowledged the debt and pressed cotton tassels and penny nails into the hands of the dumb Indians who had brought them back aboard the *Tonquin*, we might be celebrating a nation-wide Te Deum. Captain Thorn marched back and forth on the edge of our crowd, pretending not to listen.

But around a large fire, where their clothes had hung, steaming dry, they had been regaled with all the delicacies of the cedar hut, dried salmon flakes, berry blocks, and toasted, oil-steeped halibut skin, and with the grave silence of strangers who have no syllables in common, nor even a single mutual gesture to cope with the risk of misunderstanding.

The Indian men had been naked in the huge, dark, fire-strung indoors. So had they, too, been naked, dissolving in pudginess and embarrassment, striving to hold to their superiority of white skin and Scotch baronial poise in the hectic nude, benignly permitting the mirthless, inquisitive squaws to pinch their legs and find them flesh and bone.

A daughter of the Chief Comcomly had stood and stared at The M'Dougall. Her little black eyes were set awry in the crevices between her squashed forehead and her high, oily cheeks. She had greased herself plentifully in the white men's honor, and had dusted her chin with mica and bright sea sand. The M'Dougall had had to see how young she was, and how her short red legs burned

through the chinks of her bark apron, and his own nakedness had troubled him sorely then.

He loved this part of his tale. He would have told it
four times over if he had found fresh audiences. He was
full of moral indignation against the little red Jezebel.
He had given her a proper lecture, he assured us. I could
see him reaching for his still wet kilts to quell his old
bachelor belly, and how he must have turned his head
away like a true British gentleman from the solemn in-
sinuation of Chief Comcomly's closed eye.

Then, their own tobacco ruined, they had had to take
some from the Indians' kinik-kinik patch; but none of
them smoked it. A finely powdered stuff, supposed to be
crammed in the mouth and chewed with sticks of clamshell
lime . . . it had raised white blisters on their tongues.

They had had priceless bear rugs and mountain goats'
wool to sleep on, and food and fire and ever more oily
food, while they drowsed like gods among strange, obsequious little people who would not dare try to match
languages with them. Their first night there, the chief
had stayed awake for hours to supervise the fire tending
by the slaves. He could not have been more kind.

Once, deep towards dawn, The M'Dougall said he had
awakened and seen Father Comcomly squatting in a
ring of olachen oil lamps, sucking his lime stick, devoting
his tireless open eye to a stack of best quality assorted
pelts and copper shields. Another time he had Mr. Stuart's
discarded plaids spread out before him while he counted
the colors wonderingly, counted, counted, and grunted
softly back to his women nodding in their terraced quarters behind him, in their loose little aprons of cedar bark,
in their unwashed glory of fish oil and mica-daubed cheeks
and fire-stained legs.

When the canoes which brought them back to us at the
three days' end were finally gone—and with them fifty

silly little things their paddlers had wheedled or pilfered
from the deck—The M'Dougall insisted on showing us all
over again how much his mouth had been burned by their
tobacco powder. He was sure of boils on his gums and a
blister far back in his throat. He stretched his fat lips
open. The pink roof of his mouth, the plump, purplish
tongue, appeared. I looked away, impatient.

But a chuckle from Ovide recalled me. It would be
Ovide who'd notice that the stout old moralist's double
chin was unexplainably slick with fish oil, still rubbed to
a gross fiery shine with mica and bright sand.

5

They established the permanent fort site at last, fifteen
miles distant from our present anchorage on the south side
of the river. The place was called Point George. The wind
stitches in the captain's face flared bloodily when he heard
that.

They took the longboat and twelve men, mechanics,
voyageurs, their favorite Montreal clerks, food for a week,
and a full lot of tools, and made up the river ponderously
ahead of us. When we followed on the late day's tide
they were already encamped at the bottom of a small bay.

We anchored outside, a few hundred yards off shore.
Great half-burnt logs were rolling down the bank. There
was a running shock of many axes hacking at thick trunks.
Voices came over the water with all the strength of spring
and new, hopeful tasks in them. Smoke rose from the
underbrush, pressing through the tree tops' sieve to join
the smoky sky. They were burning the hill clear.

Our second small-boat was ferrying some more passengers ashore. Ovide had gone with the morning's first batch.
Perrault was with this one, carrying a formal invoice for
blankets . . . now, goddamn them, they were welcome to

all the blankets and side-arms they wanted, and the sooner the better, etc. . . . and the wholly gratuitous compliments of Captain J. Thorn, Lieutenant, U.S.N., on their choice of a name for their fort site.

But they hadn't necessarily chosen the name, I chuckled back to the captain. They couldn't precisely help it if some earlier expedition of benighted Britishers had dubbed the little peninsula after their King George.

We could make out the flames pale yellow and tiny in the daylight, and the smoke spurting after them from the feet of the straight, sunny trees. Mr. Thorn reached over the rail as though to toast his temper on those little bonfires.

"Mark the date, Lewis . . . 'n' what I promise, too. Mr. Astor'll be betrayed before a single log in their first building's halfway seasoned."

"Aye, sir."

Plots, plots, plots. I gave up grinning. For all I knew, he might be right. Or an utter fool, a bigger fool than any of them. It was only when I suspected that, that I hated him.

"Mark it, Lewis, April 12, 1811 . . . you'll see."

"If I'm still alive, sir." I remember saying that.

"They're a pack of Bible-bred sneaks 'n' blackguards, they are."

"Yes, sir, they're——"

"Tory traitors, Lewis."

"I suppose they are, sir." The devil they were, but if the devil said they were . . . so long as he played the devil, not the barking fool.

We stood in the stern, watching the small-boat shove her lane through an already bothersome cluster of visiting Indian canoes. The ship wore a deserted air. Her deck was suddenly large with emptiness. Half her humans had been gradually sucked shoreward.

"Damn glad to be rid of 'em, Lewis. Lazy, haughty, filthy lot."

"Yes, sir."

"Little clerks 'n' landlubbers."

I nodded most gravely. "So they are, sir." The fool. Fool against fools. Had I, after all, struggled only to the magnificent position of fool's assistant?

"Well, we'll unload 'em properly 'n' give 'em all their goods. . . . I'm not the one to skimp Mr. Astor's orders. But I'm off up the coast as soon as I can, I tell you that, Lewis. I'll take you with me, of course."

The small-boat had landed in the cove. That must be Perrault climbing out of her now. So slight a figure under the huge trees.

A great trunk, bare and crisped by lightning, swayed and toppled with slow arc down the sky. We heard the crash and the cheers from here. On the nearer cliff, bright-shirted against the blackening shrubs, two of the voyageurs were singing as they stamped the embers down.

"You will, sir . . . take me with you, of course?"

"I will." A gleam came into his little cold eyes, as though he had recognized the annoyance and disappointment rattling behind my respectful echo of his orders, almost as though he enjoyed the irony I could not erase from my words. "I will, indeed."

He must have known how my lean toes, sick of gripping at a slippery, tilting deck, tired of swinging higher than my head in the storming night, ached for brown ground, for the soft crunch of ferns and old acorns brittle under-foot, for all the cheerfulness and sweet-smelling common-places of a strong, fecund earth. He had not lugged in that reference to clerks and landlubbers for nothing. His manservant was no mystery to him.

"Indeed I will. D'you think I'd let you waste your time whittlin' Maypoles 'n' composin' spring poems for these gourd-headed savages around here? You've grown too useful to me, Lewis."

Play his game. I gave him a smart salute.

"You're my most useful of the whole damned lot, Lewis. D'you know why?"

That gleam in his little ice-gray eyes . . . now I knew the time I had seen it there before. It was when he was thrashing the tardy sailor, Aymes, and there had been red flecks on the cane and up his stocky forearm, and he had looked up drunkenly happy at Ovide's loud "Tiens!" from the rail.

"D'you know why, Lewis? B'cause you hate my guts, Lewis, more 'n any of 'em do. B'cause I know it. B'cause you'll have to go on hatin' me but followin' me . . . 'n' you know that, too, in return. B'cause you're a pedant, 'n' think you're a poet, 'n' have long fingers that'll never even learn how to tie a decent sailor's knot, 'n' that'll have to go on writin' things for me . . . whatever I dictate, faithfully, smartly . . . 'n' do my dirtiest biddin'. B'cause you know Latin 'n' philosophy 'n' other stuff of the land like that, 'n' I hate you—Christ, of them all I hate you worst . . . 'n' that's the best bond possible between such as you 'n' me."

I stood looking down into the icy pleasure of his eyes. We were alone on the idling deck. A canoe of Chinooks, squaws, and silent children with tightly bound foreheads, passed below our poop. We scarce heard them go by. We kept looking into each other.

"B'cause, God knows how, you've changed, Lewis, you've grown from everybody's joke butt into my man. My man . . . but a man. B'cause the man in you goes on hatin' me but being more 'n' more useful to me, to my own hate that I wouldn't squander on anything less than a man."

Had he stammered or grown the least red from the

perplexity of such unusual talk, I should have let him have full blast all the curses which were puckering my mouth. But he stayed encased in his cold, strict malice, and only his eyes in their nets of hard stitches betrayed how much he was enjoying his recess from taciturnity. He was no fool.

"Hate's held worse men than you 'n' me together, Lewis. You'll stay with me, just because . . ."

My heart bounded. No, he was no fool. The gruff fangs of the Devil himself had stroked and emblazoned my brow.

"Now, get to land, man, 'n' spend the fortnight spyin' on those goddamned traitors for Mr. Astor's next report."

6

It was Farnham who finally asked it aloud: where, all this while, were Mr. Wilson Price Hunt and his party of overlanders whom we should have found waiting for us here on the Columbia? We had all been wondering this, when evening came and the axes rested and the woods stopped hurling back the new echo of mallets and anvil . . . all grumbled it sleepily to ourselves, or, if a little bolder, whispered it to those next us around the smudge fires.

Our idle talk died, and a silence deeper than the river below our hill, deep as the black of the forest above us, replaced it when Farnham finally asked that question aloud.

Mr. M'Kay did not answer him. Mr. M'Kay sat cross-legged, watching our amateur sentinels beyond the fire-light. He smoked his long Cree pipe, with the red stone bowl in the cup of his hand on the charred ground before him. He was far away in thought, probably not listening at all to Farnham's young worry.

Far away in thought . . . a thousand miles away, maybe, beyond these coastal greens and great churchly cedars, inland in some steep pass he had himself encountered, where the mountain pines flatten to winds from a glacier ice, and the trail is venomous with arrows of hostile tribes shooting from the heights, and where white men with black tongues must stagger through the snow . . . away upon plains he knew, where the hoofs of the Blackfeet's horses drum upon the drumming of the hoofs of a buffalo herd . . . away where the little rivers betray white men's canoes to the broiling swamp or the consternation of sudden waterfalls, and where a thin nag or a sick dog or the mere exercise of a swatch of old moccasin leather between a man's dry, shrieking teeth can save him from starvation, madness, and the last unspeakable resort. . . .

So far away in thought, for all we knew, was the great explorer M'Kay. He smoked his long Bush Cree pipe, he baked his tough gnome's fingers on its red stone bowl. He did not answer Farnham.

The silence and constraint lasted a little while. It was as though we had all grown lonely.

"Pardon me, sir, possibly you did not hear me. I only——"

Ovide roared. "Stop it, give me some wine."

So we could laugh along, forgetting all except ourselves in the ruddy companionship of the woods . . . our own good selves, good friends all, laughing and drinking and falling asleep among the grimed clumps of our clearing, while the fires died and our guards stood off to the dark.

7

The partners had already had the tent raised over their sacred paunches. The rest of us lay with our faces to the stars and the cut-paper tree tops.

Restless, I woke just before daybreak. I leaned up on my elbows, listening to the first birds resuming their dismay and rage over the black havoc we had made of their woods. Their sounds were ironically sweet. It is the business of conquerors to enjoy—and never to understand —what their victims are singing.

The voyageurs had made a camp of their own below us at the river's edge. Their smudge was cold, and they slept in a sumptuous sprawl, pistols and paddles strewn around them, a thin oratorio of insects over their heads. Ovide de Montigny lay among them. I could not see him, but I knew that he lay with his mouth open and his yellow hair soiling in ashes. He had been very drunk last night.

A turkey buzzard set out on its day's hunt across the hills: I could tell it by the fat, lazy flapping of its wings upon the dawn. The sky lightened. An eagle spiraled among the paling stars, putting them out one by one.

Near me, next Koaster, the dumb Russian carpenter, Perrault slept with her head thrown rakishly against his thick, unsensing arm. The new day, creeping through the cedars, touched her small face with the soft unrest of mother-of-pearl.

A twig's crackle woke her as I rose. She lay looking up at me with strange, smiling eyes, sleepily aware that we two were the only ones awake in all the camp. Even the guard we had posted over our arms-stack was drowsing with his back against the muskets and his chin slanting deep in weariness. He had had a plaid scarf on, but during the night, no doubt, some humorous Indian had lifted it deftly off and away while he dozed.

I smiled back at Perrault, pursed my lips and held my finger up in pantomime of secrecy, as one does to a child. Like a child, too, she had closed her eyes again.

I found myself a loaded pistol for chance protection's

sake. I tiptoed down the crooked lane which all these prostrate bodies left, into the cool, beaded green and jubilant clamor of the morning woods.

Here was the forge of Roussil, our blacksmith. A bear cub waddled in front of it, heaving up its little diamond-bright snout to wonder what that rigid iron effigy of itself could be which stood on a great block close by the chain and bellows. Across the clearing, against the river mists and the far emerging peaks behind Tongue Point's green lowland, rose the stripes of our first rafters for a storehouse, and, equally silhouetted, two wild pigeons walking gingerly along a beam.

I had not gone far before I heard someone running after me. Heels made crisp reports upon the cinders of our camp ground. I turned, saw that it was only Perrault, kept on strolling. Confound her . . . I tried to be cross. She was all breath-shorn when she caught up with me.

"I thought you were taking me along," she panted.

Her famous old overalls, as ever too big for her, made her droll. I had cut her hair for her yesterday, so short that her scalp shone through like a sea shell. She looked a scrawny boy again. That was all the more necessary now on land, unless Ovide . . .

"I thought you had dropped back to sleep," I retorted. "Where are you going?"

"Nowhere, of course. Where could I possibly——"

"Oh, but in your pocket, there!" She pointed to the bulge.

"A book, that's all. Can't a man ever find peace to read?"

"A book—what book, Lewis? About the ancient wanderer you told me of—you remember his name? The one who sailed so many seas, and was so cruel to the lady whose rôle I almost sang?"

"Æneas," I informed her. I bridled at her smile. "No,

not that book. Another—well, now, am I your librarian?
Go ask such things of—of others."

"Lewis, it is no book at all. Please, Lewis . . . it is a
pistol. I watched you take it. Why?"

"Oh, I see. You silly!" Heaven only knew what desperate picture was puffing through her featherweight
brain. I made a rough effort to hide how suddenly pleased
I was with her idiotic anxiety. "Do you think Ovide de
Montigny is the only man in camp who can pull a trigger
without shooting his finger off?"

Ovide. As though one must always think of humans in
welded pairs. Ovide and Perrault again and again. As
though my knowledge of their coupling would never let
me look at her without thinking of him, too. Of his bright,
masculine mane tumbling across her throat when he bent
down to her. Ovide. His picture across my brain, and his
name poisonous on my lips whenever I looked at her or
heard her low, boyish voice.

"I happen to be strolling nowhere at all," I said, "and
doing absolutely nothing, and wanting no company."

"Very well, then, I am strolling with you, and doing——"

"Oh, are you? I have not invited you."

She stood with her absurdly trousered legs planted
apart. "I have come on longer adventures than this without waiting for an invitation from you, Lewis."

"Keep quiet! Why not wake up the whole company?
Is everyone to know——"

"No, don't scold me, Lewis, please don't." Her eyes
grew heavy. "Go along your way, then, and I shall go
mine."

"You'll do nothing of the sort. Do you think this is
the fashionable Bowery? These woods are full . . . of
mischief. Go back."

"Back? Back to what, Lewis? To——?"

Damn her and her cuteness for sympathy. She all but bowed her head. I had made a savage job of that haircut. It gave her face a startling narrowness and austerity. Once, in the room of one of my college classmates, a Papist from Maryland, I had seen an engraving of an arrow-riddled St. Sebastian with just such young, drawn cheeks and sorrowing brow.

"Back to him with my compliments." She a saint . . . the little trollop, trying her stage tricks to tease me. I laughed without humor, without mercy. The jaggedness of my voice scraped my own nerves. I heard myself snarling on: "Back where you belong, in the sag of his big, drunken, satisfied body in the ashes. Back to your brave one, your hero, your husband-to-be."

There were two things she might have done: by her look she was on the verge of those stupid tears of hers; either that or she might have been about to break into the rapid, high-pitched polyglot of Latin wrath she had used on me once or twice before. But this time she neither cried nor cursed. She was studying me patiently, almost shyly. She gave me a hesitant smile. Then the color climbed her slim neck, fought into the sea tan above her lips, into her eyelids, her forehead, and, while she smiled, pricked hotly in her scalp. I could see the waves of it meeting in her short, rigid hair.

I stood as tall as that above her. She was the one living being among them all with whom I was, and always would be, still conscious of my old gangliness and sorry address. And, as of old, I would still defend myself by upbraiding her.

Her unaccountable flush sped. We stood saying nothing, knee-deep in the pink of salaal blossoms. There was everywhere the wild smell of high, wet ferns which stormed the vast tree trunks around us.

Down the slope the river was already taking on the

olive brown of its daytime dress. Thin seams of yellow
lather drifted towards the channel under the hills of the
north shore, telling the end of the tide rip twelve miles
seaward. Far out, a lone gull tilted on the silver breeze
and dipped among the poles of an Indian salmon weir.
A black duck skimmed low, dagger straight, the perpen-
dicular beat of its swift wings almost chipping the hard
crinkle of the current.

This deep, liltless music might have been the shoreward
water's, or the evergreens' above. While we stood silent
it grew upon us in sound too broad for any sure origins or
distinguishable notes, from below, from aloft, from the
camel's hump of a mountain directly behind us, from the
river itself and the brightening combs of the hills across
the river, from out of the brook cleft which led to the little
bay on our camp's left, where birches, taller than I had
ever dreamed birches could be, glittered and clattered
upon the darker sound-surf of cedars grappling with strong
boughs and spruces shaking the last mists from their
mighty heads. It was the sound of the new sun charging
upon woods and water, the sum of all the fresh, unbargain-
able sounds which sing up the quiet of these North Pacific
days.

"I did not mean to be surly," I admitted stiffly. There,
that was apology enough.

She stood with eyes downcast upon the ferns, and I pretended not to have noticed the sudden impulse of her
hands towards mine. I turned on my heel in the shaggy
turf and started off by myself, diagonally up the hill from
the river bank. But when a sprawl of fallen tree trunks
slowed me, I saw that she still followed me, stumbling
doggedly behind me among the brambles and flowering
tangles, saying nothing in suddenly meek expectation that
I might otherwise chase her back again.

I halted to blaze a tree. I made a pretentious matter of

waiting until she could catch up with me. But this time she halted, too, and stood looking up at me from the rusty, windy fringes of a little cliff over the cove. She was twenty yards or so downhill. Under the great trees, whose tops topped even the rise on which I waited, she was insect-small, a perky, incommunicable, fly-like thing.

The destiny of a fly . . . but her destiny was all her own. Her own and Ovide's, never mine.

It would profit me nothing to stand so high above her, to stare down the chute of restless branches into the bright speck of her face, at her wind-blown blouse and her odd, theatrical stance among the blowing fronds. I stood wondering dully what she was doing, standing there aping, looking up, laughing, perhaps . . . no, not laughing, either. The black speck of her mouth in the bright speck of her face meant something else than laughter. And the way her arms put handles to her boyish hips: I had seen her use that pose before. But when, where, on what specially brave occasion?

As I watched down, I could see the tiny flicker of sun and windy fern shadows across her lifted throat. There was something lunatic about her inexplicably open mouth, her footlight manner, something embarrassing which made me look away.

Down the other wing of the bay a few renegade Chinooks had already settled themselves and their squaws as our most faithful and pestiferous camp followers. I gave my eyes all sorts of squinting tasks among them, counting their dugout boats in the white lapping of the strand, the number of women squatting shapelessly before a little fresh waterfall and kneading berry biscuits, the gusts of smoke from their camas ovens, the horse clams a little naked boy was digging as he waded in the ruffle of brown shallows.

Mean curiosity brought me back to Perrault. The tug of

a temptation to glance again at something self-forbidden.
To her, to that little insect of stiff, voiceless antics and
open mouth down there, my gaze gave back . . . my half-
contemptuous, half-pitying conjecture of what the devil
she could be doing, and why, and for whose benefit. For
she was still at it. Was she trying to say something? Was
she wanting to shout some stagy plea at me uphill against
the wind, against this whole downpour of tree boughs
swinging and clashing in their gianthood's music?

Then at length I knew. Then I saw her instantly as
though she were in Cherubino's satins, courtly and deli-
cious and an imp of the angels; recognized my memory of
her pose with young gallant's arms akimbo and a page's
lace wristlet dangling debonairly over her toy sword hilt,
and her sleek, impertinent, merry boy's face thrown back
to lift her song past the pit's ears to the circle of faces in
the lighted boxes . . . to the round red faces smiling over
satin stocks, in tune with the lightness and loveliness of
what she sang.

It was for me, this impromptu concert. She went on
with it, on and on in absurd fiasco, as if to bring me a great
gift, as if she had recollected what I wanted most in all
the world to hear, and she must carry me it with all the
frills and knee-knicks and sweet pleasantries that such a
song required. Only her gestures told me when she was
finally done with it. Her arms came up and out, her quaint
head bobbed, she managed half a curtsey in the underbrush.

I came down to her with the wind. I must thank her
somehow. I was wondering, should I risk it, should I guess
what she'd been singing? But when I was close enough, I
could see by her clear smile that she took it entirely for
granted that I knew. I need not blunder into any error.
I had only to nod gratefully back when she put out her
hand to steady me after my rushing descent.

"There," she said, "that was my return for all your bad temper to-day. By your favorite composer . . . all of it, every word of it in my best before-breakfast voice and my finest Milanese style. And all . . ."

I should never tell her that I had not been able to hear a single one of all those words.

"There is no music as dear to me as Mozart's," I assured her gravely. "I am certain of it now." But even as I said it the wind struck its thousand green harps and poured my pretty speech away.

Yet she must have suspected something patronizing, overgrateful, in the way I took her hand. Or may have known that I was going to be hopelessly awkward again about my bending over her poor, toughened fingers. She withdrew them slowly, turned away. For the second time in these few minutes she had flushed again: the creeping, irresolute, dark flush of a woman troubled and shamed.

Single file, we thrashed through, out upon the open rocks above the river.

There was a murmur of sunlight over all the stone, a reflection as watery as the little waves from which it came. We faced each other in a craze of white radiance. It was over our feet and up our thighs, a sweet, fiery enfoldment in the blaze of full morning from the water crests.

"You are a good, beloved man, Lewis," she said slowly. "What should I have done without you? . . . and now . . ."

I completed the sentence for her with a strange bounding of my heart. "And now what will you do with me?"

But we had walked by accident into one of the cliff burial places of the Clatsops. Even with the first of our words we had begun to be aware of the vile stench around us, the broken, decomposing bodies folded into their carved boxes and canoes beneath the gaudy, horrible grotesques of their memorial posts.

8

We had several interpreters among the Indians. There
were those of the Chinooks who knew sufficient Nootka
and Chihalis words to match the few which some of our
own sailors knew. Come to the worst, they had all the
trick, learned inland, of making themselves understood
by grunt and thumb signs and a jingling of the little white
haiqua shells which were their currency markers. But their
jargon was spattered, too, with the Missouri patois, with
the unholy bits of English they had remembered from our
own American Messrs. Lewis and Clarke's stay here five
years ago, and already with a little of the thick Canadian
French. Our voyageurs would add to that end of the
vocabulary, no fear.

Mr. M'Kay, of course, could converse with old Comcomly as with a tilikum, a kinsman, a friend among
friends. They would mind Mr. M'Kay and his mouth as
lean, his lips as leathery, his sense of the woods as curt
and yet as sharp as theirs, when they would listen to no
one else among us. For them he was the tilikumpapa, the
the ahnkuttie tilikum himself, of our tribe.

Sacrilege against John Jacob Astor, I remember thinking
. . . and grinning. And I remember The M'Dougall's pink
snout alive with jealousy and the moisture of offended
pride as he tried to impress on Comcomly of the One Eye
the seriousness of such an error.

The Chinook brethren and children came continually
visiting us now. They brought us the bluish, limy sand
of which we made our foundations, the olachen oil we
must use in our lamps, huge salmon still quivering from
the first spring catches, skins and bracken roots and gray
whales' blubber—a chieftain's delicacy, this, all garlanded
with feathers and iridescent with many months' rot.

Their young girls they brought us, too, fresh from their

year behind the screen, plump and giggling from the noisy
potlatches in honor of their puberty, squat, sooty, and
rancid; their breasts ruby-red with blistering oil, their
heads squeezed into gross and comical misshapes.

Ovide roared at his first sight of them. But, even so,
I noticed how his big knuckles tightened on the mallet
he was swinging at the moment, and how much sudden
shoulder strength he threw into his blow when he felt
their black, childish eyes on him, and the way his own
eyes fluttered up in command of admiration as he split
the mallet head in twain.

It is one of the best pictures I have of him: astride a
rafter, leaning back as in a saddle to wave his broken stick
at the giggling, flat-faced little virgins under his imaginary
stirrups, to roar and laugh and be boisterously pleased
with the feel of his quick muscles rippling under his embroidered deerskin and returning him to equilibrium.

The sunlight gave him a blazing, tipsy crown. His stick
was now a marshal's baton. He began to recite some ribald
verses from the Parisian revolution.

That was how Perrault and I saw him when we came
back into camp that morning. The day's work had already
started on the storehouse . . . and there he was, riding his
rafter high, swaying, still fumy from his last night's
drunkenness, hallooing the sunshine and the little red
girls and his own young handsomeness gayly. . . .

"Bebé!" he'd shout, and throw his kisses far.

Until he caught sight of us standing close down here.
His recitation ended. His face became a fury of jealousy,
of long teeth biting at his laugh. He raised the thick rem-
nant of stick, flung it at us wildly—at which of us, or both
of us, we never did know—but it struck Perrault upon the
throat, its splintered end like claws across her cry.

Before I could rush for the rafter, he had already un-
seated himself with that drunken throw. He fell thrice

his height to the ground. As I reached him I heard the snap of the arm that was under him, and I almost hit him in spite of it.

He was very sorry about that poor little boy, Perrault. He was very brave about his own broken arm. In the Chinook jargon forever after the word for a kiss will be "*bebé*."

9

One other word we learned from their constant dinning of it at us. The word "mahkook," the Nootka word for trade, for bargaining, for all the shrill war of cunning and flattery, coaxing and pretended exasperation, the jingling of haiqua shells and the grudging, suspicious weighing of penknives and tobacco twists over their stacks of pelts, all the interminable game of exchange of goods which they were willing to play with us for rainy hours on end.

Mahkook ... a bargain, a great bargain. A twilled cedarbark basket, three beaver skins, a digging stick carved out of horn, and a sardine rake blessed with special mightiness and good fortune by the magician of the Ravens, in exchange for just one of the huloima tilikum's blankets and a few of those bright iron nails.

And, very well, if the foolish white men insisted on such a common thing as an otter skin, here was a purplebrown otter skin shining like the hills behind the sunset.

A Pekin mandarin might poison his emperor or forswear his ancestors to possess that otter skin in years to come. But the Chinooks had had it, and a hundred like it, from their neighbors of the Northern bays: the kelp was full of these cheap, gentle creatures whose own gas carried them helplessly up to the hunter's waiting spear. They were nothing compared with these pouches of spruce root, these copper shields embossed with the design of the horned

owl and the legend of Semmelth, the wolf-child, which we
could have so reasonably, instead.

We made the partners' fortunes in these first few weeks.
Even after the Chinooks realized that it was skins we
wanted, and how recklessly we wanted them, and had
begun a systematic business of loitering around the unfinished storehouse to steal back those for which we had
given them the most, the trade was preposterously all in
our favor. Tenas mahkook, so cheap, so very cheap.

They came in their dome-shaped hats and their soaked
coats of rushes when it rained. The wet weather peppered
their red, plucked chins and dissolved the orange clay
marks ornamenting their mouths. The raindrops stayed
in little gray balls where they had greased themselves
most thickly.

Their feet, the short, fat, close-toed feet of a waterside
people, were invariably bare. We could hear them grating
like clam shells up the sand whenever they stepped out of
their canoes, and the clank of the squaws' anklets over
their shiny heels. In the woods it was a different thing.
There—as thousands of years of seasonal migrations to
the hills had taught them—they had the paws of cougars,
cautious and secretive and alive to each leaf they
walked on.

Fair days again, and they flocked through our encamp-
ment in freer numbers than ever. They had come to please
the Creek woman, they assured us, the goddess who lived
under the little brook and beaver pool above our cove;
and Father Comcomly was going to get her special
promise to be generous with her trout eggs in our honor.

His open eye glistened beautifully as he explained this
—and his other marked the climax of a solemn, endless
wink. It cost The M'Dougall four twists of tobacco and
a bolt of red flannel to impress him that day.

They swarmed around the new pigsty. They squatted

whole hours in the hot, trampled copse, the men stark
naked, the women's cedar aprons dragging the ferns,
while they listened gravely, excitedly, to the squealing
inside and waited—Mr. M'Kay corroborated this for me,
later—for the pigs to resume their human forms.

Not that the superstition would interfere with a successful ambition to kidnap a couple of specimens, of course.
But I think it was seventy beaver skins they had to pay
for each young porker we suspected they'd stolen. The
M'Dougall insisted on it loudly, to no avail. Mr. M'Kay
had only to suggest it. Father Comcomly sealed it immediately with his one eye.

Tenas mahkook. Wake hyas mahkook. So very cheap.
Such a bargain of bargains.

Next day he came back accompanied by his split-nosed
magician, by his favorite son and all his womenkind. They
were carrying some silver salmon, and they made an endless ceremony of presenting them to us.

Only two little requests went with the gift. We must
take care never to cut the fish open lengthwise with our
foreign metal knives, lest we offend the salmon people
and their mighty master, the killer whale. Secondly, we
should have the whole mess for just one of our muskets,
one horn of powder and a few lead balls.

When Mr. M'Kay refused him these, the black veins
swelled in the chief's neck—I noticed for the first time
how short and inevitably thick a neck it was—but his
face stayed sly and imperturbable under the blue-and-
white diagonals of paint he used for a formal visit. His
magician, waving a long head scratcher, chittered with
disappointment. But Comcomly made no protest. He sat
sucking his hot lime stick. His eye slid from lean M'Kay
to the puffed, importantly hemming and hawing M'Dougall.

A plaid of the Clan M'Dougall rewarded his tact. He

paid for this, in turn, with a bag-shaped net, stuffed with olachen. He called up his women to render the oil. We heated rocks in our forge fire for them, they dropped the rocks hissing into a canoe full of water, boiled the thousand little fish until the oil rose and spat and thickened in a golden scum.

While Comcomly's old wives squatted and howled the song of the oil try, his daughters must squeeze the hot olachen dry, pressing them ceremoniously against their squat young bodies until all were coated in a crimson rage of the heavy-smelling, lustering oil.

This took hours on end. It went on while we worked, while we toted and carpentered and finished the sixty-foot storehouse, while we rested and gaped in the noon sun.

Ovide, his broken arm boxed with a cedar slab and held slung handsomely up in front of him in one of the voyageurs' gayest *ceintures*, was enjoying the performance in his own sporting way. He had taken the chief's son back into the woods and given him a stiff cup of rum. The young boy lay sick and stupefied in the salaal, pulling at his upper lip as though it were no longer part of him, as though the glazed and reeling blossoms across his mouth were as huge as the huge trees whirling with the sky.

I found them like that when I went behind for a load of alder for our charcoal. Ovide stood chuckling down, half-ashamed to meet and give any explanation to the wretched, slanting eyes which sought his from the ground.

"Another of your celebrated jokes, M. de Montigny," I said.

He flew into his braggadocio, constant refuge when anyone found him out. "I did not play it for your benefit, old bones. Must I prove it to you? It is only my left arm that's broken."

I did not answer him. I kneeled and lifted the sick boy's face out of the hot sun.

"Well, what the devil, is it such a crime to teach him his liquor? When you know as much about the Indians as I do, and how they love it . . . Hey, Laframbroise, Lapierre! Here, Belleau, here!"

His cronies, the voyageurs, came running to join his laugh. And then, in the midst of their loud, good-natured circle, the Indian magician, screeching rebukes, and Father Comcomly himself.

The old chief pretended to take no notice of his drunken son. He stood stock still, saying something interminably which none of us could understand, softly, in woolly gutturals and the gentle, clacking consonants of a polite speech, without outward resentment or any whine, until we had helped carry the boy down to the shore and sobered him with a slash of water. Then Comcomly of the One Eye actually thanked us for our humor. There was that necklace of black veins standing out from his thick red neck . . . but he thanked us and said soft, courteous goodbyes to The M'Dougall.

But whenever he or any of his male villagers visited our camp thereafter they wore their war clothes, their armor of heavy skins or close-bound sticks. Now they had always freshly purified themselves, scorched and scraped the bottoms of their canoes anew in some clamorous ritual on their beach; and, when we let them, they now came among us carrying carved whale ribs, sharp pickaxes of jade and bloodstone, and the heavy clubs which they called slave killers.

10

Below our camp, circling the hill behind it, ran the tributary which we called Young's River. In the sunset, when the world was all amber and wine and a single star, some of us were drifting back to the Columbia in boats of the friendly Clatsops.

There were Farnham and Matthews in the canoe with Perrault and me, and a slave whom the Clatsop chief had brought yesterday to Captain Thorn as a guide, as a bodyguard, as an offering to the Thunderbird. The *Tonquin* lay close to the Clatsop village nowadays.

We had paddled up the smaller stream to see a meadow where they told us the Messrs. Lewis and Clark and their famous American party had camped throughout the winter of 1806. The log house was still standing in the high, wild grass. Still standing, but overgrown with parasite creepers, and long since broken-faced, mouldering, the doors in soggy strips upon the ground. Five years . . . the green, impatient wilderness and its allies, the rain and the coast wind, were fast blotting out all concrete memory of these celebrated overlanders and their journey to the sea.

We paddled in silence. From the canoe in front of us, manned by some of the voyageurs, floated their song:

> "*Le bruit court dans la ville,*
> *Le bruit court dans la ville,*
> *Que demain vous mourrez,*
> *Faluron, dondaine,*
> *Que demain vous mourrez,*
> *Faluron, dondé.*"

The shadows of the spruces from both banks met in great chevrons across the river's dusk. The woods were motionless. Some rose-hips glimmered from a patch we passed, and, as we neared the confluence, a clump of water-weed shone with the claret of the evening. Perrault, in front of me, shivered for the gone sun.

I could not see her face, but I knew how sad the afternoon had left her. I had watched her standing staring at the caterpillars crawling and sliming in hundreds between the logs of the deserted cabin. I had known well enough

what was passing through her chilled, unphilosophical little brain.

The Indians had shown us, too, their treasure of broken beeswax candles with the gilded monogram of the Church still decipherable on them, remnants thrown up from a shipwreck in Nehalem Bay half a century ago, the only souvenirs of all the castaways with strange black beards ... and when we asked the Spaniards' final fate the Indians refused to understand.

They had rambled on about other shipwrecks, other rare foreigners who talked a huloima wawa and taught them to pop corn, and of others and others, like their good tilikums, Lewis and Clark, whom they had guided to the sea for salt, and whom they had guarded against the sons of the Ravens and the paddleside serpent canoes of the hostile Tillamooks and Clatskanies.

And in more tentative, nervous tones they had told us of the others who had come sailing, like ourselves, far up into the river mouth on the backs of great Thunderbirds ... of those who, like ourselves, could command the god-like carrier to spread his huge white wings cloudwards, to fill the sunniest noonday suddenly with black anger, thunder, and the red lightning of destruction. They had seen it once when the Chinooks from across the river had pushed too near the shadows of the wings of another great bird, almost as big as the *Tonquin*—Broughton's, perhaps, but we never could learn for sure—but it had dealt the lesson of death which, I now remembered, had chased the Chinooks from the mere reflections of the black bone-tips of our guns.

To the master of the Thunderbird, to the Thunderbird itself, they had given this slave. Their houseposts had come alive and spoken and ordered them to do this.

There was white people's blood, the blood of the men with beeswax and strange black beards, in the abject man.

His father's father had taught him to speak the huloima wawa. Aboard the *Tonquin*—I had happened to row out to her yesterday afternoon with another of The M'Dougall's demands on Captain Thorn for tar pots and what not—the slave had squatted in the lonely forecastle, too frightened to talk or eat or take a hand at anything.

"Here, try some of your uppity Latin on him, Lewis. Get two words out of the dirty devil 'n' I'll give him to you outright. Tell him to get t' hell off my ship. Tell him to go wash his rumps, 'n' that I'm no damned nigger snatcher. Take him ashore 'n' let him sleep with the Sandwich Islanders. Christ's sake, tell him he's a free man."

That was the one thing I knew I never could tell him. He had the natural, unpressed head of the slave-born. His mother had not been allowed to squeeze his brow under the tight, torturing cedar strips when he lay in his cradle. His skull was the skull of ignominy. He would be a slave and a cleaner of fish until he reached the end of his stick of life.

He was the bow paddle, now, of our canoe. We were coming back into the low cup of Young's Bay. When we passed the *Tonquin* her night lanterns were already lit and plunging talons in the water. The slave turned, looked at me with terror in his eyes.

The tide was low, the water calm, and islands of dark reeds and sand were giants' footprints towards the breakers and the sea outside. The big, saddle-backed mountain which had come to be peculiarly ours was tissue-thin behind us in the gloaming.

The mute, desperate supplication of the slave as he rested his paddle . . . and the *Tonquin's* shadow bristling along her side, like the shadow of the wings of a great, ominous bird . . . I looked to the smoke-skein rising from the Clatsop village far down the bay, then back to the waiting slave.

I nodded. I only half knew what he wanted, or whether he was waiting my permission at all. I warned the others to keep quiet, to balance the canoe.

He slid noiselessly overboard on the shore side, away from the *Tonquin*, away from all white men, and began to swim swiftly downstream.

I knocked up Farnham's paddle. "Let him go," I ordered. I was telling myself what a weak-lunged, lazy sot we might have made of him around our camp.

At first we saw the glitter of his arms when they cut the colored water. When he reached the nearest of the sand bars we thought we could still see him running in its surf, plunging to swim again beyond it, to reach the Clatsop colony where he had been a lifelong slave.

Away, somehow, anyhow, away from the white men who spoke the huloima wawa of his father's father's ignominy, and whose heads were all the common, unpressed heads of servitude, and who lived like lice on the body of the Thunderbird.

Back, somehow, anyhow, back to the masters who would know how to beat his disobedience out of him, how to slay him riotously in the boasts of the next potlatch and fling his inconsiderable body under a house post or out into the woods without a box or any belongings or even a canoe for the final journey on the rivers shining underground and far away . . . when the forest beaks would find his bones, and the teeth and claws would split his shameful forehead into dry white splinters.

The stars were springing everywhere. Over the fires of our own camp they hung like checked sparks. We pushed homeward. The voyageurs in the canoe ahead had exchanged their song for cheery hollering to the shore. We could see the stalwart outline of the big log house among the trees, and the camp fire echoed in the brand-new sills and windows.

"Five years will be nothing in this fort's life," I vowed
to little Perrault, in front of me. "It will outlive us all."

"Perhaps," she replied. And then, in the voice of one
who must go on hoping against hope and all belief, "Us
all . . . and our sons and our sons' sons. . . ."

II

Captain Thorn sat shaving the loose fibers from a splice
he had been making to while away time and temper. He
had a heavy jackknife. Its blade was shilling-broad, and
he kept it always sharp and rustless.

His compliments to Dunkie M'Dougall, commander of
the British forces now occupying Mr. Astor's fort at
Mr. Astor's own expense—Captain Thorn's sarcasms could
be as heavy as his jackknife, if nowhere near as neat—
'n' how long in hell did they think they were going to keep
the *Tonquin* hanging around here?

I had come aboard carrying him the partners' invitation
to spend the night ashore and drink hearty with them over
the christening of the Astoria mahkook house and the
laying of the first logs for the living quarters.

The elder Mr. Stuart had bade me be sure to promise
him that bygones would be bygones and that they'd dine
in gold braid and all the possible state of the Nor'westers,
as they'd used to dine in their great club on Beaver Hall
Hill in Montreal. To save my stanch Yankee from a fit
and Fort Astor from a cannon ball, I had made up my
mind to forget these sweet inducements. Now I saw the
uselessness of delivering the invitation at all.

"More 'n' a month I've been kept waitin' on their
doorstep. Like a tuppenny porter whose load it don't
convenience 'em to take in."

"They had to finish the storehouse before they could
begin to fill it, sir. They'll soon unload completely now."

"They'd better. They'd better, or I'll have my anchors up, 'n' that's that. Collectin' mud 'n' barnacles more 'n a month, waitin' for a lot of bloody Tories to take their kits 'n' wave me pretty good-byes. I've better places to go to. Up North, around Nootka, I can trade on my own account better 'n the whole lot of 'em combined. If I can only get there afore the Russians are down from Seetka for the summer, while the savages are still standin' by to see whether it's winners for the Spanish, the English, or who. . . ."

He had it all planned. Or perhaps Mr. Astor had planned it for him, back in his office of sublime, satin-stocked omniscience in New York.

"Why, goddamn 'em, Lewis, they think they're traders. I'll show 'em what a Yankee c'n do along that line. I'll end up home with my hold crammed tight with otter."

"Home, sir? Not back here?"

"Back here? What for? Hell, Lewis, I know my orders. Why?"

I held back my smile. "Right, sir, you know your orders."

He gave me his old look of testy suspicion. It was a misty day, and he wore his weather-greened pea-jacket. All this idle while on the river he had kept it looking as correct and clean as an old maid's tippet.

"What've you been hearin', Lewis?"

"They'll expect you to call back here, sir. They were trying to decide last night which one of the partners is to go with you."

"Which one of the partners . . . what for?" His face was stitching itself purple. "What for?"

"To take charge of the trading."

"To take . . . why, the bastardly . . . I'm doin' the tradin', I tell you. Else nobody's . . ."

"I am only repeating what I heard, sir. You'd told me to—to eavesdrop."

"If it's M'Dougall I'll have him in irons in two days."

"No fear. Mr. M'Dougall would—no, it'll probably be Mr. M'Kay. They'll have to vote which."

"Well . . ."

"Mr. M'Kay's the best of the lot, sir." There was silence. I began again. "Mr. M'Kay knows the Indians, doesn't he? The Nootka tongue, too. And you'll have to admit, he's a famous old hand at trading."

I was baiting him deliberately, for some reason that was deep within me and that I could not have explained. His lull, his "Well . . ." and his pause for one decent little doubt had disappointed me.

It was the devil I wanted to see in him.

I wanted him to rage. I wanted to see him rail and snarl with insane hate of them, of us all. I wanted my right to hate him back, as one would hate the devil incarnate with blood specks up his corded arms, and to know that I had sold my soul to someone whose tongue was blacker than anyone's and whose stubby hand could clench around a knife with spasmodic meaning of fury, punishment, and utterly pitiless evil.

He started for the hatchway. He returned my salute with martinet's nicety.

"Well . . . I'll look up my orders in the matter," he said.

His orders from on high. That one dull, single-minded little money god he would go on worshiping.

The devil had known the wild pleasure of taunting the heavens above, but this neat, red-faced miniature of the devil would have to run down into his too prim stateroom and study the instructions from his infinite shipowner.

"Oh, they're not bothering about Mr. Astor's orders," I called down the steps to him. I was quite cheerful. He stopped midway.

"In fact—sir, in fact, they weren't hesitating to speak

rather badly of the Astor Empire last night. They were offering all sorts of bets that the British David Thompson 'll reach the river here long before our own overlanders. They were sure that somebody could induce the Indians to give our people what they called the long traverse . . . and they laughed. Not Mr. M'Kay so much, sir, but the others. At Mr. Astor himself they laughed."

There was a strange, cracking sound from down the hatch. I recognized it rapturously. With the still-open blade in his left hand he had stabbed the bulwark through. There was the steel in the thin wood first, then the side of his fist with a thump as the riven panel screeched . . . all within the half second that let loose his new, surcharged wrath.

"Damn you, Lewis, that's what I'll do to every whoreson Judas among 'em that talks like that. Look, by God! Come here, you, 'n' look what you've made me do to my own ship."

"Excuse me, sir." I mocked him, "Mr. Astor's ship." And fled chuckling for the rail.

12

We had sent some of our best men exploring up the river. Our camp was weak, and it alarmed us when the Chinooks began to stay away.

We heard first that they were low in stock of furs. Then, a more believable rumor, that we had offended their Creek woman with our metal frying pans and must be forbidden any more fish. Then that the sturgeon season was coming, and with it a great number of kinsmen from near-by Gray's Harbor and the Juan de Fuca strait.

The Indian village across the river grew five times its former size. Cedar planks sprang to punchions overnight, and many new long, rectangular houses poured smoke from their chimneyless roofs over the studded shore line of Baker's Bay.

Even the renegade few who had been hanging viciously around our woods and cove were paddling home to the Chinook headquarters and taking their goat mats and young daughters and their new-found love of rum all back with them. Back, they would assure us gravely, only to help stud the fish hooks with shell and to join the annual hunt for the greased and scented harpoons which the tamahnawis man, the tribal conjurer and master of the wolf-head masks, had hidden in the spruce boughs.

I thought I recognized the fine touch of One-Eyed Comcomly in the way they insisted on the innocence of their absence.

The M'Dougall and the two Stuarts wrangled away over the plans for quick fortification of our camp. We heard them at it in their tent for half the night, shouting of bastions and palisades and British army regulations for firing lines. Between the canvas and the candle The M'Dougall could be seen standing, a soft, fat silhouette, exhibiting his letter of authority from the Infinite Astor, pointing with a fat, soft shadow of a finger of the other hand to the sentence conferring on him his chieftainship.

But Mr. M'Kay came back with his exploring party the next day and took real charge. We raised the shops and dwelling house parallel to the warehouse. These and the ravines below them gave us our flanks. We cut a great quantity of pickets in the forest, and formed a square around us with little guardhouses and cannon ports at each corner. We organized a guard for day and night. In less than a week we had the place formidable to see, sufficiently impregnable. Nothing could surprise it now excepting treachery from within.

Less than a week—but long enough to send Captain Thorn on the *Tonquin* into another orgy of rage and insult

over the new delay. Long enough, too, to reduce The
M'Dougall to a realization that he would never really be
the fort's commander with Mr. M'Kay around, and to
keep him moping in his tent in true Homeric style. Every
hammer thwack they heard was gall to both of the old
adversaries.

Then, one late afternoon in the midst of all our prepa-
rations, Comcomly's daughter appeared. From nowhere,
patiently misunderstanding all our questions as to how
she had come and what had happened to the canoe which
must have brought her over and up the river, she was here.
Here, and as suddenly, as calmly, pushing the flaps apart
and bearding the great M'Dougall in his den.

We all stopped working, crowded around. We could
not hear what she was begging of him. We saw her only
from behind, the lumpy calfs of her red legs oil-slicked and
bulging up from her copper anklets, her young haunches
flaring out of their cedar-braid apron; a comical, uncouth
segment of a figure which began with bare feet on the
ground and ended abruptly at the tent flaps.

Somebody in our waiting circle laughed aloud. Ovide.

The face of our local Achilles, fiery, piggish, puffy with
moral abasement, rose over the girl's shoulder and shooed
us back. He began then and there to lecture us all on the
frivolity of our minds and manners. We misjudged him if
we thought . . . but there was such a moistness in his words,
and the drivel came so readily down his jowls, we could
see well enough what he secretly hoped we'd think.

Comcomly of the One Eye was a very sick man, it
seemed. He had sent this dear little daughter who was—
er, well—a favorite of the white men's chief, the Tyee
M'Dougall, to beg for aid, for the white men's medicine,
for one of those cures which come only in the pills of the
huloima.

For the holy magician himself, the sorcerer, the greatest

tamahnawis man of their sept, had not been able to cure
Comcomly, neither with his rattle dance nor even by
blowing on him through his magic blow tube, because the
white men, the mighty tkope, were supreme in the tamahnous of life and death and ana-in-the-belly . . . and because
the Thunderbird of the white men had clapped its wings
and told the Killer Whale, who had told the Porpoise
People, who had told the Ten Brothers of the Sea Lion,
that Comcomly of the One Eye must die unless the white
men's chief, the great Tyee Tkope, would come and cure
him.

"Come? To their village?" demanded Mr. M'Kay.
"Are you daft?"

The M'Dougall managed to fold his arms over his fat
chest. "Have I ever been one to run away from danger?"
he demanded. "I ask you, have I——"

"I said nothing about danger," replied his partner.
"I said only daft." And, giving him and the girl's smooth,
ochre-striped back another short look, turned and went
off to his pickets.

She had been cleverly coached. They had evidently told
her to avoid Mr. M'Kay's good sense. And to court The
M'Dougall's bad.

No doubt she should have appealed to the master of
the Thunderbird, out there on the river, she continued.
For some of her father's people had been uncertain which
was the greatest tyhee among us, while others had been
sure that he who could command those great white wings
across so many seas was the one, the only one among us,
who could surely cure . . .

The M'Dougall had decided. He was already half across
the warehouse, towards the few stock drugs which Captain
Thorn had parted with only a few days ago from his neat
little medicine chest.

"Ah, by the way——" very benevolently—"just what

may your father's complaint be? Don't be . . . you're among friends; speak right out, my dear."

But it needed much supplementary pantomime from the crowd of us before she knew what he wanted to know. As though it mattered to any Indian where he was sick when his soul might be wandering in the woods or the graveyard and he was sick . . . if he was really sick, of course.

An instant I fancied I caught her glancing at The M'Dougall as though she knew what a fool she was dealing with, as though all young girls must forever know the abysmal foolishness of fat old men and how to deal with it. But her sugarloaf-shaped head was glossy, and her glance went down with her face.

There, her father had ana there. She clutched her throat. And there, too, in the head. Ana everywhere. And terrible ana here, ana of the dying, most ana of all down here in his belly. Like this, here . . . and with the flats of her hands she polished her red, warm trunk. See, such belly-ana like this, like this. . . .

Six Sandwich Islanders to row them, they went away together in the longboat in the glory of the day's end and the blaze of The M'Dougall's regimentals. He had insisted on time enough to don his scarlet. He had a half-dozen assorted drug bottles and his Bible all wrapped in a plaid upon his wide-spread knees, and between them the daughter of Comcomly crouched and gazed up with wonder at the three moistly enfolded rosy crescents of his chin.

I think there must have been an Amen in many of our minds to the thought that we might never behold him again.

But we were wrong. He came back three mornings after, in the even greater state of the Chinooks' longest and reddest and most handsomely carved seagoing canoe, reclining upon bearskins and beating the measure for a dozen swift paddles as though he were the tyhee of all the red men's race. They swung alongside of the shore, and he stepped out, squudging a little from his weight in the soft strand, but still resplendent and imperial, made them a mighty dismissal speech, and came beaming up among us, his flasks and his Bible still bundled before him.

We were putting the last pickets to the fort. We had had six days' hard work at it and were tired and quarrelsome among ourselves. Those of us who had heavy tools in our hands must all have itched to let him have them hard against his jiggling guts or on the back of his round, puffed head. He went strolling among us with the distant cheeriness and condescension of an earl to his faithful, forelock-pulling tenantry.

We would oblige him by convening in the mahkook house in the noon hour to hear some news of undoubted interest to us all.

He began by chiding us whimsically for our recent alarm over the Indians' absence. And for wasting so much labor, such expert supervision—a wave and a porker's snort to Mr. M'Kay as he said it—on the erection of all these new defenses, when a little diplomacy . . . when the Holy Scriptures themselves should have taught us the easier and far more just lesson of doing unto others and loving our neighbors as ourselves.

True, he must admit, Chief Comcomly of the One Eye had not been precisely truthful with him, had not been ill at all when he sent for him. But he, The M'Dougall, had not been surprised or taken in by that. He . . . a tolerant smile around the ring of us, a nod which came to rest on Mr. M'Kay . . . was quite as shrewd as anyone else.

He had suspected from the first that he would find Comcomly sitting on his chieftain's platform in the biggest of the cedar houses, as healthy as ever, surrounded by his conjurers and warriors and all the members of the klale

tamahnawis of his sept, with no ana in his head or anywhere, and no worry except his altogether unappreciated
and misunderstood affection for the tilikums across the
river, the huloima with beards, the Thunderbird People
who were building the big fort against all of his, Comcomly's, peaceful and gentle kinsmen . . . and against him,
poor Comcomly of the One Eye, who wanted only to be
known to us all, to our Tyhee M'Dougall above all, as
the Father-in-Law of Fort Astor.

Mr. M'Kay looked up from his Bush Cree pipe. "Eh?"

The M'Dougall had an increase of benevolence. He had
not swallowed that story whole, either, he assured us.
He knew human nature . . . and the Indians.

He had looked around the great smoky house, at the
faces of all those tribesmen, threatening and awful in
the sputter of many lighted candle fish, those faces of
warriors war-striped, of the tamahnous men in their wolf-
head masks, their shway-at-sho-sin masks above their red-
painted arms and their waiting clubs, the slave killers . . .
and he had known what to do.

He had pulled out of his plaid a little bottle of orange
liquid and held it under all their eyes. The candle-fish
torches had given it fiendish glints, a wicked djinn had
seemed to writhe and burn in it and struggle against the
ceiling of the little cork.

Smallpox, he had told them. The spirit of the dreaded
smallpox, the terrible scourge which makes men etsitsa
and sweeps with fatal, black finger nails over the faces
of whole villages.

They had screamed. Many had fled. Behind the cedar
matting of the big house's inner wall a whole family of
them had hidden, howling and pressing their flat heads
against the carven images.

Comcomly of the One Eye had fallen back trembling,
his children in horror around him, that little daughter of

his . . . yes, of course, we must remember her, the one who'd . . . well, gentlemen, all of them out of their wits and penitent, and our servants and humble allies always from now on . . . and all for fear that he, the Tyhee M'Dougall, might uncork a harmless little bottle. Syrup of figs, damme, that's what it really was, gentlemen, would we believe it?

Some of us would—some of it. He was so long-winded about it. He made so much of his coup, it had a literary flavor, it was probably embroidered with flourishes from Captain Cook or some other famous explorer. What was fact and what fol-de-rol, we never did learn.

I watched Mr. M'Kay tug at his long pipe, and the smoke in his brown, deep nostrils.

"So, Dunkie, an' they did ye the great honor of choosing ye to kidnap?" said the elder Stuart. Even The M'Dougall's oldest crony had had his fill of the smallpox bottle.

"Aye, so they did, Davie, the rascals, so they did. Nothing personal, of course, but in my official capacity as commander of the establishment by written authority of Mr. Astor"—beaming more broadly than ever at Mr. M'Kay—"I was the one they'd naturally choose, gentlemen. Not that I've had anything to do with all this foolish fort-making, and I told 'em so, gentlemen, frankly—and that I've always found that diplomacy's the thing, and that true neighborliness and—and——"

He faltered for the first time in his recital. The triumph went out of his pink jowls for a moment. He had understood at last the look which Mr. M'Kay was giving him.

"What did you do with the bottle, partner?"

"The—oh, the bottle. What should I do with it? They were so sair afraid of it, they kept . . . well, gentlemen, do you know, they wouldn't let me pour it on the ground or in the fire or anywhere. And to prove to 'm how harmless it really was, I—I drank every drop of it myself."

He got something like a groan from the assemblage. It encouraged him to go on now and be the martyr for our sakes.

"Tasted bad, gentlemen, and the effect . . . most inelegant. But there you are, the Indians know me now for what I am, your governor and their—their friend." He smiled up again. His snout quivered. "I told you there'd be nothing dangerous about it, my good M'Kay."

"I said daft." And Mr. M'Kay went back into his pipe smoke.

"And now, gentlemen, the most important and, I have no doubt, the happiest of my tidings. Your strict attention, please, because I am particularly anxious to impress upon you that there's naught behind my intentions 't smacks of—of iniquitous lust, or the philanderings of— some of you younger gentlemen had best listen to me— of reckless youth. It is much for your sakes, gentlemen, to preserve the peace and further the cause of amity and dignity and our commercial prowess that I contemplate this—this purely political alliance. Beseeched by One-Eye Comcomly, as though by a vassal who'd consider it an—to whom the title of father-in-law to his overlord would be a pledge of—of——"

He got not even a glance from Mr. M'Kay to help him forward this time. His own little pig's eyes rolled over and over with the slowness of his hunt for tender, juicy words. He remembered the Scriptures again, the Book of Ruth, but began to snicker and drip in the midst of the quotation.

We must realize the honor of it to him and to us all, the pleasant and profitable relations with his father-in-law's tribe forever more, the pure generosity of his motive . . . but underneath all that ran that slobbery, secret little wish that we'd also suspect him of being a lusty old rake.

It was someone else I saw as I stared up at him over all their shoulders. The girl with her buttocks striped and flaring, the flats of her hands polishing her young, red, oil-slick belly, and how she had looked at him from under her flattened brow with the look that rewards all fat old fools, the whole world over.

"Dammee, Dunkie," shouted his crony, the elder Mr. Stuart, "ye wouldna marry it?"

"It?" The M'Dougall smiled. He indulged Mr. Stuart. Old friends are always rude about such things. Naturally . . . and nobody is ever free from his friends' envy.

"I would and I do. By both Scripture and their own rites, too, to—satisfy all parties, with a potlatch in celebration and gifts from us all—I trust I may rely upon you, gentlemen, for I am assured it is the custom—gifts from Mr. Astor and us all to my happy relative, the Tyhee Comcomly. Only a few muskets he wants principally, and —well, we shall see, perhaps a few horns of powder and lead balls to find us some venison in the hills for the wedding feast. A detail, gentlemen, a detail. . . ."

There was noise among the gentlemen. He took it for cheers and raised his pudgy fingers in a pleased protest.

All that troubled him was the tight screw of Mr. M'Kay's face behind his pipe smoke. I knew for certain now that James M'Kay would be voted to accompany Captain Thorn and the rest of our Nootka trading party northward, and that he would vote aye to that himself with all his leathery heart.

"Thank you, gentlemen. I am proud of this proof of your fealty . . . and your enthusiasm. And when I bring home my bride, I feel sure that I can rely on you all to show her the respect that is due her as your governor's wife, and to be kind to her, remembering . . . as true Brit— —as true gentlemen, remembering the momentousness of the arrival of the first woman in our midst."

The noise again as we dismissed. Someone laughing loudly. Ovide.

13

Restless, I sought the woods in the midst of a hot day's work.

I had been back and forth eight times between the *Tonquin* and the storehouse. The last of the goods for shore were finally out of the hold and off the decks and piling and trundling between the strand and the new shelves.

Both ends of the ferry had nagged me, each trip. They had fought like spoiled children over the division of the flour bags, the powder kegs, the blankets. They were still bawling at each other across the water, from hill, from rail, rich compliments of the occasion on, for instance, the number of Sandwich Islanders we should be allowed to take along. Or if not that, anything . . . and each party very valorous in the knowledge of the fact that his voice could not carry quite that far.

The woods were cool. Their quiet rose from the cushioned ground in a windless, endless shimmering of green, high to the tree tops where the fragments of the sky were as bright as sunlight on deep water. Green shadows dwindled and grew upon the shafts of green light in broken slants and verticals, and all so cool and quiet, even the multi-green ferns around my knees seemed the noiseless vegetation of the sea bottom, and I walked miles deep under the green sea.

These woods, and all the silent wealth and strength of them, the Thunderbird had claimed in the range of his bristling wings.

These woods and all the things with fur which scampered and chewed the berry bushes and tested their claws lazily upon the tree trunks, belonged by right of riches and omnipotent vulgarity to the Great One of New York. While we, his servants and his emissaries, must shatter the peace with bawling and insult, the temper of clownish avarice and cruelty, with musket shot and torch glare, click of the trap on forepaws, the slit and rip and count of pelts from still steaming bodies, and all the shrill indignity of trade.

These woods that were so green and quiet . . . and my ears yet ached with the shoutings of Captain Thorn as he straddled a sack of seedling potatoes which Franchere had asked for, to plant in the burnt patch behind the dwelling house, when, at the top of his iron lungs, he'd be damned if he'd waste 'em on young quill twiddlers and taproom clerks. And as for old Unkie Dunkie . . . the famous news had reached the ship, of course . . . Dunkie M'Dougall had already expressed his preference for red meat and fish oil over any poor potatoes. Captain Thorn's compliments to him, and a pair of cuckold's antlers from the hills. . . .

A little red fox leaped daintily across the trail. Beware, O talapus, little red fox with your bright tail bobbing in the ferns. I have beaten the moth eggs from a thousand of your brothers' pelts already in my master's warehouse.

I neared our brook, halted by its border of pungent wild cabbages and glassy moss. There was no sound the water made as it carried a garner of petals and young leaves down the green ravine. The little waterfall from the pool further hillward strung its beads of sunlight without chatter or haste. I leaned back against a giant fir. I was here the little thing I longed to be, drowned in the tree-high, fluid silence of a world without men.

Over there, in the cinder-smeared tract which men had made, one of the fattest of them had squealed at me all day in the ill-humor of an empty stomach, having promised

his new Indian kinsmen to starve himself in a three days'
fast before his wedding, so that he might approach the
blessed state of transparency which insures mutual fidelity
in the marriage contract. Squealed and squeaked and
played the lewd martyr for us all, and nudged us to make
sure we'd see he wasn't taking the savages seriously about
it. . . .

A yearling black bear sat watching me, its pointed head
between its paws, from a bough high above. Beware, O
itswoot, young black bear with shaggy bottom, I have
been sent over many seas to furnish your poll to fond old
gentry to tuck around the young girls' tender knees in
the sleighs on winter nights.

I strolled on up the falls. Through gray-green rocks,
under the moss-damp portico of a great toppled spruce,
the water splattered from the pool above with no solemner
intention than to mend its little rainbow over the pool
below. Deep, brilliant green of the jeweled ground, where
the little bell blossoms of kinik-kinik had each its tiny
clapper of spray from the tumble of the falls. I stood midway between the pools, my face running gladly with this
coolness which hurled from their steep, singing link.

The pool above, that little part of it which was on a
level with my eyes, was dark and choked into stillness by
many sunken branches. Across the throat of the falls it
must have been a beaver that had built that barricade. I
could see where the floating leaves crowded into brown
mounds on the water, and how a pair of little black nostrils nudged among them, bubbling the calm.

And you, O eena the beaver, most of all of them you,
beware. You, whose little scrubby outline is the very trade-
mark of the great fur companies, and whose skin is a necessity to the glistening of a million fops' pot hats . . . you,
most of all of them, you, I have been sent to snare and
slaughter you with iron teeth and club and hot lead balls,

you who are the pet of my master's heart and whose pelt overflows his dusty bins and the tarry stomachs of his big ships and hangs, a shiny trophy, on the wall above his beer . . . you, O eena the little beaver, most prized and most staple and profitable of them all.

Amused, I climbed a few steps higher until I had the whole radius of his swimming, the other dark, drenched bank, and all the brown, soupy industry of his dam. I was well hid and quiet. The waterfall itself outdid any sound I might have made as I kneeled in the bushes and gave myself a few minutes to watch him.

The white man's eyes are on you, little eena. Who are you that you have never heard of the white man, carrier of death slung over his shoulder and in his pistol pocket, with his traps to gnash you in John Jacob Astor's name and his eternal price tags to tie through the empty eye-hole of your skin? Who are you that trust to the peace of great woods and the safety of your own quiet building under the brown leaves, and who think you are writing your own destiny in bubbles across your little pool?

She must have been there a minute already. Perrault, I mean.

She was below me in the sunny, prismatic spatter of the other end of the falls. She stood looking into the whiteness of the lower pool, quite as I stood looking into the blackness of this one above. She did not see me or know I was here. She must have been there at least a minute, because she was already acting on her whim, tugging and wriggling out of those old overalls of hers, and it was the white light refracted from her baring shoulder that first drew my attention down. Her face and her bright shoulder from almost straight above.

I started to call out, warn her I was here. The squawk I gave was not really meant to reach halfway down the crooked rumble of the brook. I stayed kneeling, one hand

crushing some ill-smelling weed which had come among
its fingers, the other all suddenly knuckles between my
teeth to keep me from crying out to her any more.

I watched the shining wet of her arms as she reached
them out into the little rainbow, and the way she laughed
—I had not seen her laugh like this in many months—as
her shirt fell back and the cold, breath-robbing spray
pelted her quickening skin and ran in tinier waterfalls
again from off her upheld wrists.

All the pent lust of a nervous, long abstinent man
scratched within me. If I could have yelled now, it would
not have been to warn her but out of a bestial impatience
because she took so long to undress, to show herself as
naked as I knew she was going to, under my suddenly
hot eyes.

I knew, too, what price I had given life for this . . . the
whacks taken, the laughs and kicks and sickening sprawls
I had had to accept, the bruise of Ovide's boot upon me
that time when I had run in bashfulness from her puddling,
freezing body on the bunk . . . all for this, that I should
know the joy and honor of the rôle of Peeping Tom. That
I should long, as all men born of woman should, and rejoice in the heat of my expectations at the sight of the
white, slim, merry body of the female of my kind. That I
should see at last all the eager, singing nakedness I had
always known there would be below the lifted young
throat of my beloved.

Sooner or later she must look up and see me kneeling
here in the high green. She will see me through the dancing
of a little rainbow, through a curtain of flying sun drops,
and she will cry out, startled and shielding herself instinctively, before she flushes . . . the slow, deep flush I
have seen go up her face when she looks at me nowadays
. . . flushes, exclaims again, laughs softly, laughs with that
long toss of her head I have watched so often but never

until now knew could be the carrier of laughter all the way up her open and adventurous body.

And so you, too, O klootchman the woman, beware the white man's eyes upon you, the heat of his eyes and his long-bound heart and the new strength of his fingers among the green leaves. You, too, O klootchman the soft-skinned woman, O kloshe the white beloved, with your sea-soaked destiny lying in my toughened and at last unhesitating hands, with your smooth white hide so prized of millionaires and famous mountebanks, courtiers and yellow-maned heroes. . . .

I remembered in coarse parade all the details of my tutelage: the ripe, lazy breasts of the brown girl of Karaka-Koua, the dark luxury of her wide loins in among the moonlit flowers, her childish crooning over the silly shoe buckle I had given her in payment for the night, and how neither of us had ever known the other's name.

Since then, too, the sight grown common and comical and unremarkable of squat young Indian girls fresh from behind their puberty screens, their red bodies offensive with grease and ochre, their hard buttocks flaring and grotesquely striped.

So that, even as I got upon my feet and started to look down the rocks, I knew that I no longer wanted to see her.

Between the sight of her and my own eyes I wanted, instead, to raise a mist that was half disgust, half pity, a skeptical sense of the denial of anything good or anything beautiful which I had long since effected for my own heart's hardening, a knowledge of the pact I had made and sealed with the black sulphur of the powder run, and which must sacrifice even her who had been that bitter pact's chief urge.

Between her and me, the flesh of so many men who had enjoyed her, I could be sorry for her . . . but call her by the right, cheap name that she deserved. And the flesh of all the strange animal women to whom love would never mean more than a shoe buckle and a thumping and a biting in the dark.

I turned my back. Not in consternation, this time, or shyness, or overmoral shame. I had had my look. In spite of not wanting to, I had looked and seen her. In her white and lovely nakedness I had seen her. Desirable, but I had not desired her. Maddening, but I stayed sane. And weary, aloof, quickly sickened of my instinct, wanting never to see her body again.

For so I loved her, loved her that much and in that fashion. One glance had given me her body's secret, the secret of why her name and Ovide's would continue to couple themselves inevitably, inseparably in my mind . . . always, paired, glued fast in a concept of parenthood for me all the remaining days of my life.

It was true, then, and I saw in one glance that it was true, this thing which all the damned old-womanishness in me had recently suspected. One glance, and I had turned and clambered back to the beaver dam.

Out of her sight and hearing. Out of her destiny, swiftly and far away from the fond destiny gathering in her womb . . . and I laughed at myself when I saw the reflection of the gesture I made of dumping all my presumptuous romantics into this opaque black pool.

Was it at the mirror of my own self I was raging? From my own self let me try to hide it.

There were little streaks of bubbles fanning out from the little glittering nostrils. You had had your warning, gentle worker. My master, richest of the white men, does not believe in warning little beavers. That is bad business, O, eena the beaver. That is bad for destiny, whose tool is the pistol I am pulling from my pocket.

See, little eena, have you ever before seen in your black

pool so curious a reflection as this of my arm outstretched
. . . towards your glittering little nostrils, outstretched,
towards your body which will shine so prettily on my
master's wall . . . as prettily, see, as the pistol at my arm's
end? . . .

The shot brought panic to the woods. Great trees threw
the heinous noise of it back upon me, the ravine spewed
sudden smoke. Among his old black leaves, threshing and
fast muddying and bloodying the pool, the little beaver
struggled with death and died.

Thus the little German butcher's son goes forth to hunt
his millions. In Canton—I heard it as plainly as though
it had been only yesterday and I stood so close I could
see the red neck bulging with strong hair, and could smell
the excellent beer in his silver tankard—in Canton it
voult pring five huntret tollars.

I hurried back to camp. The pistol barrel reeked and
stayed hot in my hand for a short while. Then it, too,
cooled. When I was far enough away to be sure that Perrault would not know who it had been, I began to whistle
gayly through tight, icy lips.

But gayly. A goot pelt . . . a goot salute to destiny.

14

Comcomly's favorite huy-huy man, his most expert
bargainer, sat facing me beside the river over a pile of
goods we had just finished trading. He was a bony old
fellow, his face so wrinkled that it looked like a long discarded piece of salmon net with two holes rotted into it
for eyes.

He was, I knew, a sort of treasurer of this sept of the
Chinooks, trusted accountant of all the blankets and nails,
the large coppers, red flannel bolts and blue beads ac-
cumulating so miraculously in his chief's vast potlatch

house. He could count twenty on his haiqua shells. He had traveled much in his middle age and knew words of the Nootka, the English, and the Bella Bella. In our honor he had changed his name to Thunder-and-Lightning Bird. He had many names.

He nodded back at me over the painted sculpin box in which he was carrying home all of to-day's new wealth. He was in good humor. He had managed to argue a paper of gold spangles, worth sixpence, and five little spools of worsted out of me instead of the two I had originally offered him, in exchange for merely one sea otter. He would probably try to palm a sixth spool, too, when he thought I was not watching. I could afford not to watch. I nodded back, equally good-natured.

"Tell me this, old Scallighan," I said. "What does wealth mean to your master, your Tyhee Comcomly?" I grinned, knowing delightedly that he would understand only one word in seven, and that his own grin was a mask of oiliness and innumerable dirty wrinkles. "What the devil does he want with all this wealth, anyway?"

He had heard the name of his master. He had at least understood my stranger's way of pronouncing the word chickamin, the word for money, wealth. In his old crow's voice he began to give me back jargon for jargon.

"My tyhee, the great One-Eye Comcomly, is richer and mightier than any other tyhee among the Chinook. He is richer and mightier than any other tyhee among the Chehalis, the Cowichan, and the Nisquali to the north, or among the Clatsop and Tillamook southward. He has made mahkook with the tilikum from far, cold harbors where olhiyu, the seal-people, lie in wait and nenamooks, the otter, washes in with the kelp. He has made huy-huy with the huloima who know how to track swift mooluk, the elk, on the inland hills. He has sent ever more of his kinsmen in hunt of the whale, the sturgeon, all the big

and little people of creek and river mouth and pounding
sea which give men of their fats and winter oils and flames
to see by in the otherwise black night. He has built his
salmon weirs out to circle all the islands of low tide. He
has built many houses of cedar for the living of his people,
for the ceremonies of his sept, for the stowing of his furs
and copper shields and his bright blankets so numerous
that only I, who can count up to twenty, can count the
twenty times twenty twenties of his riches there."

The old rascal gave me a grunt when he had come this
far. He was turning a lime stick critically, sprinkling it
with a tobacco powder as black as his fingers.

"Yes, of course, all homage to him and his one wise
eye," I protested. "But why? You don't understand what
I'm asking you. Among—among people like yours, where
wealth . . . well, why?"

Clear shallows just under our hunching place had grown
lively, distracting, with the arrival of a school of small fish.
Their little silver bellies flashed like thrown coins.

"On the house posts of his houses are carved the crests
of the Tyhee Comcomly's ancestors and the tales of his own
prowess. No tyhee in the memory of the river has raised
so many house posts or caused such splendid legends to be
carved. None has so many wives with so many gleaming
anklets or such marvelously flattened heads, such heavy
labrets pulling down their lips. None has ever fulfilled
the customs of the potlatch so magnificently with such
thanks for his son's initiation, or flung such priceless quan-
tities of olachen fluid so wastefully into the celebration
fire until the smoke holes crackle red, or broken so many
coppers apart, sunk so many of his own canoes, slain so
many of his slaves, given away so many of his blankets and
his kinsmen's blankets to put the rival tyhees to shame."

"Bravo!" I said. "I begin to understand the ethics of
riches."

He popped the lime stick into his mouth. The suck he gave it drew his cheeks far in. Then they puffed slowly out again with excruciating pleasure, away from the burning mixture, until the old fish net of wrinkles over them had almost disappeared.

"Your own tyhee, then," he asked at length, "your far-away ruler over thunderbirds, what does he do with all the beaver skins and red flannels and blankets and blankets that are in his many mahkook houses all across the world? Has he found such grander use for all his shining chicka-min? Has it made him so much mightier and happier among you, made him so much more youtl tumtum than the Tyhee Comcomly is among his kinsmen of the river and the bays?"

I caught the undying cunning of his old, sore eyes. I was as amused as he was. The little fish were tossing purse-fuls of silver to the surface of the cove.

"I suppose you're right," I agreed. "I'm not allowed to ask my tyhee any such questions . . . so I can't be sure."

"One-Eye Comcomly has found power of life and death," he persisted softly, "over whole twenties of magic makers, live-dog eaters, famous harpooners of ehkole the whale, great corpse snatchers and secret singers of the winter ceremony, warriors and salmon spirits and the un-flattened foreheads of countless slaves. Has the chickamin of your own far-away tyhee given him power over more than these?

"One-Eye Comcomly," he added most proudly, "has twenty times twenty enemies."

I chuckled. I remembered the slow, befuddled wrath of the farmers of Putnam County, the rumors of all the hasty conferences in state council chambers of Madrid, St. Petersburg, and London when the news of Mr. Astor's new empire in the fur lands had arrived, and the Nor'-westers tasting their wine suddenly bitter in the forts and club rooms and muttering promises of the "long traverse."

My tyhee, too, had his power over great magic makers, money gobblers, soldiers, hunters, skinners of the dead, his singers in velvet and the footlights' glow, his slaves among the tea-stacks and the dusty bins, and all the flattery of many enemies.

My mind went back once more to that hot, idle afternoon in King Tamehameha's courtyard, to long-nosed prime minister Kraimoku retailing me the glories of his celebrated Eri's reign beneath the dusty palms. I heard again that dry, humorous old voice. "All people are made happy in the power and riches of one man among them."

Silver shillings scattering all around us. Silver chickamin springing in teasing profusion to the surface, to the sun. I laughed.

"But, what is your master's most valuable possession, Sir Scallighan, shall I tell you? It is this, that among his servants there is one especially crafty, a rogue so much a rogue that he knows the foolishness of being anything but faithful. As great a rogue as I am, as great as—as all rogues with sharp noses and lean legs and slow, low voices in a world of the butchers' necks of great dull domineerers."

He was not even trying to make out what I tried to say. He had sucked his lime stick to a crayon point. He leaned a little towards me between his crossed old knees, eying the goods at my side with elaborate carelessness. He would let me philosophize a little while longer.

I was indulging myself in a prodigious nonsense. I was saying, over and over, "Mr. Tamehameha, Eri Comcomly, Tyhee Astor, John Jacob Comcomly, Eri Astor, Tyhee Tamehameha . . ."

It actually annoyed me when I could no longer give one of them the other's title. As though any of the titles could be wrong. As though there were any difference.

"We rogues who know there is no difference, and yet pretend so skilfully, with such ornamental and convincing boasts, and who would commit all the necessary sins, kapswalla and mimoluse, too, in their proud, imperial names . . . we lean rogues, we fast-wrinkled ministers of villainy extraordinary to their dense, busy, power-strident minds . . . woe unto us, old Scallighan. We shall give them our bony shoulders for hoists to see Heaven. Heaven with its radiance of brand-new shillings, its æon-wide floors of red flannel, its blue-beaded dome and its angels of brown wives with dugs as big as coconut pods . . . on our thin, heel-dirtied shoulders we shall hoist them until, in spite of their short necks, they'll see well across the wall of Heaven, of highest Saghalie, the House of Myths, and speak with God as to a partner, to a kinsman, at God's own height. While we, Sir Scallighan, old rogue . . . while we three faithful rogues . . ."

He looked up slyly. He drew back his dry black hand a little when he saw me watching it.

And that set me roaring so boisterously, I surprised him into pulling altogether back. I grabbed up the sixth little spool of colored worsted and gave it to him with my loudest blessing. He grunted. He was obviously disappointed. I had robbed him of the privilege of stealing it while I talked.

The thousands of little fish flashed and hoarded silver sunlight.

15

I stood behind a circle of five old conjurers: the tamahnawis men of their tribes, those men above and apart from all others, who must never touch their hands to their own hair, and who had bones thrust through their septums, and possessed a strength of magic over other men's souls and over the dangerous souls of the dead which infest and misgovern the bodies of the living, and a knowledge of all the future in all lands.

I listened to their five varying and sagely disputatious tales of the beginning and the end of earth, the coming and the going of mankind, the forms and whereabouts, names, intentions, and experiences of the Supreme One, and when I went away I carried with me only the confused and insubstantial wisdom that has been given in a dream.

I had with me the new interpreter whom we had hired of Comcomly for our passage North. He had drifted down with the many visiting sturgeon fishermen from Gray's Harbor. A young man still, a captive of the Clayoquots in his boyhood, but ransomed and come home with a smattering of naval English and Spanish and all the Vancouver Coast dialects. And a fawning, clever air.

He stood next me, translating the venerable conjurers in a demeaning, half-derisive way, apologetic and a little angry that they took no notice of us, that they spoke such things in the presence of a rich tkope tilikum like me. If it had not been for him I should have thought I was dreaming.

Gnats danced in brown, translucent swarms over the uncombed heads of this synod, and they used their delicate scratching sticks continually while they talked.

The venerable on my right was dissertating on the nature and omnipotence of Etalapass, the Supreme One, the Saghalie Tyhee of land and water and furthest sky. The creature next along, whose septum-hole made a high, mewing noise whenever he breathed, had greater praise for Ecannum, a second divinity, more human, more man-like and more man's friend.

For Etalapass, even though he created man, created him with mouth unopened, with eyes fast shut, with unpunctured ears and immovable hands and feet, whereas the less creative Ecannum had understood the plight of man's imperfection and had taken a sharp stone and compassionately laid open man's mouth and eyes and given usefulness and skill to all his members. No more than a semi-deity, this Ecannum, addicted to several venial bad habits, such as stealing and kidnaping from his faultless fellow gods, but full of the knowledge of all the things man craved to know, and teaching him generously to make canoes, nets, paddles, to bend wood for boxes, and how to carve his weapons, his cooking implements and memorial posts. He had been even so kind as to throw great rocks into the river and obstruct the ascent of the salmon, so that man might take his fill and feast in the proper seasons.

But the priest across the circle, a conjurer of the Chehalis, shook his wild head and gave both these former advocates the lie. For it had been revealed to him that the Supreme One was a woman, a woman who dwelt aloft beyond all reach of men's joys or sorrows, sins or braveries, a woman eternally young and eternally indifferent, eternally unenlightened of the wants of earth or the longings of any of its people.

Then the one who was next to this old conjurer, and who dribbled through his blow-pipe and had many red ants climbing and slipping and climbing up again upon the grease ponds of his kneecaps, denounced them all and told how he had learned among the far Northern Haida that the Supreme One was Wigit, who reaches behind him whenever a baby is born and picks out blindly the little stick of the length of that new life.

While, for the fifth of the priests, the Supreme One dwelt nowhere unless at the end of the endless inland forests, and on this day He was a beaver and that day a land otter and another day the sweetest perfume from the House where the scents of dead flowers gather.

But Etalapass could be all these things and also a killer whale, besides, claimed the first tamahnawis man. And Ecannum, said the second, could be both killer whale and beaver-king, and a thieving raven, too. And even a woman when he wished to.

They called to their helpers to build them a fire in the center of the circle. They nagged and taunted each other over the uncomfortable flames of the hot day. The gnat cloud chased away; another of sour, yellow-veined smoke took its place.

The helpers brought masks for them to wear; huge wooden travesties and symbols of fellow animals and birds, sea monsters and nightmarish cannibal faces behind whose wooden teeth, prime-colored beaks, and muzzles the magicians gave muffled imitations in praise and defense of their contending gods.

The quarrel and the fire grew together. The old men clambered up and shook and screamed. But none could scream the others down. They clashed beak to muzzle, pulled strings and opened their huge teeth to show undermasks even more fierce, and growled and shuddered themselves into a pumping rhythm of frenzy, the poor convulsions of old men who cannot achieve more than palsy and thin sweat puckering their grease coats.

Then suddenly one of them was in the fire, screaming his Wigit's name, screaming a few times more from the unendurable pain of the trial before he came out again with his legs speckled with little oil flames and smelling of cooked ants.

And then the next was in the fire, out of it, then in again. And then the next and the next . . . so that God might be given a name and the Supreme One find a reason.

The smug piebald young interpreter wanted me to come away. He kept telling me he knew the idiocy of this exhibition. He kept assuring me he knew that God had no other name than the name of the owner of the Thunder-bird, and that the Supreme One's, the Saghalie Tyhee's one and only name was Mr. Easter.

Was it not so? Had he not attended Mr. Easter's spring-time ceremony on a Spanish ship's deck when he was still a little boy? Was there, could there be any other God so saghalie . . . as our famous Mr. John Jacob Easter?

I smiled. I said: "None other."

So I said, Lord . . . and knew not what I said. There was the glare around me of a confused dream.

16

I listened to them talking in the fort of how comfort-able the living quarters would be when they were done. The white men's talk, too, for all its plain, familiar details of blue clay, logs, and cedar-shakes roofing, came to me only vaguely and without any personal interest, as though I were hearing them promise things of some entirely foreign place which I knew I should never see.

They talked of a separate dining room. Well and good; and of a private room for each of the partners, a large apartment for the men and the artificers. They'd build them leisurely between exploring parties throughout the summer.

They must get some sort of walls around the black-smith's forge, first of anything, to keep the Indians away from the new tools and nails. Good.

By the time we of the *Tonquin* put back here—late August, or surely September, say—it would be all quite complete. Governor Dunkie and Madame M'Dougall would be out of the poor little canvas tent of their em-barrassed honeymoon and moved into a larger, more be-fitting suite of logwork and royal furs. Oh, yes, and

Koaster the carpenter had already started work on the presses we needed for all the furs already soiling in the storehouse. There'd be more presses for all the more furs we'd surely bring back. Well and good.

The *Tonquin* must up anchor positively in the next few days. Captain Jonathan Thorn, commanding, etc., had had his patience pulled taut to the end of May. June first would be the day after to-morrow. Now that the woods were plentifully green and warm and the river bank crowding with summer flowers, I should be going back aboard to walk the tar lines on a cranky deck.

I did my best to be sorry about it. I could no longer be either that or especially glad.

My head was chockful of sums of jackknives and bead strings, tobacco and sixpenny chisels we had divided— without bloodshed, at least—with the fort. Automatically I was already balancing each commodity against so and so many seals and otters, curage and export expenses, profits in terms of Hamburg drafts and China tea. Chockful, and still the quickest head among us at such things. ... "Dot wass how I, too, began to be a millionaire."

As though that were my whole life nowadays. That and, once aboard again, to rub hates with Jonathan Thorn.

I had not spoken to Perrault since the day I had seen her at the falls. She did not know why I was avoiding her. I was not trying to avoid her. I was trying to speak to her. What was there for me to say?

A hundred things should and must be said to her by someone . . . but why by me? By me, of all of us, her betrayed duenna . . . and was it a midwife's part I should be expected to play next?

The flush of a little wench in trouble and following me everywhere around the camp, as though I were her madame and supposedly versed in how . . . that was all it meant. She flushed when I turned about and tried to speak to her, and I could not say anything kindly to her, anything at all.

The captain would order her along. I almost laughed in his face when he did.

He'd be damned if he'd give the partners the satisfaction of letting him sail without his cabin boy. A no-good cabin boy, a butter-fingers and a squeaky eunuch, and 'd grow up into a morphodite sooner 'n into a midshipman. But, by God, who in hell did they think they were that they could keep his cabin boy ashore?

He was already vile about Mate Mumford. Ever since we were inside the river the mate had refused to come back to the *Tonquin*. He had had his fill (at the top of his New England voice to the all too sympathetic voyageurs and partners) of ragging and browbeating and bad seamanship. He had been sent out deliberately to drown. The captain could jangle irons at him, strike him from the log, put Job Aitken in his place, or do what he liked about it.

I took pleasure in repeating it so to the captain, and how the partners were going to sign Mr. Mumford to their company without even consulting the captain's wishes.

Too, I used that purple moment to add, as if it had just now occurred to me, that Governor M'Dougall of Fort Astor, Point George, the Oregon Wilds, had commissioned me to request the honor and unbounded pleasure of the company of Captain Jn. Thorn, etc., at his wedding in Chinook Village on the evening of June first, tides and other details of departure permitting.

And when, with proper reluctance, I agreed that all this had been so arranged undoubtedly to rob the *Tonquin* of the dignity of her going, the hills above the ship had belched back echoes of a profane, crazy fury, and Indians idling around us had paddled sharply away.

My heart bounded, as though that were my whole life
nowadays. To color that wind-stitched map of his face.
To help skin the freckles from his rough fist when he
bashed it against the woodwork and stabbed at the in-
sinuation of my tales. Secretly to exult—when secrecy
was the essence of such exultation—in my sure talent
for smirking him, baiting him, into these rages of his
which raised him from a whiny little watchdog to a devil
worth bedeviling.

17

They sent me after Ovide de Montigny to tell him he
had been selected to come with us as assistant to Mr.
M'Kay. An honor, this selection. There was not one
among the young Canadians who did not idolize Mr.
M'Kay and want to clerk for him. Now, especially, when
there was an odor of conspiracy about Mr. M'Kay's
having been voted out of the fort.

I had no doubt but that Ovide would be proud to
come. I went looking for him around the camp, tasting in
the back of my mouth the irony of my having to tell him
he was coming. These lion-haired heroes who are brought
along to ornament every adventure.

And Perrault . . . she would need him now. Need him
against all the men and the embarrassments of shipboard,
in the next few months as never before.

Ovide, alternately surly and smiling, mastiff in the
manger concerning a girl who adored him but only bored
him, and who drove him to childish jealousy whenever
her applauding eyes . . . never mind, Perrault would need
him now.

Had she told him? How much had she had to tell him?
If I could guess, mustn't he know for certain? He must
know. He must come along. He must be glad to come,
damn him

I looked for him on the river bank and down the cove. I climbed the hill and called for him through the woods.

I had a sprig of evergreen in my hand and was crushing it with nervous fingers, lifting it absent-mindedly to my nose to possess the sweet pungence of its bruises. It was an old habit of mine. I remembered teaching my school children to do it. I remembered the round, apple-glossy Dutch faces of some of them.

Yesterday I had passed a baby being tortured in its cradle—the fort was overrun with Indians and their belongings, nowadays, and their women were everywhere around—and the filthy baby's eyes had been enormous and three quarters out of their sockets with the pain of a tight forehead strap. I had stopped and bent down. A young mother had screeched and come at me with crusted hands and a spruce-wood needle. The baby had bawled with fright, all its little body shuddering up into the monstrousness of its fixed, thong-bound face. I had fled.

I was fleeing now . . . from children's faces. Digging nervously into the fibrous little wounds of the green sprig in my fingers, feeling and smelling the strong fluid of the woods in my knuckle creases and under my nails, while I fled the thought of a child that must be born into such a world of great clashing forests and no song that could ever be set to music, among men who would only hiccup at the ribald joke of it, among none but Indian women whose own children were like flies under cakes of summer flies.

Fleeing the necessity to care for her, or for anyone, or to keep even this one small, futile tie to charity and pity and a gentle past.

Let Ovide care for her. Let Ovide do the honors of shielding her, midwifing her, when the day came for her to go into the woods and, like an Indian woman I had seen, grasp at the bushes with outflung, shuddering arms and legs and let earth tear her brat down from her womb. Ovide alone should do it. It was not mine to care.

As for all the rest of them, the white men, red and brown Islanders, all this thick, uneasy splatter of natives and strangers who would live greedily upon each other in the haphazard process of extermination which they explained to themselves as a patriotic commerce, in the buzzing cycle of exchange of myths and house plans and their various money, their own hides and their old diseases, the most foolish scum of their tongues to compose a jargon suitable to their need to betray each other in a daily trade . . . as for these others, they mattered nothing at all. They mattered less to me than a beaver swollen with death and decaying, torn and upturned in its desecrated pool.

I was the shrewdest of them all at trading and numbers. I could be the most casual of them all at everything.

I had made me a universe of my own lacks and grievances, and had put a supremely thick-necked god of my own over it. A god whose neatest and most faithful servant I was remoulding at last into his most dangerous enemy.

I was the Devil's own creator in a theology of my own thought . . . and my own destiny thereby, my own self's fate self-justified and self-imposed, disdainfully sober to the thought that I, with my little fly's soul, had found power over all the other flies, the other animals, all nature, and in the end would be more powerful than God.

I failed to find Ovide. I came down again into the camp, past the Indians idling with great jabber around the forge, from one knot to another of our own men talking about the future buildings of the fort . . . and none knew where Ovide was.

At last he came to the warehouse door when I called.

He filled the door frame picturesquely. He stood nursing his left arm's sling as he leaned back upon the logs. He had a sleepy look, as though he had been in the cool privacy of the warehouse a long while. Annoyed as he was, he smiled.

"What are you doing in there, De Montigny? I have been looking every——"

"I find it an excellent place to mind my own affairs," he said.

"It was built for Mr. Astor's affairs, not yours," I retorted. "I happen to have important news for you."

"No doubt. Save yourself the trouble. I happen to have important business of my own at the moment."

His shirt was open and rumpled back. His laugh exercised all the quick cords across his naked chest. His fingers played up and down the gay pleats of his sling as though it were a woman's bodice.

"I am to tell you, you have been selected——"

"Precisely, Lewis, I could guess all that. And some other time I shall take pains to explain why I cannot accept. But some other time."

"Not accept? Not come along? Oh, so."

He blocked the doorway. There was that indefinable odor of arrogance about him, the air of a young man physically and immediately charming and aware of the ease of his way with all people . . . with women most easily.

"So," I repeated. "You cannot accept. Your regrets to Mr. M'Kay, I suppose? Shall I say, a previous engagement?"

But he could beat me any day at the game of taunting. It gave him his favorite tone:

"*Tiens*, dear James, a previous engagement . . . that will do nicely. I trust the kind gentlemen will understand, but I frankly prefer to join Mr. Stuart's canoe trip exploring up the river."

"Mr. Stuart is one of the gentlemen who invites you to the *Tonquin*, instead. Even Mr. Stuart can be unkind enough to see the uselessness of a man with a broken arm among his canoe men."

"My arm is doing nicely, thank you." He made a handsome show of proving that he could already lift it a little in its sling. "I am sure it would not mend as well in the sea air."

I was determined not to let him anger me. It did not concern me whether he came along or stayed behind. Let Perrault worry over his despicableness.

But I had moved involuntarily close to him, and was seeing two things which amazed me. The first was that I was taller than he was. Of course I was, when I stood straight . . . but why, all these months, had I never stood straight against him and known it before?

And secondly, across his shoulder in the dim cave-coolness of the furthest corner of the warehouse, a frowzy and obscene little figure, sprawling grinning and complacent on a tumble of fresh furs, I saw the young Indian girl. I had known long before I saw her that someone was there, someone like this behind him, giggling and sharp-breasted under the charge of his impudent love-making.

The impudence of him, here, in the crowded center of the fort, in the plainest daylight of open windows and men passing and repassing, as though he had deliberately planned to give the camp a flagrant peepshow.

He knew that I had seen the girl. He pretended not to know it. He shifted a little in the doorway—and he smiled at her squeal of dismay behind him when I met her eyes.

Her stupid eyes and the accidental high-lights on her grease-slicked, lumpy little body were all that I saw. She had pressed back upon the fur-mound, into the dim corner. She may or may not have been Comcomly's daughter, bride-to-be of Governor Unkie Dunkie, supposedly fasting, and praying at home in the Chinook village, in the cedar house especially dedicated to the purification of the Tyhee's women, but already planting on the M'Dougall brow Captain Thorn's wedding present of a pair of antlers from the hills. Except for the blunt humor of such a chance of who she was, I did not want to know.

"Or shall we simply say, dear James, that I prefer to stay off the *Tonquin?* . . . Everybody will agree with me that your Yankee captain is an unpleasant devil."

A devil he called him, and this made it my round to smile.

"That was Mate Mumford's excuse. Seasickness is a better one for you."

He posed for pride. "Excuse? I need an excuse? Very well, then, seasickness. The truth, you know, is that it will be a long, dull voyage without adventure or any smallest danger. . . . I am not interested in trade. I can find brighter duties here."

I could have sworn he was purposeful in the way he raised and flourished his right arm up the door frame, so that I might be sure to see the little Chinook girl, restless in her corner. His self-consciousness was of itself a complete challenge.

All these months I had never known that I was as tall as he was. I stood straight against him, staring into his eyes until the taunt that played in them broke and hid behind lids already heavy with his love-making. As tall as he was, perhaps even an inch taller . . . and once he had kicked me out of a doorway, out of a girl's sight.

"You fail to see the brightness of your duty to Perrault."

I said it slowly, intent on the inevitable twitch of his long, theatrical eyelashes, willing to give him time to establish some new telltale pose. But he was suddenly too ridiculous for further patience.

"Perrault? The cabin boy? Why . . ."

I came close to him. I did not want the whole camp to hear. I could have struck him as I talked.

"Perrault," I repeated. "You who have called me a coward time and time again. Your cheap aping cannot cover your cowardice about Perrault. Do you need me to tell you that, instead of hiding your consternation behind little rutting Indian girls and cuckolding your masters to regain your self-esteem, you have a duty to Perrault . . . to Perrault who, God knows why, still . . ."

"Finish it, friend Lewis, finish it if you can." His jangle of words and mirth made a parody of defiance. "Swear to me, by all that's noble and self-sacrificing, that of course she still adores me. M'Dieu, you should know. You should know whether you or I will be her little bastard's father."

At the very instant I slapped his face I saw Perrault herself coming down the camp ground, walking slowly and peering everywhere among the people, as though she had been looking for someone a long while.

In my rage I knew she must not see him now.

He had no chance to retaliate. My slap went across his eyes. He stumbled back into the warehouse. I drove my fist hard against his sling before he could recover, and he continued backwards past the doorway, his own single curse as high pitched as the yelp of the Indian girl when he sat down, hard-jolted and stupefied with pain, on the dirt floor.

I grabbed the door and pulled, slammed, held it shut. Panting, I held it. I shall never know why he did not yank it open. He did not try. There was no tug at all from the other side. He too may have seen Perrault coming in that instant before my hand slapped across his eyes . . . my hand which, now suddenly so red and hot from the sting of his face bones, gave off anew a soft, fanciful pungence of evergreen.

Perrault had not seen him. It was only I she saw as she came across the camp.

She stood looking at me, wondering, timidly amused, from the bastion's deep shadow. I had to risk letting go the latch and standing free to meet her.

"What in the world are you doing, Lewis? Where have you been all day? I have been looking for you everywhere."

"For me?"

With a lonely little try at her old-time coquetry she made a gesture which said, "For no one else." And her lips, already a little thickened and drained by her pregnancy, added: "Do you still mind so much?"

Under the rough pile of logs and the wild carousel of branches, she looked so lost, so small.

"Mind?" I protested. "I do not mind. But I do not care. I do not care. Nothing matters to me except . . . I do not care."

But all the while I was repeating it, I was walking her gently back, away from the warehouse, from Ovide, in and out among them all, our arms linked and quiet, bashful as two boys in a schoolyard friendship.

A great tree's shadow ran up and down her old, shapeless clothes as though a black whip scourged her. She pressed close to me.

18

The huge new potlatch hall of the Chinooks stank of a hundred impaled, furiously burning candle fish, of buried ovens griming under the big central fire, and roof beams charring above it, of carved and newly dyed food bowls all oily and brimming with seal meat, halibut heads, and the olachen-fatted puddings of berries and salmon spawn.

It stank, too, of all the women squatting in the sweaty restraint of taboo on the wooden terraces around us, and of the warriors who stamped among us with faces of ani-

mals and daubed bodies streaming under the glut and
noisy ceremony of the feast.

It stank of a dog which had been overlong sacrificed and
dead, still waiting to be buried at the foot of the newly
crested house post which the Tyhee Comcomly had raised
in honor of his son-in-law. Of the warm, riled dirt beneath
our hams it stank, and of freshly cut cedar, of bitter smoke
and stifling, imprisoned air, the many gassy, warring
greases of fish and humans, until the distaste of it seemed
almost to coagulate and drip in opaque, fire-pierced beads
from all the red planks above and about us.

Strange, dehumanized creatures sprang in and out of
the dense glare. Creatures with the signs of the sculpin
upon them, and of the raven, the sea monster, the mosquito
snout, the moon hawk, and the killer whale. Creatures
who yowled and gibbered with a terrible cordiality, who
had whipped their bodies sore with hemlock branches in
fresh water, but who stank.

Around that fat white cherub, the bridegroom, they
clustered and rattled, squealed, pranced with showers of
mica down their hot, oiled legs, and sang the song of the
wedding bear.

Around the bride her relatives, defying the heat with
sweated robes of sea-otter skins and broad queues of
Tlingit ermine, chanted over and over her virtues and
beauty, the generosity of her royal father, the great price
the groom must pay for alliance with so royal a family,
with a maiden of such celebrated fertility and allure. Between them, at the foot of The M'Dougall's tall crest pole,
the dead dog waited with the teeth marks of cannibals
still welling in its hairy throat.

The conjurers were giving some foolish sleight-of-hand
performances perfected in the winter plays; they had un-
clothed a woman for execution, whirled a sharp paddle
and seemed to cleave her with it, straight through her

shoulder, down into her breast. Blood gushed from somewhere—from a hidden bladder, probably—and great lamentation began as the tamahnawis man dragged his gory victim underground. A few minutes later he brought her back, wholly cured and scatheless, a miracle, alive and shrilly self-proclaiming.

In another corner, giggling and secretive, some girls were tying up the little cedar-string figure designed to be the core of the bride's diary, the long ball of daily knots, plain or beaded or red-ragged, which would hold the tightly rolled history of her private life. Perhaps there would be gilt buttons tied into it at times, or harsh-colored threads from a voyageur's *ceinture*. Or golden hairs from a young man's mane, unexplainable to anyone else, hard for even herself to remember in the years of hagdom ahead.

We—Farnham and I, for he was not coming on the *Tonquin*, and these were the few final hours before she sailed— sat together on the ground, our backs against one of the rude mounting-steps, grease stubborn and malodorous on the planks behind us where we had wiped our hands free of food.

"See, the giving begins."

One-Eyed Comcomly had mounted the potlatch platform. He and the men of his family were tossing blankets down into the crowd. Red blankets which bellied and sank in gaudy bloat before the rival chiefs and their henchmen gathered them, cheering, and rolled them up for some future potlatch in return.

The women's clamor broke. A rush to the platform's edge. Red arms, a red forest in storm, reaching up, wriggling, fighting for finger space, for room to clutch and hold the prized possessions which were being tossed down in a climax of the feast.

Native goat-wool blankets of heavy yellow and blue designs, thick-fringed, years of faithful weaving in them, thudded down and were hallooed, acknowledged with wild business, carried back and away. Cheap red blankets from out of the *Tonquin's* hold, pitifully prized with even more delight because of their garishness and newness. Big black bowls, beaver handled, abalone eyed. Boxes of bent wood, startlingly carved, roofed and painted in miniature of the cedar houses. Furs from swiftly demolishing stacks, furs tossing down with red gleams and twirling paws into the shrieks and clutches of the guests. Blankets, blankets like red faces with wind-filled cheeks, and more blankets.

We had brought liquor to the feast with us. In spite of Comcomly's request, The M'Dougall had made us pass some of it out among the Indians. A wedding without hiccups . . . not for him. He was nettled because neither Mr. M'Kay nor Captain Thorn had done him the decency to come. They'd betrayed their jealousy, that was all. Jealousy of his good fortune, his luck with the lassies . . . y' canna keep a true Scotsman away from 'em . . . jealous because he was conducting himself like the pious Nor'- wester he still was. . . . And by God, give 'em all to drink. So that, in the annals of the river, there was never a pot-latch like this one.

From the platform Father Comcomly looked proudly down on his awed, befuddled debtors. Now he was giving away his copper shields. No tyhee among the Clatsop, the Tilamook, or any of the Salish tribes could possibly have as many copper shields to give away. One to each sept's chieftain, another to each nephew of the chiefs, and still the burnished stack of them was not yet gone.

Comcomly's single eye burned in its shrewd socket. Behind him his favorite old huy-huy man, he who could count twenty twenties on his haiqua shells, remembered all that his master gave away, what and how much to each of them, and what each of them would have to return with vaunting interest, twofold, threefold, in future potlatches

to preserve his reputation, his credit, his very chieftainship, the glory of his totem.

They kept immaculately sober, Comcomly and his
treasurer. The stinking candle-fish torches spattered them
with greenish light, lit up their almost sweet complacence.

Carved spindle whorls, alderwood urinals, beaters and
shredders and war clubs of whale's rib and jade. The
slaves kept bringing them in from the heap laid out upon
the beach for public admiration.

Floats and hunter's boxes, bailers and checkered mats
and fine baskets from the Northern straits and far Alaskan
islands. Each guest, according to his rank, the honor of his
presence, the extent of his gifts to the house of Comcomly
in potlatches of old, must be rewarded, impressed, confounded . . . and indebted.

Carved harpoon rests, dancing aprons, dishes of mountain sheep horn, monumental settees, dentalia hair binders,
blankets. Blankets, blankets.

Let each drunken chieftain, and each groggy member
of his sept, remember to his dying day the richness of the
mahkook house of the Chinook tyhee and die beggared and
broken-hearted in some future attempt to outdo the
generosity of Comcomly of the One Eye, ruler of the river
mouth, father-in-law of all Fort Astor.

"They're such children about it," said Farnham. He
had all the loftiness of a tipsy reformer.

I nodded. The din grew ear-splitting. Comcomly had
given stone drivers into his slaves' hands and had ordered
them to break the remaining shields. He could afford to
break a half dozen coppers, with horned owls' faces en-
graven, and throw the pieces into the sea. Which of his
rivals, covetous of his prestige, could ever outdo him here?
Let them drink of the oil of humility and acknowledge
his kingly wastefulness, his prestige over all.

"Such damned children about it," shouted Farnham

again. "They'll all be beggars before we're done with 'em. Men of your sort, Lewis . . . so much smarter . . . they'll all . . ."

Out of the hellish racket leaped tall flames. For a final challenge Comcomly had ordered precious reservoirs of olachen oil to be thrown upon the fire. Heat and insufferable, brightness fled outwards from their own deep roar.

A young harpooner, drunk, his face a revolting smudge of sweat and ochre, staggered past us towards the river-door ladder. He was naked, his mantle of wood-rats' skins held up in his hands in front of him and loaded with gifts of the feast.

Men of your sort, Lewis. So much smarter. Men with the genius of profit in them. Of profit and destruction.

I shouted to the young harpooner. He stumbled, stopped. Bat-eyed against the flaring, roof-high fire, he came back a little way, stood leering down at us.

"Trade, trade," I whispered to him. "Mahkook!"

He knew the white man's way. The white man who never gave back twofold, who never gave back at all, who traded without feast or laughter or honor to anyone. He pulled the ends of his mantle high and tight to keep us from seeing its contents.

"Halo mahkook!" He started to go by us a second time.

"Well, a proud beggar," said Farnham. "I like him for it."

Nettled, I grabbed up a bottle from under Farnham's knee. There was a little rum left in it, a small band of black at the bottom of red glass when I held it up before the fire.

"Mahkook." And as I repeated it I dipped the neck of the bottle slowly in the drunken young savage's direction.

He had stopped again, dribble-mouthed, agonized, watching the glass go down until a first, fire-red trickle of liquid reached the ground.

"Lum," I said. "Mahkook for lum."

The ends of his mantle sprang away as he grabbed. He made a tragic, beastly sound. All that he had been carrying fell down around us, ours for the patronizing and the pocketing. We both chuckled at the depth of the bottle neck down his throat.

So it would be with all of them. In time. In good time with them all.

Flames climbed upon flames. Into the central fire, around which in stolid defeat the rival chiefs must stay seated and drink each his spoonful of humility, the slaves of Comcomly still poured his priceless olachen oil. Black clouds charged at the smoke hole and, sped by the heat whorls, stampeded back upon the walls and down upon us. A multicolored blaze ran between ground and roof, pressing so solidly upon both that it might have seemed to emerge from either. It had the deep, gusty, contrabass note of broad flames. Across it, sharper than wolf barks, the rhythm of sparks against the roof planks, the breaking and clinging of little brands over our heads.

I kicked the harpooner's fallen goods out of my way as I got up.

"You can settle with this young sot," I said. "Good-bye, Farnham. I'm going aboard."

"Oh, yes . . . good-bye."

He said it as carelessly as I had. We liked each other well enough. We had been together since my first days in Mr. Astor's Liberty Street establishment.

"Say good-bye for me to Ross and Franchere and the rest. Don't let them neglect their diaries."

He gave me a thin New England grin. "You'll be back before . . ."

"Of course, before the summer's over."

"It'll all be bigger by then. We'll have the living quarters up, you know."

"Yes, I know." I would not give in to the unexplainable heaviness that pressed upon the silly little things we said. I did not like him well enough for that.

"And the new fur racks," I said. "Don't let them delay them. We'll be bringing back otters by the thousands, worth millions."

The roof around the smoke hole had begun to burn. Flickering edges of yellow ran out along the planks. Through the red smoke I saw the closed eye of Father Comcomly, the climax of a wink, and the livid, puffy face of The M'Dougall disgraced by fright.

"Like a good Yankee, keep the British away from our flagpole," I said. Farnham took it for another joke. It might have been.

All the upturned foreheads, misshapen, black-tufted, running with sweaty ruin of the paints they had had upon them, upturned towards the final sport of putting out the fire on the roof. All the broad, drunken faces as happy as faces of children just after a first exhibition of fireworks in Vauxhall. I made for the beach door across rows of greasy knees. I climbed the ladder, halfway out.

A cannon sounded from mid-river.

"That's your sweet-tempered Captain Thorn," shouted Farnham. "One of his famous old blank shots. You'd better hurry. I wish you joy of him."

Joy of him. I stumbled out into a cold night air, into the cleanness of a moon-white sand and coarse, silvered reeds which bordered the path down to the boats. I wanted for a moment to go back to Farnham . . . I was almost certain I must go back . . . and tell him to say good-bye for me, too, to Ovide.

But I got no more than my head back into the blistering hall. The stink of it. I no longer liked anyone that well. I thanked my own pet god that I did not. The brush of the sea came through the clinking salmon weirs, from far around Cape Disappointment, the disorderly, white deadness of the smell of the waiting sea.

From under the risen wings of a great bird, red-eyed in river darkness, another cannon thundered of her haste and umbrage.

THUNDERBIRD

VI

Thunderbird

FIVE days we tacked and scraped in the river mouth, in the surf across Point Adams's bar and the tide rip yellow and gorged with sand. Then at length we carried free of the cape and out upon the ocean, into the north again.

Mr. M'Kay made no complaint of tardiness. This commercial survey would be tame work, a tiresome indignity which the politics of his partners had foisted upon him. Moreover, the longer we were in the river, the larger chance we had of hearing that Hunt's overlanders had finally arrived. Mr. M'Kay smoked his Cree pipe alone at the foot of the mast where all the voyageurs had formerly been around him.

There were few of us: seventeen white men, twelve Sandwich Islanders, and the Indian interpreter from Gray's Harbor. Once in blue water, and we should feel the roominess of even a little three hundred tonner like the *Tonquin* with only thirty men aboard her.

The crew worked well. The captain was undisputed. This was his pet expedition, his own special proof of worthiness to Mr. Astor. He and Mr. M'Kay could almost be friends. They sat together at the cabin mess. Sometimes they talked.

The spray had the sun in it. Gulls, from the moment when Tillamook's huge rock sank in back of us, were in holiday around our spars.

Once Louis Bruslé, who had shipped in Ovide's place, pointed out to me a sprawl of loosened kelp that floated near the coast. Its long stems were slimy of the sea. It had a torn look. The stems ended in brittle, staring bulbs. Christ, what did they remind me of? demanded Bruslé.

Of nothing. Of nothing that had been or that would be. Time was now, and time was pleasant. Now was my respite. All else waited on these days of a blue-white water and the white gulls in sunny rigadoon against the blue.

2

I stretched a back of spare canvas for Perrault to rest against when we sat sometimes at the stern rail. There the long sunlight was clearest and most warming; over the lazy tail feathers of our blue wake she could watch at ease the search of a little single cloud for its shadow far out at sea, and the mountains with low folds of snow behind the many bays we passed, and down the silver distance of the straits.

While at night, when the cabin wanted neither of us, and the hold and its stacked wares were all clamped away, we had the stars, a suspended shower, and the old white horn of the waning moon butting the hills apart before he could show, too, his watery, brown-gold, winded beard with a spangle of wet stars upon it.

But, no, the moon could have no beard, said Perrault. For the moon is a woman, and every woman carries the moon beneath her heart . . . I must not ask her why or how.

She said it in soft, desperate haste, as though she were saying too much. As though I were a little boy whose innocence demanded fables and ridiculous evasions. As though I could know nothing about herself or what was in her eyes, when yesterday she had asked me where we'd be five months from now.

Stammering as she asked it, and neither I nor any other

man had been in the thoughts she had tried to keep hidden
behind her eyes.

When I leaned down to give my jacket to her cold,
wind-modeled shoulders, it had seemed to me that I leaned
endlessly out and to no avail, into a mystery of private
fortitude against all pain and mad predicament, towards
the kernel of an ecstasy of life which all the tissues of her
own life were secretly preparing, to some moment five
months hence around which all the quiet sluices of her
mind and body were already pouring a protective thankful-
ness and pride, and which neither I nor any other man
could possibly reach or ever understand.

I felt the thinness of her shoulder blades, the bright wind
on my bony wrist as I held the old jacket there. She had
said a *"Gratia tant'"* . . . absently, as if the careless Neapolitan stage words were of her mother tongue and the
first to occur to her. Absently, with her face half turned
and showing me only the young, high line of her dark
cheek, every daily change of which I had watched and
knew so well, and her short black hair that curled so un-
governably in the salt air.

But *"Gratia tant',"* she had said. She had said it happily.

I remembered it now in the night, when she talked such
nonsense of the moon, and when I must agree with her
gravely, digging into my recollections from a college
mythology class to piece out our pauses with proper in-
struction. She did not seem to heed my lesson. She swayed
a little towards me with the fluid swing of the stern. She
blotted out a star or two, and where her head had been
upon the sky a few new stars sprang forward.

"Ancient peoples almost invariably regarded the moon
as feminine," I told her. "It was a goddess they worshiped
up there. Artemis, for example, or Diana, to give her her
Roman——"

"Yes, of course, I know. *Diana Amante.*"

Then quickly, for fear I'd be in a scholar's huff at such a frivolous interruption and might fail to ask the meaning:

"Oh, a famous old opera of Leo's, Lewis, *Diana Amante*. You should know that. I sang it twice in Parma, in a tunic of white pleated silk, so severe but . . . with a bow and arrow. Not silver, though. I was very jealous of the Diana herself because her bow was silver. I cannot think who I was. I have forgotten what I sang."

"One of the huntresses, probably."

"Oh no, not just one of the huntresses. Those were small rôles."

I should have known better. I begged a diva's pardon.

We were too content to laugh. She spread her hands upon the dark. "It was only a few years ago, but a lifetime. . . . Once I might have stabbed you joyfully for less than such a little slur on my singing. How stupid of me. We have left whole lifetimes behind us, Lewis."

"You have never told me half of yours," I said.

"A singer's."

"But a—a woman's, a——" I was trying to halt myself.

"No, I would not have you know it. Not now. But you," she said, "I think your youth must have been a good one, Lewis, to give you so much peace and kindliness."

The night was my refuge. There were some things about me, too, that she should never know. If she saw peace and kindliness in me, it was enough. Enough for now.

"If ever I had a son, Lewis"—was she trying to tell me it?—"I should pray to the Infant Jesus that he might have your heart."

"Oh, stop. The Infant Jesus——"

But she would not stop. "The heart you have always held around me as you did your old jacket this afternoon. Is it your mother I should thank for that . . . for you?"

My voice was as dead as my mother herself when I tried to speak of her. "She is long gone. I cannot remember her."

I saw her hard little hands upon the dark again, and then the sudden clutch they gave at the moon as she raised them over her head. I wondered whether she knew without my adding it that Diana had also been the goddess of childbirth. And of whom she demanded it; did men always forget their mothers?

I started hastily to tell her of the operas I loved. Of Mozart. Of the old man, the librettist, fabulous and ghost-like in the murmur of a fountain that had been like a miniature of the murmur of this water under our stern, so many thousands of miles away. Of why I had been in the inn garden at all that night . . . until I remembered why I had been, and stopped short.

She was too drowsy to insist on my finishing that part of it.

Instead, I told her again of the first time I had heard her sing. She could not hear it too often. Of how I had marched home through the mud and rain humming her song, and of the face of the old city watchman with the drizzle and the street-light on it as I splashed merrily by. And of the time she had been so amused at me from her high carriage seat on the Battery green. We could be amused together, now. Her head was against my arm.

"You are sleepy," I said. "Go in." She had retaken possession of the little chart closet, of course.

"It is black in there. Let me stay with you. See, I'll not take cold." Her old overalls gave a funny screech upon the boards as she curled close. "And I promise . . . I'll not try to climb the rigging, Lewis, I'm too tired. . . . I'll not, not now." She said it so serenely, lazily. "Go on, tell . . . talk. . . ."

What plays were they giving there now? Were Signor Comoglio and his company still singing between the acts and in those elegant concerts at the Commercial House? The newly repainted Park Theater, fawn, French gray,

and purple, with white and gold boxes where they sat, the
rich ones, with plump, winy faces over their satin stocks.

She was asleep.

The Northern dawn would come early. On one hand we
should have the far diffused reflection of a sunrise at sea,
and on the other the mountains wadded with clouds and
streaming faint colors of the mist down all their cataracts.
The light would grow gay, and in the blue sky the white
gulls would begin to swing and glitter in fresh play around
our ropes, and would sit drying themselves along the rail,
so close to us that we should see the merry red dab on
each one's golden bill.

I brought the end of my coat up as best I could and tried
to cover the gap which the night breeze had found at the
bottom of her throat. Her breasts were enlarging. The gulf
that would run between us . . . of mother's milk.

She must have felt my hand there. She murmured something in her sleep. Someone's name, perhaps. It was not
mine. It was nothing. I did not mind. She smiled in her
sleep as she murmured it, and the mother moon showed
me the same untroubled, silvered face she had worn when
she had said that *"Gratia tant'"* to me . . . to this little time
that was mine.

3

The young Indian interpreter was giving me lessons in
the people we'd trade with here: the Nootka and their
island neighbors, the sober Cowichan, the lower settlements of the Kwakiutl, and the Queen Charlotte dwellers,
the Haida, whose isolated, hostile villages we should swing
to on our way back from Baranoff's otter land.

Past San Juan de Fuca's waters we must meet the Clayoquots first. An embittered little tribe, the Clayoquots.
They had been badly used in the days when the Spaniards
had wrangled with the British in near-by Nootka Sound;

and only recently a Yankee Captain Ayres had broken faith with them and left a dozen of their best hunters to starve on a desert island of Drake's Bay. The Russians from Seetka, a bullying and groggy ally, alone knew how to handle the Clayoquots.

In Clayoquot Sound . . . oh, yes, please, I must pardon his impertinence, he should not need to suggest it to any noble tilikum of the great Tyhee Easter, but if we carried a boarding net and it was not too much trouble . . .

There was something sultry about Kasiascall, our little Indian. His very name was illegitimate and suspicious. And since coming aboard he had been stealing single pieces of clothing from all our ditty boxes, so that he soon had a wardrobe of sorts, a collective dress of all his employers, the white men, which he wore in front of us with sleek anxiety.

He assured me often how fortunate he was that his mother had been so attractive to Spanish sailors, attributing to her hospitality all his own superior knowledge of the ways of white men's ships and all the Indian tongues and tempers of the inner bays, the whole Vancouver Island west coast, up to the furthest Alaskan glaciers of the bold-shirted Tlingits.

I never could learn what tribe had first borne him, owned and probably disowned him. He was a jack of all tribes. He despised them all, he told me in great confidence, especially the sturgeon-fishing tribes. Once he had been a prisoner among the Tanu, who had taught him sturgeon fishing. He preferred the white men's ships, where one need only sail, nor bother about hook, spear, or paddle.

On one white men's ship, when he was a little boy, he had learned perversion. He thought all the huloima practised it. He was always shiftily around our Sandwich Islanders. When I caught the vice in his look at Perrault I would not let him near her again.

The bright summer weather held. But it grew colder, and when we sometimes turned to reconnoiter in the inland passages the clouds hung in torn veins upon the tree tops to both sides of us.

I saw more and more of that upflung kelp, with its brittle, fright-cracked eyeballs sliming in the white seams of the tide.

It must have been a mile below our hull that the bases of the mountains met and gave us these green channels from the sea. On our portside an occasional glimpse of the ocean was still light blue. But here, in the haphazard narrows and bays, except where the water feasted coldly on cold rock and sucked the black lips of the shore line's rough shadow, it had grown slowly green, the intense, malachite green of an ice too deep to be truly melted, only its physical texture submissive to the sun.

The gulls were dwindling. These past few days, so Kasiascall made me understand when he saw me looking after them, they had all been absconding to the rimy ledges where they mate. He stood there, obsequious, pernicious, and unclean, watching me and doubtless wondering what I saw in this last flapping of white wings, and why I was so clownishly sad at our release from the nuisance of their fouling and their noise.

But, "Nah!" I said. "Look . . . yahwa, nah!"

For it must have been one of the very last of them I saw go wheeling seaward. A little one, sunset-breasted, tilting up from our wake and going in sharp, eager arc over a peninsula of hemlocks.

The same evening glow showed me Kasiascall's flat face piebald with the faulty mixture of pigments of the evil bloods in him, and how his purplish, slanting eyelids squeezed shut when Perrault went by in her boy's old clothes.

There would be no birds with us any more excepting a

single huge black gony. We saw it only now and then. But sometimes I thought I knew it in the formless shadows of a mountain range, and it followed us into the black night of Clayoquot Sound, where are the islands of the dead.

4

The captain's good-humor lasted yet a little while. He had me down into his stateroom to give me a cup of Teneriffe and the benefit of his advice on how we'd trade with the Indians from now on. He'd show M'Kay.

I sat uneasily on his little horsehair sofa, waiting for him to drink first, and for the fretful things he would find to say about our future conduct. About my coddling that boy Perrault too much, for instance.

About the Indian interpreter, the only savage he'd ever seen in his life, by God, with right nautical manners and a proper respect for a ship's captain and no need of a cat-o'-nine-tailing.

About Mr. M'Kay, too, of course. He was all right, M'Kay was, but thought he knew the Indians. Had tried to persuade him to keep away from the Clayoquots.

He'd show M'Kay. He'd make him admit in front of all those jelly-bellied partners, when we got back there, that Jonathan Thorn was a Yankee born trader and knew how to treat the filthy bastards as they deserved. And 's Mr. Astor had intended we should treat 'em in the first place, instead of mugging 'em, marrying 'em.

One fair price, a knife and a blanket for every otter skin, and that was all. Handle 'em in his own sea captain's way and he'd have more furs from 'em in one round of ship's bells than we'd wheedled in two months down at Fort Astor. He'd show M'Kay.

"Knives, sir? Blankets, yes, but might it not be better to . . ."

He had worked himself into a pink, bullet-headed pet
through merely telling me what he'd do. He pounded down
on my remonstrance. One price, by God, and they could
take it or no, then go, get off the ship. But no haggling.
He hated the dirty red ignoramuses when they tried to
haggle.

He had on his old weather-greened pea-jacket, folded
back—he would never throw it carelessly back as the rest
of us did ours—and his buttons were scrupulously polished.
He finished his wine with great unction. I reviewed the
strength of his thick, stubby fingers around the cup as he
wiped the bottom of it and set it fussily down, and the
wild, incongruous bristle of hairs on the back of the hand
he was using for such a housemaid's task.

The little stateroom seemed almost to burst with the
pent air of uncomfortableness there was between us.

Or did he never know it? How much I wanted to honor
him for the hate I bore him . . . and how much I despised
him for the hate he was wasting on a few naughty little
beads on the bottom of his cup.

"But knives, sir? May I not remind you respectfully of
Mr. Astor's letter, sir, quoting you General Washington's
instructions to St. Clair? You must remember it, sir:
how Mr. Astor warned you of too much confidence in . . ."

It was not necessary for me to complete it.

Did he ever know, either, how much I envied him his
seaman's god, his shipowner, whose ultimate orders he
must go on obeying with all the doggedness of a small,
cruel, honest man? His jaws flared square as I started to
give him these handsome verses from his own private
Bible. The wind stitches drew swift maps upon his cheeks.

"Damn you, Lewis, there be times when I almost think
. . . Get out of here."

Rage followed his irresolution, but a sufferer's rage. The
little silence as I rose had a leer in it. He raged, to avoid

sacrilegiousness, not against his god but against me. It
took him a time to settle back. His thick shoulders creaked,
and where his coat was folded over them they bulged in
exaggeration of his body's great strength.

"Send me old Weeks," he said. "See to it that he has a
correct list of the condition of our guns 'n' muskets. Half
of them wooden shams, 'n' our powder, thanks to those
miserly traitors at the fort . . ."

"Yes, sir." I was already half out into the cabin. I stood
bent in his low doorway, playing a soft tattoo on the woodwork behind me. His cranky ear heard it. "Very well, sir."

"Lewis . . ."

"Yes, sir?"

"Lewis, I've been damn faithful to Mr. Astor. You
know that."

"Indeed I do, sir."

"None of 'em's served him like I have. Stop that pesky
noise, d' y' hear?"

I stopped. I wrapped my hand around my thumb to
make myself stop. The knuckle cracked. "I'm sorry,
sir."

"A year ago you weren't the man I'd 've told this to,
Lewis. But I like you, Lewis, I've got to have somebody
to trust. M'Kay . . . all right, but he's one of the partners,
'n' those goddamned partners . . ."

"I think I understand, sir."

"I know you do, Lewis. Y' know my navy record. I
never did like that letter of Mr. Astor's, that's the truth.
You know how I fought at Tripoli. They gave me a medal
for it. I can handle savages like none of 'em can. I've
proved it. I don't need any ten commandments from—
from New York—or General Washington's instructions to
St. Clair. Or do I?"

"Indeed you don't, sir."

It was all too easy, provided I say only what need be

said. "I thought, myself, when Mr. Astor dictated that
letter to me, sir, that he was giving you too little credit.
Of course, I couldn't say so. One is naturally never
permitted to say such things to the all-wise Mr. Astor.
But——"

"Yes, he did dictate it to you. I'd forgotten that. To my
own clerk, by God! Well . . ." He would not look at me.
He sulked to himself. Then, suddenly, the subterfuge
again: he resumed railing at me, and in a voice more high-
pitched than I had ever heard him use before:

"I told you to stop that damn drumming." And:
"Damn you, Lewis, get out, get out!"

I got out, across the cabin. It was all too easy.

5

Did he know even now what I had been making of him?
What the nervous tapping of my fingers, not half so strong
as his, could do to his growly dog's mind?

Too easy to give me any of the triumph of ascendancy
I might have had a month ago. I did not want it now.

I sought Stephen Weeks, who was not in the powder
run. When I had climbed down the ladder and stood in
that narrow, stifling dark, I had a feeling of loathing of it
which drove me straightway back.

Here I had once lain the whole of a warm Owhyheean
night, wiping the moist hate from my face, sniffing the
smell of black sulphur, tasting the tart powder on my lips
when I drove my teeth into them. I had discovered here
the necessity of villainy that shrieks in all despair. I had
sworn . . . I had tried to give the whole loveliness of life
away as a bribe against a satirical little Frenchman's paragraph on destiny. The more fool I.

I climbed back out of the pitchy run. I had not even
waited to accustom my eyes to the lack of light. I knew

that the powder barrels were there, a huddle of round, smooth, tightly fed guts. I did not want to see them. I abhorred the dark and the malevolence of its cramming of possible disaster. I was suddenly mad for the kindliness of the world above the deck. A little square of the noon sky shone through the open hatch.

One had only to give in to God. God would place a bracelet of sunlight upon one's outstretched wrist and quell the greedy rattle of the nerves that go all up one's arm. One's fingers would grow light and quiet, as though they were resting on a sleeping woman's breast and feeling the hope of God alive in her body below.

How presumptuous of man to declare that man had been created in God's likeness. Truer by far, and humbler, too, to admit that God is created in man's. That each man's God is the giant idea of himself which he sets up over his own soul and his own lonely want of power, pity, or high rapture.

Until one knew one's own self ultimately, how could one possibly know one's God? Until, in this last, blinding instant of infinity, I know the destiny that my own soul must complete, how can I dream the truth of the face of God?

Chance is the only eternal. All living creatures are opportune even of their deities. The dog that sinks its head upon its master's shoes, the fly that hurls itself into the flame, or under an irate slap, or into the mandibles of some larger, fly-devouring insect—what glorious appearance does God's destiny wear for these littlest flies of your philosophy, M. Voltaire? The shadow of a fat man's finger or a spider's jaws?

Over the temple doors St. Paul had seen it written: "To the Unknown God."

God was a Babe all radiant in a rough-hewn cradle to one of us. Or God was a thick-set master of sagacity, a superhuman orderer of untold sailing ships, owner of far coasts and mighty harbors and rich cargoes which must be carried neatly, profitably home.

I had almost been jealous of Perrault's God. I had almost robbed my captain of his God. One does not sin against God when one robs a man of his God. One sins against man—and that is so much worse, the unforgivable, superlative sin which only minds as great as God's can commit with impunity and praise.

Take away a man's God and one leaves him his Fiend. Who knew that better than I?

Only the savages were civilized enough to conceive of God as great enough to be both good and evil. For the peace of tired Christian minds like mine, God must be always good, a gentle, unbegrudging God, suffering, abstaining, self-sacrificing, a God of forgiveness for the sake of pain, of ecstasy in His hurts, of self-recompense, self-beatification for His own unselfish, unembittered part in life.

I had never been really happy unless I suffered. Unless I served. Unless I relinquished. Unless I could throw down my loneliness, my sensitiveness, all the gangly comicality of the form which fate had given me, under people's feet, for them to tread upon and kick and muddy.

That was why I was here. That was why I was happy . . . because I had been given the one reward such a nature as mine could truly cherish and use.

A woman was grateful to me. A woman, who carried another man's child in her womb as bravely as she had ever carried a song in her throat, had loved me with a smile upon her sleeping face . . . and had murmured another man's name. But she had been klootchman, the woman, to me for all these months. She would be kloshe, the beloved, to me all my remaining days. In her all my happiness, the hope which turned me back to the one joy for which such as I are born, the everlasting love and mercy. . . .

All this I thought as I stood there that moment in the little square of gray-gold light from the deck above and wondered of the truth of the face of the Unknown God.

I shall see Thee, Lord, when my page is written. The end is almost here. Then I shall raise my eyes, scarce daring, blinded . . . the smashed and splintered blood pools where my eyes had been . . . and I shall see. I shall know.

6

We had our choice of either an inner or an outer harbor.

In a dusk that was printed with black mist we met the first guardian islands of Clayoquot Sound, low, rocky islands, small and several, with a scrub growth writhing out of the waves' reaches, their bottom stones spewn with sea moss and surf.

There were two villages, it seemed. Sometimes, when our bow was between them, we could see their evening smoke. Then, later, the vertical oblongs of firelight in cedar doorways and, from the further settlement, the luster of the fire on an apron of wet sand.

The near village, seaward and low and close to us behind the breakers, was probably no more than a fishing station for the other. There, down the shadowed race, two canoes were already darting to warn the people of our arrival.

I was on the quarterdeck with the captain when Mr. M'Kay finally persuaded him to stay outside. Or, rather, the interpreter persuaded him. For Mr. M'Kay could only clamp his pipe in his brown-stained teeth and leave it to this twitching, piebald little Indian to be eloquent in an assortment of dreadful dialects about the whims and customs of the Clayoquots.

Morning would be time enough for Mr. M'Kay to go

ashore and make them a proper representation of our good
intentions and our generosity in trade.

We found a hemlock cove that would take care of us,
this side of the narrow arm that led from bay to bay. The
night became a gruel of clouds from the steeps and inlets
invisible all around. The ocean was noisy on the island
rocks behind us. Ahead, uncertain until the next noon
in the foggy calm of that mountain-hung harbor, we stared
towards more islands, many and small, which sent us a
thick, sweet, greasy, crazing smell.

We established an extra rail watch in addition to the
seamen's. All night, whichever one was watching thought
he heard the secret, quick sound of paddles in the cove
around us; and Bruslé, whom I relieved, swore he'd recognized the light scrunch and gurgle which only a canoe can
make as it touches alongside a ship's wood. He had rushed
railward but not been able to light a tar flare in time, and
neither he nor the sailor with him had seen anything.
Neither could I, when I came up.

Perrault's closet door was half open as I passed. I
paused and spoke to her a moment. She was sleeping
badly and afraid, but she would not say so.

The strange smell all around . . . did I know what it was?
I did not. I really was not sure.

I did not answer, but found a little horn lantern and lit
it for her in the cabin, so that, with her door on a crack, she
might have some light to keep her in better spirits through
the night. It was so black in there, I remembered her once
saying.

The thin blade made a cut of gold across her face. She
stepped back a little, blinking, putting her head restlessly
slantwise, for now the light was in both her eyes and showing me plainly the strain on her wakeful pupils.

"I am not frightened," she assured me. "But . . ."

The little hollow in her throat was like a dark pearl on

a chain of tiny brilliants of a sweat of fear. When she saw me looking at her neck she lowered her head to hide it from me. A few months ago she would not have done that. She would not have minded what I saw her do.

"But what?" I said.

"No, but nothing. I am not frightened. Not now."

"Good, I am glad of that."

Chuckling a little, suddenly elated and warmed, I started to move on. At the end of the cabin I turned and saw her still there at the door-crack. Only a pencil's width of her, but still standing there, lamp illumined, looking after me.

"Kasiascall tells me . . ." I began.

But I did not go on with what Kasiascall had told me. For two reasons. First because of the strange, hasty padding of bare feet I heard up the hatchway when I said the name.

And secondly because what Kasiascall had told me was that in Nootka, the next large sound, we might meet with a Spanish missionary priest whom the English had allowed to remain, or that in Baranoff's Seetkan castle there would undoubtedly be a father of the Greek Church over the Aleuts and serfs . . . and now was no time to go on with the rare plan which had been quarreling with my bashful heart for the past week.

Those two seconds, when I stood hesitating, gulping my words down, looking back at the bright, narrow panel of her desperate prettiness, were a complete postlude to all that I had been thinking when I had stood here this afternoon. And to all the loveliness of kindly life, the abstract fantasy, to which I had been born and to which I had gratefully returned.

"Good-night," I said. I had never been so happy. So should she be. If my whole life could make her so, so should she be.

In those two seconds I had given someone a chance to reach the head of the hatchway and be off. I wondered, as I went up, who it could have been, and why he had been eavesdropping.

At the rail were Bruslé and the sailor, a Sandwich Islander, their flare smoking damply and wasted on giving red edges to the waves and the misty hemlocks on the hill above us; and behind them, straight, tense, panting a little, his face towards the hatch and me, his greased body shining and evilly blotched in the dying of the torchlight, was Kasiascall.

"They are all around us," whispered Bruslé. He was tired and badly scared. "You will hear." He told me groggily what he himself had heard, and how he and the sailor had looked in vain. Their canoes were like moths in the dark.

And the smell . . . he did not know what it was, but the smell was the worst of it.

I was looking at the Indian, Kasiascall. He knew. He wanted to be asked. He had regained his breath, but he hung back, taut and restive, as though he had been caught by accident in this little group and had no liking for it.

Bruslé went to his bunk. The sailor moved off to his old station. There was the broad quiet of a sleeping ship, full of the little sounds, less than sounds, of rope and board, iron and anchor-strain and the lap of the water line.

It was cold on deck, and yet so stifling. Spar chains and spars, the masts themselves, were cut off, halfway up, by the heavy blackness of this air which a ring of snow-topped mountains had let slide. The islands, the sky, the sea behind, all else of the universe excepting the fog-swollen bottoms of the structures of the deck, had disappeared. But there was still the smell.

The little interpreter was moving off, too. "Where are you going?" I asked him.

"Halo kah. Nah! Those the islands of the dead," he said. "There the Clayoquots bring tilikum when they die, lay them unburied on rocks above waves, or in little trees, with all their worldly goods around them. Tyhees they lay in great canoes."

I should have guessed as much. I recognized now for certain the cloying, lugubrious taint which Perrault and I had met once before in the Clatsop woods, and remembered the sudden reek of putrefaction which had sprung from within a mouldering canoe as we crossed the rocks. This reek was the same, but hundredfold.

"Moochos ignorant, these Clayoquots, fear their dead. Always make paddle fast past the little islands. Only bravest hamatsa, cannibal pight men, corpse eaters, ever not afraid to visit them."

I let him edge another pace away. In the dark his body still gave off an uneven, sticky glimmer. He had nothing on but a beaded breech clout.

"Where are all those fine clothes of Mr. Easter's you were so damn proud to wear?"

"Oh, yes . . . but among rude Indians like these . . . they would not like to see me in the huloimas' coats and shoes." He was barefooted, too. "They moochos foolish, wicked tribe."

His too smooth tattle about his own people disgusted me. I did not believe in his corpse eaters. That was something out of his own tainted mind. I let him pad away. I watched after him for the short space the fog gave. A yellowish patch on his back was almost phosphorescent, and then he was gone. To fawn obscenely on the Sandwich Islander, I thought.

The quiet was denser than the dark. There was only the ship's bell to time it, and now and then that rustle like moths' wings which may have been the paddles of unseen canoes or merely the spatter of the chilled mist from the trees that were wind-bent over white, corrupted skulls.

I remembered genial Mate Fox standing at the watch, much as I stood now, and telling me with pink, embarrassed moon face that love and death are the whole of life. And how he had hastened to assure me it was decent love he meant, married love, love for the smaller pink moon face of a son, for instance. . . .

I smiled into the dark. I snorted death out of my nostrils. It would be a love so decent we'd bring to the priest to publicize, with my love only like an old coat around her shoulders, and hers for the babe all radiant in a rough cradle.

It had to be, then, as though from a world's end, and I alone heard her, that I heard my dear one scream.

7

I bounded down. The lamp had been extinguished. I heard a door close quickly and the latch tongue click back. Then there was the silence of someone crouching on bare feet, hiding from me in the blackness of the cabin.

I rushed for the chart room. A corner of the mess table caught me in the groin, doubled me down. On the other side of the table someone leaped softly past, glimmering, agile, the yellow blotch on his back already halfway up the hatch.

I heard her shocking and terrible shudders through the door. I threw it open. He had not had time to lock his work behind him.

When I tried to make a light she struck at me with weakly clawing hands, crazed and not knowing who I was. She lay contorted on the bunk, the blanket with which he had smothered her first cries pulled off her body and twisted over her lower face, her eyes unbearable, rolling and wild with the pain of his thumbs' pressure on them and with the shock of the desecration he had done. I did not try to make a light again.

I closed us in, so none should hear her. I groped among the maps all scattered on the floor for a clean shirt which I had made her only yesterday. When I found it and started to divide it into bandage strips, the sharp snarl of ripping cotton set her shuddering again, and her knees thrashed and thwacked against the bunk edge in a delirium of recollection.

I discovered a puddle from an overturned water bottle, dipped a strip in it, and laid it over her eyes.

"It is Lewis," I kept saying. "I, James Lewis, I . . . I."

A bitter spasm left her stiffened. She was not listening to who it was. She lay over my arm like a savage corpse over a tree bough.

I clasped her shoulder. My fingers went nail-deep into a wet tear his teeth had made. I wanted to cover it. She began to fight me all over again, sobbing, panting unbearably, her legs thrown up and flinging in an agony which wrung crackling noises from every tendon of her body.

"Go away," she gasped. "All of you . . . all go away."

"But it is Lewis. Alone."

"Go away, away." Then, when she finally knew me: "You, too, Lewis . . . dear, good Lewis, you most of all. . . ."

And I could no longer stay there.

8

I had picked up her little dagger in the dark. I went like a maniac up the fog-filled hatch.

I prowled the deck all the remainder of the night, running and yelling murderously at man-shaped things of wood and iron, climbing into the misty rigging and the small-boats, hacking at every glimmering chain and the yellow patch of the ship's bell on the black.

The Sandwich Islander on watch with me thought me gone mad of fear of the Clayoquots. He gave me a leaf to chew, a piece of the forbidden tupso from the Columbia. He took it out from under his belly band and went through a grave play of showing me how to crumple it under the tongue and let its juice bring me a few hours' quiet and forgetfulness.

I took it from him on the dagger's point. I carried it to the galley and brewed a drink of it for Perrault. She was soon asleep.

I went on searching the ship. I searched the hold, the forecastle, the tarry quarters abaft it where Bruslé and some of the others were stretched out. They cursed me for waking them. I stumbled on with a long laugh, still hacking at the dark.

Until, hidden from the daylight as the Indian hid from me, I was back in the powder run again . . . the powder run which was the black heart of all the blackness of the ship and the blackness around the ship, and which I had told myself I loathed . . . and there I lay, at length prostrate, and loved again the dry black vomit of final and total ruin which clung upon the barrels and in the floor cracks under my outflung arms and flattened lips.

9

No sooner daybreak than the captain moved us into the narrows. Mr. M'Kay departed for his visit to the chief, Wicananish; a half-dozen hostages came aboard with sea-otter rolls and crow-calls for our interpreter; and the channel mist rose upon a stage of many painted canoes.

Now, nosing towards the inner bay, we saw the shag of the woods in an upward-sweeping circle, the ring of white sand below, the iron-gray pot of mountains all around. There was one especially high and dark directly over our bowsprit, a mountain tiger striped, ice faced, tightly collared in clouds; at the foot of this one, dead ahead of us, the mainland village strung its cedar houses to the beach.

Someone loaned me a glass and pointed out to me the many old totem poles, a man-made forest fantastic and richly colored from even this far distance, which raised their strange, animistic crests above the roofs. They were like trees out of hell, armless, rigid, evilly infused, bewitched with the harsh and unintelligible carvings which crawled up and down their trunks. I gave back the glass without comment or feeling.

With plain eye I could see now all the jagged little islands of the bay, the dead men's islands of black, moss-corrupted spiny scrub, and their isolated hemlocks with bleached bundles everywhere around them. Between the sparse branches the sky whined.

I saw some pale things stirring among the stones; they may have been only the last ghosts of the mist. On one island, sacred to their former conjurers, were stacked the carved burial boxes of that distinguished caste, the broken and doubled bodies often mixed in awful bursts with the broken cedar of their shells.

By day the smell of the islands was not so strong. The eye shared the shock of their affront.

And, seeing them, one knew better what they were, and thought more clearly and amusedly about them. I stood, for instance, thinking of how soon it must be when the white men's empire of busy mills and axes and missions and many trading posts would brush their living from the beach, their dead from these noxious little islands, and how the trees would go down . . . blazing and splitting down, alike the high, rough, living trees of the woods and the rigid, intricately colored and meaningful dead trees of their great memorial poles . . . and all the mighty single trees, too, which had opened their hugeness into red, amazing flanks for the canoes which were now gathering around us. . . .

Canoes of the otter hunters from the nearer village. There were no women with them, and they came without ceremony or any song, with none of that ballet of eagle feathers to which Father Comcomly had first treated us. Their pirogues were loaded with skins. They drove their paddles deep, quietly, as quietly as though it were deep night, and no lather had time to spring behind their blades.

I heard the captain whistling me to get ready our own wares. I was on the point of shouting back something about waiting for Mr. M'Kay's return. I did not shout back anything.

I made a handsome laying-out of our stuffs on the deck, blankets and red and blue cloth, some papers of penny fish-hooks, the usual little bags of china beads. And knives, too, damn him . . . since he insisted on knives.

Before the day's trading would begin I dashed below for a moment. None had missed Perrault. She was still asleep, a stricken little bundle. I did no more than glance in at her and lock the door. When I came up the Indians were aboard in large numbers.

The interpreter, Kasiascall, had come out of hiding at last. Out of his night's perch in the forward chains. When he saw me he slipped behind a pair of natives as ugly and scabrous as himself. He had managed to put a whole Indian tribe between him and me.

One Nookamis, nigh a century old, was their huy-huy leader. In the strange ways of making mahkook with the gruff, stiff-witted white men he was supposed to be incomparably well versed. He was long nosed, lank, and withered of limb. A son of the Tyhee Wicananish stood

on either side of him, supporting him, ayeing and applauding him, holding up for us to see closely the precious rolls
on which he discoursed with such wheezy, insinuating
patience. He was the world's last man to deal with Jonathan Thorn, late lieutenant, U. S. N.

I kept to the edge of the ring around our goods. I had
our ledger open. The Indians undid their rolls, laid some
of the furs down, glistening bait beside our bead bags.
In London or Canton a single one of these otter backs
would buy two tons of such trash as we had brought.
They cheeped as though they knew it.

The captain had thrust his big hands into his pea-jacket
pockets. He was not listening at all to the interminable
skookum wawa of Nookamis. With his boot heel he
dragged a couple of the skins aside and kicked down a
blanket to match them. So much for so much.

Here, where was that goddamned smart interpreter?
Tell 'em to hurry up and call it a trade.

Under my stare Kasiascall came, cocked head and scaly
fingers, into the ring. His slanted eyes stayed on me, and
when I made the slightest move I saw how the purplish
pucker of them excreted a minute grease. All the while he
talked between the captain and the chief he looked at me.

These Clayoquots were a too wise, deceitful people, he
confided to the captain. They delighted in scolding and
boasting, in taking offense, in quarreling with the great
Mr. Easter's countrymen particularly. . . .

When he attempted Mr. Astor's name four eyes were
on me instead of two. Captain Thorn was remembering the
sacrilege he had imparted me in his stateroom only a few
days ago.

I pressed down a new ledger page and, with Perrault's
little dagger, began deliberately to shave a pen.

"Offense? These filthy, flat-headed savages take offense
. . . what about?" demanded the captain.

They had not liked the way he kicked their furs around, it seemed.

Kasiascall went into long, glib discourse about it with the still glibber old Nookamis. Kasiascall was even more at home in these squirrel noises of their tongue than in his execrable Cockney seaman's Spanish-English. He was so polite. He spoke very quickly, and almost nothing he said was understandable to us.

Once a greedy little smile rippled down Nookamis's long, furrowed face, and the faces of the two warrior sons creased up upon their dented foreheads in result of something he said especially softly. Mr. M'Kay would have understood. I went on sharpening my pen and wishing Mr. M'Kay were here.

I wished nothing of the sort. I felt the captain's eyes on me, as though he wanted me to know he'd show me now, by God——

"What's he sayin'? Here, you, what's 'at he's sayin'?"

The little interpreter let the tip of his dark tongue travel his mouth's whole slit before he explained. While he explained the old huy-huy man cheeped on, complaining dismally, chuckling with slow drools of lime-hot saliva over his bad gums and down his unplucked chin.

He was one of us, this old rattle-boned, long-nosed rascal—one with Kraimoku, the lean prime minister of Tamehameha, and with Comcomly's verminous old treasurer, and with me . . . with me, expert in the intricacies of mahkook and the foolish vulnerability of ordinary man and the mightiness of millionaires . . . with me in the bloodless, wheezy, miserly old age I could foresee for myself in years far enough ahead to bring me forgetfulness of a ruined woman's love and of her desecrated motherhood. . . .

I heard that damnable Kasiascall explaining to the captain. When I looked up I saw their four eyes on me, and the neat, chesty strength that pushed at the seams of a pea-jacket and made its polished buttons stand up with such righteous insolence, and the disease-dappled skin of the other, the brown, discoloring blotch over one of his semi-male nipples.

"... 'E say 'e know Mr. Easter reech man, oh, moochos reech man, Mr. Easter tilikum must pay moochos fine goods, blankets, knives, for fine otter tupso. ... 'E say, Mr. M'Kay say, Mr. Easter say pay moochos fine goods an' no please kick tupso with lepee. ..."

He reached out with a mottled foot towards one of the furs to show us what he meant by that. One of the young warriors pushed him back. Screaming explanations and protests began all over again.

In the dapple-gray sky above the mountains the noon sun was indistinct, a gray fuzz which laid the rigging's shadows messily across us all where we stood at the foot of the mizzenmast. But there was, too, a complex shine of the reflection of water from over the rail, and the deck lapped light, the brown legs of the Indians danced without motion, and the topaz-brown fur heap glowed like an unholy grail in a wild white fire.

"Mahkook," wheedled old Nookamis.

Kasiascall talked on between the two parties, making us purring, ingratiating assurances of what shrewd things he was saying to the Clayoquots . . . and all the while, as I stood paring my quill with Perrault's little dagger, his eyes never left me.

Captain Thorn kept still. He had set his price, and they could come down to it. His square face took on the autocratic petulance of a spoilt boy's, his lower lip swelled, the lobes of his ears and the neck below them were colored with his vexation . . . and all the while, as I stood pretending not to watch him, his eyes never left me.

"Mahkook," droned the old huy-huy man. He took

another pair of fine skins from his chief's sons' bundles and laid them out slowly on the deck. He had seen the others' eyes on me. His own sought to address me, too, as though I were some mysterious and final arbiter with all the great Mr. Easter's powers concrete in the pen and paper I held above his outspread goods.

"Mahkook, mahkook . . ."

So that suddenly, when I realized that all of them were waiting on me—on me, the clerk who had nothing to say, whose business was only to write their barterings into my book, so much for so much, but whose lowered eyes were the goal of all their own suspicious, estranged eyes—then I realized what I should do.

"Please only," Kasiascall was saying, "Mr. Easter's excellencies please not kick pile with lepees. . . ."

I kicked out at the pile. The furs scattered, flapped their paws, threw back the ragged pieces that had once been heads. Before they settled I kicked at some of them again, and there were the simultaneous scuffs of my boot sole and the seasoned pelts along the white-fired planking.

"There, sir!" I kicked their prize skin clean to the rail. I had sirred the captain . . . but let them all have the satisfaction of it. Let them all bawl out, squeal and rage and grab down for their insulted treasures. "There! And there!"

"By God, Lewis! . . ."

But whatever the captain might have wanted to cry out at me was torn into unmeaning noise in the uproar around us. What happened next threw him entirely to my side.

Old Nookamis had seized one of the rescued skins and was holding it indignantly up with dirty, palsied hands an inch below the captain's nose. Mr. Thorn snatched it, slashed it back across the huy-huy man's face, slashed with it at the faces of the two chief's sons, too, before he flung it down, kicked at it and the other skins around it with all the wrathy, purple-faced pleasure of a little boy sanctioned to be naughty.

The strength of him, though . . . and the hulk of his short body and solid arms as he collared the old Indian and kicked him after his pelts. The rapture of cruelty which tore his coat away from its neat buttons and turned his thick fists into mallets upon the heads of the amazed and routed savages.

They were gone like that, in one shrieking, ignominious instant, and their anger grew as thin as the buzz of flies as they lengthened their canoes' distances from our side. Like flies they would go away for the night, keep their shrilling and their greedy energy for the next day. We watched them paddling fast away to their beach stations, and the wing skeletons of their blades in glittering rhythm over the gray fire of the inner sound.

I stood behind the captain as he watched. His broad shoulders had not yet quieted down. The red still banded the back of his neck. He had done his part magnificently —at my boot toe's prompting.

"Here's M'Kay back," he said, pointing to our boat coming hard across the water. "Now for a solemn pipe smoke, I suppose, on how badly I've treated his savages, 'n' how we'll have to duck out quick 'n' all that. And now, by God, he'll know who's master here! . . ."

He looked around. It was Kasiascall, the interpreter, he was looking for.

"Time they all knew," he continued. "That's right, Lewis, isn't it? By God, 's time they all . . . even . . ."

"Yes, sir," I said, stepping very close behind him. "That's right, sir. Even Mr. Astor."

"Where's that damned half-breed? He ran away the minute the trouble started."

"Oh, did he, sir? I did not notice that."

Out of the corner of my eye I could see Kasiascall

crouching in the bow, hunched over the silly little wound
I had given him. In the first of the squabble, as soon as
I had been sure I should not be seen, I had run at him,
caught him as he ran, and let him have it. He squatted
there now, as hidden and far away from us as he could be,
staring down with wide yellow eyes at his piebald arm and
at Perrault's little dagger pinned upright into it.

10

The silly little wound I had given him. Payment of only
a short spurt of blood, and the knife belonged to him now.
Yet I was glad it did when Perrault asked me for it a few
minutes later.

There she lay in the closet's rank, exhausted air, past
fright and derangement and the forlorn crisis of her pain,
too weak for tears. I thought she was still crying when I
found her pillow so drenched. But then I touched her
temples and cropped scalp, and knew it was the moisture of
a fever sweat, and how close she had been all day to her
death. To an agonizing, obscenely accidental death,
blasting the little life within her. . . .

"Your hand is good, Lewis," she managed to say.

I kept it there until it grew as hot and wet as the forehead under it. My long, bony hand. My good hand.

"Lewis, I . . . I had a . . . a little dagger. Do you remember?"

"But——"

"Lewis . . . I want it . . . Lewis."

"Oh, aye."

She had not strength enough at the moment to lift
herself up and witness all this profuse fiction of my search
for it around the room. She only moaned when I told her
I could not find it. Moaned and drifted into a short doze.
She had not even strength enough to want terribly to die.

She lay slack and grief drugged, silent. At length one of her hands succeeded in coming up her sore, spent body and meeting mine.

"Would you have loved the child, Lewis? For, you see, dear Lewis, it would . . . would almost have been your child, Lewis. I used to think . . . and now . . ."

"*Tais-toi!*" I said, as calmly as I could.

Why I said it in French I did not know. Ovide would have said it so, and I was thinking inevitably of Ovide, whose great, handsome body had begotten this child in hers. I had thought of Ovide so little of late. This was one of the last times I should ever think of him on earth.

I thought of his gallant, careless, golden body upon hers, begetting the child which had almost been mine. . . . And then I thought of the fiend's body, mottled and evilly maddened, which had flung upon her and soiled, slain, travestized this last shy kindness of our lives.

The colorless little closet danced suddenly with faces and naked bodies, brown, red, and white, a pinwheel of reckless lusts and jealousies which, stopping and twirling as suddenly in the opposite direction, showed its shrieking heads and writhing, unconnected limbs in a new prophecy of horror and bright damnation. . . . Then it exploded utterly, and there was only the colorless air again, and a sick woman too dispirited to keep my hand in hers, or to weep freely, or even to want to die.

I locked us in and sat beside her all the night. Sometimes she moaned a little in her sleep, or babbled childishly about the discomfort of her uselessly swollen breasts, or woke to ask me why the whole world had grown so deathly quiet. . . .

So quiet, I could hear no rustling of the hemlocks ashore, as I had heard last night, nor any breathing of the bone-strewn islands all around us, nor the scurry of a single canoe.

In the deathly quiet and the utter dark I sat beside her all the night, and had to do many menial things for her, to stanch and ease her . . . and thought of the strange day it had been on deck, and of the incalculable day ahead, and of the silence everywhere which, thank God, she was now too sleepy to ask me to explain. . . .

In her half-sleep, once, she began to sing for me. Or for the child which had almost been mine. In a sorry, keyless, lifeless voice . . . "*Voi che sapete*," that young Cherubino's song of Mozart's . . . her voice sharping miserably and absurd with drowsiness and long, dry sobs . . .

"*Voi che sapete che cosa e' amor?*"

Once again the pinwheel of wild heads and limbs exploded into a blaze of darkness, nothingness. Once again, just at daylight, and the hail of the watch on the deck above to the first Indian canoe, my hand hushing her poor bruised mouth and its pitiful song . . . my good hand . . . and, when I leaned down to her a last time, my own tears cleaning the piebald pervert's teeth marks in her tired but still quivering flesh.

The last of my tears. I left her with the summer dawn's bland light upon her sleep. I left her . . . humming to myself, instead, the Canuck paddle song which the voyageurs had taught us on the Columbia:

"*. . . Que demain vous mourrez,*
Faluron, dondaine . . ."

II

Someone was knocking at the captain's stateroom door. "There's seven boats of 'em around us now, sir. Mr. M'Kay's askin' o' the boardin' nettin'—'e says——"

"Oh, says he?" Mr. Thorn came out across the cabin.

"The boardin' nettin', no less, says he? Well, my compliments to Mr. M'Kay 'n' will he please to mind his own godda . . ."

I followed them slowly up the hatch. I felt a bit unsteady. None of us had eaten much in the last twenty-four hours. Excitement had kept our stomachs turned; and the strange smell of the islands, though our nostrils were grown dull to it, made appetite impossible. There'd be tea with a touch of grog in it in the galley. That would do me.

The deck was damp-brown from the already disappearing fog. Where the sun reached it it steamed slightly and was as mottled as an evil creature's back. Sailors were peeling the night's tarpaulins from our piles of goods.

The boarding netting had been brought up, but lay jammed, a tightly corded bundle, unopened in the bow. A greasy mist browsed on it. In the mist a black gony cawed and scolded and, resting an instant in the dripping furls, clawed and shuddered itself free of a dangle of seaweed.

Over the ice-bright cleft in the mountains the sunlight came, a spinning cone, and laid a faster spinning cone of light upon the harbor water and the rocks around, and on the many canoes coming out to us from both villages. How many we could not count then . . . thirty, perhaps, fifty within an hour more.

They came slowly enough. But not timidly, either. In many of them the women paddled, the men lying back lazily with their fur rolls behind their backs or between their spread legs. On a few of the stacks I saw babies cradled.

That was Wicananish, the Neweetee chief, standing up in the first canoe to reach us. He wore no regalia, went through no more ritual than the usual spreading of his arms and short-kirtled legs to show us he could have no weapons on him and had come only to trade.

There was a friendly tone to all their chatter. Whatever they were saying, they gave us proof of it with the sample pelt which the chief skimmed over our rail, straight to the captain's feet.

Ship's tailor, an able seaman by day, had had to spend the night righting the seams of Mr. Thorn's famous old pea-jacket. The captain looked unalterably neat. Those navy buttons shone back at the sun. His heavy, close-razored chin shone in concert, and his little water-gray eyes snapped with self-satisfaction as they looked down on the flawless otter skin.

"'N' give 'em just one blanket for it, Lewis. One blanket 'n' no more. We'll trade my way to-day."

Three men came aboard with the tyhee. They were all unarmed, quiet, anxious to trade the captain's way to-day. The women slid the canoe a little away from our side, out of the sleepy shadows of our guns, and the next canoes neared us.

"Why, they've all their bitches with 'em," said the captain. "Tell Partner M'Kay. My compliments to him 'n' he ought to know from old times that when the men mean war they never . . ." He had an old navy whistle in his right hand, and waved it over the crowded, fast noising shipside. "You know that, don't you, Lewis?"

"Aye, sir, even I know that."

He enjoyed it as though I had made a right respectful jest. He scraped the ring of his whistle with a thick and fussy thumbnail, and he glanced fore at Mr. M'Kay. "Would've wanted me to raise the boardin' nettin'," he said.

"So would Mr. Astor, I presume, sir," I said.

He must have heard me, but only his little eyes replied. It was to Wicananish and his second canoe load of trades-men that he nodded.

The bartering went wonderfully. The Clayoquots had

learned their lesson yesterday, perhaps. They argued once
or twice about a blanket, but good-naturedly, knowing
there was no use in words without the absent interpreter
—where the hell was that whoreson Kasiascall, anyhow,
the captain kept wanting to know—and they always
ended by rolling the fat red cloth around themselves like
a playful armor, or by throwing it cheerfully down to the
women in the canoes.

Mr. M'Kay came through, saying nothing, drawing
slowly at his pipe, his eyes hard on the savage chief, then
down along the deck to count the number of Indians already aboard by the number of pelt piles glistening at their
feet. He started to speak to the captain, thought better
of it, went away again and leaned, half sitting, smoking
steadily, against the taffrail.

"I'm showin' him how to make mahkook!" said Mr.
Thorn. "By God, 'n' I'm showin' the great Indian expert
. . . look y', Lewis, just 's I said I'd do . . . we'll be rich
men."

"There'll always be one richer," I said.

He was too vastly busy to guess whom I so obviously
meant. "Get over there by the blanket pile with your
ledger," he ordered me. "Bruslé, take charge of the knick-
knacks and tobacco. Trade quick 'n' sharp with 'em. No
nonsense. We're not millionaires . . . yet."

He was almost knee deep in priceless skins. We had
never seen such beauties, or so many so carelessly tossed
us in one session. When he turned them over with his
boot, and kicked them to a sailor to pile prettily up, the
Clayoquots had no complaint to-day.

To-day was bargain day. To-day was windfall and triumph and rich reward for his good, stiff, honest Yankee
methods. No haggling to-day. No dawdling or dirty finger-
ing of the blue beads before they'd take 'em in exchange.
No time for such small tactics. No room on deck for . . .

Christ, there must be nigh a hundred of 'em, 'n' each of 'em haulin' a roll of ten 'r twenty skins. Beauties. For a dollar blanket apiece.

To-day was bargain day. To-day he'd show M'Kay how to make mahkook ... show him and us all how he'd taught 'em their lesson 'n' could kick away at the pile 'n' they'd only grin 'n' like him for it.

"Aye, lepee on tupso!" And he kicked away at the pile, and they only grinned and liked him for it.

In all this din he did not hear my "Bravo!"

Fully a hundred of them, three of them to every one of us, and they kept on coming. I watched Mr. M'Kay as he lounged, half sitting, against the taffrail and smoked. He was trying to catch the captain's eye. Once again he started to say something, but he would not shout it, and whatever he wanted to say was smothered in the din, too.

My blanket pile was dwindling. The sailors were dragging up another. A few minutes, at this rate, and it would have to be another and another. An hour, and all our blankets would be gone. Luck unheard of. An otter or three, four, a half-dozen perfect beavers for every dollar's worth of rubbish ... for a shilling sash, for a sixpenny package of tapers, for a jackknife.

At this rate there would be nothing left for us at the end of the day but to turn around homewards, all the silly junk and trifles cleaned out of our hold, all these precious, world-worshiped, shining tupsos tossed high in their places and overflowing, deluging us with riches ... riches. ...

Over my depleted pile I could see across the rail. They kept on coming. Their canoes hung close around us, the squat little women making their long, sharp, sunny paddles scratch deep into the sunny rim of water which enclosed our stern. Their little deformed faces were all upturned to us, smiling. Their slicked striped bodies gleamed. In and out among the drooped shadows of our guns they scrabbled watchfully, as though we were a great bird pinned and helpless on the ground, and the time for the swarming of insects must soon arrive.

I heard myself yelling something at the captain.

"What's 'at?"

"Nothing, sir," I said.

But he must have understood me in the first place. "Why, y' yellow-livered school teacher, I tell ye, there's not one hatchet 'r club a-hidin' amongst the whole bastardly lot o' them. How could there be? What 're y' a-feared of?"

"Of nothing, sir. Nothing."

He jabbed his whistle at a grease-coated young pight man who had edged in too close to him. "Stand off, sojer, heave your tupsos down there!" It was all so successful. So deliriously so. "Now, you, Lewis, what're y' a-feared of, now?"

"Of nothing, sir, excepting Mr. M'Kay's fearful looks."

The pight man had stumbled obediently back and dropped three otter skins before us. He grinned along.

"And of Mr. Astor's special instructions to you, sir, if I may make——"

He did just what I wanted him to do. He began to spatter me with insult.

Over the ochred shoulders of the Indians crowding between us he hurled the dirty deck mop of his favorite epithets, the scorn and blessed hate he'd have of me until the very last instant of his life . . . repeating himself stupidly, testily, until he reminded me—what a thing to be reminded of, now—of the little oven bird who used to scream, "Teacher, teacher, teacher, teacher," in the woods outside my schoolhouse window and give the children something to laugh at and mimic. . . .

"Teacher, teacher, teacher."

It was I who laughed now. I so enjoyed these final honors of his everlasting hatred. I so loved the cold, correct temper of my voice against his.

"May I not remind you, sir, of Mr. Astor's apt quotation of General Washington's celebrated advice to St.——"

He saved me the trouble of quoting further. He burst into devilish obscenity. Bravo, I knew he would. He thrust some Indians aside, kicked his way to me through furs, plastered his thick, discolored, purple-stitched face up close towards mine. . . . Bravo.

"To hell with your Mr. Astor! I'm captain here—I, I—I."

He had done it. He had said it. He had shouted it aloud before them all. He had renounced his master. He had cursed his god. He had grown into the full stature of—of him I should gladly serve in any hell's pet mischief.

It was said. It was done. To hell with Mr. Astor.

A few more minutes and the blankets were exhausted. The Indians wore them wrapped around their oily loins and backs and bellies, and twisted across their upper arms, like a blood-red humorous armor.

From somewhere in the fishy crush of them I heard the voice of Kasiascall for the first time to-day. "They say, please, jackknifes . . . Mr. Easter's excellencies please trade only jackknifes."

I could see nothing more of Mr. M'Kay but his pipe smoke above confusingly many heads. Flattened, distorted, weirdly grinning heads, a watchful company of jet-haired, slant-eyed, inhumanly misshapen heads afloat and jostling on a wave of blood-red wool. I could see only Mr. M'Kay's pipe smoke when the captain bawled down for a bushel of jackknives . . . and how the pipe smoke stopped for a moment, as though Mr. M'Kay were trying to say something which we could not hear in all this genial mêlée of the Indians, and then began again, an angry plume thrashing up from his leathery, clamped old lips.

Still the canoes kept coming. Slowly enough, and put their furs aboard, and scratched with long, sharp paddles in the sunlight and the idle shadows of our guns. The women watched with upturned, serenely ugly faces, and tiny children slept and sucked the ends of their torturing head bands in the bottoms of some of the canoes.

"Wicananish people promise moochos fine otter tupsos for every little jackknife."

There must have been a hundred and fifty of their men aboard us now. Whale headers, sturgeon hunters, pight men all, clansmen of the wolf and the raven, brown and watchful as their little kin, the beaver folk, and all trading patiently, peaceably, apparently unresentful of yesterday's insults, immediately agreeable to any absurd mahkook we'd offer them to-day.

I saw the nephews of the tyhee throw down a whole roll of otters for two rusted jackknives and carry them fondly, gravely, up to the bow to show them like delighted children to the old conjurer who squatted there, pierce nosed and lousy, on the big, sunny bundle of our long since forgotten boarding netting.

No warehouse had ever held so many gleaming furs as these which tumbled on our deck, under our feet, everywhere around us in such crazy festivity of wealth. Every four-footed thing on all Vancouver Island, and all the flappered creatures of the straits to northernmost Alaska, must have been stripped to give us this Astorian holiday. A fortune lay flashing in the sunlight: soft, jewel-lucent browns from out the kelpy bays, rich, dark hides as shaggy as the hills from which the inland tribes had hacked them, as lustrous as the waves in which the sea people had speared them. . . . A fortune, thirty fortunes, wealth and all the gay things which wealth can buy for every one of us on board. A fortune lay flashing . . .

Like the flashing of the jackknives, now, in each red-armored Indian's quiet hand.

All the gay, dear, pleasant things which wealth could buy for all of us. For our simple Sandwich Islanders, who could return home now and own pigs and countless pigs, and bring silver shoe buckles without number to the girls flower-girdled on their clean mats. For old Stephen Weeks, deaf, failing, and anxious for just a few last years in a decenter air than a ship's black powder run. For all the sailors . . . and for me, too, in some warm, singing land of poppies and white temples, far away. . . .

"Christ A'mighty, what're ye laughing at like that?"

The captain had heard me above all the hubbub. He had grown nervous. He himself had noticed at last that there were five of them to every one of us.

I had laughed when I thought of Perrault lying hurt and spent and inconsolable in the closet below, and how all the wealth in the world could never bring back the lost child to her womb, or the song to her throat as young Cherubino must sing it.

I had laughed when I remembered the pink, rueful moon face of Mate Fox, shoal battered, sea rotted now, with sand eels dragging through its eye holes, and the fins of strange monsters rasping against its unmindful brow, and how all the wealth in the world . . .

Most loudly I had laughed when I remembered, in that same instant, that all these furs and all the rejoicing wealth of them belonged not to us but to the millionaires, to the kings, to the oak-necked masters of our destinies, to the Tyhee and the Eri and the Great God Mr. Easter, in whose eyes we were no more than proper servants, slaves, flies . . . most loudly of all I laughed at that.

"All the wealth in the world," I said to my captain in explanation of my laugh.

He gave me a quick, barbarous stare. He was certain I was lecturing him for that greedy, drunken arrogance which feasted in the stitches of his face, for the cocksureness of his success. . . . Teacher, teacher, teacher, teacher . . . the fool who hated me, thank God, for teaching him the measurements of a famous devil.

"Bruslé, aloft with six men! Make ready sails!"

He had carried his coup. We should ride out of Clayoquot Bay pelt-laden, proud, chuckling at our own invincible Yankee ways. We watched the sailors pushing to the masts among the many dumb, waiting Indians. I remember how, as the first man gained the mainmast rigging, he seemed to be climbing over the glass-striped mountain behind it, and that this was a fantasy which would never end.

"'N' now, damn you, Lewis, you poor, shiverin' lank, you can close y'r ledger. We're clearin' the deck, sails unbend 'n' anchor up in three minutes. Savages ashore. Clear the deck, damn y'all."

And then, when he saw how each of us was hemmed about by five watchful, scarlet-padded, steel-handed figures, and how the warriors had formed so dense a throng upon the stern that even Mr. M'Kay's pipe smoke was cut off from us, he buttoned his old jacket with quick, thick, steady fingers and was suddenly himself, remorseless, undespairing, unafraid, a stocky old tyrant with slits for ice-gray eyes, with veins like ropes in his red neck, and with a little tin whistle stuck deep into the center of the bursting cushion of his cheeks.

He blew. Shrill to his last breath.

That was the signal. Five jackknives tore up at him as the screaming and the massacre began.

12

All this happened in those same three minutes his little whistle gave us to put the savages ashore. Out of our thirty men they left five alive.

In the first minute, as they rushed screaming upon us from the stern, I saw the body of Mr. M'Kay swaying hard on the taffrail, his hands gripping air, his Cree pipe dropping with red spray past the new and wider, redder mouth which had sprung suddenly below his old mouth with the instant gaping of a great cut across his throat. And I saw the captain stagger and stumble back from the knives which had found him, stumble stupidly among the furs around him, and saw as much as heard how he sobbed with bullish rage. I saw men bagged and tripped and marked with red, writhing ribbons as they fell, and the ribbons running in swift crisscross on the deck. I saw one Sandwich Islander spring high, and another go down with his bronze loins split and spilling, and a white sailor wriggle back against a capstan clutching at the gathered blades before him like a puppy at a porcupine. And I heard the cheerful yells of the women in the canoes below as they tossed the war clubs aboard, and I saw—I know I saw— one tiny baby sleeping, sucking peacefully, in the sun.

All this and more I must have seen at the endless start of that first minute before I saw, too, the red-wrapped arms which dashed at my own head and body and could not be struck down or away when I rebelled against the steel-hot, hissing pain of many wounds.

Darkness I saw in the second minute, and then behind the darkness a spinning, blazing sky, and behind the sky an ice-aflame mountain, and, twirling upon the darkness and the mountain and the sky, several thrown bodies somersaulting out across the rail before they splashed. I saw the empty taffrail where Mr. M'Kay had been, and I heard the sharp paddles and the sharper laughter of the women below as they killed off the helpless wounded in the water. I saw Captain Thorn streaming twenty streams of blood down all the little fissures of his face, and down his desecrated clothes, and dabbling the furs on which he stumbled, fighting bravely, stubbornly fighting back, with his own big jackknife in his thick, flaying fist, and that look of utmost pleasure in his little, light eyes which only the sight of blood could bring there. And through the red dark I saw seven seamen caper and gibber on the rigging above, and one of them fall like a spattering egg into a thicket of berry-red knives, and another of them leap madly clear to the canoes and the red-threshing paddles, and a hundred war clubs rush at the rest of them as they slid for the near hatch. I saw to the red-dark distance of the prow, over the tumbled clothes mounds of the dead and the dark gurgling of the scuppers, to the dung heap of our discarded netting, where the conjurer already crowed to the sunlight on the glaciers.

All these things I surely must have seen as, lying face downwards in the blood-pool from my own many wounds, I managed to raise my face and see, hear, sense it all, in that eternal fraction of the second minute before another knife drove deep into my back, and the world and I went down and wholly dark a second time.

Musket fire gnawed at nothingness somewhere in the final minute, and I saw the holes of flame it bit into the black puddles of my eyes, up the black bigness of the shattered hatch, as the survivors gained the cabin gun rack and fired for their lives. I saw the monstrous toes of a hundred Indians as they ran close by me, over me, treading in the red bog of me, away from the wild shooting, away from their own panic, overboard to their canoes. I saw the deck chased clear of living men by a few blind musket shots, and the dead lying doubled and quiet, bashed and unrecognizable and quaintly resting, among the litter of burst bead bags and forgotten, up-churned, bloodied furs.

I thought, in that third minute of forever, that it must be Death himself I saw, when I saw the dainty, tortoiseshell evil of the face which twisted in from over my back to make certain of my own face before its owner sprang sleekly through the musket fire and perched in the anchor chain. The knife he had left in my spine would need no seeing. Perrault's little dagger had come home.

And over all, centuries of minutes of red darkness over all, I saw the white shreds of transparent gun smoke drifting and settling like the sunny goosefeathers of a festival of peace.

13

I could move my hands, and they knew I was still alive. Three men had found me among the corpses. By the way my hands throbbed in the hot and half-dry blood they knew I was alive.

"Ovide," I said.

But it was not Ovide. It was Bruslé. A grimy, ash-faced Bruslé.

"Look," he kept saying to the other two, "he is not dead, he is not yet really dead."

Old Weeks smelt hellishly of burnt musket powder. The third man was a Sandwich Islander.

". . . the only one alive on all the deck," said Bruslé. "But look at him."

"Ovide," I said.

They tried to bind me as best they could. When they would have raised me a little I began to bleed again. I felt the wet, hot crawl of it across my raw mouth, and out of the gashes in my chest. But from the deep, numbing stab in my back I could not feel it at all. They bound my back tightly around, so tightly they almost squeezed the blood-pink breath completely out of me, and I could no longer quiver in my pain. It was only in my upper body that I felt the pain.

"But it's no use," said old Weeks, fumbling. "Ye can see how his . . . poor Lewis, a young man like him, he'll be . . ."

The Sandwich Islander could say nothing to me or about me. He had my head in his hands. He looked down at me with fright-stretched eyes, pitying me dumbly. His eyes finished old Weeks's sentence for me. I did not mind what Weeks had said. It was the smell of burnt musket powder about him that I minded, and the dullness of his old fingers as he fumbled at my legs . . . and the knowledge that it was actually my legs that were dull, leaden, immovable in the sick stink of the sun-dried deck.

I kept calling on Ovide. There was something I had to tell Ovide. About Perrault it was. About Perrault after I . . . after . . .

They brought some grog to my lips, but I could not swallow it. The noon beat down on me over the half-furled, dangling sails. I could move my head. I let them bandage it. The bandages at least kept off the glare.

I was fully conscious now. I managed to ask them about her.

"Her?"

"Perrault."

"Oh, that lad of yours."

"Christ, tell me."

"Why, he's safe enough, absolutely unhurt. He was in that little coop of yours all . . ."

I could nod. The bandage kept off the glare and the flies.

"And the others?"

Neither Bruslé nor old Weeks answered me. They need

not. There was everywhere the fat buzz of gorging flies; and from overboard I heard the first gulls in many days as they quarreled for the floating prizes the sharp paddles had left them. I wanted to shudder, but my body stayed still. I got my arm up across my eyes.

Gleaming white gulls which tumbled in a blue, idyllic sky and, sunset-breasted, had flown off to their mating where the mountains could not see.

"Bind me tighter," I told them. "Still tighter. Now."

They could lift me now. "The Indians are gone," I said.

"Hours ago. They'll not come back to-day. They'll not dare while we're aboard . . . with our muskets."

"But to-morrow."

"Aye. . . ."

What would to-morrow mean to me, Bruslé was thinking. I could see it in the way he turned aside, and in the Sandwich Islander's soft, frightened eyes. I should be dead to-morrow.

"Aye, we'll none of us be here. To-night we'll risk it. You too, of course, Lewis. We've got to. The small-boat. We can fill her, lower her in the dark. We'll all row . . . all but . . ."

"But me. Where to?"

"God knows. Out of here, anywhere, back to Astoria if we can."

"If you can . . . as far as that, with me lying paralyzed in the bottom of the boat, unable . . . maybe unable even to die."

Old Weeks groaned for me. "Don't say things like that, Lewis. We shan't leave you here. To-morrow, when they see the ship's plight—for we can't sail her, Lewis, without . . . to-morrow they'll come back for their booty, and they'll . . . no, we've got to take you along somehow, Lewis."

"Perrault," I said.

"Of course, Perrault, too." They promised it hastily, too stoutly.

"The small-boat can hold us all," said Bruslé. But I saw he thought the opposite. "Though young Perrault's puny and strangely ill and won't be able to pull an oar. If any-one stays behind——"

"You will take Perrault," I said.

I said it as strongly as I could, so that deaf old Weeks should hear it, too. Blood came into my mouth, choking me.

"Sit me up against the capstan there."

When they hesitated I tried to pull myself up. They had to help me. Thousands of years ago a seaman had wriggled back against this capstan, clutching and yelping at the onrush of the knives. Here, this was he who lay here with his foolishly lacerated hands gnarling dry and black in the noon sun.

The dead, the many dead, and behind me, beyond the rail, the worse than dead and the white gulls' banqueting. And I must not fling my gaze away, lest the stuff in my mouth become a sudden torrent and I die too soon.

"Leave me here," I said. "I am well enough. . . . You have much to make ready."

But when Bruslé and the Sandwich Islander were going I motioned Old Weeks to stay, to come close to me, so that he might hear what I had to ask him.

"Perrault," I asked him, "does she know . . . that I am alive?"

He stared at me. He may not have heard me rightly. "Perrault," he said. "Yes, yes, we've promised, Perrault comes along."

"Does she not ask for me? Does she think me . . ." I tried to wave my hand at the many dead.

He shook his head, but continuously, as though in a pitiable doubt, as though his head must shake this way and that in answer to his own old nerves, and not to my question.

"Perrault's ill," he said. "Ill and . . . but unhurt. Lies there, crying, crying for someone. Sometimes for you, I think. I can't hear well, you know. But sometimes for you."

The dead, the dead around us, and the bloated flies.

"Shall I bring Perrault to you?"

"In Christ's name, no."

"You don't want——"

"No. Hear me, hear me. No, do not tell her . . . I could not bear that. Nor could she. Tell her nothing. Do you understand? Nothing."

"But, Lewis——"

"Tell Ovide, instead. If ever you reach Astoria, take her to Ovide and tell him. . . . See, old friend, I trust her with you, tell him. . . ."

But what was there to tell? What Ovide had done to her, and I had done to her, and God in His Heaven so high above the glaciers and the devil so deep below the black-green sea had done to her, and to the flower in her throat and the song in her womb. And so long as I lived I should not know whether the old man heard me at all, understood what I was trying to say through the hot, salty stuff in my mouth.

And the dead, dead, dead, the many dead who buzzed up at me through crusted lips, demanding why half my body should still be alive. My body especially of all their bodies, my brain that had urged death to all their brains.

"The *Tonquin?*" I said to the old armorer. "A slow fuse?"

He knew at once what I meant by this. He had grown old in the powder runs of so many ships. His white head shook, and his hands trembled in his thin, horror-crisp hair.

"You must," I said. "Or they will take her as a prize, with all this and this . . . and these. A slow fuse. That is your business. So that after you are gone, and I am . . . gone——"

"With us," he swore, "with us."

"Aye." I had not life enough left in me to contradict him.

He was a good old man with fumbling hands, with a palsy, a whimper, a uselessness of fright. He might try to do what I suggested, but . . . he would not.

He backed away from me, reeling, fading, gone in the glaze of the noon. I was alone, head and shoulders alone living, paining, draining, tied to dead legs among the many dead.

I let myself go down sidewards from the capstan's prop. I lay bent upon the deck and, crawling with my arms, straightened myself out face down, slowly, carefully, lest . . . and I could drag myself for greedy and tormenting inches at a time.

To the nearest body, peering, pawing, and past it to the next. To all the dead in my path, the caked and stiffening dead enormous across the low way I crawled with my arms, until, close by the riddled hatch, at last I found him.

I knew him by his buttons, some of which still shone clean, by his own big jackknife stubborn in his fist, and by the navy whistle sun-frozen into the broad clot which had dried upon his jacket.

He lay rigid, somehow achieving order and dogged righteousness again in the stupid, chunky gallantry of the hard way he had died. His face was gone. The war clubs, the slave killers, had finished him and stove in his face. It was a devil-red mass, and—crying out in an agony of warring pity and revulsion at the sight of it—I dragged myself upon it, lay covering it with my numb legs to shield him from this last indignity of the buzzing of sunny black wings.

Hours I lay there. Oh, my captain, my mischief master, this last, dying salute to your neat little soul. What need had we of an Astor or a God? See, see, with these already dead legs of mine I can curb the destinies of a thousand flies.

14

The three men worked in the short night. They made no lights, and as little noise as possible. The Sandwich Islander struck sounds as soft as mice among the galley pots as he gathered a few handfuls of broken hardbread. Bruslé went by me slowly rolling a water cask, creaking deeply on the crooked path he must take down the crowded deck. Sometimes there'd come a pause in the creaking, then a sullen little thump, and I might know how the barrel had met a grisly obstruction and had to be rolled directly, desperately over it.

Old Weeks was long below. Where? Preparing Perrault? In the powder run? He came up only once after the sun was gone, and I heard him searching for me, whispering my name as loudly as he dared, chirping. . . . Once he fumbled straight past me, never scenting where I had crawled to, nor how I lay face down and motionless in a burrow of furs. He went below again.

The others joined him there. Why did they delay? The night would be so short here, and they needed the dark . . . and I, too, needed the dark . . . and they must hurry, hurry. I could clench my fingers. They clenched around cold, night-wet metal buttons.

15

Bruslé and the Sandwich Islander were carrying her to the small-boat. I could only guess it. I did not dare

look up, did not want to, could not, when they came up
the hatch again at last and passed me.

The blanket they had rolled her in dragged one of its
corners along the deck. I felt the soft scrape of it against
the side of my face as they passed; it tickled me for an
excruciating second. I heard Old Weeks whispering to her
how he'd searched everywhere, and Bruslé muttering her
an order to keep her damn sobs down, and that it was all
for the best . . . aye, better for me, too. . . .

Once, long later, I must have dreamed that I heard her
cry out my name. My hands had gathered some pelts
into little hills upon my ears, so that I could not possibly
have heard them in the small-boat below, or the despairing
stealth of their taking to the oars, or any cry she gave
in the clawing night shadows of the islands of the dead.

Nothing could possibly have come to my blood-clotted,
bandaged, vindictively buried ears excepting a voice I had
dreamed. Nothing lived aboard the whole ship excepting
me. Excepting half of me.

TO THE UNKNOWN GOD

VII

To the Unknown God

IT MUST be done. By the hacked, slowly draining half of
me which still aches and so I knew still lives, it must be
accomplished without flinch or fail or any merciful philosophy.

Through the short Northern night I must will myself
alive, must use the wakefulness of this single, final purpose
as a weapon against the drowse of my emptying veins,
must lie in wait, conserving my poor strength, stretched
on the hardening body beneath me, praying that some of
the strength which has been smashed down with him will
pass with his last warmth from his body into mine. So
the savages sometimes believe. So I pray. To Whom? To
what Unknown?

I only know that it must be done, and that I must do it.

2

What a game to play . . . of keeping alive. And yet who
ever lives and plays another? This lifelong pastime of
securing, extending all life of one's own, of exterminating
all life set up in opposition to one's own. Every living
thing plays it on the little gameboard of his world of ant
hills, cities, woods or peaks or sterile sea, and every dying
thing must clutch his counters and risk the last move of
his life against the next few ticks of time.

To gain what? Applause or execration, a dump of
wealth, an ecstasy of fictions and forgivenesses, the blinding glory of the face of God?

I must will myself alive. I must live on until I feel the dawn chill creeping on my fingers, and know for certain that a new day's color bends from the mountains to scrawl red, fateful signs on the cold slate of the bay, and that across this gleaming writing the fleet of their canoes will come, a holiday assault of gaudy, greedy prows and adzed flanks blatant with scarlet and ochre.

For this I have lived and been let live: to exterminate the centuries of other lives regathered in barbaric celebration on the dead-strewn, loot-heaped gameboard of our deck. And for this born: to be the instrument of the destiny —or against destiny, I know not—of two villages, an entire tribe, which will never even know my name.

In the hot amazement of my arms hundreds will go down with me and couch upon the flowers of the sea, and be immediately dead with me, nor even know my name.

Dead they will be as the corpses now cold around me, under me, cry out that they must be. Dead as the Great God Astor, from the tall dump of his throne of white man's gold, has designed that they shall be. Dead of their own sly fiendishness, dead of the white man's righteous and magnificent wrath, of the revenge which tidy cities always take on the blundering hostility of the wilds . . . justly wiped out and forever dead in the name of that law of the tyhee and the eri and the millionaire, the builders of tall mahkook houses for the forest empires near and far, the law of an eye for an eye and a pelt for a dollar blanket.

To kill them all in the rose of the dawn I must keep myself sufficiently alive. Dear Christ, Thou knowest how in the lonely, blood-heavy heart of me I longed to die too soon.

3

I should remember some pleasant things: the apple-red cheeks of little Dutch school children in a snowy yard, the soft greening of the spring on hillsides looking towards Connecticut, and the orchards bubbling with bloom.

I should peek across the Threshold at some curious riddles and uncertain fates: the British frigates hawking around Sandy Hook, the Yankee flag on the log bastion of Fort Astor, the whereabouts of Mr. Hunt and his starving, tattered overlanders, and the way the olachen-sleek, plump hams of The M'Dougall's bride must wither and seam in her old age.

My gaunt, prissy college days came back to me, and a wonder of what the weather would be in the dawn's trail to-day, and a recollection of many dawns bygone . . . the one of thaw and winter muck in my childhood when my mother had died, the one I had met in a window overlooking the town's roof tops when I glanced up at last from my first Virgil, and this one through which I had come reeling home drunk under the twirled poplars of the Bowery, and that one when they had rowed me out to climb aboard the great bird stiff-winged and brooding in the Long Island mist . . . a wheel of dawns cogged with a wheel of dusks where the steeples were like inverted torches and the rounded cooking fires under the palms glowed like young Owhyheeans' breasts . . . a whirring of past things and future, distant, imminent, recent, indistinct. . . .

My good, dull landlady's kitchen, the purring of a kettle, and the sweet, soft feel of the baby's absurdly tiny fingers bringing my big finger down to suck.

Babies . . . in the early sunlight over the coming canoes there will be some babies, too, asleep with the greasy ends of their torture bands in their slobbery little mouths, or staring against the flies, bawling for the red milk of women who can wield sharp paddles and shriek for the hurtling wounded to finish off in the water.

Babies . . . but I will not think of Perrault in the past.

She is gone, I have heard her last cry across the night. Perhaps she will reach Ovide again and make him bend his sulky golden head to the first realities of his rash, histrionic life, and she will know him, win to the human that he is . . . that we all are. . . .

Or in the night, perhaps, to-morrow or the next night in the weary hiding of some cave along this Clayoquot coast, the pursuing remnants of the savage tribe will discover the little boatload and wreak some unimaginable revenge. . . . It is my own cry I hear upon the dark this time.

There will be only one Kasiascall left alive to interpret the tale months later, when he is ransomed out of slavery, to the dumfounded people of Fort Astor . . . the sly, obsequious, tortoiseshell-dappled tale as he will tell it to the not entirely displeased Unkie Dunkie M'Dougall, to the indefatigably journalistic Gabriel Franchere . . . the single oily, insinuating key to the green-dark oblivion in which the far-burst particles of hundreds of exploded bodies drift and turn to fish food and white rot and soak in the good fate of being clean forgot.

4

He sits close by me, as though we are at table in a midnight garden and there is nothing in the world except ourselves and the dear music we remember. I see him, the faint glitter of old teeth and preposterous jewelry which are all of him, sitting there surely and without astonishment or blur, a delightful old liar who can almost make me believe he has come whistling in from under the trees where ripe fruit drops into the dark, or has leaped straight over the moon-grained fountain, or has merely shuffled himself out of an upturned beaver hat.

"Da Ponte, sir . . . librettist to Wolfgang Amadeus

Mozart in his most charming operas." The shabby laces shake like little white flames around his wrist. "And I, sir, am . . ."

My cheeks are grown too sunken and my lips dry. I want to whistle along with him, to hum the light harmony his foolish old voice requires. I can only drum the rhythm with my knuckles on the deck. At first he nods and does not mind.

His white hair glimmers . . . or is it a mist?

Death should come like a young girl, laughing, teasing, light-footed, her slim throat uplifted to the moon, and not like a rigid stranger with a purse and a guttural command to hurry, hurry.

Aye, so you once said, my famous old poet.

Death may come like a jangling bundle of parched bones, or like a cool star behind a fire. Some see Death in the shadows of the guns of a great Thunderbird. . . .

But you've told me all that before, my little old Jew grocer.

My hands drum fast, drumming some tuneless something of their own accord, glad of the sting of the deck in them to help keep me wide alive.

What are you drumming there, young friend? More slowly, I beg of you, more lightly, happily . . . in time with my song, my loveliest of all songs . . . do you not remember, there are some so fortunate and gentle, they are permitted to hear Death in a song. . . .

But faster and faster the brittle and involuntary rataplan of my knuckles on the boards, on the hard, broad skull of the corpse beneath me. I want to stop and heed him, apologize to him for the bad manners of my hands, promise him they will keep grateful time hereafter to his song. I cannot stop. Faster, faster, the dry, splintery roll of cruel and importunate noise . . . I try to cry out to him above it. My cry is as bitter as desolate.

This too is music, my fine old fraud. For this is the drum roll of those who must see Death in the cracked, drifting eyeballs of a mess of uprooted kelp, in the piebald face of their own necessary evil.

He makes a curious, courtly old gesture. He is astonished, disappointed in me, sad for me, offended . . . he had remembered me as very fond of Mozart, and of this loveliest song which only the most fortunate and gentle men . . . His laces are ragged white fire around his wrists as he bows me his adieux.

Aye, these are the heel beats of the march of my thick-necked domineerers, thomping with masterly crash and destruction into the empires they have marked for their fat own. And these are the cedars toppling after their fresh red footsteps, and the totem poles snapping down and burying blood-proud legends in the shorn, rumpled earth, and even the mean, rimy trees of the furthest islands of the dead reduced to sudden stumps and splinters under this music of mine, old Lorenzo da Ponte di Niente . . . you with your little song all crushed and noteless under my masters' broad, hard, businesslike heels. . . .

Your silly little song of beauty which they robbed me of. Your dead little tune of klosche, the beloved. Hear this, instead, and this and this . . . and wait, you shall soon hear the loudest note of all.

5

In the dangling sails a white wind stirs. There is its faint moan through the shrouds before I feel it on my knuckles. I feel it in the lift of little hairs on the furs around my ears. It is an ice-white wind from the mountains and from over the wet crescents of the village strand, and I know it for the announcement of the dawn.

I can do it. I must do it. If I do not do this thing . . .

I drag myself for ages to the rail. The dying upper half of me drags my dead legs. It needs forever. Face down, hands clawing at the planks, at the rail, at the nearest capstan, to pull myself along, pull myself up to the view above the rail, and almost to stand there in a travesty of standing on dead legs.

Once I let go and fall down on my back. I lie there a dim eternity, newly exhausted, wrung, until I regain life enough to try like a turtle to turn myself face down again ... if I can only do it in time. I must do it. My hands are so sore. I have rolled both of them in furs, wrapped them in beaver mits, and I pull myself somehow forward, up and to the rail again. This time I will not fall.

It is still night in the villages, and the ceremonial fires blink all along the beach. Only in the mountain cleft above the eastward shag of woods the darkness is wounded and slowly stains the spruce tops purple.

How many thousand thousand times will the sun rise and slay the dark and ride in triumph around all the earth before the mountains are low plains again, and the waters have receded, and deep in the drying clay ruts we shall lie, the absurd and indefinable remainders of things which were men and ships?

I nigh fall again. I must not. I must hold here somehow until I see for sure and am surely seen. I let my arms go over the rail. I hang upon it on my armpits, like a scarecrow hanging on a cross.

The breeze has passed, the useless sails say nothing more behind me, and the pelts I am still holding in either hand hang limp. I let the one in my left hand drop. The other will do well for a flag, for a playful signal, when I wave it. I must wave it soon.

They must see me. They must be made to know there is only one of us left aboard, and this one half-paralyzed, helpless, suppliant for the mercy of their war clubs . . .

and they must see, too, the sample of booty awaiting them, waving, inviting them. . . .

The little fires all along the beach are turning yellow and smoke-gray. I know what these ceremonial fires mean. For hours now, under the conjurer's command, the Clayoquots have been scorching the bottoms of their canoes. Red fire alone can clean away red blood. Red fire is the toast these carved prows drink in honor of the killings of yesterday, the rich plunder of to-day.

Then they are coming, surely coming. That is what it means. As surely as the sun itself has come into the cleft and the steep woods and the blanched islands flower with colored light and the bay is covered with an instant red writing. Rose is upon the peaks, and crystal as a thrush's note the new-born sky behind them . . . and the canoes are coming now.

I am waving, waving. Do they see me from the shore? I grip the rail with the shrieking muscles around my left arm. My right arm is free to wave. The pelt of little eena, the beaver, glistens . . . ah, a perfect pelt, my almighty millionaire, which glistens, for a perfect purpose . . . and I know that the day has come and the canoes are coming.

It is far to see to the strand in this soft light, and my eyes are the eyes of the dying. But I see the gray stir of tiny people as they pour out of the houses, over the water's ribboned edge. The whole village is coming.

From the fishing station closer to the sea a huge canoe of the pight men is already in the surf, and I can see them wading knee-deep with her, tossing their long paddles before they mount. And another canoe, and . . . both villages, the entire tribe.

I am shouting. My mouth will give no exit to this weak, fatally wasteful noise; but down in my stricken bowels the spasm squeals and calls to the upper part of me which

still lives and holds me up and can wave the entire tribe
Tonquin-ward.

I lose the fur flag. It goes down shining, slaps and
spreads upon the water.

How many fine furs will hurl and go burning down and
float in blackened tatters . . . and how many . . . of an
entire tribe? As I fall back upon the deck again, rejoicing,
self-reviling, my eyes stare up into the awful sky where
dwells that Unknown, that Master of the House of Myths,
whose law is a pelt for a pelt, and for a handful of sailors
. . . an entire tribe.

6

I have turned myself over. Farewell to thee, sky, and to
thy white lady of the moon, and thy schoolyard of countless
children's faces twinkling to be stars. I have turned myself
face down for a last time. I am dragging to the hatch.

Teacher, teacher, teacher, teacher.

I am dragging myself over the dead who lie thickest
about the shattered hatchway. Over the spoiling bodies of
the several companions whose deaths require this last
antic and revenge. My dead legs grate on theirs as I cross
them. Farewell to ye, strong bone and lively flesh. Farewell to the bodies of us all which had the shapes of men
and the seed of heroism in our hearts. On some proud hill
above the Columbia a hundred years from now, perhaps,
they'll build us a monument in tall conjecture of this deed,
and wreathe this monstrous finale to our opéra bouffe
with the gilt of our great patriotism, and in all the school-
rooms over the land the children will be taught the brave
scheme of my celebrated sacrifice, nor be allowed to pale
or sicken when they hear it.

Stork, stork, gaunt, gangly, shy young man with a
weak chin and a long beak and drooping loins, luckless
with women, nonsensical among men, Ichabod self-

apprenticed to spite, greed, and the Devil. Teach them that, too. Tell them this was an American hero, and that he whimpered like the youngest, weakest of them whenever, clawing his way down into the hatch, he caught his bleeding fingers in the bullet-split boards.

I go down the hatch steps on my belly, my bleeding chest, my elbows. Halfway down my arms give way and I go the rest upon my face. The heavy dead legs behind me do not bounce, but shove me faster to the bottom. My head bandage has been brushed all off. The bandage they had tied so tightly for me around my middle is a ravel of dirt and blood.

I must hurry. I must live these ten minutes more, until I am across the stale disorder of the cabin, and down, somehow down . . .

Farewell to morning and the mountains and the clean, sunny air above, and the smells of the sea and woods, the strange smell of many islands, and the smell of ship's tar I have come to love. Drink, comical nose, this bitter whiff of yesterday's musket fire which still hangs upon the cabin bunks and in the dead men's scattered clothes and books and foolish things, and which is the heralding scent of the deep black sulphurous smell of the powder run down there.

Old Weeks has not left the run door open. I cannot possibly get to my knees to open it. I must break the pane above the ladder. I reach for something, anything, sufficiently big and hard in the litter of cabin and stateroom stuff around me. I must smash the opening as clean as possible of glass.

A stiff-covered notebook. This will do. Something of my late captain's. Pages already ripped out of it . . . by Bruslé yesterday in frantic need of paper to wad their musket powder down. My own handwriting. Jno. Thorn, lieutenant, U. S. N., commanding . . . in neat and untiring complaint against the perfidy, mutiny, stupidity, and constant misbehavior of the partners, the Canadians, Tories all, to John Jacob Astor, Esq., of New York.

I smash the glass. What the book of Astor will not do I finish with my raw hands. The way to the ladder is open wide and black.

Farewell to you, lastly, great Eri Easter. Months later, when some mail ship out of Owhyhee brings you the grim rumor from these straits, you have the kind permission of three hundred dead to be a little disconcerted, to flush a winy flush, and to regret God's will for a few moments piously but slightly resentfully, as though it were the treachery of a Tory partner or a lesser millionaire.

But go to the theater that night, our glorious John Jacob, promise our lost souls this . . . go sit in your plump, satin-lined box at the Park that very night and see the play through . . . the polite and charming play you'll see behind a rain of bloody remnants of your people and your wood beasts and water beasts and your whole grandiose plan . . . disappoint me not in this, my Great God Astor, as I do not disappoint you in this last display of fireworks in honor of your plan.

Stolidly, strongly, view the pretty play from your satin seat, and you may even yawn a little towards the evening's end. And when they wonder at your fortitude in being there, ask brusquely, gutturally, and with famous despisement of all sentimental cant, did they expect you to stay at home and weep?

Through a cracked port I can hear the paddles of the first canoe as it nears the ship's side. I pivot myself upon the cabin floor. I push my legs ahead of me into the black, glass-jagged hole.

Nor ever, John Jacob, stop for a single moment in your evening game of draughts and stare into the dark bubbles in your tankard trying to recollect who was a clerk named James Lewis, some impudent school teacher who might have become a millionaire, and whose memory now pretends to the nation-wide fanfares of a great patriot; a white men's champion, an American hero to every school child in the land.

I hear the jangle and voices of many from the first canoe on the deck. Their cackles come down the hatch. They are running among our dead. They are scrambling for penny beads. They are like children. I hear them calling the other canoes closer, and the swift, hissing drip from paddles all around the ship.

I find a broken jackknife blade in the shallow rubbish of the floor. I scrape it up into my hand. I know the powder run so intimately, I know there is the old flint hanging there that I can use with this steel sliver.

I shall do what I shall do . . . out of my own lack, out of my own necessity, out of the clamor of Me who was born in the black, sulphurous stench of a powder run . . . lest in some future life a light girl should laugh at me, a glossy horse piss upon me, a stupid farmer spit tobacco juice on my best coat, a handsome swaggerer call me a coward and kick me away from the silver cup of a woman's navel . . . to justify Me to my own self and my own man's life, which is all of a man's life, and all I shall eternally remember . . . I must do what I shall do.

I shove myself clear into the hole, descending the ladder hand under hand. My dead legs pull me down. It is hell-black and narrow here.

I am wedged in by the powder casks. The firm, full, pot-bellied casks. I have lain here a whole night at a time. Now I must hold to the ladder and stand . . . if I can still stand. I want for some whimsical reason to die standing, to do it with my dead feet planted and whole and solid on solid planking a last time.

From far above I hear them climbing aboard, swarming, shouting as they run everywhere, shouting jubilantly down to the canoes in gay packs everywhere around the ship's side . . . the deck is seething with them, and they run heedless up and down it, and into the shrouds to catch at the flapping sails. . . .

They will try to take the *Tonquin* into the inner bay, to beach her, to strip her at leisure. They laugh in crowds. They overrun her. I can only hold to the ladder, wedged into the claustral, lonely dark, digging the steel sliver from out of the palm of my hand, desperate for room to reach over to where the old flint hangs above the firm, fat casks.

Room, room, John Jacob the butcher's son, give me just this little room for the little time left.

7

Old Weeks has not set a fuse. The old fumbler could not. I have known all along that he could not.

I use the quicker means. I work the bung out of the keg before me. I hear the thin, dry trickle of powder from the hole. It is a full keg. So are they all, sufficiently full, and firmly laid.

I cannot see to die by. And when I shall strike the flint and steel at the bung-hole's black lips it will blow back at me . . . and whatever of blazing light there will be must blow me out into nothingness before I can see.

A thundering, blinding nothingness of bits of things in red-gold revolution in the air, things too thick and numerous and suddenly disrupted to be seen in mid-glare, falling back through their black gases to the red quench of the sea . . . back upon the bursten, charred canoes and the maimed, charred women and children floundering in the belch of the riled sea.

But, dead, I shall see. And, dead, I shall know.

And raise the little rounds of nothingness where once my eyes had been and look at last on God. On the God who is good to suckling babes, the God comprehensive of all evil, the God who is so much everything that each man may create Him in his own puny image. . . . Dear timeless and illimitable God, shall I see Thee at last as I have dreaded so long to see Thee: as a rich, strong, righteous, domineering God, with a neck of red mountains and a brow of cliffs and caves, awaiting my stammered excuses for the perfect pelts which I have blown to worthless shreds and wasted on the sea . . . the shining, priceless pelts which might have adorned Heaven's wall behind Thee. . . . Shall I, dear God, must I see Thee so?

The entire tribe. Above me, close around me. Some of them shouting down the hatch to some already in the cabin.

It is time. Time that was and time that will be in this thrust of the flint and steel to the powder's lips. The roar and the terrible radiance of eternal annihilation when I click them together for a tiny spark.

8

I, James Lewis, dead and standing forth . . . I clicked the flint and steel together for a tiny spark.

I, stripped soul of him that was James Lewis, relating these things out of bewildered memory of my life so lately left behind, with His terrible bright gaze upon the page whereon I wrote, write Finis now.

And raise my soul's self's eyes to look, to search the thousand thousand years of the blank skies, to see, at last to know.

.   .   .

Room, room for James Lewis in history.

.   .   .

Room for James Lewis in hell.

THE END